SCATHACH

by

G. H. Lauziere

PublishAmerica
Baltimore

ISBN: 1-4241-7611-5
PUBLISHED BY PUBLISHAMERICA, LLLP
www.publishamerica.com
Baltimore

Printed in the United States of America

SCATHACH

CHAPTER I

The heavy rains had come and gone, leaving the early morning with a chill that covered their naked flesh with a breath of cold air. In this drifting, dank fog the warriors waited in silence, unmoving among the forest of larch. Droplets of rain fell from tall branches high above and dripped down their waxen hair to their open backs making them shiver. Several of the Turanian horses snorted in puffs of white, twitching anticipation of the next command from their rider. The sixteen women reined them hard to keep them steady and quiet. Any movement too soon would bring disaster to the mission. And every woman among them knew it. The horses knew this too. Silence and patience is the key to success in this endeavor; just enough time for the Roman soldiers to get half way beyond the edge of the forest.

"I'm not sure I can do this Skitatsya," a young girl whispered beside her. "I'm frightened." She shivered violently in the cold, but she utterly refused to move about unnecessarily for fear of Skitatsya's punishment. Some say it is worse than death itself. Harsh training and discipline were ultimate tools for becoming a woman warrior. Anything less was not acceptable. And it wasn't always that Skitatsya herself would appear at the front of an attack. This had to be something special for her to leave the camp. Indeed, for now she straightened on her horse and looked ahead in recognition.

"You will be fine," she whispered back, straining her eyes to see further ahead. "Perform as you have been trained. Do not hesitate or you will die."

"Perhaps," the young girl lowered her head. "Perhaps, I could marry later."

"And let Aoife take your man for a play thing?" Skitatsya spoke sharply.

"Aoife is your sister." The girl snapped her head up in anger. "If she wants a man she will take one. If he happens to be the man I desire, I will simply have to wait for the next."

Skitatsya settled on her horse's back and looked sternly at the girl. "If you allow someone, anyone, to come and take your man from you, you are even less than a woman who squabbles for food to feed her wretched children!"

"But she is your sister," the girl insisted.

"Blood does not count in these matters. You are Sarmatian! Act Sarmatian! Kill your enemy and bring home his head to show your family. And then you shall marry. It is the law! It has been the way of our people for two hundred years. But be swift and do not delay. The slightest hesitation will cost your life. This is not a training session."

Arieoles was sixteen and older than most for marriage. She shifted nervously on her horse. The command to attack would come at any moment and she waited, quietly. Her deep blue eyes scanned the forest's edge until they met the enemy who suddenly wandered into view on the open grassland. She looked to Skitatsya in anticipation.

"There," Skitatsya announced dangerously. "Second from the end. He is mine. All others you may do with as you please."

The sodden earth silenced their attack from the midst of the larch until the first arrow struck down the lead rider. With the shaft buried deeply in his throat he slumped to the ground twitching just as another was launched, hitting the second man in the middle of his chest, piercing his steel armor and exploding into his heart. Confusion and disruption of the quiet morning caused the Romans to falter momentarily. In the next instant their morass had settled to quick caution and they swiftly drew their weapons. The last four riders immediately surrounded the one who apparently was their leader, the man Skitatsya had intended to kill by herself.

From the slope of the larch taiga came a blood-curling cry that cracked the still, cold air and sent a shiver down every Roman's spine as they looked first to the forest and then to the low-lying valley where the echo returned to haunt them. Of the twelve soldiers, two had already gone down, four continued to surround the leader with eyes fixed in every direction and six turned their lesser breed of horse around to face the Sarmatian women emerging from the forest.

They came with awesome fury, their intent written all too well in their eyes and in their screams. Their growing reputation for quick victory across the eastern lands was not tainted by this endeavor. They charged against the Romans, who were obviously strays from a much larger company moving east. With swiftness and speed they caught them by complete surprise. Skitatsya had planned well, sending scouts to search and watch the plains of the western Altai Mountains for Romans moving about Mongolia. Rome had already moved tens of thousands of men into Gaul and much further north. Some claimed that Roman power had reached as far north as Brittany and perhaps beyond. Now they planned to move east to take more land that did not belong to them. And what was worse was that China was seeking an interest to the west. While China was yet the lesser threat, the Scythians caught in the northern Caspian Sea were being forced to join the Roman legions or suffer great deaths as only Rome can imagine. Skitatsya wasn't about to let that happen. Not here. Not yet, at least. Not while she had the skill to kill. Her father had taught her how to fight long ago, before she could barely speak, in fact. The Mongols murdered her brother nearly twenty years ago in the Altai. Now only she and her sister, Aoife, remained of her entire family.

The clash came hard with steel against steel, the death cry of every woman echoing throughout the valley below. Arrows were of no use at this distance and the only way to get the head of your enemy was to cut it off up close. One has to look into the eyes of their adversary as the head is taken. It is believed that the spirit of the man inside is claimed along with the head. And so it was on this day that Arieoles took her first swing in battle against an enemy she did not know. He was much older and she could see that he was battle hardened with years of experience. There were scars on his left cheek and a healed gash above his right eye, splitting his brow in half. A strange smile formed on his lips as she approached, as if his delight in battle would be emphasized ever more by killing one of the famed warrior women of the east. But her intent was not on his glory, but in hers. Today she would have the head of an enemy. And that head would allow her to marry her love. Thinking now that she would never allow Aoife to take him from her, she waved her sword back and forth menacingly. With all her strength, she raced her powerful, golden mare into battle, screeching like a hawk on the hunt.

His smile disappeared and a look of evil gripped his dark eyes as she neared. She never noticed the change in his features. When he was within reach she slashed at him immediately, quickly chopping down and slicing rapidly to the side before speeding by in search for the next Roman to kill. She never looked back to see if her strike had any effect. Yet, her sword was brushed aside without effort as the huge Roman also ignored the first attacker and turned to meet the next female warrior coming for him. While Arieoles had failed to kill Bracus, she managed however, to swipe the sword-arm from the next Roman who had much less experience than the first. He sat, mounted and bleeding with a starry-eyed gaze before the Sarmatian charging in behind her lopped off his head. It rolled from his shoulders and fell to the ground with his mouth gnashing open and shut. Then Bracus, the first Roman, had turned his beast around and charged at them from behind.

Skitatsya, meanwhile, had raced to the rear of the party and dispatched the first two guards from her focus. They were no competition for her superior skill. Immediately, the remaining two came forth, ready for her. In the midst of the attack she suddenly crouched upon her horse and lifted her legs and feet to her Turanian's hindquarters. With a quick shove from her powerful legs, she leapt into the air like a salmon moving upstream, spinning and writhing and twisting. In mid-leap she severed both heads in one swing before curling, flipping and landing back on her horse. The eyes of the Roman leader registered utter shock at her amazing yet accurate movements. Never had he seen a thing such as this. Without hesitation, he dropped his weapon to the earth in surrender.

Bracus however, fearless and hungry for Sarmatian blood, now moved at them with full speed. It was Arieoles who turned first to meet him yet he had caught her by surprise. There was no time to bring her arm up to attack. There was no time to move away from his approach. All she could do was defend herself in the best way possible, but she knew it wasn't good. He had the advantage. His sword came down at her with deadly accuracy and she bent low as the edge whistled just above her head and close to her right ear. The blade had missed her head, but a sharp pain suddenly creased the flesh of her back, ripping through muscle and tissue and bone. It rendered her mindless and sent her brain into complete numbness. Before she had the chance to turn about and face him again her hands let loose of the reins and she fell from her horse. A moment later she lay unmoving on the thick grass.

Bracus was happy with his efforts. He had cut back with his sword and taken down Arieoles, a warrior of the eastern plains, splitting her naked back with a deep gash and nearly cutting her in half. But it was a momentary victory that forced him to concentrate now on escape. A quick search of the area told him he was now alone with Suetonius surrounded by Skitatsya and five other warriors. There was no chance to save him. All he could do was race for the open plains and pray he made it back to the larger company moving in this direction.

Shardai had taken up the attack where Arieoles had left off and chased after Bracus on a chestnut stallion. Her Turanian was fast, but not as swift or talented as Skitatsya's golden stallion. She was certain to cut him off long before he got to the lower valley where escape was certain. He watched as she neared and lifted his sword to attack. An arrow soared by and struck him in the upper shoulder. In a vain attempt to trick the Sarmatian he slumped over his Arabian and played dead just as she reached him. He knew she would take his head. She would cut it clean off and carry it back home to her family. Then they would clean his skull and cover it with leather workings and pin gold and silver ornaments around it before using it for a drinking vessel. No. That was not for Bracus. He had seen what horrible things these people do with the heads of their enemies. He would not be a part of their drinking wares.

Skitatsya watched from above as Shardai moved to Bracus to take his head. Something was wrong and she could feel it. Something about the way his body slumped on the back of the horse told her that Shardai was in trouble unless she got away now.

"Watch him!" she ordered the five who now surrounded Suetonius. She put her heels to Khutalk and sped him to the edge of the grasslands. "Shardai!" she shouted. "Stay away!"

It was too late. The moment Skitatsya called to her, Bracus was in motion. Before Shardai could recover, Bracus had pinned a knife between her ribs and watched while she jerked and flailed to break loose and get away from him. He held her, pushing himself closer, watching the life go from her eyes and waiting for the end to come.

Another arrow caught him in the middle of his back and he jerked. He had to let go. He would have to move now if he was going to survive at all. Without conscience, he dropped Shardai to the ground, grasped the reins and kicked his horse forward onto the open plain. Wounded and bleeding heavily he was off for the safety of the forest just ahead. Escape was inevitable. And Skitatsya watched him disappear; drift off like dust in a storm. There will be another time, she thought, but her attention was brought back to the prisoner.

"What do you want?" Suetonius demanded. "Do you realize who I am?"

"I don't really care who you are," Skitatsya replied as she drew up close. "Do you know what I want?" she asked.

"I have no idea," he lied. His hair was curly and ash blonde; his nose straight and narrow even though his nostrils flared indignantly. He had the stamina of a schoolboy, protected and nurtured in politics and diplomacy; and Roman sarcasm as well. Yet he was easily broken. The will to live always outweighed the assignments of Caesar. And cowards, such as Suetonius, always buckled at the first hint of death. Not at all like the Gauls or the Scythians Romans had murdered along the way. Those people gladly gave their lives to protect what was theirs. Suetonius was pure sheep, waiting for the wolves to herd him to his own demise.

"The stone!" Skitatsya demanded.

"What stone?"

"I won't play games with you Roman. I know you and your people. I have fought you across the entire Turan. I have followed you to the southern Ural Steppes and now to the Altai. I know what you have collected from the Mongols and now I want it."

His deep, blue eyes squinted with danger. "Do you know what Nero will do to me if I return without the stone?"

"So…, you have the stone, then?"

"I'm not saying that," he defended his words.

"I'm going to have your head if you keep wasting my time," she warned.

"I can't just give it to you," he told her. "I'm a dead man if I return without it."

"Return? Return to where? You are already dead. I just want you to tell me where the stone is so I don't have to waste the time searching for it. But if I have to, I will waste the time. Now…, where is it?"

A small attempt to search for escape proved useless, yet he searched anyway. Perhaps there were friends hidden among the larch that would suddenly come out and help him. Not a chance. Not with Skitatsya monitoring the land in all directions. In fact, everyone's attention shifted to the open plain where a rider approached; a female warrior. A round object was held high in the air as she came.

"It's him, isn't it?" Suetonius directed to Skitatsya as he watched the rider close in.

"Yes."

"You knew he wouldn't escape, didn't you?"

"I have too many eyes in this land. His end was certain. I have been watching you for more than a month now."

"So you know that I do, indeed, have the stone?"

"Yes. And I want it," Skitatsya ordered.

"I see I have no choice. What will you do with it?" he asked quizzically.

"Use it."

"For what purpose? It is only a stone."

"Is it?" she replied. She knew better. Romans don't simply cross thousands of miles of foreign land to gather strange stones for no reason. There was great purpose in this stone. And while Suetonius may not possess the knowledge to understand the item or its meaning didn't mean that others were ignorant of its purpose. Surely Nero knew the value of the stone. Why else would he have sent such a loyal follower? Somehow he had gained the knowledge of how to capture it. Perhaps he even paid lots of gold to acquire this stone. But no matter, Skitatsya had been following this item for some time. For more than a year she had been waiting, listening to stories and tales of its movement throughout the mountain people and then the Mongols and then to other places. Only now was she able to actually get her hands on it; or part of it. And she wasn't about to leave without it.

"I have no use for stones," Suetonius told her. "I am but a puppet on a mission. What is in it for me to tell you?"

Skitatsya smiled at his pungency to preserve his miserable life. She could have dispatched him long ago and searched among the dead bodies for the item. Instead, she chose to let him live long enough to question him, per chance he might deliver it without quarrel. Now she became irritated. Her smiled suddenly disappeared and she slapped him across his face like an insolent, thieving child. "I like a good challenge," she said to him with a strange thought. "I will offer you the safety of the open plain beyond that forest," she pointed to where Oseida rode in with the head of Bracus and displayed her treasure among the remaining warriors. "After that, any of my warriors are allowed to hunt you like a rabbit and bring you back. If you survive, it is by your God's hand only. That is what I offer. Do you accept?"

He searched the faces of all the women gathered about him. Each was attractive and possessed the appearance of the beautiful women that usually bring a good price in Rome and Athens as slaves. Yet they also possessed muscular features where the fair women of his homeland would not have them. Whether rain-sleeked skin or sweat from this skirmish, their bronze-hardened bodies shined even in the grayness of the new day. It aroused Suetonius with seductive thoughts of his hot baths in Rome. There were so many gatherings then, he thought. Then he wondered if he would ever see Rome again. He returned to the present situation. What choice did he have? He could die here and now at the hand of these beautiful women or attempt to gain some distance and make it to safety. The latter seemed to be the only option if he was to survive. "I accept."

"And the stone?" Skitatsya reminded him. "There," he pointed to the fallen Roman soldier. "It was planned long in advance that the youngest would carry the stone. If any of us returned for certain, Nero thought it would most likely be the youngest and most handsome. It is unfortunate," he said looking at the severed body.

"For you, maybe." Skitatsya sent Rwan to search the body of the young, headless soldier. A moment later she returned with a dull stone, grayish in color yet nearly oblong, like an egg. "You can go," she directed, not really paying attention to him any longer.

"Remember my name, girl. It is Suetonius. Someday we shall meet again," he said to her as he started to turn away.

Her smile returned to mock him. "If we do, it will be with your head at the end of a pole."

"That may be. But remember this, warrior woman, Nero will come for you. And I will be with him," he replied then turned from her.

"I look forward to the visit. Now be off, before I change my mind."

With the stone secured, Skitatsya now began looking through the dead and wounded. "Where is Arieoles?" she asked as she searched, suddenly remembering that the girl was afraid to fight.

"Here," another announced, looking at a body that was nearly cut it two.

Skitatsya looked the girl over. She was to be married soon. All she had to do was sever the head of her enemy and get away. The marriage would have been sealed forever. Aoife will have her way with Arieoles' man now, Skitatsya thought. And there would be no one to stop her. She turned away. "Rwan…, Oseida…, go below and return with Shardai," she ordered. To the remaining women she said, "Prepare the *kurgan*."

The day had been swept away in preparation for the grave. The *kurgan* was dug deep enough for both horse and warrior. When the time had come, Skitatsya ordered the choice of horses to the ceremony. Shardai's chestnut stallion was older and no longer of much use. It was not a problem to decide its fate. However, Arieoles's healthy mare had many more years of service and Skitatsya elected to allow the golden horse to live. When all were gathered about the *kurgan*, the chestnut and a dun mare, old and nearly lame from many years of fighting and mountainous traveling, were brought forth. "The hammer," Skitatsya ordered then. An iron hammer was brought forth as a burst of flame from a pile of dried limbs and leaves erupted at the head of the grave. With hammer in hand, Skitatsya stepped forward and approached the chestnut stallion. Two Sarmatians held him steady from either side with rope. "You have served your master well in this life. Follow now, and serve her well again, my friend," Skitatsya said and let the hammer fall with a quick and powerful blow to the stallion's forehead. The beast collapsed with a terrible shudder. It was immediately dragged to the hole where it was set beside Shardai who lay with her weapon resting upon her chest and her personal belongings ceremoniously placed around her body. After another powerful blow to the dun, in the same manner, she was set beside Arieoles who also carried sword and personal belongings to her eternal life. And when the flames died down and the light of day had nearly gone from the sky, Skitatsya ordered the hole covered and a mound of earth and stone built atop the *kurgan* to mark the location. All that remained was the purification of those who attended and to return and tell the story to their families. That was the way of the Sarmatian.

A small shelter of long branches covered in hemp cloth was erected on the site and Skitatsya surveyed the small fire burning within. When the flames were hot enough she scattered small stones inside until they burned red. She then tossed calyxes seeds onto the flame until a cloud of heavy smoke bellowed from the front entrance. All who attended the ceremony of the *kurgan* passed through the shelter in purification.

"What of the Roman?" Rwan asked when everything was packed and ready to move on.

Skitatsya looked out over the horizon, to the west, where night was taking over the last light of day. She felt suddenly generous. "We'll let that one live. Someone needs to go back and tell Nero, I suppose," she answered, then turned Khutalk away and led them down into the valley. They traveled in the same direction as Suetonius, but they did not follow him. There were more important things to do now that she had the stone. *Father will be pleased with her,* she thought. He had been searching for the stone for quite some time. And Aoife will be there also, waiting for Arieoles to return.

After a day of travel they reached the Zaysan, a lake west of the Altai that offered a brief rest and a moment to clean the battle from their hardened flesh. It was a time to reflect and a time to silently mourn for those who had been killed in battle. A meal of hot stew was prepared with the meat of two fresh rabbits Oseida had killed earlier that morning. While there were no fresh vegetables to add to the stew they flavored the meal with herbs found along the way. After several hours they mounted and continued to cross the Turan until they came to Lake Balkhash, a relief to Skitatsya, for this marked a quarter of the way home. At the Balkhash, they could fish and wash daily for almost a week, eating and drinking as much as they like. And the food they gathered and the water they carried would support them for the next ten days while they crossed dryer, colder lands until they came to the Jaxartes River. Then they would follow the Jaxartes northwest to the Aral Sea and push on to the Caspian.

Their movements over land were uneventful. Only small bands of traders and gypsies traversed the plains with them, mostly keeping to themselves and at great distances. The reputation of Sarmatian warriors, it seemed, was everywhere. No one wanted to exchange words with a Sarmatian. Not if one wanted to live, that is. Yet, Skitatsya saw no signs of soldiers or mercenaries in these parts. Not even the tracks of Suetonius' horse could be seen beyond the Balkhash. Perhaps he had moved south at the pass between the Balkhash and Sasykkol lakes. The land would become more desert there, harder to cross than the way Skitatsya had chosen for her warriors. If he wasn't smart enough, he could get himself caught in the Tien Shan mountain range or maybe captured by Hans who still hid within the mountains. No matter, Skitatsya cared less for his safety, though she absently hoped he would make it back to tell Nero of his encounter with the famed females of the east. Until then her attention was on the Jaxartes and home.

On the forth day beyond the Balkhash the weather had changed and their mood had become irritable. They slept little and talked even less. Conversation was reduced to more or less directions and warnings of dangers in their way from scouts sent ahead. Romans, with the assistance of Scythian trackers, were seen moving along the land, and some in great numbers. Some moved east while others pushed more northward, into the forthcoming winter weather. Skitatsya smiled. Many of them would not survive this voyage into unknown lands. And there were more traders on the land, some in much larger groups than normal. So she kept to the cover of forest patches whenever possible, keeping her warriors obscure from all sight. Meals of raw fish caught from passing streams and *kumis* (fermented mare's milk) were consumed while they rode. The weather had cooled from the rains that had come with the changing season and snow would fall soon. This was another reason to return quickly. Already, the mists of the mountains far to the north grew darker with each passing day.

On the fifth morning, the sun rose bright and warm. It brought another change of mood, one more light and pleasant. Oseida rode close to Skitatsya most of the morning in silence. She had been wondering about Shardai and Arieoles. Skitatsya felt her uneasiness, but remained to herself. When Oseida was ready she would speak. At the Jaxartes they halted for a short rest.

"What will you tell them?" Oseida asked when they had filled their skins with water.

Skitatsya knew exactly what she meant. "I will tell them the truth. They died in battle."

"That is all?"

"That is all there is, Oseida. Their parents will expect nothing less."

Oseida looked away to where the other women were gathering the sun and feeling the warmth upon their flesh. Most had picked out a shade tree and rested. Sentries had been set to keep watch. "It all seems meaningless. All Arieoles wanted was to get married. She wasn't one of the strongest warriors we have trained. Why did you allow her to fight when she wasn't ready?"

Skitatsya looked cross and would have cut another for such talk, but she proffered to answer. "It was her choice, Oseida. I asked her to remain behind until I thought she was ready for battle. She chose differently. For the love of a man she wanted to marry, she was willing to risk her life. She has done so. And she has paid the price. There is nothing more."

Oseida wanted to argue the point, but the loss had affected Skitatsya in a strange way also. Oseida could see it in her eyes.

"Skitatsya!" one of the scouts came racing in. "Men. Coming in from the south."

"How many?" Skitatsya was in motion. At the sight of the scout coming to the river the others had mounted without being told and stood ready, eyes searching every direction for danger.

"Thirty, maybe forty at the most."

"Soldiers?"

"Not Romans. I believe they are Xiongnu moving toward us from Bactria. They are armed and not in a pleasant mood by the sounds of them. And they are riding fast."

"Xiongnu? What are they doing in this area?" Skitatsya asked openly. No one answered. She looked around. There wasn't much cover at the river. Most of the land around them was open also. No matter what they did, they were sure to be spotted before they could find a place to hide.

"Do you think they want...?" Oseida motioned to the place where Skitatsya had hidden the stone.

"Possible." Skitatsya thought for a moment. Why should the Xiongnu push north after all these years? They were a tough nomadic tribe who had controlled much of the land from Mongolia to the Aral Sea a hundred years ago. They had raided the borders of China many times against the Hans and the Chins—at least until the Great Wall had been built. Even then they continued to raid the border people. But they had settled in the Tien Shan Mountain region, many of them disbanding and living quiet lives among the farmers and traders. Some even became Han. Most had taken a wife and raised children. Why have they suddenly armed themselves and moved to the north?

"They are not far behind, Skitatsya. You must act quickly," the scout warned.

Again, Skitatsya looked about. Only a few trees and the river, which was too deep to cross, stood before them. Yet, there had to be something. She didn't want to move to the north and certainly not back to the east... "East," she suddenly said out loud. "Traders. They were traveling to the east. How far?" she asked the scout.

"We crossed them early this morning, just after sunrise."

"They will help. They have to," she insisted and mounted Khutalk. Waving her hand in the air, she pushed her horse back to the east, away from the river.

17

"Why east?" Oseida asked as she rode hard beside Skitatsya.

"We'll join the traders. That's what the Xiongnu won't expect. They know we'll have nothing to do with traders. And they also know the traders will have nothing to do with us."

"Yes, but won't the traders try to run?"

"They can try, but they cannot outrun these horses. They will have no choice but to accept us among them. They will accept or die," Skitatsya informed her. And Oseida knew she was good for her word.

By mid-afternoon they had moved far enough east to see the serpentine band of traders stretched along the horizon. And the traders appeared to have seen the group of women coming for them at a rapid speed and took to pushing their animals and wagons to their limits just to stay ahead. But Aram of Samarkand, leader and taskmaster to this marching troupe, knew there was no way to outrun the horses of the Turan. Eventually, the drummer—hired to keep a steady, even beat on a goat-skin drum to maintain a constant pace for the traders to move along the miles of trails and passages—stopped playing and the men, many of whom were mercenaries hired to protect them from such raids, stopped and armed themselves. Each man was prepared to die to save his goods. It wasn't the first time someone had come along to steal from them. Traveling in larger groups tended to keep away dangerous raiders and thieves. But sometimes the thieves were hungry and greedy enough not to care. Many times complete bands of traders and merchants were found murdered along the winding roads and pathways, their goods and wares taken as part of the victory. Not so much recently, due to the enormous trading being conducted from Rome to China and throughout this region, but one could always trust in the possibility of it occurring.

Skitatsya slowed when she could see the leader of the band sitting atop his draught waiting for them to approach. A large, impending sword hung from his side. He, himself, was a large man. She could see the heavy burden of his weight on the horse's awkward stance, an advantage she would surely have if he were to initiate a fight. His eyes were dark and daring, as were his features. One blow from his powerful fist would send any one of her women to the earth, but her speed would undo him easily.

When she was close enough she stopped, held the others back, then proceeded alone.

"Is it a fight?" he asked when she was near enough to hear.

"Not unless you wish to die this day," she answered.

"You are Sarmatian," he stated flatly. "We don't have many dealings with your kind. We are merchants and traders, not much more. While we outnumber your women three to one, I already know you will win if a fight is what you intend. But," he said and his lips creased into a smile. "It is not like the Sarmatian to plunder what does not belong to them. So what matter is it that you come to us?" he asked.

Skitatsya knew he had already figured it out. While he was large and perhaps slightly lethargic, he was quick with wit and knew how to handle his words. Reasoning and diplomacy were perhaps his best qualities. She realized there was no sense in delaying the truth. "We require the cover of your company to protect ourselves from a band of men believed to be Xiongnu. Even now they travel close behind us," she told him.

"And why should I protect you? You are warriors trained to fight and kill. You are famed in nearly every corner of every land to die the greatest of deaths. Surely you are more skilled to defeat the Xiongnu than we? Why do you seek assistance from poor travelers of meek goods to be traded?"

He was starting to annoy her. There was too much talk and not enough action. "They are too many for us. Will you help us?" she suddenly became serious.

"Which tribe are you?" he asked her, unworried about her situation. After all, it was her situation, not his to worry about. He had no quarrels with the Xiongnu. In fact, they had become fair traders themselves when Aram passed their way.

"What?" she didn't understand. She absently squeezed the hilt of her sword.

He folded his huge arms across his chest. "Tribe. Which tribe of Sarmatian are you; Alans, Roxolani, Aorsi…?"

"Roxolani," she interrupted. "But what matter is that?" Among his qualities of diplomacy and reasoning, she realized, he was also partially intelligent. Perhaps too much so.

"It matters greatly to me. This tells me you are from the Black Sea area. You are most likely from the Dnieper region and quite a distance from home," he continued.

Now she was curious. He knew entirely too much about her people for he knew exactly where she was from. "And…?" she questioned.

"And…?" He laughed then; a hearty boast. "And that is good. The Alans are gathering in the Caucasus Mountains. There is not much luck in them, I believe. But what do I know. We have traded many times with the Roxolani and the Aorsi, but not so much with the Alans and the Iazyges. They are not as friendly and willing to accept the trades of our merchants. But I don't understand what takes the Roxolani this far from home," he said and sat thinking with a finger on his cheek. "Ahhh…," he said then. "You have been to the Sayan Mountains, maybe?"

He knows of the sacred mounds, she thought then. This man, she realized, was no ordinary man. If he knew of the burial mounds in the Sayan, and knew of her homeland near the Dnieper, then surely he was a dangerous man. Her eyes suddenly searched about for men ready to attack without warning, but all seemed secure. All eyes were on her, waiting for her reply. "No," she spoke the truth. After all, there was nothing to hide. "We did not come from the Sayan."

"I'm glad you said that," he said, and his smile grew. "It is entirely too early in the season for ceremonies. And entirely too early for telling lies."

That was it. Skitatsya needed some answers. "How do you know of these things? You are not Sarmatian. Only the Roxolani know of the time for ceremonies for our dead and about the lands we live in. Where do you get your information?" she questioned hotly.

His belly rolled with a chuckle. "Please, I am but a traveling merchant. Normally, I would not know of such things. My son, however, knows much about them. He is a scholar, you see."

"Riders!" Oseida warned.

"We haven't much time, merchant. Will you protect us?"

"What is in it for me?" Aram asked. "You really don't have anything we need." he continued as he looked them over. "I certainly have no use for heads," he suggested with a nod at the sack hanging from Oseida's horse.

"What do you require?"

"Well…," he dragged on, his eyes locked to the open skies.

"Hurry, or I swear I'll take your head long before these men take mine!" she threatened.

"We will decide later. I believe I have something in mind. But I think your situation requires attention more quickly. Come, follow me," he said and led the way into the huddled group of traders and merchants. The mercenaries kept their weapons ready and scanned each woman as she entered. When they had gathered about, Aram spoke to them all.

"The Sarmatian warriors require our assistance. I have agreed to hide them among us and provide them security from that group of men moving in the distance." All eyes searched to the west where he pointed. They could just pick out the dust-filled air from the multitude of horses moving over the land. There wasn't much time to waste. "Vlad," he spoke to a sorrow-faced man, older perhaps than most of the others and much thinner. "Have your sons remove one of the wheels on your wagon and make like you are putting on repairs. Mharc," he issued to one of the mercenaries. "You and the others get these horses under rope. It seems we are now trading horses this trip. Tie them together so it appears they are one group not to be separated. Lose the bridles in one of the wagons. As for you women," he said then, and looked directly to Skitatsya. "Hide in the wagons and do not make a sound or it shall be your life." Of the remaining wagons, four were open and seven were covered. The women were quickly hidden in the bottom of the covered wagons, out of sight, while their horses were tied together and hauled to the outer edge of the working area. They immediately took to grazing. While the wheel was removed, everyone else went about checking their wares as they would if a real accident had occurred. Aram walked about barking orders as he went. By the time the wheel was off the wagon, the horses had been gathered and tied and the women had been safely hidden away, the Xiongnu had come into the camp. Aram met them at the western edge on his horse, just as he did when the Sarmatian women arrived.

"Can I be of assistance?" he asked them with a slight bow of his head. His language was unknown to Skitatsya, but she listened closely from behind the covered wagon nearest him.

"We are looking for the female warriors," replied a gruff man who showed that he hadn't bathed in quite a long while. His hair was matted and stringy and he smelled of dead animals and dried sweat. Lice moved freely in his hair and on his skin. His black eyes were dangerous and impatient. Dirt caked his flesh so that it was difficult to tell if he was tanned or black of nature. The mountainous living made his skin tough like leather and his face was a map of deep crevices.

"We have not been confronted by any warriors," Aram commented stiffly.

The Xiongnu leader looked at the hoof-marks in the dirt, then back to Aram. "You have seen no one?" he asked.

"Oh, certainly we have seen them," Aram caught the other's observant eye. "They are far ahead of us. We merely follow their tracks. You know how they move across the land. They always find the best ways to travel this region."

"Yes, they do. How many are they?" he asked then.

Aram shook his head. "I was not counting, good sir. I merely followed their tracks."

"I see. So why have you stopped if you are following them?"

The big man shifted his gaze to the repairs being conducted on the wheel of Vlad's wagon. "Repairs, sir. One of our wagons has lost a wheel." He smiled then, ignoring any dangers that could possibly appear.

"And where are you going with your wagons?" he questioned.

"To China and then to the Mongols. We have gold and silver and fruits to trade for their silks and other fine fabrics, which we will return to Rome. Are you to join with us on our travel?" he offered.

The Xiongnu shook his head disinterested. "No. You have nothing we want. But take warning," and he looked carefully at the sweating herd of Turanian horses that suddenly caught his eye. "If you have lied to us, we will return and take all that belongs to you, including your lives," he said and moved aside, pushing his mount ahead in search for the Sarmatians.

"And a good day to you, sir. May Maodun bless you," Aram replied in his own language. Dust filled the air with the passing of the Xiongnu tribe. In all, there were perhaps twenty-five on horses and an additional ten more on chariots; each carried a bow and a spear. The stench of them left him partially sick, but he overcame the nausea and moved back to Skitatsya. "It is safe," he announced.

"You speak their language," Skitatsya commented when they could speak openly.

"I speak many languages. I must to survive and deal with the many different tribes of people we visit along the way."

"Who is Maodun?" she asked then, remembering his departing comments to the Xiongnu.

"Ahhh…, Maodun," he commented to himself. In the next instant he was looking over his shoulder. "Piladius," he called loudly then continued. "As you know, the Xiongnu were given their name by the Chinese; Xiongnu, meaning illegitimate offspring of slaves. They are really nothing more than nomadic Mongols who continued to fight for land of their own. But…,"

"Yes, father," a weak voice sounded behind him. Skitatsya watched him approach and thought nothing of him. He was not built for fighting and posed no threat. His arms hung loosely to his sides as he walked in a scholar's gown and his mind and eyes were elsewhere than on his surroundings; not much of a hunter, she thought. A leafy scroll swayed back and forth as he came, obviously something he had been studying. His hair was sandy brown and cut more to the scholarly style one would find in Rome or Athens and he appeared quite dainty in stature.

"I want you to meet my son," Aram said with a great smile. "Piladius," he welcomed with a big hand on the small man's back. "This is someone I want you to meet. She is Roxolani and very strong."

"She is a beast! And she smells of horses," Piladius protested.

"Yes, yes. But, please tell us. Who is Maodun?"

"That story is old Father but, if I must. Maodun was a great Mongol who collectively coordinated his people to rule the area west of Mongolia to the Aral Sea. All this land was theirs," he said and spread out his hands showing the lands about him. "The Chinese called them the offspring of slaves and their name, Xiongnu, has remained ever since. Maodun was their bravest and most powerful leader. If not for his death, the Xiongnu would still rule this land. The Chinese tore them apart, even after the raids…," his voice screeched with excitement.

"Piladius, Piladius, enough, enough," Aram calmed him.

"I am grateful for your services. We won't cause you any more trouble. We shall leave immediately." Skitatsya told him.

"Ohhh…," he boasted in a haughty laugh. "But, there is a payment to be made," he insisted.

Skitatsya looked gravely at him. "What do you wish?"

"Ahhh…," he eased beside his son. "At last there is justice in the world," he commented with a big smile. "Come, sit with me while Vlad replaces his wheel. We will discuss payment terms. Piladius," he held him. "You stay here for the moment."

They sat under the shade of a tall oak while the horses were untied and made ready to depart. Skitatsya listened to Aram's terms while the sun continued to shine brightly. If not for the interruption of the Xiongnu, the day would have been one filled with laughter and joy during their travel westward. They were a week from reaching their homeland, but the day would have made their movement much more pleasant, especially with the change of season approaching.

"I have carried a burden with me for quite some time," Aram started. "I don't have much use for him as a merchant and he certainly won't make for a Taskmaster. His mother saw fit to school him in all things that are rich and pure in all lands before leaving him with me. Therefore, he is educated and quite gifted in the ways of intelligence. But he is not much else."

"And what does he mean to me?" Skitatsya asked.

"Ahhh…, yes. He is going with you."

"Who is going with me?"

Aram turned his head over his shoulder, much like an owl does when searching the night for strange animals moving about in the darkness. "Why…, Piladius of course," his smile broadened.

"I will not!" Skitatsya refused.

"Oh, but you will. That is my charge. For saving your life, I entrust my son's life with you. You can do with him as you will, but no matter what you do, he is yours."

"And what good can he be to me. He has no strength. He is not a hunter. He will not survive," she complained.

"And here I thought the Sarmatians were honorable people."

"What do you know of honor?" she nearly cursed him.

"We are done! That is my charge. Now take him and what belongs to him and leave me. You may have his wagon too. We have made a deal and now it is time to move on," he bellowed loudly and moved off. "Vlad," he yelled. "We go."

Skitatsya had no choice. She knew she must take the young man with her. It was the price paid for life and she would accept it.

CHAPTER II

"You have found the stone?" he asked at the first sight of her.

"Yes, Father," she confirmed. "I have found it."

He smiled and welcomed her. "You have been gone from us a long time. Aoife has been worried for you."

"Aoife has never worried about anyone but Aoife," Skitatsya answered with distaste. The moment she returned, Aoife stood at the entrance to the village looking for Arieoles to arrive so she could taunt her about how she seduced Torak, her husband to be. But when Arieoles failed to arrive with the others, Aoife turned with a smile and went to report it to Torak herself.

"She is still your sister," her father reminded her. "And she does care for you." He sat among a patch of pillows and threw more seeds into the fire. The tangy scent of hemp rose to the air and he breathed it in heavily. His arms were covered in tattoos, mostly depicting that of *Epona*, the horse goddess, intertwined with those of *Tabiti Hestia*, the goddess of nature. Skitatsya, and Aoife too, had these tattoos on her body, but only on her upper arms so that it was not a distraction to those looking at her beautiful visage.

"She is also the village whore. Is there no man she has not taken?" Skitatsya complained.

"Do not judge her so, Skitatsya. She is one of the greatest warriors in this village. I would be hard pressed to match you against her should she ever challenge you. Now, come and show what you have brought me. I have waited so long."

"I have lost two warriors for this stone, Father. I trust it will be worth the loss?"

"Thousands would have died if they knew what powers this stone possesses," he told her.

Skitatsya removed the stone from her sack and presented it to him. He glared at it with resigned indignation for there was nothing special about the way it appeared. It was almost a disappointment to him, but he knew better. Things were not what they seemed. To someone not knowing what to look for it would have the appearance of an old rock, oblong in size with a flat bottom. A series of three lines in three locations were etched in circles around the middle, top and lower parts and there was a dark, grayish sheen about the surface; opaque in nature. "Have you looked at it and touched it?" he asked her.

Odd, she thought, that he should ask that. "No. I simply brought it back here."

An old smile, perhaps one of salvation, claimed his features and the cracks in his forehead and corners of his mouth split wide to show his excitement. "Go, now," he said. "Clean yourself up and tend to your horses. When you are finished, returned to me."

Cleaning was the perfect idea. Already, the women who had joined her on this mission were celebrating with their husbands or husbands to be. Oseida had posted the head of Bracus outside her home on a pole for all to see. The flies feasted mercilessly on her victory. She stood beside it proudly waiting for everyone to come and congratulate her. Skitatsya praised her in passing. Bracus was such a big man with such a big head. Nearly everyone gloated over the size of it. Skitatsya suddenly wondered if Suetonius made it back to Rome to tell Nero.

"So, where do I stay?" came that screeching, pathetic voice of a man-slave.

"Why don't you go find a place?" she told him.

"Where...? Here...? This place is filthy!" Piladius complained as he studied the area. Children ran dirty throughout the village in all directions, yelling and screaming as they went. Small fires were kept burning in front of worn out homes where mothers and daughters worked on cleaning vegetables and preparing meats for stews. Hides of animals hung on lines between homes at nearly every turn. The scent of cooked meat, rotted animal hides, decaying bones and feces varied drastically from one step to the next, stinging his nostrils. And he complained again.

Skitatsya stopped. She had had enough of him. During the last two weeks of her travel home, he slept and ate and read from his books and scrolls while lazing in the back of his covered cart. He cited poetry to vacant ears from a book he found in Anatolia. He read parchments from Greece that no one understood. His favorite book was Homer's Illiad. He carried it with him everywhere, perhaps for luck. And he read inscriptions from Plato and Aristotle. These he acquired from a port south of the Mediterranean while Aram traded spices and silks. When he was bored, he studied Latin with variant forms of Istroromanian, Dalmatian and Aromanian. In vain, he even attempted to teach Rwan—who was chosen to be driver of his covered cart—Finno-Ugrian and Sanskrit. Each ended in failure. Rwan was not the type to pick up foreign languages quickly. He pouted and sighed often. He whined and complained every day that passed. It was no wonder Aram wanted to be rid of him. And now Skitatsya wanted nothing more to do with him. "Here!" she cursed and sped off to a home settled near the edge of the village. It was of moderate size and made of hardened mud and clay, the roof covered in reeds and thrashes. Reaching beside the entrance, she lifted a wooden bucket. "Go to the river and gather water in this bucket," she commanded.

The look on his face nearly made her laugh, but she remained stern. "Move!" she barked with a voice that made him flinch and reach desperately for the bucket. "And be quick about it," she ordered.

By the time he returned, only half the bucket was full of water. The rest, she was certain, covered the front of his scholar's gown from top to bottom. She watched him stagger and trip all the way and held in the laugh that she wanted to release. He was awkward and clumsy and had no control over the way he moved his body. When he reached the door she opened it and removed the bucket from his limp grip. She noticed he was completely exhausted. "Get another!" she barked as she dumped the water into a larger bucket inside the doorway.

"What? I can't! Look at my hands!" he complained.

She looked. Red marks had seized his palms where calluses would soon erupt, but not before the blisters burned his flesh, she knew. "Yes, very nice. It's working," she commented dryly and pointed back to the river.

He rubbed his burning palms against his gown. "What?"

"Now!" she screamed. He took the bucket and ran, fearful of her. He had seen what Sarmatian women do to a man who didn't listen. There was no other choice here. He moved quickly to the river, but he would complain the moment he returned, he thought.

Sweat streaked his pointed little face and his hair was in complete disarray. Only a quarter of the bucket was filled with water when she took it from his grip the second time. He leaned heavily against the side of the house. "Am I finished?" he asked carefully.

"Go away," she ordered. "I will be unavailable for several hours," she told him and closed the door. It didn't bother him. He had a place to stay for now. The cart was small, but he could sleep and read and eat there. At least for now; at least until his hands healed.

Skitatsya rested a moment before cleaning herself. Reaching across an old wooden table, small and simple for her sparse home, she took a stone bowl and filled it with cypress, frankincense and cedar. This she pounded into a paste, dripping water occasionally to create a good mixture. When the paste was complete, she covered her body in the plaster and lay down on the thatched corner-bed and slept. It was her first comfortable sleep in weeks; nothing to worry about; nothing to harm her here. By morning the paste had dried to a caked crust that she peeled and brushed away from her skin beside the house. After rinsing with water, she combed and preened her fiery, red hair into a tail. Her body was refreshed, her skin radiated in the rising sun. When all was prepared she went to see her father. She knew he would be waiting for her.

"Much better," he initiated as she entered his much larger home. Her eyes sparkled a piercing blue and her hair radiated in the sunshine. Her spirit had rested well, he knew. His attention was immediately brought back to the stone. A hard gaze kept him captivated on the glowing center.

"Yes, you do look more attractive when you're not carrying the road with you," Aoife said beside him. She smirked and gloated with her head canted to one side.

"What are you doing here?" She shifted to confront Aoife.

Aoife stood, defiant. "He's my father too, Skitatsya."

"Yes, but I'm beginning to believe you had a different mother," Skitatsya replied.

"Enough!" Brona said to them. He looked tired. The stone, Skitatsya realized, had probably kept him up all night. He needed rest, she could tell from the way his eyelids sagged. But he would not hear of it. His gaze went back to the object in his hands.

"Don't bother," Aoife told her. "He has been that way since I came here. Nothing I do changes his mood. That rock obsesses him so."

"Father," Skitatsya moved to him. His face strained to looked deeper, concentrate harder on the object. His eyes appeared dull and his mouth drew down in what she thought was misery. "What ails you?" she asked close to his ear. "Father?" she called.

"I told you," Aoife said beside her. "He doesn't hear you."

"Let me have the stone, Father," she told him. He ignored her. "Father," she said again.

There was no answer from him, only the staring and bitter concentration. Without waiting, she reached down and grasped it from him without concern for herself.

"Noooo...!" he wailed as the stone was taken from him. "What have you done?" he shouted dangerously.

"You are not listening, Father. The stone had you in its spell. You were gone from us. I had to do something," Skitatsya screamed back. "What has happened to you this past night?"

He slumped against a feather cushion and tried to regain himself. "We are lost. We are all lost. There is no more time."

"What are you talking about, Father?"

"Skitatsya, he is burning with the fever," Aoife said leaning over him and feeling his forehead. "We need to get a fire burning."

Skitatsya was in motion. She fled from the house only to burst forth and knock Piladius to the ground the moment she exited. He had been waiting for her just outside the entrance. His Illiad was cast to the ground several feet from him. He scrambled to retrieve it before standing and moving to her. "What is wrong with you?" he asked casually.

She grabbed him by his dusty garments. "You..., fetch firewood and water and bring it back here immediately," she ordered.

"I'm not your slave! You fetch it yourself. Look at my hands. They still hurt from...."

"You move or I'll slay you before another word leaves your lips. And if you spill one drop of water, I'll slice you just to watch you squirm for a last breath."

He grunted loudly and turned on his heals headed for the bucket of water.

"Father," Skitatsya returned.

"He is sleeping. The fever has him harmless. What is that stone he was looking at?" Aoife asked.

"I'm not sure. That is what I returned with on the last voyage. That is what Shardai and Arieoles died for. And it looks as if Father may die for it also. Where is that water?" she asked absently looking for Piladius over her shoulder.

"They died for a lousy stone?"

"Obviously, it's not just a stone. Look at what it has done here. Where is that water?"

Brona stirred and grunted. "Skitatsya..., Aoife..., you must prepare yourselves."

"Father, you must get some rest," Skitatsya told him.

"Here!" Piladius flailed in with a bucket of water. Some of it had spattered on his garments, but she ignored him and tended to Brona who was delirious with fever. She dipped a cloth into the water and wiped it on his forehead several times before she noticed that Piladius was still standing behind her.

"Well?" she said turning back to her father.

"Well..., what?" he asked. "I brought your water."

"The firewood. Did you bring it?"

"There isn't any. I'd have to scavenge the woodlands to find it."

"Well...?" she said, ignoring his slight whimpering.

"What? Go out there alone? I'll get dirty and no one knows what kind of wild animals are out there. Can't you send...." he stopped and watched her stand, slowly, her hand reaching for the knife sheathed at her side. He knew she would use it. If she touched it and lifted it, he was dead. He wasn't about to wait. Like a crazed, wild boar charging into thick brush, he was racing for the exit. Anything in his way was kicked or pushed aside as he scrambled.

"You sure have that one trained." Aoife commented with a slight laugh. "A little skittish and awkward, but at least he moves when told."

"Not quite, but I'm working on it. He's lazy and clumsy, a complete oaf. What's worse is he's useless."

"Give him a chance. He looks a bit handsome. Maybe a little skinny for my taste, but a little muscle and a little more fat in the right places and he'd make for a chase in the forest."

"You keep your hands off him, Aoife. You touch one hair on him and you'll be looking at the end of my knife."

Aoife scoffed. "A little testy this morning, aren't we?"

"Don't push it, Aoife. We have to get Father back on his feet, and quickly."

"I know, sister. I'm just teasing."

"I don't like the way you tease," Skitatsya said dryly.

"Here!" Piladius dumped several sticks of dried wood on the floor at her feet. Aoife nearly laughed out loud from the sight of him and Skitatsya did all she could to control herself. His hands were nearly black and his robes were covered in bark and dirt. There were scrapes and cuts on his feet and a trickle of blood oozed from his big toe from a scratch he received looking for wood. She had forgotten that he was wearing sandals. "Is there anything else I can get you while I'm slovenly and filthy with dirt? Look at me!" he cursed and spread his arms out to give them a good look. "This is ridiculous! I'm not made for this kind of environment! I'm leaving!" he shouted at her.

"And going where? You have no idea where you are. You'd get lost and then you would starve. Then you would die and get eaten by some poor wild animal looking for an easy meal. Not, of course, to say that you wouldn't be an easy meal alive. You are quite helpless."

"I don't have to take this!" He turned and stamped his bruised and battered feet out of the small house. Both laughed at his departure.

"Skitatsya," Brona called her. He had slept through the night while she cared for him. Aoife had left his side during the early evening hours to walk the village. She was never one to stay in a single location for too long. It was a daily chore she attended ritually, just to ensure every male knew she was around. Already, they were calling for her, their voices ringing out in whispers from dark corners. And why not, Skitatsya figured? Aoife was, by all standards, a beautiful woman. She was a tall figure, slim and slender yet muscled and hard. Her face was a statue and her long dark-red hair was always combed neatly—at least when she wasn't traveling the countryside. Her lips were full and her breasts were perhaps quite the gift of the gods for no man walked by—except for Piladius; who wouldn't notice that she was even a woman—without searching the cleavage of her low cut attire. Indeed she was a beautiful woman. A woman most men would fight and kill for. But she was also a warrior and a dangerous one to be sure.

"I am here, Father," she replied.

"We must talk. I have seen the end."

"Don't talk nonsense. You have been ill. You have been cursed by that stone."

"The stone, Skitatsya. Where is it?"

"I have it, Father. It is safe."

"No, you don't understand, child. Bring it here. I must show you."

She left him and returned with the stone. It had changed some from the last time she saw it. The glow that penetrated the air from the center was now dull and obscure. She handed it to him.

"Here, drink first," she told him and held a cup to his mouth. He drank deeply and sat up.

"Look hard, Skitatsya. Concentrate on each set of lines. Notice how similar they appear when looked at for the first time." She agreed with a nod. They did appear even and similar all around. "Now," he continued. "Look at the top set of lines and then the bottom and move your eyes up and down between each set of lines until you see the change." She did as he requested and saw the stone melt away, almost abruptly. She smiled at the ease of it, yet it forced her to concentrate harder at the lines and to look between them. The gaps, the open spaces between each set of lines, suddenly opened to her and engulfed her whole. She found herself standing on a battlefield beside a stranger whom she had never met. All around her was death. The stench made her gag and she held a hand to her mouth trying to hold whatever she ate last inside….

"Skitatsya!" Brona called her.

"Father! I have seen it. What does it mean?"

"I cannot tell you that. It was for your sight only. It is something that will occur sometime in your future. Perhaps tomorrow…, perhaps next season…, perhaps next year. One cannot be certain. But trust in the vision, Skitatsya. It will happen."

She gaped at the stone. "This cannot be, Father. There is some trick of magic here. It is an evil thing."

"No, Skitatsya. There is no magic here, and certainly nothing evil. I have been waiting a long time for this stone. So few of us know the secrets of the stone. Now, listen carefully. Soon you must gather your sister and all that belongs to you and move away. There is great danger if you stay here."

"You are coming also, Father?"

"No. I must stay. I have seen it in the stone."

"Then the stone lies. I will not leave you here. I will fight for you, Father."

"Oh, daughter. While I admire your courage and strength, I fear they will be too many for you. I have seen it all. Trust me."

"But where will we go? What shall we do?"

"You must travel west. They know your name, Skitatsya. They have marked you for death and they travel to find you. They will think you travel to the east to escape. That is why you must move west. Mix with them. Change your name and stay clear of them."

"Who, Father?"

"Rome!" he said and lowered his head.

Suetonius, she thought. He has made it back to Rome. She was almost happy to know it, but frightened at what the cost would be for giving him his life and his freedom. Surely, Father would remain to fight with the rest of her tribesman. Was Nero that hungry for bloodshed? Or was it purely the stone that he desired most? He must know that the Sarmatian tribes of this area, or any other area for that matter, would cause great, if not severe, damage to his armies. And then she thought of her own vision. Yes. She could see it clearly: death by the thousands. Bodies lay everywhere and she had no control over anything. The resolve of the battle was not hers to command. She was but a pawn in the midst of the struggle with little to do but fight for her own life. But at least she would have Aoife beside her.

"When does this happen, Father?"

"Soon," he replied.

"Can we bargain with the stone? Can we trade the stone for the lives of our people? Surely there must be something we can do," she pleaded.

"There is nothing, Skitatsya. They have marked you. A man has called out your name amongst the evildoers and he has cursed your name forever more. If we offer the stone, they will ask for your head as well. You know as well as I that our people would die before they offer your head to anyone without a fight."

"Why then do Aoife and I get to live? Why not tell the village so that we all may live?"

He looked at her with love and adoration. She was strong, he could see. She was much stronger and wiser than Aoife, but perhaps a little slower than Aoife in her movements of battle. There was so much of her mother in her. Marianne was of strength and beauty also. If not for the difficulties of labor, she would still be here, he realized. Aoife was to be her last child. He would have loved a son to carry his name, but looking at Skitatsya and all her beauty and strength made him realize that no son could have made him any prouder to be a father. "It cannot be, Skitatsya. They will destroy everyone they meet along the way. Even the innocent will be killed. If we scatter and settle among other tribes, they will push to all corners to find you. It is not fair to them. Rome knows where to look and they will come here, directly."

A spark of insight grabbed her. "But what happens when they discover that I am not here? Surely they will continue searching until I am found."

"I will take care of that. You must simply escape with your sister. Tell no one of your plans, Skitatsya. And above all…, remember to change your name."

"My name? I have had this name all my life. I am known far and wide for my name. Am I to simply give it up? Pretend it never existed? Father, you ask too much."

"You must," he warned. "For your own sake."

"And what of the stone?"

"Ahhh, that," he looked at it closely. "You will take it with you. You will find it very useful in your life. But you must never tell anyone of it. Not even your sister."

"What manner of evil is this stone, Father? How can you trust it? Perhaps it tells lies."

"No!" he shouted. "It does not tell lies. I can see the truth when it shows itself to me. You must trust it always."

"I will not!"

"You must and you will! Now go…, leave me. I must rest and prepare for what must be," he told her and turned away so that she would leave without further confrontation.

The night brought a bitter chill that made her shiver when she left his home. The sun had come and gone and she never got to see the day pass. The village had quieted with only an occasional haughty laugh from one of the men drinking and sharing stories among the other men of the tribe. The women were most likely keeping their homes warm and tending to their children, their weapons or their animals. Soon the winter would come and they would have to be ready for it. That was their way. They would hunt the forests equally with their husbands and bring home deer and rabbit and cook it up as stew, sharing it with as many neighbors as they could before returning to the forests for more. There was always plenty of cheese and *kumis* and fish and vegetables to go around. Meaty stews were always special to them. No one ever went hungry. And there were laws they obeyed: laws that the elders had put together for everyone to live by. A hand for a hand was the general rule. There was never much crime when the rule was applied. Death was a common result with nonconformists.

"I know about your sto…"

Her hand came out and struck him before he could finish. In less than a heartbeat, she was standing over him with a knife at his throat. He had startled her, but more importantly, he had nearly gotten himself killed. The instant he squirmed and writhed on the ground she knew who it was. For a moment she almost considered performing the deed, ending his miserable life in one slice, but chose instead to keep him around. "What is wrong with you?" she asked of his stupidity.

"You…, you…, hit me…," he whimpered and brought his hand to his mouth. He spit blood to the side and leaned on an elbow. "You didn't have to do that."

"You're lucky to be alive, my little scholar. I should have run you through so I wouldn't have to listen to you whine any longer. Why don't you show a little strength, a little backbone? You are like a Scythian woman mending the leather of her husband's boots."

He sat up as she moved away from him. "I just wanted you to know that I know about that stone."

"You close your lips," she ordered as she spun around, her eyes darting the surrounding area for listeners. "You know nothing!"

"Oh, yes I do. I know more than you think, little princess of dung." A look of death grabbed her features and her mouth curled in a way that made him wish he had not made that last statement. He knew she would end his life if he didn't say something to amend his words quickly. "But, I can help you understand what it is you are searching for in that, ummm…, object," he attempted to smile, though he rubbed his chin where she struck him.

She reached down for him.

"No!" he screamed like a woman.

"Shut up, flea. I'm only helping you to your feet," she said and pulled him up effortlessly. He brushed himself off and looked at her. "Come with me, and keep your mouth closed," she said then and moved off. Inside her small home she sat him at the small wooden table with only a single chair. There were never guests in her home. She took a seat at the edge of her thatched corner-bed and studied him for a moment. He looked out of place. He was also dirty and in need of a good bath. It was obvious he wasn't used to living without the comfort of a daily cleaning and a change of clothing and someone to look after all his needs. But that wasn't her job. It wasn't her responsibility to mother him. No. It was her job to make him a man, she thought. And that was something she was determined to do…, and soon.

"So, tell me," she said dryly, before he started to spatter off about how she treated him.

"Tell you what?" he said stupidly.

"Don't make me…."

"Oh, the stone…, yes, yes," he reminded himself. "Well, practically every scholar knows the story. Mostly, they consider the stone a myth, and perhaps there have been great stories of legend come about the stone. But no one really believes it to be true."

"So, tell me the story," she insisted.

"Fine. Like I said, it's only myth. The stone is claimed to have come from the sky. It has been described as a stone of fire from among the stars. This stone was broken into three great fragments and sent to different locations so to keep them apart from each other. The myth says that each stone belongs to a greater mass, a monolith that once told the secrets of all life as it exists. By combining the stones with the monolith, the secrets shall be released. And it was not just life here, but life everywhere, even among the stars themselves. It is said that the stone is the key to everyone's destiny."

"So why, if it is a myth, do I have it here with me at this time?"

"I don't know. Like I said, it was supposed to be a legendary stone that no one really expects to exist. But if you do have it…," he thought some. "If the stories are true, then you have used it?" he asked.

"Never mind that. Tell me more of the stone and its use."

He thought for a moment longer. "There isn't any real use for the stone other than the energy it is supposed to produce. In Buddhist and Taoist writings, there is a story of eight immortals or masters who reside beneath a secret mountain near the border of China. There is a city, known as Agartha, deep within the Kun Lun mountain range. This valley, it is said, hides great treasures from the beginning of time. It is also claimed that they are a gray people who live there. But no one can get to them. There have been hints of underground tunnels leading to the city, yet no one ever returns to tell the tale; so it is forgotten. At least that is the story, as I know it."

"So where did the eight immortals come from? And why are the people gray?"

"I suppose the legend goes that they were made of air and clay, formed, so it is written, by Mu Kung, the ruler of the eastern winds and Wang Mu, the queen of the western."

"That's a lie. There are no such people made of winds," she scoffed. "I wouldn't doubt that you are telling me complete lies about the stone to protect your hide."

"Skitatsya, I have no reason to lie to you. I only tell you what I have read or heard in my life and on my many visits around the lands. If you don't believe my answers, try another scholar. He will attest to my very words, if he is indeed a knowledgeable scholar," he said irritated. "Now, I will retire to my cart," he said and stood indignant and defiant. Before she could say another word, he was outside.

She slept uncomfortable and with bothersome dreams throughout the night only to wake to the clash of battle cries and horse whinnies. Aoife rose early, starting to train the next group of young girls how to fight on horseback. She had been working with them for almost a month now. The girls aged from eleven to fourteen and their untrained screams were piercing to Skitatsya's ears. She rose and went out to see.

"Did you sleep well?" Aoife asked on a pass by, following the last group of girls racing to the edge of town before they turned about and rode as fast as they could back.

Skitatsya looked on, dazed and still rubbing sleep from her eyes. No answer followed. From the corner of her eye she saw him coming. Piladius was cleaned and groomed well. She realized that he had probably had enough dirt on him to finally go to the river and wash it off. Even the cuts and bruises on his feet were cleaned and looking better.

"Did you sleep well?" he asked cheerfully as he neared. He was obviously in a better mood.

She squinted against the rising sun in the distance. "What do you want?" she remarked sarcastically. Her head throbbed.

"Nothing. I feel better today," he commented.

"I thought you were leaving. I thought you said you didn't have to take this anymore?"

"I've changed my mind."

"And what made you change your mind?"

"That's none of your business. There's a lot to learn here and I'm writing it all down."

"Lots to learn? Like what? We train to fight and hunt and kill and cook and clean. What could you possibly want to learn from us?"

"There," he pointed. "Do you see what those men and women are doing over there?"

She scanned the dusty road and looked at the smoke rising in the air from the fire pits. "Yes. They are making Brona's things. You want to learn how to make weapons and pottery?"

"No. They don't just make weapons and pottery. They make them with a new metal that they claim came from Brona's idea, a new mixture of earthly chemicals. That is new. They have called it bronze, to keep it Brona's. Nowhere in all the writings of the world is there any mention of bronze used for weapons or anything else. And your women are making pottery and plates and vases of this same material. That is incredible. I must stay and write it all down," he said excitedly.

Skitatsya thought better of his plans. "I'm sorry, Piladius. That won't do. You won't be watching much bronze making. It won't fit in your schedule."

"What schedule?"

"As of today," she decided. "You begin learning how to hunt."

"But I don't want to hunt. I don't have the clothes for it and I don't have any weapon for it. I won't be very good at it either. So, you'll have to find someone else to hunt for you."

She laughed. "You won't be hunting for me, Piladius. You will be hunting for yourself. You see I have already spread the word to every home that you are not to be eating of their kind pots any longer. From now on you are killing, cleaning and eating your own food, Piladius."

"Fine," he said with a sense of arrogance. I'll feed myself, but for now I'm writing all of this down."

"Do as you will, but don't come back to me whining about hunger. I have said my last on this subject. When you are ready to hunt, come and find me. I will teach you."

"I won't be looking for you, Skitatsya. I'll make out just fine on my own."

She left him then. Going back to her little house, she dipped her hands in the bucket of water she always kept at the entrance and washed her face. There was not much time. She had to speak to her father. There must be another way for her people to survive.

CHAPTER III

"You look troubled, Skitatsya," Brona said in greeting.

"A terrible pounding in my head, Father."

"Come, sit with me. We must make preparations for your departure."

She sat on the carcass of a great stag that her father had killed many years ago. Most of his home was covered in animal skins. It kept the ground warm in the winter and amazingly cool in the summer. He joined her after serving a cup of cold water treated with special herbs that he had picked himself. "Here," he said giving it to her. "This will help."

"Father," she started after a good drink. "We must find another way. I cannot let this happen to my people."

"I know how you feel, but there is nothing you or anyone can do to stop it. The wheel is already in motion. You can slow the wheel down, but you cannot stop the wheel from reaching its destination. What I saw in the stone will happen. It is just a matter of when."

There was a sudden knock at the entrance and Brona invited Oseida and Rwan into his home. They had waited for Skitatsya to come first, watching from across the way as Brona had instructed the night before. "Please, come in," he invited with a smile.

"Father, why are they here?"

"They know what is about to happen, Skitatsya. I have told them the story and they are here to help you. You must explain to them all that you know. Oseida is to take your place at the head of the battle, Skitatsya."

"My place at the head? But, I will be there myself, Father."

"No, my child. They already know that you will be far from here. That is why you must teach them all that you know about yourself, your family, your life. It is most important that they know everything so as to trick the Romans. Otherwise our efforts are completely lost and so are our lives."

"I cannot. I will not!"

"Skitatsya," Oseida interrupted. "If we are to survive through you, you must tell us everything. We are prepared to give our lives for you, but you have to allow us to know all that there is to know. And when this is all over, we shall wait for you in the new life. Your father has told us everything. We are ready for this battle, Skitatsya. We won't fail you."

She shook her head. Why must this be? How could she let this happen? It was all her fault and there seemed to be nothing she could do to stop it. Yet she knew that she had to give in. What else was there? From a bent head that searched the floor for answers, she started:

"My name is Skitatsya. The name was given to me by my mother, Marianne, of the Roxolani tribe. My name means *to wander* in the native tongue of the upper Steppes. My father is Brona, the tenth generation great grandson of Rashada, mother of Alexander the bold. Young Alexander and Rashada, who is known as Roxane, are the wife and son of Alexander the Great. Upon the death of Alexander in Babylonia, they were sent back to their homeland in Macedonia, only to be executed some ten years later. But they were not murdered. Instead, they were saved by Perdiccas and taken to the western shores of the Caspian. From there they would travel east to Sogdriana, Rashada's home. You see, Perdiccas was wounded in battle and she saved his life as he crept about the countryside searching for a way back to her, and safety. To repay her for her services, he rescued her from certain death and offered her and her son safe passage home under the guard of several loyal soldiers. However, the general and his men were killed by a band of mercenaries after landing on the eastern shore of the Caspian, never making it to her home. Roxane stole her child away and settled among the people of the Alan tribe. She was a strong woman and so taught her son to be strong. Soon, she was seen as an outcast. It was not right for women to teach men to fight and hunt. She moved north with her son and joined with a group of gypsies who had prospered from the Steppes. Together they settled in a location just east of here, between the Scythians and the Sarmatian tribes of the Alans and the Aorsi. It was there that they called themselves by the name which we go by today, Roxolani. It was Roxane and the Alan tribe combination that she chose to call herself and the tribe has remained since. Alexander grew to become a mysterious man who died, some think by poison, when traveling to the southern shores of the Black Sea. Though he never married, Setra was born of him. From Setra came Clovis and Boris. This lineage continues for over two centuries to my father, Brona, who now keeps the name of my family a secret. No one else knows of this lineage. And it must never be spoken from your lips. Certain death will find you should you speak the names I have said today. It is only because my father has asked me to do so that I have given them to you. My sister, Aoife, knows her heritage, but chooses not to remember her namesake. Only in her horse's name, Bucephalus, does she know that her blood is always that of the great Macedonian. I, on the other hand, shall always be proud of my family lineage."

"Indeed, Skitatsya, that is quite a heritage," Oseida said to her, surprised. "To be born of Alexander the Great! There are many stories of his deeds across these lands. We never knew. Now we can see how you are so strong and determined. But for us to completely fool the Romans we must learn your fighting techniques. You must show us the leap of the salmon. Surely, the Roman you captured on the Turan knows you are the only woman alive who can perform such a feat. Now you must show us. If he sees this, he will be certain that he has found you."

Skitatsya looked at her with dread. She had known Oseida for many years. They had grown together and fought beside each other many times. She had scars from many battles on her arms and legs and a patched hole on her inner thigh that Skitatsya had mended herself after a wild boar attack. They shared many evenings under the stars wondering what would greet them come the following day, never quite knowing if they would live that long. And they had shared many tears over the *kurgans* they had built along the way. There would be no more *kurgans* after this battle, she realized. "I will show you," she said sadly. Brona nodded his approval.

She spent the rest of the day in a far off field teaching Oseida and Rwan, who would take Aoife's place in the coming battle, how to leap from the ground like a salmon leaps from the water going upstream. She never realized that her headache went away. Brona's drink had done its job. While she concentrated on teaching Oseida and Rwan, she kept her eyes open for onlookers. This was not a feat she wanted everyone to know. There was virtually no one, anywhere, who could perform such an act. Not even Aoife could do it quite the way Skitatsya could. And while she continued to train them, she thought about her name. She had to change her name, but not here. Not where everyone who knew her would question the sudden change. No. Sometime after she left she would change it. And what would she call herself? She had no idea, but there was plenty of time to think of one. For now she would concentrate on getting Oseida and Rwan trained as her father instructed. The day was actually quite perfect for it, though she knew winter's winds would come very soon.

It was sometime during the afternoon when she heard the crashing through the brush. It stopped Oseida in the middle of a practice leap, causing her to fall to the ground hard. Rwan already had a short sword ready for whomever or whatever was coming out for them. Skitatsya stood beside her, her eyes searching all directions at once, waiting somehow for Romans to come charging in. Then the crash came again, closer and more focused on an exit from the thickets. Then he emerged. He was scratched from thick brush on his feet and his face and he was covered with bronze from head to toe. He looked utterly silly yet angry and determined.

"You!" he shouted across the field. "I've been looking for you everywhere!" he continued to shout. Rwan and Oseida simply looked on with giggles. They had never seen such a pitiful excuse for a man.

"What do you need, Piladius?" she stifled a laugh herself. He was wretched.

"I'm hungry!" he shouted and stopped at the edge of the field. "You've told everyone not to feed me and they won't let me get anywhere near the food pots. I'm hungry and you had better feed me!" he demanded.

The drawn weapons went away and Skitatsya approached him casually. "I told you before," she started then slapped him across his pointed face like an insolent child. "You have to learn to hunt for your own food. No more handouts for you, my fine young scholar. You'll learn to hunt for your food, or die of starvation. Your mother and father are no longer with you. You are on your own. The choice is yours."

He stood there near tears, but refused to let them fall. Suddenly, she slapped him again, provoking him. He stepped back in surprise. No one ever slapped him. He was a scholar. Scholars don't get slapped. They slap others with words and philosophy and intelligence. Yet, here he was, getting slapped by a woman and for a second time. There was something wrong here. No woman ever touches a man in such a way. Not where he comes from anyway. Yet, she was not an ordinary woman, he told himself. Still, it didn't matter. Anger filled his veins with fire and his face turned red. His fists closed into tight balls. His eyes darted left and right, never quite looking at anything, yet seeing what his mind thought he should see; Skitatsya on the ground begging for mercy. She saw his features change and watched his eyes squint, hinting of action, any action. He leaned and she caught the shift in his balance. Before he could bring up his arm to swing at her, she simply pushed him further, making him stumble. By the time his arm came up in a swing he was tumbling to the side like a drunken fool. With insight enough to know, she had seized the opportunity to reduce his attempt to strike back and knocked him down before he could act at all. There he sat, on the ground, staring out at nothing. There was nothing he could do. He was at her mercy. Whatever she had in store for him was going to become his life. It appeared as though he was going to become a hunter. At least, he thought to himself, he could learn to hunt and then leave this dreadful place on his own, knowing he could survive on his own. Yes, that would become his plan.

"I will learn to hunt, Skitatsya. But I need food first," he begged.

"You'll be fed, but only after you have hunted."

His eyes rolled in defeat as he stood, brushing himself off. Oseida and Rwan went back to the village without comment. Skitatsya would be busy for the rest of the day, they realized.

The next few weeks went by without mishap. Skitatsya's schedule had become a daily task of teaching Piladius to become a man, much the way it was when she was doing nothing but training women to fight. That had become Aoife's job now. While she rode the young girls to the ends of the village and back and showed them to fight with sword and knife and spear, Skitatsya occupied herself in the forests, showing Ploppus—as she now called him because of his refutable gestures—how to hunt with a bow. It took a good week just to teach him to hold it properly. Once he became used to the weight and the pull of the gut against the alder wood, he became quite efficient. He had changed his attire to hunt also, enjoying the comfort of leather boots (though they chaffed his feet during the first week) and pants that kept his thighs from being rubbed raw while he learned to ride a horse. A shirt was given to him from Torak's brother, Joshuba, who was about the same size as Piladius. The combination of riding a horse and pulling a bowstring at the same time took another week, but he managed, much to Skitatsya's disgruntled attitude about his slowness to achieve. During the afternoon hours she would teach Oseida and Rwan the leap of the salmon and other fighting techniques that only Skitatsya would know. They had become quite adept at learning her moves, though they were somewhat awkward about them at first. A little more time, and they would surely pass for her in a battle against the Romans, Skitatsya knew. Piladius would tend to working with bronze in his afternoon hours, creating interesting plates and jewelry and cups and even weapons.

A week later the snows came, but only for a brief time. A day later it melted to leave the ground in a soft mush. Skitatsya felt her time to depart was soon coming. Under her father's supervision, she had consulted the stone twice. Each time she saw the same vision; death, bodies askew on an open battlefield, a golden haired man with curls that bounced from the sides of his head. It all meant nothing to her and she ignored it each time. But the weather could not be ignored. Already, the women were preparing their homes for winter's harsh breath. Pelts from the hides of deer and bear were being prepared to greet another cold season. Skitatsya knew she had to teach Ploppus quickly. She had other things to take care of before she left. At this rate, he would only slow her down. Therefore, he would have to hunt on his own. And she knew he was ready for it. He had grown accustomed to getting up early and washing his face and hands in a bucket of water she made him tie to the side of his wagon. He filled it daily, without losing a single drop. He had managed to gain a good state of balance with his body, standing up straighter and taller than he had before. And there were calluses on his hands that he didn't seem to mind. Yet he whined on a daily basis about being fed. Apparently, you can teach him how to hunt, but you can't teach him how to gut it, clean it and cook it too. Skitatsya was willing to sacrifice the dirty work just to keep him at the hunting. Cleaning and cooking the food he hunted would come in good time, she knew.

"Skitatsya," Oseida called running to her on horseback. "Come, quickly. Brona wants you. He says it is urgent!"

She left Piladius to find his way to the village on his own as she dashed back on Khutalk, her golden stallion. Piladius had been in this forest many times. She knew he would return safely.

"Skitatsya," Brona said when she entered his home. "Gather your sister. You must leave on the morn."

She shook her head momentarily. "It is time, then?"

"Rwan has been sending scouting parties to all corners. They have returned with word of a Roman invasion. We have no choice, Skitatsya. The time has come."

"I cannot, Father!" she nearly wept.

He took her hands in his. She was beautiful…, and strong. "You must. If you delay, all that we have done here is for nothing. Tell no one, Skitatsya. Leave in the morning as you would on any other day to go hunting. And never look back, my child. Remember everything, but never look back."

"But Aoife teaches the warriors in the morning hours. Surely they will know something is wrong if she doesn't appear."

"I have arranged for that. Oseida will replace her in the morning. Aoife will be assisting you in training that young man of yours tomorrow. But be easy on him, Skitatsya. He has a way about him. There is intelligence within him. I can sense it, Skitatsya. Now go, and keep your name in your children and them in theirs," he said.

She leaned close and held him. She hadn't done that in many years. Not since she was perhaps ten and when he had shown her how to hunt large game. He was much younger then, she remembered. He smelled of smoked wood, a scent she had enjoyed since childhood. It was his way of saying the winter season was upon them. "I love you, Father," she whispered.

"And I you, daughter. Be mindful of your sister, Aoife. She is a wild one, but a strong asset in battle."

"I will," she replied with a kiss on his bearded cheek. Then she turned and walked away, never looking back to see him standing at the entrance watching her go.

"Skitatsya?" Oseida called her.

She turned to look at her longtime friend. Without a single word each knew what was to happen. "Before you go," Oseida said. "I wanted you to have this." A decorated bowl was removed from a sack and given to Skitatsya.

"What is this?" Skitatsya asked.

"The skull of that Roman I had outside my home. It started to stink badly so I removed it and made something for you. It was too large to make into a cup, but I managed a bowl for you to take along on your journey."

Skitatsya studied it. Indeed, if this were the head of Bracus, it would never have made for a cup to drink out of. It was much too large. But a bowl seemed quite appropriate. A pleasing combination of bronze and gold horses crowned the exterior of the bowl and the interior was polished smooth. Had Oseida not told her it was a skull, she never would have guessed. "Thank you, my friend," Skitatsya said, then embraced her with eyes full of tears.

"What is all this?" Torak came around the corner and caught them crying and holding each other.

"None of your business," Oseida replied before Skitatsya could.

"Women crying in the streets? Surely that is someone's business. Especially," he stopped as Skitatsya turned to face him. Her knife came up and she stood ready. There was danger in her eyes and he read the signs immediately. "I…, I didn't know it was you, Skitatsya," he tried to apologize.

"Be gone, Torak," she warned. "Or I'll place you beside your sister who is ten times the warrior you'll ever be," she threatened.

He left without another word, but kept looking over his shoulder to see if she moved after him. Even though he towered her by a foot, he knew she would kill him before he ever put a hand on his own weapon. No one ever confronted Skitatsya. Not if you expected to live for another day.

"What's wrong?" Ploppus rode into the village and met them.

"Get your things ready," Skitatsya told him. "We leave tomorrow."

"Leave?" he questioned. "Where to?" he asked, almost excited.

"West," she answered while looking at Oseida, then turned away and walked to her home. It was the last time she would see Oseida. In fact, it was the last time she would ever see her village again.

CHAPTER IV

"And why can I not take my books?" he screamed at her.

Without waiting for another word, she turned about and slapped him hard across his mouth. He didn't fall, but stood there with a bleeding lip, looking at her with hate in his dark eyes, a hate she had come to know many times in her past from training women to fight. There were many who wanted to strike back and attempt their fate at fighting her. But like all those before him, he backed away, knowing she would kill him without hesitation. Yet Skitatsya was not without heart. She realized that he had saved and maintained a collection of knowledge that far exceeded her entire village. For him to simply leave his entire life's work in the hands of Romans didn't seem right. And she knew she couldn't take them along. Surely the villagers would become suspicious. No. Their departure from the village would have to be as if it were another hunting trip and nothing more. With the exception of a silver coin Brona had given her several years ago, all her personal belongings remained in her hut. The silver coin, a Tetradrachm he had called it, contained the facial impression of Alexander the Great on the front. It was all she had of her heritage.

"I am ready." Aoife rode up on Bucephalus. She loved to travel, yet realized that this would be a long journey. It had not occurred to her that she would never return. She wore a leather harness designed to carry her bow across her back, her arrows, hunting knife on her right side and a sword sheathed on her left. A spear of alder wood was stuffed between blanket and horse and within easy reaching distance if she needed it.

Skitatsya looked at Ploppus. "You can take three books with you and no more. You won't have room for anything else."

"But they are all important to me. I cannot just leave the others."

She thought for a moment. "Pick three to take with you. The others we will bury nearby," she said.

Instantly, he stuffed Homer's Iliad down the front of his shirt then removed three more tombs from his cart to place in his sack. Of the three, one was on the work he had done with bronze that he had been writing himself. From now on, he realized, he would be writing everything that happened on paper so he would never forget. The rest of the books he packed neatly in piles and placed them carefully into sacks to be buried. He would mark the site with the hope that he might someday return to get them back. Of the other two he would take along, one was a hard choice between Plato's *Republic* and his *Critias*. Both, he recalled vividly, told of Plato's philosophy and belief in the island of Atlantis, which has never been found. In the last moment, he chose *Republic* only because it portrayed a contrast in the corruption and ill use of diplomacy Atlantis exhibited while using Athens and its positive culture and stately virtues as a backdrop for the dysfunctional city Atlantis had become. He had traveled to Athens with his father, Aram, on a trading journey long ago. It was then that Piladius first became interested in reading and writing, watching scholars translate Latin and Sanskrit from ancient books and the many other languages throughout the ages. And the storytellers were numerous and great. Yet *Critias* was Plato's cousin, he remembered, who narrated the story of Atlantis. It was *Critias*, he also recalled, who retold the story from his great-grandfather, Dropides. It was such a hard decision to choose.

"We have to hurry," Skitatsya warned.

Republic went quickly into the sack along with his personal tomb that he considered calling *Piladius, a Journey in Time*. He hadn't confirmed the title, but had given it some thought. Perhaps this next journey might shed light on a different title for him. "I'm almost done," he told her. The third book was a collection of poems from the masters. These were plentiful, for no man was a writer or an educator or a scholar who did not study the art of poetic form and speak the tongue of the poet. While he fancied himself as a true poet in writing form, his audience for storytelling and poetic formula was not his forte. His was more the subdued, concentric style of writer who visualized his writing being recited in the marketplace or on the corner street in the fashion of old tell-tale storytellers.

With his books collected and stored on a provision horse that carried enough supplies to keep them for ten or more days, he begrudgingly carried the remainder of the tombs and secretly buried them behind Skitatsya's home. This he marked with a piece of dried wood he staked into the ground. The wood was carved in Sanskrit on the bottom of the backside facing the forest, where no one could see it. If a person accidentally happened by who knew how to read the writings there, they would know that a treasure of history and worldly writings was buried beneath. Only, he admitted, a true scholar would find them and use them properly. Unless, of course, he returned to get them himself.

At the edge of the village, Brona greeted them with saddened eyes and a heavy heart. He had seen the end, knew what was to be. At least he had the chance to save his two daughters. The rest of the village would fight relentlessly for their honor and none would give in until the last fell to his death. Before pushing off to the west, he grasped Skitatsya's leg and forced the stone into her hand. "Before you depart, Skitatsya, I would like to know what name you have chosen for yourself? I ask only so that I may know you when we meet again in the next life."

She looked at him as if for the first time, knowing that it would also be for the last time. "Father, I have not chosen one," she announced.

"I thought as much," he told her knowingly. "I would like to offer a blessing for your new name, a name I have heard from within the stone. From here on, you shall be called, Scathach,"

"Scathach," she repeated in a strange tone.

"You disapprove?"

"Not at all, Father. It is a good name. But it will take some getting used to."

"Yes. I suppose it will," he said with a quick smile. "But go, now. You must be off before it is too late. My blessing goes with you," he said, then turned and walked away from them. As he moved off, Skitatsya noticed Rwan and Oseida, who she thought she would never see again, watching from among the forest trees. As the new protectors of Brona, they obviously saw fit to observe the departure from afar, yet close enough to protect Brona should the need arise. Without speaking a word to give away their watchful eyes, she pushed her horse forward, ahead of the others. It would be several hours before anyone spoke again.

"Scathach…" *(Skee, yach)* Piladius repeated after a quick stop and a rest for the horses. It was the first word she had heard since leaving the village and it caught her off guard. "It sounds like a good name," he said. "Better than your other, I think," he confirmed. "Much bolder, if I must say."

She mulled it over in her mind. Yes, Father had chosen wisely. But where did he get the name? Who had given him this name to speak? She would have to find out, she mused. "Go out for food and be leery of heavily wooded areas. We don't know the land here as well as our own," she told him. "If you find danger, come back here quickly."

The last part of that statement bothered him, but he had learned to hunt well and had become quite good with a bow. If danger lurked behind bushes and trees he knew he could get off an arrow or two to protect himself as he bolted back. Before long, however, he had returned with a rabbit strapped across his back. Unfortunately, there were six arrows missing. He would have to cut down branches and form new ones to replace them, she realized. Yet, nothing had moved in the area, he commented silently. The land was peaceful and serene. And while Scathach prepared a fire to cook the meat, Aoife demonstrated to Piladius how to skin the animal and prepare it for cooking. This, he hated most of all. It was the flesh of the animal that really bothered him; the ripping and tearing of the hide away from the meat. It made him sick, but he stayed where he was. He knew that she and Scathach would make him hunt and cook his own food all the way west if he squirmed like a little child. The longer he played stupid, the better off he was going to be. Perhaps he would find a nice little city to settle down in while Scathach and Aoife shuffled across the countryside. Then he wouldn't have to worry about cooking and cleaning his own food. Just walk up and buy it already prepared. That was the life. Perhaps he would find a wife that would do all that for him, like his father's slaves who captured and cooked all his food for him his whole life.

"We have to move north along the trees," Aoife reported as she rode in on Bucephalus. He was a magnificent animal with a broad chest and an excellent display of muscle that shimmered in the afternoon sun. And Aoife was in good shape herself, Piladius noted, as if for the first time. She was extremely shapely and pranced around like a peacock strutting about the fountains of Greece. It aroused him slightly, but he fought off the urge to speak of it for fear that she would beat him mercilessly.

They waited until the meat had been fully cooked, then cut into strips for storage, before stamping out the fire, packing and leaving the area. They had plenty of food to last for several days, but sooner or later they would have to stop to hunt. Under their current situation, they took their time preparing the rabbit. There was no need to hurry. But with Romans moving to the east, there were certain precautions that had to be taken. As soon as the fire was out, they moved north and followed the line of trees that spanned the horizon. If danger happened by, they would make a dash into the woodland trees and disappear only to meet again, approximately one mile north and one mile west. This was a training tactic Scathach had taught for many years, though Piladius knew nothing of the move. If they actually had to run, he would have to follow her closely, she thought.

The night settled with a bitter wind that howled out of the north and threatened an evening storm. They took cover among the fir, huddled around a small warming fire, nothing that would give away their position. They slept in the folds of the furs they carried while the horses grazed on the low grasses. Before morning, they were covered in two inches of snow and shivering. This worried Scathach, for her trail would now be visible to anyone who tried to follow. And the Romans would also be visible, she thought. With winter getting closer, they would try to keep more to the south, allowing her to move freely to the north. "Come," she said as she rose stiffly. "We have to move further north."

"But it's cold!" Piladius complained.

"It's going to get colder. More important is that you're going to freeze if you don't move around and get that body working."

Reluctantly, he stood and stretched; shaking the snow off the hides he slept beneath. Aoife was already up and moving. She had learned not to waste time when the weather was cold like this. The thought of a man beside her kept her warm enough to endure the chill. Yet, looking at Piladius made her regret the thought. Still, she considered, he was shaping up into something that could become potential in the future.

They moved north and west as Scathach directed for nearly a week, trying to cover their tracks as much as they could. In the forests where the snow was caught in the tree branches and heavy shrubs, she pulled them forward, further and further until the cold bit at their flesh. If there was a trace, it wasn't much. Eventually, the forest got so thick that the snow had barely enough space between the branches to reach the ground. Here, they resolved to walk the horses. Only the silence lasted. Yet, Piladius didn't seem to mind the quiet, steady pace. He hadn't really said much along the way. His thoughts lingered on the dreadful outcome of the Romans invading the village far away. It was slightly colder here in the deeper forest areas, but his movements kept him warm. And he reflected upon his life as he pushed forward. All those years of sitting and lying in the back of the cart reading Plato and Socrates and eating delicious fruits; being waited on at every turn. The warmth and comfort of a covered cart being pulled by someone else while he relaxed in the folds of an Athenian quilt eased the chill. He wished, briefly, that those days were still here. Still, there was so much more he had learned since leaving that life behind. He could hunt and ride a horse with the best of them. He could fight, if only to defend himself. He had learned of bronze and how to shape objects from it. And he had become somewhat stronger, he knew. He looked himself over to certify this. Yes, much stronger. Not only was he smart, he was strong. That, he knew, could be a very dangerous combination. In his travels, you were one or the other; smart or strong. Smart was the man who could win a battle with words of diplomacy. Strong was he who could smite down the enemy with a single blow and never look back with mercy or pity. His father, Aram, was such a man, he considered. Aram was twice the size and strength and intelligence as he. Perhaps someday they would meet again. Perhaps then his father would approve of him.

The forest cleared slightly and a vision of another setting day was visible in the distance. "There is a village ahead," Aoife announced. "Shall we stop and rest for the evening?" There was a sort of glitter in her wicked eye that Piladius caught and recognized as opportunity. Yes, there were men in this village. And she would seek out the first available man to take for a companion; if only for one night. Somehow, he wished it were he that would be the lucky one. Reality dictated that it would not be so. And Scathach would not even look at him in such a way. She barely recognized him as a man to begin with. He was equal only to the animals whose instinct told them they must hunt down their prey to survive. And survive he would, he considered.

Scathach nodded. "Yes. The horses will need food and fresh water. I'll go in first to see if all is safe."

Only moments had lapsed before she returned with good news. No Romans had been in the area for a long time. It seemed that the night would be spent in warmth and comfort after all. Piladius smiled.

The animals were settled with hay and a good portion of grain and oats that the town seemed to have plenty of. The sacks of food and miscellaneous weapons they carried were stored for the night. Additional money, mostly that which was stolen from victorious Roman skirmishes and battles with the barbaric tribes of the northern steppes, was spent to ensure the safety of their sacks and horses, though there didn't appear to be any need. Still, it was best to be safe, Scathach told herself. Gold and silver coins were good everywhere, no matter where it came from.

The village had been established for quite some time, they noted as they traveled the dirt road. Most of the buildings were made of carved stone and wood, some possessing unique engravings on their doors and around windows. Wooden signs that Scathach and Aoife could not read hung on the wall beside each door or on wooden posts at the front entrance to most of the buildings. Piladius realized that civilization had surely made its way here.

"Do you know this language?" Scathach asked him as she listened to the keeper.

"Yes, Scathach, I know the language," he answered with a smile. Finally they needed him for something. He knew they would not get much help here without his knowledge. "They are speaking a poor dialect of Ugrian, but I can make it out."

"Ask them if they have food and rooms for us to spend the night," she told him.

The keeper was typical for the job; short, plump and happy. He was more than eager to assist strangers and didn't seem to mind that there were women traveling during this time of year.

"Interesting name, Scathach…" the innkeeper commented as he overheard Piladius speak her name. "Not very common in these parts, but a good name, I admit," he added. "On your way to the market?" he asked.

"Market?" Piladius asked him.

"Yes," he stated matter-of-factly, "one of the biggest in the area. People come here from the north to spend the night. In the morning they always move on to the south and the market. They virtually come from everywhere to buy and sell their wares. Are you buyers or sellers?"

"Buyers," Piladius answered quickly, although he thought it may have surprised the keeper. "We buy rare books and oddities," he shoved in.

The round fellow smiled and his belly rolled slightly with laughter. "You'll find enough there then, lad. Are you familiar with books?"

"Enough to know what to look for," he told him.

"Well, then, that's good." The keeper didn't push the issue.

"What are you two talking about," Scathach asked. There was a hint of caution in her eyes. "All I want is food and some sleep. No need for idle talking with these folks."

"It's nothing," he told her. "I've ordered a meat stew and bread for each of us."

As they settled to eat, Aoife searched the room. "Not much to choose from," she commented as a gruff fellow returned her stare. His hair was matted and slick with body oil while his face was pocked with deep craters. Patches of whiskers claimed the sides of his face and on his chin showing that he wasn't experienced enough to shave properly. Aoife had a reputation for men, but she also had taste. And this man was not on the list.

"If this is all they have to offer for men, I'll be glad to leave first thing in the morning," Aoife scoffed.

"There's always Ploppus, here," Scathach directed with a nod of her head, though her eyes never lifted from her food. And still, Piladius noted, she kept a watch on all sides as she ate.

"I'd rather a mule!" Aoife spat to the side then turned back and devoured the stew.

Piladius never lifted his head from the table. He had seen his father in places like this. Father told him to divert his eyes from those around him, otherwise one would attract the attention of wrongdoers. The lesson was well learned. Of course, he was also taught that if trouble was inevitable you had to be faster than your opponent. If you couldn't beat them, make sure you can outrun them. Piladius, though never toughened enough to perform in combat, could surely outrun any of these men. But he had worked hard over the months and knew he could perform well beside Scathach and her skills as a warrior. These men didn't appear to be outlandish, just dirty and unkempt. Surely they would not attempt anything in this place.

They had eaten uneventfully, bathed and settled for a good night's rest. Aoife wasn't about to be let down, however. She managed to eat, bathe and move about the town freely, in search of a good man to taunt. It was her way. Piladius took to reading one of the tombs stuffed in his shirt and Scathach slept without worry until Aoife returned, slightly disappointed by the sounds of her obnoxious entry sometime in the late evening hours.

By morning they were rested and in better spirits to continue their journey west. The horses were well fed and watered, their hooves cleaned and made ready. Outside the inn they packed their belongings and mounted in the brisk weather.

"I would move south before pushing off to the west," a sly fellow commented. He stood, leaning a shoulder against the corner of the building as he spoke. His eyes were narrow, keen, his nose long and straight. His flesh was smooth, untouched by scars of battle. Certainly he was not a warrior, yet he possessed poise enough that he might be an acrobat or an assassin. Perhaps he was a spy. A knife was in his right hand and he was shaving strips of meat from a leg of lamb.

"We intend to," Scathach replied. She noticed him the moment they walked out of the building, had watched him the whole time, but paid little attention to him.

"Why are you so eager to move that way?" he asked. "There's only death there. Gaul, you know, is under attack and the legions of Rome are everywhere. Best to go to the market and leave the west alone," he said to no one. It was as if he spoke to the air around him.

"We intend to," Scathach repeated, a little more disdainfully.

He knows your language," Piladius commented. "Is he to be trusted?"

"Not likely," Aoife whispered to him.

"Why do you tell us this?" Piladius asked the stranger.

"I have been watching you. You have no intension of going to the market, even though you say otherwise. Would you like to know of your village?"

Scathach suddenly studied him closely, dangerously. "No," she said dryly.

"And Brona?" he asked her.

Piladius knew not where the arrow came from, but it was launched with a swiftness he never would have believed. In the second that it took to lodge it, the stranger's coat was pinned to the wall and he struggled to free it before Scathach was upon him. He was too slow. A knife was at his throat, his arm caught against the wall, struggling to free itself from the arrow. His knife had fallen to the ground at his feet. Now the man was pinned, his eyes darting anywhere, everywhere for help or assistance. "Please," he nearly begged, "Skitatsya," he whispered. She faltered slightly. He knew her, by name.

"Who are you?" she asked, though the knife remained at his throat.

"Please, I know you well. I have not followed you this past year to be killed so easily, warrior. I merely state that your travels should drive you south rather than west. I will not pontificate my commander's reasons for tracking you, but you have fascinated me for a very long time. I now only want to see your safety through to the end of your journey."

"You want to see me to the end of my journey? Where is it that I go?"

"It has been foretold, Scathach. That is what you call yourself now. I like it much better than your other. Please," he said and put his free hand up to the knife and lowered it. He stuffed the last piece of meat in his mouth then gave the arrow a few tugs until it loosened and withdrew from the wall. He handed it back to her. "We need to find a place to talk."

"We will talk on the road. Do you have a horse?"

"Yes, wait for me," he said and went behind the inn where his horse was standing ready. He was back before Scathach mounted Khutalk.

On their move south the stranger started. "You Sarmatian are extremely impressive." He let it sit in the air a moment before continuing. "I have watched you for a long time, Scathach. You fight very well, better than most men I have seen in any land. And there are many lands that I have traveled over. You are far better than any woman of my own city."

"Let's get to the point. What do you want of me?" Scathach stopped and addressed him just outside of the town limits. There was no sense in pushing on if he had ill intensions. Besides, she had the cover of the forest around her to get away if a trap was about to be unleashed.

"Fine," he said. "My name is Phaedrus. I was sent by Nero in Rome to find you. Suetonius has told him about some ancient item, a stone I believe, that he was returning with to give to him. You managed to recover that item and he wants it back."

"So, you are Roman?" Piladius asked with caution. Oddly, he reached for the bow strapped across his back. It was awkward how he moved and Phaedrus saw the shift, but ignored it as an inconvenience.

"No. I am Greek, from Lacedaemeon," he commented proudly.

"Truly!" Piladius replied and released the hold on the edge of his bow. Even if he tried, he could not slip it from his shoulder any faster than Aoife or Scathach. "You are Spartan?"

"Yes."

"Then you are either a spy or," and his hand went back to his bow.

"Or an assassin," Phaedrus continued then nodded with a thin grin.

"If you are an assassin, why are you telling us this?" Aoife asked. The story of his occupation was little cause for concern in her mind. She could kill him any time she wanted and very easily, she knew. It was best to get as many answers out in the open first. Then she would decide what to do with him. After all, he was probably the most handsome man she had seen the entire trip.

"Because," and he looked directly at Scathach, "you are remarkable warriors. And…I don't really care for the Roman way of doing things; too much political anxiety in the air. They are a very ambitious yet untrusting people. I'm sure it was only a matter of time before they drummed up a charge to have me put to death."

"I understand," Piladius jumped in. "You are Spartan. I have been to Greece before and studied in Athens for a year while my father traded, bought and sold throughout the city. It bored him so much that he took to traveling the countryside looking for new wares to ponder on people. And I was subjected to a reclusive life, confined to the back of a covered cart where I could read and write and study by myself; a place where my father didn't have to listen to me, or even look at me for that matter."

"We're not here to talk about you!" Scathach finally shoved in. He thought she raised her hand to slap him, but hesitated and brushed her arm so as not to give her intension away. "Tell me, Spartan..." she looked at him, "if you are an assassin, why am I alive, and what do you know of my village?"

"My dear, lady," his features softened slightly, "we must move along from this road. Too many ears pass this way for us to speak idly."

She agreed without replying and turned Khutalk about and started off. When they were a good way down the road, Piladius picked up the conversation again.

"So how does one become a Greek assassin?"

"Ahhh, yes...the curious philosopher," he commented. "I have watched you too. And when the time is right, I have a special talent to teach you. But to answer your question directly... My mother was a *herlot*, a slave if you will. My father was of the manner of *perioeci*, a merchant himself. In this respect I can admire your father's decision to move about the lands to the east and west for Greeks have the taste of fanciful wares that tend to stagnate and become obsolete very quickly. My father did not last long as a merchant and trader, becoming a slave beside my mother in the olive fields. I also have an older brother, Crecuphus, who managed throughout the years to lie and steal and cheat his way into the aristocracy of the Greek democratic society. In his lies, he has secured a position on the *ephorate*. He now guides all aspects of Spartan life with the assistance of four brethren, who I believe have no claim to the seat they possess. In knowing that I could pose a threat to his position, my brother sent spies and assassins to kill me. I barely escaped and found myself living among the people of Rome. They have trained me well."

Aoife scoffed. "You don't seem that intimidating to me. But now I want to know about our village. What happened to our father?"

"Gone, I'm afraid. The two you had trained to take your place made a wonderful display of battle tactics, another reason for admiring your talents. Your father too, was a great adversary to the Roman legion that marched upon your village. In the end, he was murdered as testimony to Caesar's strength and might over any land this side of Rome. And know that he died bravely."

Scathach lowered her head, tears nearly falling from her eyes, but she held them back. She knew father would have fought his best to the last.

"The Romans burned the village to the ground and gave up the stone for lost. That is what was reported to Nero back in Rome. Unfortunately, the head of your father and the two young women who fought as you do were taken back to Rome as proof of the victory."

"So now it comes to the matter of killing us or following us, is that it?" Aoife asked saddened by the news of her father.

"My dear lady," the smile returned, "if I wanted you dead, I would surely have killed you long ago. In my culture as a Spartan, our women are trained to fight just as the men are trained. Each pulls his own weight in arms, unlike the Athenian women who quilt and sew and cook and clean. Your women are similarly strong and well trained. But you possess something quite unique to your style of fighting and I enjoy watching it, have admired it for quite some time, even if from afar."

"Were you a soldier as a Spartan?" Piladius asked to break his stare at Scathach.

"Yes," he answered, but did not avert his eyes.

"A *hoplite* or *peltast*?" Piladius prodded.

The smile disappeared. "You are educated!" he remarked. "Does it matter?"

"Perhaps not to them, but to me, yes."

"Then know that I was a *hoplite*. But my time as a soldier was very short lived."

"So you are a trained assassin? Are you a good horseman too?" Scathach asked.

"I am adequate. But I must admit your Turanian mounts far surpass the gelded horses of Greece or Rome. Given some time, I would love to ride one of those hot beasts."

Scathach and Aoife both pat the necks of their mounts. Bucephalus snorted approval. "So if you are not going to kill us, why are you still following us?"

"Like I said, dear lady. I merely want to see you to the end of your journey."

She stopped and faced him. "And the stone?"

There it was, out in the open; the only question left unanswered. What happened to the stone? She hadn't used it since she left her village and her last encounter still left her questioning the reality of the vision. Could the ethereal proclamation dictate her future? She was uncertain and thought best to leave the stone in its hiding place.

"As much as it seems intriguing, the stone is of no consequence to me."

"And you are telling us to move south because...?"

"Caesar has invaded Gaul. He marches there himself; and with fifty thousand in his army. There are more than three hundred thousand already waiting for him to arrive. He intends to destroy a man some call a king, who has created effective skirmishes against Roman soldiers. Caesar is determined to win. Your move across the western lands will only end in death, Scathach."

"But the winter season is upon us. Surely they will set camp and wait for the warm season to arrive before starting their wars again?" Scathach was sure. She had fought them many times herself in the past. Romans did not like the cold weather and always settled their camps until the winter faded to spring. They would continue to train and practice war skills and they would build large buildings to sleep and eat in and they would build boats to move through the winding twisting rivers of Gaul when the land thaws, but they would not move far from their self-made habitat.

"Not this time." Phaedrus confirmed shaking his head. "Caesar is pushing his army further north and weather is not a concern of his. He has lost many men to the cold and the snow, but cares not. His sights are set on the death of this so-called king and bringing Gaul to its knees."

"Who is this king?" Piladius asked, thinking he might know of him since he traveled many places over the years.

"Vercingetorix," Phaedrus answered. "Do you know him?"

"I thought I might, but the name is unfamiliar to me."

"Not to worry. The Arvernian name will mean nothing when Caesar is finished with him."

"So we go to the market in the south," Scathach told them blankly, resigned at last to make the decision.

"I believe that to be in your best interest," Phaedrus told her. "Besides," and he looked at Piladius, "it will give me time to teach this scholar pup a thing or two." He smiled at Ploppus who shied at the thought of being taught by an assassin. Aoife, however, seemed dazzled by the idea of his company, yet his attention was directed mainly at Scathach. While Aoife was a seductive nymph whose ability to taunt even the gods could be possible, she was not the sophisticated, mature vixen of a woman Scathach had become. When most men would shove a knife in their own heart to bed a woman like Aoife, others would cut off their own heads just for the thought of a night alone with Scathach, her beauty unsurpassed even by Athena's, Phaedrus thought to himself.

CHAPTER V

A heavy fog kept them smothered from sight almost the entire way as the warmer southern air met the colder north. It was a relief for the most part, yet Scathach kept her ears listening all around for any strange movements. Khutalk and Bucephalus also kept alert for strange sounds, their ears twitching and shifting in all directions. The fog kept the earth damp, almost marshy. Their movement over the hilly land was as silent as the still air that encompassed them.

"How long to the market?" Piladius asked him.

"A few days, perhaps a bit longer. It depends on the weather."

"And what will we do when we get there?"

"I suggest we take winter quarters there until the season passes. The weather threatens to be harsh this year."

"So why do people go to this market so late in the year?"

"Because this is the time of year they sell everything they possess and move all the way to the southern shores to restock for the next season. Most will loose money on the bargains, but they will sell them anyway, just to be rid of them. They won't move south unless they have sold everything. They will carry nothing with them except the animals they use to haul their goods. They will procure new carts and carriages on the southern shores and start all over."

Piladius looked at him closely. "My father is a trader. He has been all over these lands. Why haven't I heard of this place before? Do you take me for a fool?"

There was a hint of caution in Phaedrus' voice, but he maintained a constant tone. "Your father was probably a seller of finer merchandise. Perhaps he sold wine or silks?"

"Yes, among other things."

"Then it could be possible that he has never come here, because there are mostly those who sell jewelry, and gems and blankets and clothes. A seller of silks and treasures of the extraordinary would not be found here. They are the ones who continue to travel across the land from destination to destination with a specific buyer in mind. Tell me, did you not repeat your travels from one place to the next? And did you not see the same faces from one place to the next and meet the same people to bargain with when you got there?"

Piladius never realized it, but Phaedrus was right. Always it was the same people Aram had traded with along his journey. Piladius only saw it from the back of a wagon. He was never really allowed to take part in the trading or the buying or selling. He was always in the back of the covered cart reading or eating or sleeping on large, goose-feathered pillows.

"Yes," he answered, almost ashamed for being so ignorant of the trading business. But it wasn't his fault. Aram kept him away from it. He rarely confided in his son about anything in the trading business. The only time he really spoke Piladius was to discover information about a certain type of people or language they spoke or custom they administered in their region. Other than that he was left to himself to squander in luxury and comfort, to lead a blissful life of laziness and self-indulgence. Aram had no use for him. But somehow Piladius knew that was changing. He had changed over the months. He had become stronger, his skin tougher, his direction in life more defined. He had intelligence and strength and the combination suited him.

Khutalk snorted and stammered slightly to the side. This told Scathach there was danger about. "Silence!" she whispered menacingly. Her sword came loose and she bent low on the withers, ready to spring. Her two feet slid up the sides to rest on his hindquarters. She was ready for anything. Phaedrus sensed it also. His knife came from hiding and was shoved between his teeth while a short stick slipped unnoticed from under his heavy mantle. Scathach had never seen such a weapon. There was no point or blade on either end. It was nothing more than a stick in her opinion, yet she was curious. Then her attention was directed all about her where fog had closed in and concealed them and whomever lurked along the road in hiding. Aoife strayed to the rear, giving them each enough room to swing and jump and leap if need be, but maintained a distance close enough to render aid if required. Her bow was ready as was Piladius, though he had no idea what was going on. To him it may as well have been an animal in the path that Scathach thought she should kill and clean and cook to take along on the trip.

Khutalk became skittish and jolted to the right. A bulking figure jumped out from behind a tree and raised an axe. Scathach was ready for him. She threw herself into the air and cut off the hand that carried the weapon long before it could strike. In the next instant she squatted on the ground listening in all directions for the next to come for her. Two others had jumped in from behind the moving troupe. Aoife dispatched them with an arrow in their gurgling throats. Piladius nearly screamed and bolted for safety but somehow managed to clench the reins tightly in his teeth and raised his bow. A burly man garbed in heavy fur leaped in front of him. The arrow shot out in surprise more so than conscious effort and struck him in the upper chest. He grabbed the shaft and fell to the earth. Piladius reached for another arrow strapped to his back. His eyes darted everywhere, first for danger then for safety.

Scathach heard the next coming and spun about to pin him against a tree with the point of her sword. She drilled it through him until the blade struck his backbone and then the tree itself. With a twist, she snapped his spine in two and withdrew the blade only to hack the next man swiftly across his neck as he moved for her. He staggered and fell, twitching and writhing on the muddy earth with his mouth gnashing up and down in a lost struggle to survive. His head dangled loosely to the side by a flap of skin that held it on his shoulders.

Then it was Phaedrus who sprang into motion. The man was pure grace in the art of killing with minimal effort to lose energy in the process. The first to come for him danced a jig with his throat cut by the knife just deep enough to spill his blood in spurting rivulets. The second was stabbed deep into this heart and gashed completely to his right side where his heart was transplanted and then stripped from his body completely. The third bore the knife full in his right eye with the bleeding heart of the previous man attached to the hilt end of the blade. He went crashing down never knowing he had participated in the battle. And then the stick came to life. Phaedrus was a master. His movements were smooth and even, his breathing controlled and concentrated. With every strike he exhaled with a whooshing breath, forcing more energy on the impact of the dual blades that suddenly sprung to life from each end of the stick. It spun in circles to keep the enemy at bay then in figure eight motion to slice extremities that got in the way. Then he jabbed and stabbed and killed nine more before the skirmish moved off to screams of retreat.

Piladius nervously dismounted and joined the others. "Who were they," he asked, bewildered at what he had just seen, and done.

"Celtic mercenaries," Phaedrus answered. "Usually, they sell themselves for tracking and hunting and killing to the Romans. I don't think they managed to find employment recently. Normally, they would not attack without a reason."

The blades disappeared inside the stick and Scathach marveled at how easily and how suddenly it was hidden beneath his mantle. Aoife approached from behind. "Here," she said and handed an arrow back to Piladius, its tip stained in blood.

"Thank you," he proffered, yet receded against a fir tree in the next instant.

"And this is yours, too," she returned.

"Put it down! You're evil!" he shouted as he waved her off with his empty bow.

"It's your head. You killed him, you keep him."

"I don't want him. Throw it away. I can't believe you cut off his head!"

"It is our way. Is he not your first kill?" Scathach asked.

"Yes, but I don't want his head!"

"Fine!" Aoife screamed at him, "Then here," she said and shoved a second arrow in his hand. "This one belongs to you too," she said while handing him a leaf. There was a hole in the middle of it.

"What is this?" he asked, feeling better to have the leaf in his hands than the head of some dead mercenary.

"That is the leaf you killed with your second shot. It went straight up into the air and came down to land in the earth. Keep it. It's your second kill of the day," she laughed at him. He scoffed at her and moved to his horse.

Aoife grabbed the head by the straggly beard and threw it into the forest with a disgusted look at Piladius before brushing her hands on her pants. "You'd better get used to it, Ploppus, sooner or later you'll have to do it yourself." She mounted and waited while she watched the others.

"You are quite gifted with that stick," Scathach told him. "And you are extremely agile in a short battle. Perhaps you could be useful for a few things," she commented, yet didn't quite ask him to teach her how he had done the feat.

"And there are things I'd like to learn from you as well, Scathach," he replied.

Piladius put up his bow and regained his mount. "Let's be off. I don't like this place. Do you think there are any more like them on the road to this marketplace?"

Phaedrus looked about. "One can never know. I do, however, suggest that we move on as quickly as possible. If those mercenaries decide they can maneuver about to kill us, they will do so, even if we have won this skirmish. I don't know how many there were, but you can trust in a return if we don't move on."

Their eyes and ears were sharp for the next several miles, never encountering another ambush, which was a relief to Piladius considering the availability of an ambush to hide in any of the cracks and crevices in the craggy, mountainous region. He had never killed a man before. The memory stung in his mind and he wondered if it could have happened differently, perhaps a wound that would have kept the man down long enough for him to survive. But then he knew if he didn't let loose the arrow, it may have been his own head being thrown into the bushes. How could these women, as beautiful as they are, be capable of ripping a man's head from his body and carrying it like a trophy, without guilt or remorse?

Before the day had come to an end the fog had moved off, leaving the road visible for a long distance. The land became clear and wide open before them. Somehow, Phaedrus thought to himself, they managed to skirt the heights of the Carpathian Mountains and had prospered further south than he had expected. Jutting hills and staggered mountain peaks claimed the horizon to the north and east as they moved further south. They rested just short of nightfall and decided to push on before first light. No further attacks came for them.

Five uneventful days had passed in leisure before they reached the market the Innkeeper had told them about. The site of the city brought a relief, especially to Aoife who had watched every move Phaedrus made throughout the trip. He was handsome and molded in a shape that pleased her. She taunted him with sexual pleasures during the night and even sometimes during the day. While she was dressed warm for the season, she let a bit of her flesh show at times when she wanted him to take notice. But his eyes were on Scathach the entire way and that bothered her. She was just as attractive as Scathach and much more ready for the task of pleasing him. All he had to do was agree and he could have her, anytime. Yet he chose not to. Instead, he talked incessantly about wars and battles and Rome and Greece. Aoife wanted nothing to do with stories. And seeing the city rise before her gave her new hope of finding someone to please her, someone who would accept her for her beauty and charm, and also her ability to fight.

The city of Pannonia was extraordinary by anyone's standards. Hot springs, some of which the local inhabitants called healing springs, were found everywhere and people relaxed in the bubbling, healing properties offered by the warm, enigmatic waters. The Pannonii had built houses and large open rooms around the heated waters, offering the owner of the facility more privacy to operate the hundreds of springs running everywhere throughout the city. Stone waterways were constructed and large earthen dikes were established to control the flow of drinking water. Underground canals were engineered and designed to carry waste out of the city and into the swift flowing rivers. Most of the local Inns and Eatery places were accommodated with private rooms to urinate and defecate, completely unlike the barbaric places that offer bowls that had to be hauled away after each use. Even Scathach's own village had not seen the likes of this technique; using open trenches to deposit waste products, then burying the contents under sod. The city itself was extremely clean.

There were stone paved streets and tall walls of brick on the outer perimeter and stone homes with thatched roofs on the interior. Statues of bronze and iron and even some of gold were spotted here and there, many designed of heroes or gods and deities known and unknown throughout time. And there were people of all races and places walking the streets and searching the trader's stock for a good sale. There were Romans—who didn't seem to take notice of anyone or anything out of the ordinary—and Galatians and Celts. There were people from Egypt and from Iberia and Germania. No one seemed to mind that anything else existed outside the city. People gathered here for one purpose; to buy and sell wares. Music filled the streets and a parade of musicians marched over a cobblestone pathway every four hours. Bartering chants roared throughout the market square that surrounded a fountain where people could sit and relax and watch the trades taking place. They ate and drank freely. Storytellers herd children to the far corners of the market to capture an audience with stories of gods and myths and monsters. And there were seers, though they tended to hide for risk of persecution and ridicule from the local authorities. And yes, there were guards here. They carried huge axe-like weapons and wore violet turbans wrapped about their heads that extended to their shoulders and around their necks. Though winter was present, they wore thin shirts of silk and breeches made of pressed sheep's wool. They seemed to look at no one and everyone at the same time. The city, Scathach realized, was large enough that they would not be spotted so easily.

Among the many city buildings Piladius discovered a library and a school of arts where poets and musicians and actors lived out their dreams, if simply for the commoner. Philosophers seemed to have attended an oratory where one was allowed to speak his mind without being accused of any crimes. The only rule was that one could not inject any action based on conjecture—basically starting a war because of religious, personal, biased or vengeful convictions. Guards were set to observe the statements and comments made by all, but did not interfere in any way with the orator. Those who were convicted of disregarding this rule were immediately sentenced to death in private. He managed daily to seat himself among the others, listening and commenting softly to those who chose to discuss subjects without much validity in a more secretive manner. But he had learned and studied and occasionally offered his personal experiences about his travels across the land. It was surprising to discover that he had learned so much more in the past year training with Skitatsya than he had in all the years studying from the back of his covered wagon.

Aoife found more than enough entertainment to suit her needs. There were many places where men and women bathed either separately or together and much, much more. Steaming rooms of naked bodies were numerous and she took her pleasure of many young men in the time she had spent in the city, even under the watchful eyes of strangers. She didn't seem to mind that anyone looked on, never knowing what the onlooker was missing by not being allowed to touch her. And there were so many smells and odors of numerous scented oils and perfumes, so many decorations of jewelry and silk and glass. She took it all in with a new breath each time she moved about the city. And she trained as well, keeping her skills sharp and ready. Soon, she realized she would move on with her sister to the north and beyond. Yet she strayed from Phaedrus and Scathach and even Ploppus. Mostly she kept to herself, training either alone or with a variety of fighters who chose to keep up their skills as she did. There were new moves she had discovered here in the city too. She honed her warrior tactics and developed strategies to take out an opponent even faster than before. And rather than share this information with Scathach and Phaedrus, she chose to keep silent, hoping someday to surprise them both with her skills in battle. She was sure Phaedrus would take notice of someone of her talent after that. Then she would have him.

"Tell me," Scathach started. It was first light and just before the sun rose up on the horizon. Piladius was already gone, spending time with other scholars and philosophers who subject themselves to the dank recesses and dark corners of ancient buildings to study scrolls and parchments and documents from time immemorial. Aoife too had departed early, to start each day with a hot bathing. It would be way into the night when they would meet together as they had for the past ten days. "Why did you not kill me when you had the chance? I have seen you in a fight and I have seen you practice. Your skills as a fighter far surpass any that I have ever known. Surely you could have assassinated me any time you wanted."

He smiled. "Yes. I could have. But I will tell you again. You have fascinated me for a long time. There is something in you that I have seen in no other woman. Even as gifted a fighter as your sister is, there is something most interesting about you that no other woman possesses. I am determined to discover what that is. And I am patient. I will wait until it reveals itself to me. For that reason, you are most assuredly alive."

"Explain then how you dispatched those nine men with a simple stick and without ever losing your wind. I could have done the feat, but I would have been sorely exhausted."

"You must learn control, Scathach. If you can master the control of your body and the control of all things around you, you can open new doors and new wonders in the art of combat."

"So you will show me this stick feat?

"It is not a stick! It is pugilism, an ancient form of combat from my homeland," he nearly snapped. "They say that the mastery of combat is passed on to men by the gods themselves. And I have known many men who are thought of as gods because of their combat skills. In time, I too could have been a god among men. If only my height and brawn were as kind as my skill. Theagenes of Tasos was a master—first in pugilism and then in pankration. And Diagoras of Rhodes was a master as well."

"I have never heard of such nonsense!" Scathach told him. "I have seen many men who are extraordinary fighters, but I have also seen such men die."

"Oh, yes. We all die, Scathach. Yet it is what we leave behind that matters most. Will you leave this land void of your talent and skill, or will you share it with others so they may develop it further and enhance your abilities to make it even greater? Are you not great because you developed a skill beyond that of your trainer?"

She thought for moment. Yes. Her father had taught her the leap of the toad from the back of a horse and she developed the salmon leap from that same technique. "Yes," she admitted. "So explain this new fighting skill…this pugilism and pankration so that I may know it."

SCATHACH

Again, he smiled. "It is not so easy to explain, but I will teach you if you are willing?"

"I think I am willing to learn. I have seen you fight. I may need the knowledge of your own skill to defeat you in the future, should the need arise."

"I will be hard pressed to accommodate, but I will educate you just the same. Perhaps this is what I have been waiting for."

The afternoon was swept away in a cold breath while Phaedrus and Scathach trained in secrecy. In the far corner of a vacant stable on the outskirts of the inner-city walls, they managed to establish a soft floor of old hay and straw they had gathered from the area. His first lesson would be one of complete silence and control, sitting her down in the middle of the self-made arena with her eyes closed and her complete attention on her breathing. But that was an easy accomplishment compared to the task of getting her to remove her clothing to start the exercise.

"Take off your garments," he ordered.

"I will not!" she warned and took up a stance to fend him off.

"Scathach…I cannot train you unless you are willing to open yourself to total and complete understanding of the training itself. Nothing, absolutely nothing, can interfere with your concentration. If you cannot do this simple task, I'm afraid I cannot train you at all. You must trust me."

"Trust you?"

"Yes," he replied and let it sit on the air for a long moment. Neither moved a muscle, each staring the other in the eye in defiance.

"Fine," she finally gave in. What choice did she have? She needed to learn about his skills in fighting if she was to combat him on even grounds. While she may have the ability to kill him at any time with her present skills, there was certainly great opportunity to learn something new to use on an opponent in the future. And it seemed that Phaedrus had many such skills that she would like to understand and learn for herself.

Though he kept his mind on the task he ensued he nearly gave it all up for a simple touch of her flesh when she undressed before him. He had forgotten how long had passed that he'd seen a naked woman. And if Scathach were beautiful with her clothing on, she was superfluous without it. It took all his concentration to keep his eyes on hers and not the parts of her body that glimmered in the sunlight, aching for his caress.

The chill air made her shiver, but she refused to let her body subject to the convulsion it would have shown had she been alone. No, she would stand up to this Spartan and show him how a Sarmatian warrior could stand any conditions.

"Now…sit," he commanded.

"What about the stick?"

"In time," he told her and pointed a finger to the ground.

Obediently, she sat and waited.

"Now concentrate. Close your eyes and concentrate on everything around you. Listen to everything and nothing at the same time."

A long time passed in silence. Then the distant beat of a drum and perhaps a trumpet or two told of another parade in the streets far off in the middle of the city. A cheer suddenly went out from observers in the coliseum as another prisoner fought a lion or tiger or another prisoner for his life. These were the only sounds around her, nothing more than that. Then there was the sound of her breathing and the silence of the training arena itself. It hummed and rang in her ears. Only when she thought that her heart would beat out of her chest did she succumb to the empty silence and scream out just to hear another noise. Phaedrus knew then that she had found the place inside that she must learn to control. After this he started. First he showed her balance techniques, though she didn't need much practice here. Her abilities in balance surpassed even his, but it was a test just the same. And then came the stick. It was awkward at first, but she soon gained control of her movements and discovered a comfortable relationship with the object: swinging, jabbing, spinning, and tossing. Mostly, it was a test of balance and a relationship with a foreign object in her hand, completely separate from her sword and bow technique. And above all, she was forced to listen to the air in all directions, to measure how the motion of the swinging stick disturbed the air, how it whistled in mid-swing. This she practiced hour upon hour until the day drifted away. And only when the training was over did she realize Phaedrus was watching her naked body dancing in liquid motion to the training exercises. She dodged and flipped in the air, dashed from one corner to the next. Suddenly she stopped.

They looked at each other from opposite sides of the arena. While she stood proud and defiant on the other side, her breathing slightly raspy, she ordered Phaedrus to gather her clothing and deliver them to her. He obeyed without hesitation. Of all things, he was at least an honorable man, she thought. Never were his intensions contrary to the training of Scathach. Yet being naked was not unusual for Scathach either. During the summer season, that is the way she would fight anyway. She would paint her naked body and fight with Khutalk underneath her. And her sister Aoife would do so as well with Bucephalus and so would Oseida and Rwan and all the other women in her village. Only during the winter season did they really concentrate on wearing clothing. But being told to remove her garments by a Spartan bothered her somehow. Though not all that unfamiliar, it bothered her to see him watch her train without clothing, but she did so nonetheless.

On their journey back to the city, they talked. There were stories of great men in the world and those who would be greater still. Scathach told of several she had encountered and defeated in past years. Some were among the Mongols and the Xiongnu who she considered extremely fierce warriors. But the stories Phaedrus told were far more interesting than the men she had encountered. He spoke of men from legends whose feats of strength and endurance were far more advanced than anyone she knew.

"So what happened to them?" Scathach asked after Phaedrus had told her of Creugas and Damoxenos, whose exhibition of pankration lasted until sunset without a winner, each man fighting and hitting and grappling throughout the entire day.

"It was decided that the *klimax* be applied," he told her.

"Klimax?"

His smile was a wry shift of his lip in the form of mockery. "The *klimax* is applied when a winner cannot be decided. Each opponent has the right to strike the other, once in turn, without the other dodging the blow. The attacker is allowed to tell his opponent what position to adopt before striking him. Once the blow is concluded, the other has an opportunity to return the blow. By drawing of lots, it was decided that Creugas would be first. Standing squarely, he ordered Damoxenos to keep his arms low and punched him powerfully to his face. Damoxenos took the blow without losing his ground. Then he, in turn, ordered Creugas to raise his arms above his head. In the next instant Damoxenos swung with all his strength and connected with the underside of Creugas' underarm, shattering the man's ribs and sending them shooting into his heart. Creugas fell dead in an instant," he finished.

Scathach stopped along the path. "And you are going to teach me this?"

He laughed. "No. I will teach you to fight and win. These are stories that took place a long time ago. The men of those days did these things at the games in Olympia and Nemea and in Delphi."

"You are telling me that men did these deeds for sport?"

"Yes. Though not all men died as a result of the competition. When one has had enough, all he has to do is raise a finger to the air in defeat. The game is then over."

"And you have done this?" she asked him.

He turned and walked on. Only when she caught up with him did he answer. "No. I am a Spartan. I am alive," he said and raised his arms out to the side in observance. "If I participated in any of those games, I would surely not be here for Spartans do not give in to defeat. Never has a Spartan raised a finger to an opponent to give in. He would rather die than subject himself to the ridicule of defeat."

"I see," she told him. "So how do you know how to fight in such a manner?"

"I said I didn't participate in the games, or in open competition. I said nothing of training for it. I have used the knowledge of pugilism and pankration to gain many victories over my enemies during my life, including those sent by my brother to assassinate me. When I have taught you to do these things, I too will ask for your knowledge in combat," he finished as he looked at her.

"And with this knowledge," she held his eyes. "You will attempt to assassinate me then?"

"It is not my intent. But if I have to, I *will* kill you, Scathach."

"And if I too gain this knowledge, will I have the same advantage of killing you?"

"Yes…I suppose you will. But remember," he pulled her along the path. "There are many more forms of combat out there that you are not aware of. And there are techniques of combat that can destroy you long before you reach for your bow or your spear or your sword or even this simple stick," he warned.

"And where would one find such men?" she asked him.

"Who said it was a man that could do such things?" he retuned.

"Surely, you cannot tell me a woman teaches these things? I am far superior to any woman alive. My skills in battle are never beaten."

"Spartan girls are trained when they are very young, Scathach. That is what fascinated me most about you when I first saw you. When my orders came from Nero, I had only one thing in mind: kill you and return to the luxury of living in Rome. Nothing more."

"So any Spartan woman can defeat me, then?"

"I did not say that. I am saying that Spartan girls, like you, train at a very young age. Some, again like you, have great abilities in combat. But there are men too who have great abilities. There are those who can even kill with a word."

"How can one kill with a word?" she asked him incredulous.

"Tomorrow," he stopped and looked at her. "Tomorrow we will go to the coliseum. I have been there every day to see the amusing fighting techniques of some of the finest warriors in the world. There is a special display being held tomorrow. I believe it to be in your interest to attend with me. Then you can see what people are capable of doing."

CHAPTER VI

Morning came early and her bones and muscles ached from the day before. Though she knew she hadn't strained herself in training, her muscles groaned mercilessly when she woke and attempted to stretch.

"I did not see Aoife this morning," Phaedrus said to her when she joined him on the balcony. The air was cold, but vibrantly awakening.

"It isn't like her to not come home," Scathach replied. "Perhaps after the visit to the coliseum we will seek her out. I'm not too worried for her. She is a good fighter, perhaps even better than me at times."

"Oh, I agree. Yet she lacks your spirit. Her interests lie in the flesh of men and not much more. She will grow tired of it some day. But until then she will test many waters before drinking."

"You think she will marry, then?"

"In time, perhaps. At the moment she is too busy living," he finished.

"I have learned so much here." Piladius entered the room and greeted both of them. "If I had to stay here I would not complain," he smiled at them.

"That's because you wouldn't have to hunt and clean and cook your own food. When we leave this place your training will continue, Piladius," Scathach told him.

"But what if I never leave?"

"You would rather live here for the rest of your life?"

"I could get used to it."

"And how would you pay for your food and a place to live?" Scathach asked.

"The scholars and philosophers get their food from donations the city provides, so long as progress is made on the translation of the scrolls we have found and those that are brought here from outside."

"And what about a place to live?"

"I have seen many of them remain at the library and at the oratory."

"Piladius, my good fellow," Scathach moved behind him and put her hands on his shoulders, though he shied, thinking she would strike him as she always did. "You cannot survive in this place. You have no skills to sell. You can translate scrolls and perhaps tell a few tales, but that is about all. You will need work that pays. And for that you have no skill."

"I can scribe!" he refuted.

"For whom? How will you keep clean? Who will wash your clothes? Who will keep you from hurting yourself?"

"I will!" he shouted at her, but moved away in fear at the same instant.

"Only because I have taught you how," she told him.

"Please," Phaedrus joined the conversation. "He's right, Scathach. He does have skill. Far more skill than I, I'm afraid. I can always find work as a mercenary or an assassin, but work for scribes is very challenging and extremely tasking. And it does pay, if you can find someone willing to pay the right price. The skill to sit and write all day long and hover over parchments and the labors involved in translating…. It is extremely difficult to accomplish these things. Yes, I agree with Piladius. It's much easier to remain in a place like this where life is stable and not so demanding on the physical being. Besides, I hear there is a young man who has come to Pannonia looking for a traveler to write tales about. I think he is perfect for the job."

Both looked at him as if mad. What was he talking about? He spoke in riddles.

He noticed their blank expression. "Scathach," he came to them as they stood there staring at him. "We've talked about this several times. Someone will be needed to tell of your travels. I don't have the talent for it. If what I suspect is true, you will need someone good to write the story and I believe this fellow can do the job."

"When was this decided?" Piladius asked, looking at them both. "Why wasn't I asked?"

Phaedrus looked at him up and down. "You are not ready for this task, Piladius my good man. The writer for our travels must be an asset to us in both fighting and writing. You may be able to write, but your skill in fighting is not at all what we need. I am deeply sorry my good fellow."

"What do you mean? I'm as good a writer as anyone out there. And after this past year, I can cut my own in battle."

"Yes, we can attest to the dead leaf," Scathach mocked.

"That was pure accident. I can be this man, Scathach. You know it. Will you defy my father's request and send me away before you have finished what you started?"

Scathach caught on to Phaedrus' idea and now she played along. It was a good trick and one that worked well. "I am only giving you what you want. And it seems that you have decided to stay here. If that is your intension, then I will honor it. You are your own man now, Piladius. I was but a means to get you away from your father who thought you a burden. Now we are all happy with this turn of events. You can remain here in your scrollful bliss, your father will continue to trade without the burden of a blathering bookworm and I will continue to move north and fight as I have done my entire life."

He gave it all a hard thought. Then, "Scathach, I can do this. You know I can. I may require a little more training, but I can do this. Please, let me continue on with you."

"You don't have the stomach for it, Piladius. You don't even have the necessary tools to write about our travel."

Suddenly he gleamed. "You're wrong, Scathach. Wait here," he said and dashed to get his writing tools. "Here," he said when he returned. "I have been writing about everything since we left your village and even when I was *in* your village I was writing about it. I have kept a journal the entire time. Look for yourself."

She took the tomb and looked at it. It made no sense to her. She was not educated enough to understand a single word. Yet she was impressed that he had managed to take it with him among the three items she told him he could carry along. She didn't realize that one of the items would be a chronology of his time with her.

"Well, Scathach? What do you think?" Phaedrus asked. He looked at her closely. She was more than beauty in his eyes. Her fiery red hair and blue eyes thanked him without ever having to speak a word.

"You start today!" she told him. "We are going to the coliseum to watch a display of combat skills. You will join us," she informed him.

For the first time he smiled and accepted. "I will be ready," he said. He suddenly became the schoolboy of many years ago, eager to dive in and learn something new only so he could write it down to reflect at a later time. It was almost unbearable for Scathach to watch, but at least the ploy of keeping him along had worked. For that she was satisfied, though she absently wished she had not talked him into continuing on with her and Aoife. Much as she delighted in the fact that he was anxious to learn, she hated that fact that he possessed the qualities of a subservient waif. Then she considered Phaedrus. What were his intensions? Would he stay along with them through the journey and see it to the end? Where would he go? What would he do? She would wait for now. But sometime soon, she would have to know what he had in mind.

The coliseum was relatively filled by the time they arrived. It was odd to see so many people gathered here during the winter season. It was a time for gathering food and collecting blankets and warm clothing, not for watching fights in the open cold air of the coliseum. But they joined the crowd who waited patiently for the events to begin, many of them huddled together under warm mantles and even some who gathered in bunches around small burning fires here and there. And then there was clapping and a slight cheer went up and out over the enclosure. A small fellow came forth from beneath the stadium. From the mouth of the tunnel he walked to the center of the arena and stood naked, looking at everyone in attendance. His body was covered in oil and his long black hair was tied behind his head and folded up in a bun. He bent and gathered sand in his hand from the arena floor and threw it into the air. Most of it landed on his body and was caught in the oil. He ignored it and took his stance facing them.

Scathach didn't think much of the man. He was massive in muscle, but his height wasn't much of a hindrance for a trained warrior like her. He didn't appear to be of any consequence to become an opponent to anyone of importance. He was more childlike than man, she thought. Arieoles, as weak a warrior as she was, could have defeated this man. If she had not died on the hills of the Larch Taiga, she would have been married and perhaps would have moved on from the village to start a family of her own, Scathach considered. Somehow it was not meant to be. In the next instant he was moving around the arena, alone. No one attacked him. No one provoked him. His arms and legs moved about in straight angles as if hitting and kicking the air, but never touching another person.

"Is he fighting a spirit?" she asked Phaedrus.

"No. He is using his Skiamanchia. We also call it *Pyrrhichia*. He prepares himself mentally for his next battle, concentrating on the precise location of each blow."

"He is hitting nothing more than the wind," she told him.

"Remember what you learned yesterday. Listen to the air around you. That man is doing the same thing. He listens to the air at the end of his fingers and his toes to find the most powerful blow he can deliver. Trust that you would not want to be at the end of his fist in the moment that it reaches full extension. He has compressed so much air that the force would break your bones like the twigs of a dead tree."

"But he is so small. Surely he cannot be much of a threat?"

"Watch and you will see for yourself," he told her, smiling.

The man continued his concentrated movements for quite some time. Scathach and Piladius nearly became bored. But then he stopped and lowered his head, his eyes looking to the sand at his feet. The audience clapped, but Scathach could not see why. He hadn't done anything worth talking about. Now another figure moved from beneath the stadium.

"A lion?" Scathach marveled, seeing the creature lurk forward slowly, menacingly, circling the man and sniffing the air. "He has no weapon! The beast will surely kill him. Is that the feat we are to observe today? Watch a naked man get eaten by a lion? He has no chance of winning against a beast such as that."

"Scathach!" he scolded. "Watch and learn. This is not done for the sake of feeding a hungry animal. Watch and you will see what some men are capable of doing. No matter his size and strength."

The lion circled a third time then moved straight for him. One leap and the beast would knock him down and rip out his throat. It would be over in a very short time and everyone could return home knowing that the lion had won. But that didn't occur. As the lion lunged forward, seeking unprotected skin to tear and eat, the small man reached in for him and continued the flow of the animal's motion, rolling backward and throwing the lion several feet behind him before leaping back to his feet and waiting for the lion to return. The beast staggered up on all fours and immediately circled, looking for an opening. Again, he lunged for the naked man and was thrown to the sandy earth where he shook it off angrily and circled in the opposite direction. The audience cheered each time he was thrown.

Several more attempts were made to get the naked man on the ground, but the lion was unsuccessful. When the audience became used to the same employed tactics to render the lion harmless, they became agitated. And the naked man sensed it. It was time to end the display. When the lion circled for the last time he shifted his feet and faced the beast head on, waiting for it to leap and capture him. There was no possible way the man could grapple with the lion and throw him in this kind of stance. The only thing he could possibly do was hit the beast and everyone knew that it would not work. He was much too small to do any damage to the lion. The beast was much faster and of greater weight than the naked man. It would take a lot of force to knock the lion down.

The lion pranced three steps and lunged with his mouth wide open, ready to tear into his flesh. In the next instant the small man bent on his legs, brought his right fist back to his side and his left fist out in front of him. When the lion was sure to have him, he let the right fist come forward with such a speed as to undo the lion completely. The blow barely hit the beast in the middle of his forehead as a loud, ear-splitting battle-yell escaped the small man's lips. The lion stopped dead and fell to the dirt. The stadium went silent. Everyone stood in awe at the amazing feat. Surely the man would have been dead had his talent not saved him. He remained in the same position for several seconds before acknowledging his victory, bringing his hands to his side and bowing to the audience who clapped loudly.

"I must admit, that was entertaining," Scathach told him. "He must have a powerfully strong hand to have done that."

Phaedrus laughed. "Not at all. The strength in his hands had nothing to do with killing that lion. It was his voice."

"His voice?" Piladius commented.

"Yes. Would you like to see?"

Scathach was beside him as he moved from his seat. "Yes."

Tunnels ran everywhere beneath the stadium seats. Every twenty steps or so the halls opened up to a large stone room where men talked of fights and beasts and weapons and such. Cells had been built into some of these rooms where prisoners waited for their turn to visit the center of the coliseum. Most were expected to die of course. Those who lived were set free, for they were few and far between. If a prisoner was set free however, he was ordered to leave the city immediately and could never return.

"There," Phaedrus pointed. "Suren!" he called, though not so that anyone else could hear the name.

The bulking man was a statue with his back to them. "If I didn't know whom it was who calls me by that name, you would surely be dead by now," he said confidently in a whisper.

"I know this too well, my friend. Come, I have someone for you to meet."

"You know this man?" Scathach asked.

"We were once brothers. Until his father was killed and he returned home."

"Brothers in training, I trust," Piladius interjected.

"Yes, but brothers just the same. We have many things in common. Training to be assassins is just one of them."

The man was rather short for his size, Scathach noticed, but his muscle tone was overwhelming. His flesh was dark, his hair black and he stood on bare feet. "My name is Mahendra," he bowed as he introduced himself in a soft voice.

"I am Skitat…," she stopped and caught herself. "Scathach," she finished. She had never spoken her new name before. It sounded awkward hearing it come from her own lips. "I thought Phaedrus called you Suren?"

"Names are not important to me," he answered. "Suren is a name I want to lose. My real name is Mahendra."

"You are Parthian?" Piladius asked him.

"You are perceptive," the other replied softly.

"Let us leave this place," Phaedrus told them. "There are always ears lurking in corners."

When Mahendra's things were gathered, they departed the tunnels and returned to the arena seating area where loud cheers went up as another warrior entered the arena. In the far corner, she sat atop her horse waiting for the signal to begin. A helmet of bronze masked her face and her shoulders were draped in golden armor, all of it hiding the tattoos. Her javelin came up over her head and pointed to her enemy who stood on the other end of the arena waiting with nothing to protect himself; no armor, no weapon, no way to escape. Scathach recognized Bucephalus instantly. And if that were true, then the rider was most assuredly, Aoife.

Bucephalus burst forward with all the stamina and speed of the Turanian breed and though it was cold his coat shimmered in the sunlight. The audience was in awe by the powerful animal, but not so much as the awe they shared of the remarkable skill in the unarmed warrior. He patiently stood waiting for her to come for him.

Scathach was in motion. "No!" she shouted and performed her salmon leap as she stretched herself beyond the walls of the coliseum and landed flat on her feet in the dusty arena. Aoife saw her coming. The javelin was loosed and went sailing through the air at the unarmed warrior. With a quick twist of his wrist, he caught and spun the shaft about, twisted his body to slow the speed of the missile and turned back with the javelin pointed directly at Aoife.

Scathach bolted for the center of the arena as Bucephalus continued his maddening pace. Surely, she thought, this man will kill Aoife if she didn't interfere. But she was too far away.

Aoife continued to move forward then oddly twisted her body to the left, allowing him the opportunity to strike her on that side. In another fancy twist of his wrist, he had the javelin in both hands. When Aoife was within arms reach, he bent back and swatted her full in the chest with the blunt end of the weapon. Aoife went down in a dusty ball.

"No!" Scathach shouted again and leapt into the air at him. There was no time to react. His attention was on Aoife who scrambled to achieve her footing—and complete the next move. Bucephalus pushed on a few steps without a rider and stopped abruptly. Scathach slammed her entire body into the warrior, before he could think. The javelin went flying away as Scathach rolled over in continued motion and captured it. Before the warrior made it to his knees, she was in front of him with the javelin pointed at his throat. The audience was ecstatic at the scene. But above all, there was Mahendra.

"Stop!" he bellowed. If his battle-yell was ear splitting, this voice completely shattered them. The air stopped moving entirely.

Now, in all her battles and in all her days of training to become one of the finest women warriors of her tribe, Scathach had never been distracted from her objective. First and foremost was the death of the man who attempted to kill her sister. And her intent was substantial. But in that single moment of hesitation, the voice that burst forth from the audience shattered every thought and rendered her attempt meaningless. She stopped, dropped her arms and looked to where the voice had come.

Everyone in the coliseum stared at him. Those who stood beside him, most noticeably Phaedrus and Piladius, held their ears in pain. The entire stone framework of the coliseum trembled and cracked momentarily, then settled. Their eyes shifted back to Scathach.

Scathach ignored the man on his knees, threw down the javelin and went to Aoife who stood looking at her in anger. "What are you doing?" Scathach asked.

"Me? What are you doing? This is a display of battle tactics. I was supposed to fall from my horse. I have been practicing that fall for five days now. You have ruined it all."

"I thought you were in trouble, Aoife."

"Trouble? I could have killed him any time I wanted. It is much harder to fall safely from your horse than it is to kill an enemy. You've ruined it, Skitatsya!" she shouted.

Scathach searched the arena seating. No one seemed to have heard her name. Either that or it had no effect on them.

"Just leave me alone! Meddle in your own affairs and leave me alone!" she shouted then stammered off, out of the arena. Scathach searched the area. She needed to be out of there and the leap that took her into the stadium was the same leap that got her out. When she was finally beside Phaedrus and calmed she looked at Mahendra. "What you have done with your voice is not possible," she told him.

"All things are possible," he whispered. "Come, we must move away from here now."

Mahendra led them through a maze of streets and small homes to his residence that was settled on the northwest corner of the city. Servants were there to greet his arrival and clothed him and his guests in warm wraps and footwear made from the hide of goatskin. Inside his comfortable home, a fire was lit that kept the entire space warm. When they were settled among the many sofas with cups of broth gathered from a brewing pot above the hearth, Mahendra finally looked at Phaedrus and smiled. "It truly is good to see you," he whispered. "We've been apart too long."

"I came here looking for you several days ago. I thought perhaps you had moved on until the winter quarters had passed before returning. I received word yesterday that you would be making a demonstration at the stadium today," Phaedrus commented.

"Yes, I returned yesterday. They came for me the moment I arrived and asked if I would do this for them. Another drifting fighter failed to make it here on time. It gets worse as the years go by. He was probably taken prisoner by the Roman soldiers. They have been pressing the region for fighters to win their battles. If I didn't need the coins to support this haggard staff I have here, I would have declined the offer. But I do what I must to survive. And you...?"

"I was sent on a mission from Nero to kill this one." He pointed to Scathach. She ignored the statement and continued to search the house. Art had definitely come to this place. Vases inlaid with gold and pottery displaying gems and precious metals found nearly every corner and crevice. Statues, some small and others life size, adorned many of the corners while others stood beside entryways. The goddess Athena with her hand held out carried a large candle that burned incense into the room. Another of Zeus was beside her.

Piladius took it all in and smiled at the sight. "You are Parthian, yet your home shows more Greek art than that of your homeland," he commented.

Again Mahendra smiled. "Yes," he whispered. "I consider myself more Greek than Parthian. But that has nothing to do with the art I have here. I simply like the style of the artists who make them." Then he looked at Scathach. "So, I see you are still alive. That is something," he said admiringly. "If Phaedrus wanted you dead, you certainly would not be sitting here. What, besides your compelling beauty, could possibly have made Phaedrus abandon his mission? Surely you know he is doomed and can never return to Rome? Of course, I must admit that you have something special about you. I cannot put a finger on just what, but there is something."

"There is nothing special about me," Scathach told him. "I fight and I live."

A moment later the servants returned with wheatcakes and cheese and fruits scattered on platters and placed them on the tables in front of the sofas. Mahendra dismissed them as he devoured a handful of grapes.

"How did you become so wealthy," Piladius asked him.

"Ahhh," he sat back and wiped his lips. "Two ways. First, my father was Suren and all that was his before he died is now mine. Second, I have been trained as an assassin and much, much more. I gain a wealth of coinage for my small displays of ummm, courage," he laughed at himself when he finished.

"That was not a small display of courage. You physically abused that lion in the arena," Scathach said with credit.

"What is this Suren?" Piladius asked. "I've not heard of that title before."

"Another time, my good fellow. At the moment, I am more curious to know why you seek me out."

Phaedrus moved closer. "You have seen her, Mahendra. Yes, you know too that there is something about her. I don't know what it is either, but I know I must help her somehow. And now I have come to you to ask for your help."

"What can I do for you, my friend?"

"I want you to find those who can train her to be the best. You and I have been here before, my brother. We have fought with the best and won. Now, I need the help of others to do this. I need her to learn what others only dream. Can you do it?"

"Phaedrus, Phaedrus. Is she ready for it? I mean look at her, such beauty, and the purity of her red hair and the darkness of the blue in her eyes. Her nose is long and straight and her lips full. She is best made a wife," he told him.

"You have no idea, Mahendra. She is far more ready than you may think."

"Because she can jump coliseum walls and land on her feet?"

"Just look at her, Mahendra. She has the strength and skill I tell you."

Mahendra turned to her. "Tell me. Can you kill me right now?"

Scathach did not hesitate. "If I had to I could kill you, yes."

"Let's put it to the test, shall we?"

She looked at Phaedrus then back to him in question. "What kind of trickery is this? You invite us to your home to kill you?"

"Let me be the one to judge that," he commented. "Come with me outside."

Behind the large house was a garden that had all the fine makings of being gorgeous in the springtime and in the summer. At the moment it was a cold, vacant array of barren trees and leafless bushes waiting for the winter to pass on.

"Here," he pointed and told her to stand. "If I move to the end of the path there and told you to run at me with all your speed and then kill me when you reached me, could you do it?"

"Easily."

"And will you allow me the opportunity to stop you if I can, no matter the manner in which I employ my tactics?"

She nearly laughed. He was small and stout, but he was full of hard muscle. His jaw was square and locked tight so that the muscles in his cheeks stood out. His eyes were as dark brown as his hair and intense, yet passionate. He was strong and perhaps capable, but she knew she could take him with no problems. He was nowhere near the speed and agility of her abilities. "Yes, you may attempt to stop me. But if I catch you, I *will* kill you and then what will Phaedrus think?"

"Phaedrus will think as he has in the past; on his own. But first, you must get to me."

"Oh, I will get there," she assured him.

He moved off down the path and turned to face her. When he was settled, he waved a hand to call her on. She ran with all her speed to kill him and have it over with. Then she and Phaedrus and Piladius and Aoife would move on and continue to push to the north and west, away from Roman soldiers, away from Greece and Pannonia and everything else that reminded her of home; away from it all.

She was nearly on him and her mind set itself up for the next move. Which battle tactic would she use to kill him? Would she spin in the air and catch his throat with a quick backhand swing or should she continue forward and crush his chest in with her foot? There were so many options available. But now the time was getting short and the distance narrowed drastically. Mahendra never moved, but kept a keen eye on her approach. And when she finally chose the means with which she would bring on his demise, he began his attempt at stopping her. It was amazingly effective. Before she could collapse on the last ten feet of her approach, he bellowed out in a voice that shattered the air and stopped her in her tracks. She stumbled with her arms flailing to push forward and accomplish her task, but the sound of that booming voice forced her to succumb and drop to her knees. Her hands came to her head, keeping it together. She grit her teeth to keep them from cracking and falling from her mouth and she folded her head in her arms and wept. The noise stopped abruptly.

She stood.

"Scathach?" Phaedrus called behind her. Both he and Piladius had held their ears.

"Would you like to learn?" Mahendra asked her softly, ignoring the others. His voice was sincere. He knew this was how it would turn out. Now all she had to do was want to learn. Want to learn it all.

"Tell Phaedrus where to meet this afternoon and I will be there," she replied. She was embarrassed, but not stupid. If this voice technique can be learned, then she would gain the secret and use it herself.

"There are many things you can learn if you are interested, Scathach. You have only to ask and I will teach them to you. Phaedrus is a good man and a good ally. He is dedicated and loyal to his beliefs. You will find none better than he to help you in your goal. I will tell him where to meet me. But you must bring your heart with you when you come.... if you come."

"Who is he?" Scathach asked when they had returned to their own apartment.

Sitting comfortably at a table Phaedrus answered. Piladius, though pretending not to pay attention to the conversation, wrote it down as it was told. "Mahendra is the son of Suren. Suren is the loyal family name chosen to serve Orodes II, ruler of Parthia. Mahendra's father was Suren. Suren had sent Mahendra off to study combat skills and the art of war. He traveled everywhere and learned from the best the world knows of. That voice technique was learned from a master who lived on a small island southeast of China. He spent a year there, learning how to break pots and vases using only his voice. From there he was sent Gaul where he studied a form of art he called *fotan*. And from there it was Galicia and Greece where we met and then off to Rome where we both learned to become assassins. Each time, Mahendra's skills surpassed the greatest in the land. He trained for many years to take his father's place beside Orodes II. However, last year, Rome had moved against his people. A Roman aristocrat by the name of Marcus Crassus led his army into Parthia. Crassus was himself a trainer of slaves who taught the art of combat."

Piladius stood up. "I know of him. He trained many slaves and sold them for sporting purposes. Of course, Spartacus was one of them. They say he was a deserter from the Roman army. He rebelled and took thousands of slaves to Mount Vesuvius. He was eventually captured and killed. I remember hearing and reading about that story. It wasn't very long ago. And this Crassus, I believe he created the first fire brigade. It was claimed that he would buy up pieces of property at a very cheap price before he would put out the fires. He became very rich, to say the least. It is written in one of the books I have hidden in your village," he directed to Scathach. Suddenly he quieted.

Phaedrus continued. "Crassus may have been a trainer of slaves, but he was ignorant of war tactics. He disregarded the advice of his officers and his generals and decided he could conquer Parthia on his own, through the might in numbers. His men far outnumbered that of Orodes II and Suren was certainly looking at losing the battle. His confidence of a victory was his undoing. Mahendra's father had won the battle and as is the custom, brought the head of Marcus Crassus to Orodes II. Then, to repay Suren for his loyalty and dedication and the victory of the battle, Orodes II had him put to death. Probably to keep the next Suren in line and to show that no one is excused from death's grip. His father's fortune has allowed him to live here comfortably since *Sahmain*."

"What will he do now?" she asked him.

"Live. Teach others."

"And you think I should learn from him?"

"I think you would be foolish not to learn from him. The people he will gather and the things he will teach you will be overwhelming. The problem exists in the fact that it must be done quickly. If Caesar has pushed north through the Alps during winter quarters we will find ourselves in dangerous lands come spring. We will have no choice but to push on as soon as the winter has gone. Rome is moving east as well as north. If they have attempted Parthia once, they will try again and push on even further."

"Why not," Piladius said. "The Macedon did it once. Why not Rome?"

"That was long ago," Phaedrus told him. "We must concentrate on the now."

"Where are we to meet?" she asked.

CHAPTER VII

"The Master wishes you to pack your things and join him," a slave announced sometime during the early afternoon hour.

"Everything?" Phaedrus asked.

"Quarters have been made ready for your party," he claimed as if recited several times along the way.

Phaedrus was in motion and Piladius was nearly ready himself. "What of Aoife?" Scathach asked openly.

"The Master has already sent the invitation for her to join you. She declined, but said she would be nearby when you are ready to leave."

This news bothered Scathach, but she knew Phaedrus would be anxious to join his friend and Piladius actually seemed anxious to begin this next part of the journey. Still, Aoife could gain so much knowledge if she were to accompany her. Together, the two of them could be unstoppable in battle anywhere. It would have to wait till later, she realized. Perhaps she could talk her into it then. Yet there was one more thing she had to do before she left. It had been bothering her since the day she left her father, Brona, and her friends to die at the hands of the Roman army. She had done it once and it scared her and she wasn't quite sure she should do it again, but the thought of it nagged at her like the itch from the poison plants in the forests. She had to use the stone before she moved on.

"Phaedrus," she said as he and Piladius moved for the door. "I need a moment...alone."

"Your womanly duty?" he asked suggesting his knowledge of such things.

She was confused, but realized what he thought she was saying. He had seen women when that time of the month visited and understood the need for privacy during this time. He respected her wishes and told her they would wait at the corner. She thanked him for his understanding and let him go, ignorant of the real reason for the request.

When the room was empty she went to her things and removed the stone. It was just a simple stone, she thought as she studied it carefully. There didn't seem to be anything special about it, but she knew differently. She had seen the power possessed by it. And she needed to see it work again. It was almost as if the stone called to her to look at it, peek inside at the future. Then she remembered Brona's warning. 'Do not misuse the power of the stone and the stone will not harm you. Use the power sparingly to seek that which you wish to know. Abuse the stone and it will devour you to the point of insanity.'

She took the stone in her hands and gazed between the sets of lines etched in horizontal patterns. Her eyes shifted between them moving from top to bottom, staring between them until they faded entirely and a new view had taken shape. It didn't take long before she saw herself standing again on that battlefield. A young man stood beside her. He was tall and made from the finest muscle the body can find. Together they observed the death and destruction everywhere. Tears filled his eyes, defeat was written in his features. And she could see he was giving in. There was nothing left to fight with. All his men were gone and he had nothing left to do but surrender. But surrender to whom? What was she doing there? Where were Phaedrus and Aoife and Piladius? Something was wrong with the vision.

The scene departed instantly in a sheet of black. It was as if a page had been turned on time itself. Something new was happening and she was shaken abruptly. It scared her, but she knew she must see it through. The stone was taking her to another place, another land and another time. A young man sought her out. She could see him from a distance and she could feel his need to speak with her. Yet she fought to keep him away. She feared him, yet respected him. The stone told her it was safe and he could be trusted. But it also warned to be leery of him. Guide him and teach him and he will do you justice. It wasn't spoken, but she could sense that the stone was telling her this. She became disoriented and shook herself to clear her head. In the next instant she was back in her room looking at the dull stone. Nothing had changed, nothing had happened. She hid the stone and went to meet the others.

"Are you ready?" Phaedrus asked when she joined them again.

"Yes. I believe I am."

"You have come," Mahendra commented dryly as he studied them standing in the entry. He was sitting cross-legged in the middle of the floor with both arms extended to his front, hands resting on his knees. "Your things will be brought to your quarters. Please choose," he said to Scathach as she glanced throughout the room. It was open in all directions, a home made to train warriors only, she considered. Nothing occupied the open space with the exception of the weapons that hung on the back wall behind him and a thin matt of wickerwork across the floor.

"Choose?" she asked, though she knew he caught her glaring at the marvelous swords hanging directly behind him. Altogether, there were eight of them.

"Yes, pick the sword of your desire."

If was not common for someone to offer her a weapon such as the ones she looked at. They had to be forty or fifty thumbs long and maybe four thumbs wide where the steel met the hilt. Mostly, she had to fight an enemy and kill him to get a weapon such as this. She looked carefully. They were identical in many ways, yet the steel had variations to it, she noticed. It was difficult to decide. Was there a right decision? What if she chose wrong?

"May I hold them?" she asked.

Mahendra stood and joined her at the wall. Piladius walked to the wall and also studied them closely. Phaedrus stood back and watched.

"Yes, you may take them down and hold them. Feel how they sing in your hands. I would expect nothing less."

"I like this one," Piladius pointed.

"You...?" Mahendra asked and looked back to Phaedrus.

He laughed. "That one will go with me," Phaedrus told him. "He is a pup and requires much more attention than the girl."

Mahendra nodded understanding.

"You mean I don't get one of the swords? What am I supposed to be training with?"

"This," Phaedrus said and reached outdoors. He pulled back a bow with several arrows in his hand.

"You're joking?" Piladius stammered. "I want to learn this."

"It is not your time," Mahendra told him. Oddly, Piladius stifled and walked back beside Phaedrus. "Meals will be prepared whenever you desire them. My slaves are yours for the duration, my friend. If you need me, you will know where to find me."

"Thank you, my brother," Phaedrus said and turned about. Scathach was left with Mahendra.

Piladius smiled. He had slaves to cook and clean for him again. Life was looking better and better all the time. At least he didn't have to hunt and cook his meals.

"Have you decided?" he asked her.

"They are all similar, but they are also very different. It is almost as if they have a soul. It seems that if I choose one, it must be from the spirit inside me rather than the sight from my eyes." She tested them again, each one with her eyes closed.

After several attempts she made her decision. "This one...."

"A wise choice. That one is *Visamana*, made from black iron found in the Anupa country. Its name strikes fear in men. From this time forward you will be known as—'*she who strikes fear*,'" he said and opened his hand to take it back.

"Is it not my weapon now?" she asked him in confusion.

"No. This one is mine. Come with me."

Behind the training facility was an open-air building where slaves controlled a bellow forcing cold air into a fire pit of coals that glowed red. "Anupa," Mahendra told them. A slave departed and returned shortly after with a slab of black iron in his hands. "Here," he said and gave it to Scathach. "This is your weapon."

"I cannot fight with this," she told him.

"Not until you mold it into a sword. If you want to learn to fight with a good sword, you must first learn to make a good sword. You have chosen your weapon and now you must shape it."

"That is man's work or work for the slaves. I will not be lowered to slave work," she retorted.

"The making of this sword will be performed by the owner. We will not continue until you have done this deed." Without further confrontation, he turned and walked away, leaving her standing there with a slave waiting for her to proceed.

"What am I to do?" she asked the slave.

The slave was ignorant of her language. Perhaps it was best, she considered. She demonstrated her lack of knowledge with a shrug of her shoulders. The slave helped her. He carried the iron to the fire and put it in. Handing her a pair of thick, leather gloves he showed her how to stoke the flame, bellow the air and turn the iron in the pit. When the iron had turned red hot, he instructed her to pull it from the flame and carry it to the anvil where he handed her a hammer. It weighed heavily in her hand, but she managed to lay the iron across the anvil and bang out the edges of the blade. After a certain degree of success with rounding off the edges, the slave assisted her in setting the iron into a cold bucket of water before returning and thrusting it back into the fire. Again she bellowed the coals until it was hotter still. After heating the iron again she returned to the anvil to continue banging out the edges of the blade. Though the weather was cold, she managed to sweat under the intense heat, brushing away perspiration after every several swings. By the time the sword looked like it was shaping into something familiar, her muscles ached. She had to give in and return to finish it another time.

Mahendra knew she was there watching him, but did not interrupt his meditation. He was practicing his *Pyrrhic*, or as Scathach called it, spirit fighting. No one opposed him yet he moved across the room as if he fought some mysterious force. Then in a swift movement, he was at the wall where the various weapons hung. She barely blinked her eyes when a wooden pole, one similar to that which she had seen Phaedrus use against the mercenaries who attacked them, flew across the room directly at her. It nearly hit her, but she dodged fast enough to catch it in her hand

and stand ready for anything, even though her muscles refused to assist her. Suddenly, her arms drooped to her sides.

"Good," he commented. "Never get caught unaware, even when you are exhausted. Now that you have it, use it to stretch yourself. I can see that you are not used to working a smith's job. You will do well, though. I can see it in you. Trust, as I do, that your weapon will be a great work of art when it is finished. And take pride in knowing that you have done the molding of the weapon by yourself. Now, sit," he said and walked to her casually.

When she was seated on the floor and the pole resting across her lap, he assisted her. "Put the pole behind your head and curl your arms around it." When it was done he continued. "Now, lean your body to the right and touch the end of the pole to your left foot." She stretched to reach her foot and groaned in pain. Her muscles refused to work. "You can do it," he told her. She tried again, until she finally felt the muscles loosen and give way to her coaxing. "Now to the left and touch your right foot," he told her.

When this was done to his satisfaction, he made her stand. "Keep your hands curled behind the pole. Again, lean to the right and touch your left foot."

She did this with a little pain, but her muscles trembled then gave way. "Now to the left and touch your right foot," he urged.

After several minutes of stretching back and forth with the pole across her neck he made her stop. "The rest of the day is yours. Tomorrow we start early. My slaves will come for you. We shall meet here," he said and returned the pole to its place on the wall. She left obediently and without a single word. She was exhausted, yet she didn't know why. Was it the hammering of the iron? Was it the events of the morning at the stadium? Was it a combination of the stone and the day's events? It didn't matter. She felt she needed the rest.

A Hindu woman waited at the entrance for her to exit and directed her to her quarters. The room was small but clean and drinking water was set on a small table against the wall by a bed of pillows. She devoured the water then turned sharply.

"I've had it!" he shouted at her from the doorway. He looked wretched.

"Ploppus, what is wrong now?" she asked though she really wanted to laugh. He was covered in dirt and his garments were torn.

"He's a crazy man! He expects too much from me. I cannot learn to be a warrior in such conditions. I'm not made for it!" he complained.

"Piladius, I am too tired to slap you. We'll have to talk about it later. I need to wash and get some sleep."

"No! You have to talk with him now! He's thinks I'm getting a drink and wants me to return to start again. I'm going to die! And he's going to be my murderer!"

"Ploppus!" She shouted. "He will not kill you. Trust me, you will feel better tomorrow."

"But how much longer do I have to practice today?"

"I will talk with him. But you cannot be asking me to treat you like a child. You are a grown man. Act like one and someday you may wake up and actually be one."

He left disgruntled, mumbling the entire way until he was out of sight. When he had gone, Scathach beckoned a slave to direct her to a place for washing. She was covered in iron dust from smashing the hammer and taking chunks of metal off the edge of the sword she was making. It covered her hair and her face and ran in the rivulets of sweat running down her shoulders and arms. A moment later she was escorted to a private room where a hot spring bath had been made ready. It was refreshing. If anything, Aoife was right in the fact that the natural hot springs running in and about the city are extremely soothing on aching muscles. She knew then that Mahendra had chosen his place of residence wisely.

The morning came quickly and she woke with a stir. The muscles that she worked yesterday complained long before her feet hit the floor. It took several attempts to stretch without feeling the pain in her arms and legs. After relieving herself in a room designed to carry waste out of the city through the manmade ducts underground, she ate a bit of cheese, drank little of the *kumis* and went to the training house. She met no one on the way yet Mahendra was waiting for her inside. She absently wondered if Piladius and Phaedrus were already up and training. She had forgotten to speak to Phaedrus the night before, falling asleep shortly after taking the hot bath. But her attention was brought back to the room. From one end to the other a rope had been fastened to the wall. It was nearly three feet off the ground and pulled taught.

"Phaedrus has told me that you have excellent balance," he commented.

"Phaedrus boasts, but I do well to live by," she replied.

"That is good. Remove you clothing," he commanded.

Somehow she was not as uneasy as she was when Phaedrus had told her to remove her garments. She removed them and set them to the side. The sight of her nakedness reflected no concern in Mahendra's features. Only a skilled master such as he could avoid her beauty and continue uninterrupted.

"The stick," he said and removed it from the wall. "This is where we left off yesterday and we shall continue. Show me now how to touch your left and right foot with the pole across your shoulders."

She obeyed by stretching the pole to touch her left foot and then her right several times.

"Pugilism is a strong art," he told her. "Many things can happen for one who masters this art." He walked to the center of the floor and called her. "Sit here," he said and watched as she moved. "Close your eyes and listen to everything around you,"

She looked up sharply. "I have done this before," she told him.

"That is good. You will do it again. This is meditation and concentration. Now do so," he ordered sternly, but kept his voice barely at a whisper.

For nearly an hour she sat on the wickerwork floor listening to everything around, but there was nothing to hear. Only the drumming of the constant beat of her heart came back to her, though she stayed completely still and silent.

"Now," he whispered beside her. "Stand straight up. Do not assist yourself by putting your hands on the floor, just stand."

She did as instructed though short stabs of pain jabbed her muscles and they almost rebelled to the point of not working at all. Still, she forced herself to stand without the use of her hands.

"Now show me what Phaedrus has shown you."

Quietly, she went through a short demonstration of what Phaedrus had shown her the day before, jabbing, thrusting, spinning and jumping. Balance was first and foremost on her mind always keeping the pole ready for a strike at any moment. Mahendra realized that Phaedrus was again correct. She possessed outstanding balance technique. But now he would test it even further.

"Good," he said when she had finished. "Now do it here," he said and pointed to the rope attached to each end of the wall.

"What, on the rope?"

"Why yes. I have seen many people do wonderful feats atop a rope such as this. Jugglers and jesters and actors and acrobats have done marvelous things from a rope such as this. Surely you can do a few maneuvers of your own on such a rope?"

"I have never tried," she admitted.

"Then now is the time," he urged. "Come, leap onto the rope and keep your balance there," he instructed.

She looked at the length and thickness of it. She touched it with her hand to see if it would hold her. It barely moved. A moment later she leaped into the air and stood straight up on the rope, though she started to weave slightly back and forth.

"Now walk the length," he told her when she regained balance.

"Why do I do this?" she asked, her arms were stretched out on both sides keeping her steady.

"For balance," he informed her. "If you possess excellent balance on the ground, you should have no problem with your balance in the air on that rope," he stated. "Now, walk."

She took a step and immediately fell, jumping off to the side without hurting herself.

"Back up," he told her. "Walk," he instructed when she had claimed the rope.

She attempted another step and jumped off before she fell again.

"Your balance is not as good as you thought it was," he commented much to her disappointment.

"You do it," she told him disgruntled.

"And if I do, what reward shall I get?"

She thought for a moment. "I will never question your reason for doing anything again. And I will follow your instructions without hesitation," she conceded.

Mahendra smiled at her offer. "That is fair." He leaped onto the rope and stood straight up, arms at his sides, then stretched out far to keep his balance. The rope remained steady and when he was sure he had control, he bent his legs once, bounced into the air and flipped backward, landing on the rope again. He took two steps forward, one step back and then another three forward, sliding his feet along the rope as he went. His feet never actually left the rope, she noticed. Then he bent low and grabbed the rope in both hands. Slowly he rolled forward until he was sitting on the rope with one leg dangling off the side and the other laying flat out on the rope in front of him. He bent his leg and stood on the rope with the left one still hanging off on the side. Again, he took two steps, sliding his feet under him like a lion after prey. At the end of the rope, he stopped, shifted his weight and spun around facing the other direction. Never did he lose focus, never did he lose his balance, nor did he ever fall.

"Where have you learned such things?" she asked him when he was beside her again.

"Many places do this rope feat. There are those in a far off island to the northwest who dance on ropes such as this. They play games on it and sometimes they fight. Mostly, they demonstrate their acrobatic skills. But there have been those who fight to the death and those who base their decisions on the outcome of the rope feat such as marriage, property rights, judgments and even weighing the results of serious crimes. Now, up," he said and offered her the rope.

When most of the morning had gone and she had made several attempts to walk the rope, he instructed her to stop, eat a light meal that was already prepared and return. When she arrived back in the training hall she was met with Mahendra and two other men who seemed odd to her. They were skinny and tall, their hair long and flat. They could have been twins, except one had a flat nose, the other long and pointed. Each had dark eyes and wore similar breeches with stripes woven into the fabric and long silk shirts. They smiled at her when she entered.

"Very attractive," one commented openly.

Mahendra blocked his view. "Remember why you are here," he warned.

"Yes, I will, but you must admit, it is always a pleasure to teach one of such beauty. It helps to make it worth our while," he smiled.

"You will be paid for your time and nothing more. When you are finished I expect you to be gone from here. But I will give you one warning further. This pretty little thing as you see her, will kill you just as fast as I will should you attempt anything other than what we have discussed. Do you understand?"

They both looked at her. How could someone of such beauty and strength be that dangerous? She was certainly tall and they could see the muscle tone in her arms and legs, even through the garments she wore, but could she really kill them? Best not to question it, they considered. Besides, they have worked with Mahendra before. He was good on his word for killing them himself. They would stick to the training schedule. "Yes, we understand."

Mahendra left her alone with them. And he was right, she realized. She could kill them without ever thinking twice about it. They weren't much of challenge, she could see. They possessed no muscular tone on any part of their body. They were lanky and sort of awkward in stature. No, they would pose no threat.

"Do you know what we are doing here?" the first asked.

"I have no idea," she answered.

He stepped forward. "My name is Hahmir-Hahmir," he introduced with a stiff bow. "And this is my brother, Ouatu-Hahmir. We have been hired by our friend Mahendra to teach you to juggle. Do you know of this thing?"

"Juggle?" she reiterated.

"Yes, to throw and catch items in the air before they fall to the ground. It is very simple, but takes long hours of practice to reach a stage of success and accomplishment. We are here to instruct you to do such things. Are you well to do this?" Hahmir-Hahmir asked her.

She had never heard of such a thing, but figured Mahendra must know what had to be taught. And she had made her bargain with him. She would not question him again. "Yes," she answered and stood back to watch.

A sack was opened and several items were thrown from it. They each gathered three and went several paces apart and faced her. Suddenly they began tossing the items into the air and catching them. She was fascinated by their ability to do so. It seemed like fun; a game that children should learn to play when they are very little. She couldn't understand what this had to do with training to be a better fighter, but for the moment she would watch and learn.

The brothers slowly turned to each other on a silent command and suddenly began throwing the items to each other, each one catching it, throwing it into the air and then returning it to the other over again. It was truly an interesting game. Then, almost abruptly, they stopped. They each took out two more items and began again. Now they were tossing five items in the air. Again they faced each other and tossed one at a time to the other until they tired and halted, catching all items as they fell from the air. Not one item hit the floor.

"That is what you are going to learn," Hahmir-Hahmir told her. "Are you ready?"

"Let us try," she told him.

It was extremely awkward. It took several attempts to control the tossing of three objects in the air, but she finally grasped the mathematical equation to set them in motion. They often hit the floor and even more times they went flying off in different directions of the room. Before long, however, she could actually control her movement to juggle the three items steadily. The brothers were impressed by her innate ability to learn quickly. With that learned, though not perfected, they attempted to move on to a fourth and fifth item toss. This was much more difficult and the mathematics with which to accomplish such a task was overwhelming for her. She dropped them more frequently, lost control of them often and occasionally threw them in the air out of frustration. Yet by the later afternoon hours she had accomplished a great deal of success and they ceased the exercise. After bidding her a good day, informing her that they would return on the morrow, they departed. Mahendra had returned at their dismissal.

"They have told me you are extremely talented. I'm not impressed. You have much more to learn, and not much time to learn it."

"Why is this?" she asked.

He looked towards the entrance. "I have been informed that Caesar moved his legions during the winter quarters. They have broken through the snows that bar their path through the mountains into Gaul. The casualties were significant, but Caesar has done it none-the-less."

"It appears that we will be on Caesar's heels, does it not?" Scathach smiled slightly.

"Yes. I believe you could kill a great many of his soldiers, but to take on a legion of his finest would undo you completely. Your training here and in your future would be for not. I will have wasted my time and efforts. You will learn what you can here and now then continue on your own under the supervision of Phaedrus when you leave. Are you ready for the next?" he asked.

"Yes," she answered dryly.

"Good, remove your clothing," he told her as he too removed his. She obeyed. Both stood naked in the center of the floor. "Sit," he instructed.

When they were seated beside each other facing the wall of weapons, he began. "Breathe...deeply. Hear everything around you and concentrate on it. Listen carefully to my voice as I instruct you." He paused for several long seconds so she could adjust.

As always, he spoke in whispers. "The voice can be a very powerful weapon, Scathach. It can smite great enemies with words of aggression or it can heal with words of sympathy. It can completely change a nation with words of diplomacy or it can conquer the heart with words praise and admiration. The voice is above all, one of the most powerful tools one can possess. The use of that tool is vitally important. I have studied with many masters. Yet there is one, a master of the orient who has taught me most. Though I have never seen him do so, it was often said that he could kill a man with his voice. I have seen those who can shatter pottery using the vibrations of their voice. Everything around you becomes attuned to the vibration until it shatters. Another master, it has been claimed, can, as I do, only speak in whispers for fear that buildings will collapse around him. This art is called *kiai* and you must learn it. Not everyone can perform this feat, yet there are many who can use it to an advantage. I wish you to learn it so that you may gain an advantage in combat. To learn this art completely would take a long, long time of practice. That is time that you do not have. Therefore, I will teach you what I can. The rest will be up to you," he told her then rested a moment.

"If you are ready?" he asked and became silent. A moment later, he began. "Close your eyes and force your voice in a low humming tone. Feel the sound resonating inside your throat." She nodded that she had done so. "Now, take your hand to your neck and feel the vibration there. Slowly open your throat by pushing more air through it, but you must maintain the same constant tone in your voice. When pushing air through, you will naturally want to raise the sound of your voice, but you must concentrate to keep that same resonance inside. You have to be louder, but maintain the same tone."

She understood what he wanted and she could feel it with her hand at the front of her neck, but the more air she forced through her throat the higher her pitch became. She fought to keep the tone at a guttural sound where the vibration was deepest. And Mahendra could hear her doing so also.

"That is where you will find the most power in your voice, Scathach. Continue to practice that each day and the sound and volume will grow. Remember…some only achieve a small amount of power with their voice. Some voices are not designed to handle such power at all. But nearly all who attempt this exercise, with patience and practice and over time, achieve a significant degree of result. Now," he said and stood. "I want to you to take this." He went to the entrance and returned with a parchment of plain scroll leafing.

"You want me to write?" she asked quizzically.

"No. I want you to feel the vibrations on your hand through the scroll. Hold the parchment up with one hand and place the other behind it. Let your voice sing out and vibrate until you feel it on the other side. When you are certain you can feel the vibrations of your voice there, move the scroll further away from you. Eventually you will gain a distance that your voice will achieve results. Try it now," he told her and assisted in setting her hands where they should go.

She sang, or hummed as he called it, until she could feel her voice vibrating on the page. The scroll was perhaps a distance of six thumbs from her mouth. She moved it further away until the vibration faded.

"Yes," he commented with a smile at her understanding. "Eventually you will feel that same vibration a horse's distance from you. Of course this will require the assistance of someone else to tell you that they can feel the vibrations in your voice at such a distance. And if you pursue the challenge, you can double and triple that distance. But you must be patient and you must concentrate. The hardest part of this exercise is that the more distance you gain, the more energy you are forced to use. You will become exhausted much faster than you ever have at doing anything else, including fighting in battles. However, your stamina and endurance will increase twofold. Now," he said with a degree of satisfaction in the day's progress. "It is time for you to continue on your sword. If you are to be known as *she who strikes fear*, you must create a weapon that will produce such a threat."

She knew where to go, though she dreaded lifting the heavy hammer repeatedly in the air and shaping the blade into a sharp edge. Though the pain was there, she worked hard so that it didn't last as long as it had the day before.

CHAPTER VIII

In the next few weeks the snows had fallen heavily, leaving the land white in all directions. Not many strangers came to Pannonia nor had the people of the city moved very far from the city walls. The hot springs continued to bubble and boil which brought a relief to all who enjoyed the pleasure of the healing properties and the warmth of the water against their bodies. It appeared that the people drank and ate more during this part of the season than any other. Hunters were seen going out daily to the nearby forests to capture game and return to the city where they would sell their catch and stock up on food supplies. They also kept themselves busy in the local rivers and lakes—when the ice could be broken—to provide fish for many. Musicians who paraded in the streets were now slumbered in dark corners of lavishly decorated halls or sitting by fire pits where they played subtle music to entertain those who enjoyed meals or games or even sex. It seemed that no one really cared what went on here in the city; except during tax time. There really was no king to speak of and an occasional diplomat would wander in to assume a post of political power only long enough to be executed. Those who wanted to rule were seldom heard of for very long and those who managed to get a brief taste of the power cared not for the end result. Many rapidly left, never to be heard from again. The taxes collected throughout the year were evenly distributed among the city proprietary, yet the tax collector himself was changed quite frequently. Everyone seemed happy with the distribution efforts. And they managed to put aside some of the wealth to build new buildings, refurbish demolished ones and expand those that existed. Pannonia was a city that had been defeated many times in the past by barbaric Celtic tribes: only to be given up just as easily as it was taken. Now it seemed that Rome had an eye for the city. There was a great deal of promise to acquire substantial wealth. And where wealth was concerned, Rome surely had an interest. Lately, the people of Pannonia had developed an ally with its neighboring Dalmatians and were looking to the Illyrians for the possibility of future trading. Hope for a strong coalition between these neighboring factors could result in a substantial unity for trading in the west and in the east without restitution to outside influences that demanded tribute for free trade. Rome was such an influence.

Scathach trained hard during this time. The cold felt good on her body and she liked the frigidness of the air after a day of training. And she finished her sword as well. It took much longer to make than Mahendra had anticipated, but when she was done, the weapon was one of the finest he had ever seen. She continued to work the hammer against metal long after her sword was completed. Many knives and swords passed through the bellows under her hand. Each was a miraculous piece, never making two of the same weapon. Her ability to work iron and steel far surpassed Mahendra's expectations, especially for someone of her experience. The strength in her arms had doubled as well. Then she juggled and walked the rope and worked pankration and pugilism until every muscle ached. Yet in the evenings, Shamina, the Hindu woman assigned to provide her with everything she needed, treated her with herbs and potions to loosen stiff muscles and aching bones. Oddly, she was ready for a new day of training each morning because of it. Eventually, she learned the remedies used by Shamina to cure the aches and pains and the normal maladies that occur with vigorous training. And her *kiai* had increased as well, though after the first week she had worked her voice hoarse. Lately she found herself talking much louder than normal, even though she barely opened her mouth to speak. Mahendra had told her it was normal.

Aoife had not been seen since their confrontation in the arena, but Scathach knew she could take care of herself. There wasn't a man alive who could defeat her. One way or the other, Aoife would win. Yet, it upset Scathach to think her sister deserted her when she only tried to protect her. When the winter quarters were over, she knew, they would be together again and moving across the land. Somehow, she thought, the delay in Pannonia made her nervous. Traveling over the land had been common for her. She rarely stayed at home for long periods. Trouble was always on the outskirts of her village. Men always wanted more power, more land, and more women. Barbarians were always coming to kill off the men and steal the women and children away from the village. She traveled if only to catch them on the verge of an unscheduled attack and dispatching them without remorse and carrying their heads back to show Brona. That was the reason why few ever tried to capture her village in the past ten years. As long as Scathach were alive, her village was safe and everyone, everywhere, knew it. Unfortunately, that village no longer existed. Brona and all her friends had perished to keep her and Aoife safe. And she would never forget that. And regardless of the confrontation with Aoife at the stadium, she would be there for her always, if only for Brona's sake.

Piladius was rarely seen. Phaedrus understood the need for Mahendra to concentrate on Scathach and her training. He had seen many great fighters in his time and though Scathach was among them, she was about to become one of the best if not *the* best. With that in mind, he kept Piladius away and taught him horsemanship and above all, how to mount his horse without looking like a child. It was during practice with a spear that Phaedrus remembered. "Here," he said and took the weapon from him. It took him all morning to make it, but when it was finished the spear was returned and towards the bottom, near the head of the weapon, was a hook just large enough for him to put his foot into. "Run to your horse now. When you get to a place about an arms distance, thrust the spear into the earth and step onto the hook to lift yourself up to the back of the animal." It took several attempts—two of which he landed head first into the side of the horse, scaring it away, but eventually he figured it out. For the first time, he smiled at his ability to learn something not found in a book. He knew Scathach would be pleased.

During the evening hours, he spent his time writing about what Phaedrus had taught him and then sharing his time among the scholars at the oratory. They too noticed a change in him, as his features broadened and his arms and calves took on a more muscular shape. Some of the older friends he had gained started to back away from him for fear that he was traitor to the scholarly ways. Much as he tried to keep them abreast of his situation, they continued to grow skeptical. Then there was a young man who joined them. Enjoying a short break from Athens he ventured in the cold temperatures for a brief taste of the natural hot springs that flowed year round in Pannonia. Quintus Horatius Flaccus and Piladius became close friends from the start. The younger was extremely eager to learn all he could while taking as much time to enjoy the pleasures of the hot waters that seemed to soothe the soul. A student in philosophy, he and Piladius spent many hours together. He came to be known as Horace to those who suddenly took a liking to this vibrant youth. Together he and Piladius studied and performed transcriptions in the oratory, talking about politics and religion and all things that scholars employ to keep the minds alert. Horace especially took a liking to the poets who seemed to cling to the darker recess of the oratory to perform stanzas more silently and reclusive.

But the day was coming for the small group to move along. They all felt it, though they refused to mention it when in the presence of each other. Time was not one of the comforts they had, had they not been on the move from the Roman armies. Caesar was looking to conquer all of Gaul, but there are only so many women warriors anywhere with red hair and possessing such beauty as Scathach that surely someone would notice her. Eventually someone would report back to Nero that she had surely survived. Even though Rwan and Oseida had performed their best to the end, it might not have been enough to convince Rome that she was truly dead. If this were true it may not be long before Caesar was ordered to move to Pannonia and find her. That was something she had to avoid at all costs. But until that time, she realized she would train hard. Mahendra had done exceptionally well, she thought. While she felt as if she had known how to do all these things before, she now knew that her physical abilities in all areas had enhanced significantly. She would remember to thank Mahendra when the time came.

The days of training became longer and she worked harder to keep it all together. She was now juggling seven fruits, keeping them in the air for several minutes before losing her concentration and letting them fall to the floor. Hahmir-Hahmir and his brother Ouatu-Hahmir had progressed not only to juggling them while on the floor, but also while balancing on the rope. She had become confident in her ability to maneuver herself along the rope, juggle five apples and turn about when she reached the end. She now practiced pankration and pugilism while balancing on the rope as well, contending with Mahendra whose ability in balance far surpassed hers. He constantly knocked her to the floor with swift moves of his hands and feet only to order her back up. She obeyed without hesitation. Then he would repeat the exercise with wooden pole, knocking her off with very little effort. But now she was getting an advantage by mimicking his moves and steeling his ideas. Yet every time she learned his tricks he would alter it slightly to confuse her and knock her back down. When this part of the day was completed, she would stretch for long periods and practice her *kiai* at the same time. Instead of working with iron and steel, she took to throwing knives and axes and shooting arrows at smaller targets. And she learned to throw a spear as well, though this too she made with her own hands and with Mahendra's instruction. On a bitter morning, Mahendra took her to the garden and in a sort of silent ritual cut a branch from an Ash tree there. It was not allowed to touch the ground so that it would cleave to the element of air, always flying straight and true, he told her. He informed her, as he produced the branch, of a famous spear brought to the island of Ire by the Tuatha De Danaan from the city of Gorias. The spear was of such power that it would never miss its target and was kept hooded when not in use. Though her weapon possessed no unusual powers, the branch she molded and shaped with a knife met the standard. When finished, it was another work of art. Again, Mahendra was impressed with her talents, and her ability to learn quickly.

The snow was deep but the sun rose untainted by storm or cloud. In the brightness of the new day, they gathered in the eatery and sat with Mahendra at a large dining table. It was the first time they had been together in one room for weeks. The arrangements to meet were made by Mahendra himself. "We have news," he informed them between bits of cheese and fruits. "Yesterday our population increased by more than a thousand, all of them refugees from the war with Caesar. They are coming in droves from the west. Caesar is moving his soldiers out of winter quarters and the Celtic king, Vercingetorix, has attached interests from the Parisii, Senones, Pictones, Cadurci, and others such as the Aulerci and Lemovice. All the tribes bordering the ocean have unanimously consented to his supreme command as well. He has also secured hostages from all these states and has established a fixed number of soldiers to be sent to him immediately while he commands from the lands of the Biturges who live just south of the river Loire. His most trusted Lucterius, the Cadurcan, has moved a large force of men to the country of the Helvii. It is reported that Caesar has pressed through mount Cevennes, which separates the Arverni from the Helvii, and cleared snow six feet high to reach the Arverni territories. Lucterius was forced to retreat. I don't need to tell you that the war will indeed move to all parts of Gaul. I understand that Germans are joining in the war if only for territory purposes. The tribes of the northeast, namely the Treveri and the Nemetes, are sending most of their men to aid Vercingetorix. In their absence, the Germans are crossing the river Rhenus (Rhine) to conquer greater lands."

"What does that mean to us?" Scathach asked him. "Are we not safe here?"

"For now, yes. But if hostages have made it to our gates in search of safety, you can rest assured that Rome will follow shortly behind them."

"What is Caesar's intention at this point?" Piladius asked him though Phaedrus was thinking the same and nodded his approval of the question.

"Caesar wants all of Gaul, though he prefers the Celts to rule the lands according to Roman principals and laws. Nonconformists will suffer the emperor's whip and Caesar will ensure that it happens. Already, Vercingetorix has sustained great losses at Vellaunodunum, Genabum and Noviodunum. But he has started smaller skirmishes in the wooded lands and marshes where Romans have been foraging for corn and other provisions. These little attacks have gained him an edge. Roman soldiers care not for deprivation of food and supplies that normally are available during winter quarters," Mahendra told them. "Take them away from the surety of these quarters and they know supplies are scarce. This tends to make them slightly fiercer, yet apprehensive to wage war with anyone."

"Then we must leave and aid the Arvernian," Scathach told him.

Mahendra showed a wry smile. "I know you dislike the Romans and for personal reasons. But mind you, Vercingetorix is also malicious and cruel. Crimes are severely punishable under his hand. Hundreds are returned to their homeland without ears or the loss of an eye as a lesson to those who may decide not to obey his orders, even if he isn't near to give those orders directly. He is brave, but be leery of his temper," he warned. "Already, his own people have accused him of treason because he was camped too close to the enemy, but he managed to resolve the dispute diplomatically. His power to lead is two-fold with his people again."

She looked at him. "Will you come with us, Mahendra?" she asked.

The smile changed to a sort of grin, one that said he would enjoy the challenge and the chance to test his superior skills again in combat. A moment later it faded as he realized the consequences of such a decision. There were personal things he had to tend to in Parthia—things pertaining to his father and his father's murderer, Orodes II. "No, I cannot. But you will have Phaedrus at your side and your sister as well. I have kept up on the activities of the young scholar too. He has learned a great deal."

She looked to Piladius. Mahendra was right. He had changed significantly. His hair was pulled neatly behind his ears and tied tightly. His face was clean-shaved, his jaw showing tension and muscle as he worked it nervously from side to side. He had gained strength and much more confidence, she could tell. His posture no longer slumped, but poised erect, his chest and chin more efficacious. Phaedrus had worked him hard. She felt sorry for never getting back to him that first night there, but he seemed to have worked out his troubles, she sensed. Still, she hadn't seen him in action. He may be stronger, but he may not be able to handle himself in battle quite yet. "We shall see," she replied. "I must contact my sister, Aoife, to inform her of our plans."

"That has already been arranged," he informed her. "A message is being delivered to her as we speak. I suspect she will be joining us before midday as it may take some time for my courier to find her."

Scathach raised her eyebrows. "She will not come here," she informed him. "I will have to seek her out."

"She will come," Mahendra assured her.

"I trust you to think that, Mahendra, but you do not know Aoife as I do."

"Scathach...I ask that you always trust what I say to you. Do not waste your time looking for her in the city. My courier will find her and she will come immediately."

She didn't know what to say or how to respond to that. Mahendra was not one she would ever mistrust. If he told her the sun would rise in the north on the morrow and settle in the south, she would believe him. And she would do so now, she considered. "I believe you, Mahendra."

"Then is it decided?" Phaedrus asked. "We leave on the morrow?"

Each looked to the other. "Yes," Scathach answered and stood. "I will be with Khutalk for the rest of the morning."

When all was said and done, they each went their different way to gather their things and prepare for departure. Each felt saddened to be leaving yet glad at the same time. Even Piladius, with his incessant need for slaves to assist him, felt as if a cumbersome weight had been lifted. Whether knowing that he wouldn't have to train every hour of the day with Phaedrus or the fact of moving across the open land, he felt a greater desire to be away from Pannonia. Perhaps it was all those years of traveling with Aram across the endless plains in a covered wagon that made him homesick to push along. Just because he didn't necessarily see the lands as he traveled through them, didn't mean that he didn't feel every inch of the way as his cart bounced over the terrains of nearly every habitable area, though the thought of moving in the winter season did bother him slightly. Most of all...they would miss the heated baths they took daily.

Phaedrus, on the other hand, spent the entire day with Mahendra. Together, they reminisced of times long past, of training days and fighting enemies. "I will miss you, my brother," he said over a goblet of rich, red wine.

"May your journey be as successful and rewarding as mine," Mahendra replied. After that, the master fighter disappeared and was not seen again. There were no gifts of gratitude, no words of encouragement, no regrets. He had come to them like a ghost and had departed in the same manner. Though Scathach knew he would never be forgotten.

Aoife did appear by midday, as Mahendra had predicted. Although beautiful, she was in a state of dishevelment. A look of curiousness, yet anger, set firmly in her features and she carried her sword in her right hand ready for action. Her left hand was balled in a fist and her eyes cast glances of danger to anyone who got in her way. "Where is she!" she barked at the door, ready to strike the first who would come for her.

"Aoife," Piladius said with a greeting from the sofa as she stood at the entrance. Behind her the slave was sobbing and shaking his head. He held all her belongings in his hands as he stood there.

"Where is she!" she barked again.

"Your sister? Why, she is with her horse of course. She's probably on her way back here by now," he replied unalarmed. He had seen Aoife before when she was angry. This sour greeting was no exception to any previous encounter with her. He always sensed that she disliked him anyway.

In one swift move Aoife was in the room with her sword pressing against his chest. "Ploppus, you'd better be telling the truth or I *will* run this straight through your heart and then I'll take your head and hang it where the beasts can feed off your flesh till your skull is all that's left of you. Now, where is she?"

Piladius was taken aback. He had never expected her to attack him outwardly. His skills in diplomacy and tact swiftly came forth. "Aoife, I don't know what you've been told, but your sister is in great care. She is the one who has asked that you come to this place so we can discuss out departure."

She immediately withdrew. "Departure?"

"Yes," he responded as he checked the blood spilling from the slight cut in the middle of his chest. "You didn't have to stab me!" he spit.

"What would you have me do? I was told she was in grave danger and I had to come or she would die." She suddenly turned about to stare at the short, stubby courier. He wet his pants, dropped her clothing and personal items and ran as fast as he could for safety. Aoife didn't have the heart to chase him. She could only laugh.

"I do apologize, my fine scholar," she cajoled. "I didn't mean to hurt you intentionally, but know that I would have killed you if I knew you had harmed my sister."

"I trust in that. I'm just glad you're on our side." He shook his head.

"Oh, come, come, scholar. Look at you.... You've shaped up over this time. My," she soothed and moved closer to feel the muscle that flexed as he tended his minor wound. "I always knew you'd shape up to be of use someday, but you've become quite something," she teased. He flushed in the face and a prickly heat caressed his flesh until he broke out in an uncomfortable sweat.

"I think I have things to pack," he told her as he scooted out from under her pressing bosom.

"You do that," she giggled. "I'll just go find Skitatsya on my own."

"That's Scathach, Aoife. Get used to it," he called back to correct her. Skitatsya was a name she would never use again, he knew.

CHAPTER IX

The territory was unfamiliar to Scathach who had never been this far west of her homeland. Most of her travels took her east across the Turan and into the Altai and the Sayan once or twice a year. She had become used to the lakes and streams and rivers there and the route she would follow each time, noticing only minor changes in the landscape. On this occasion, however, she managed to let Phaedrus lead the way. He pushed them ahead on the north side of the river, Danuvius (Danube), the entire way with only small bands of travelers and early season traders moving in the opposite direction. Several settlements had been established on the banks of the river as well. While the weather remained tainted in cold breezes that blew constantly at them from the west, they continued to move on, taking shelter as often as they could in the villages they found. During the travel, Scathach took time out every day to practice her skills in shooting, throwing, juggling and even her *kiai*. In the evenings she would visit with her horse and practice movements with the pole that Mahendra had given her. Eventually, she knew, she would design one similar to Phaedrus', with knives swinging freely from both ends.

They remained silent during their journey, no one sharing anything of their experiences at Pannonia, though each had a significant awakening there. Each had matured to a level that demanded respect. They could see it in posture and feel it in conversations that emerged from decisions to rest or eat. At times, the air seemed as tense as it was cold.

On the third day of travel they came to the city of Vindobona

(Vienna), which was almost forty miles west of Bratislava in the northeast part of Noricum. While only commoners and seasonal settlers moved about in Bratislava, a terrible discovery found them searching for ways inside Vindobona without letting the keepers of the city know who they were.

"Where do you hail?" the centurion asked gruffly. A garrison of armed men flanked him on either side and at least a legion of them had set up quick shelters for winter quarters all about the area. The centurion's features were well sewn for the season, rough and leathery. His teeth gnashed back and forth mercilessly. Obviously he had a terrible ache in one or more of his teeth and it bothered him.

"Greek mercenaries," Phaedrus announced. "We have been in winter quarters in Athens and have come to seek employment within," he told him with a nod in the direction of the city.

"Greeks, hey?" he commented as he studied them. "And the women, are they mercenaries as well?" he smiled at Aoife.

"My fine Roman, you have no idea what these women are capable of," he said in warning, though the hulking centurion paid no attention to his comment.

"What if I ask you to continue on without the women? Would you leave them in my care?" he asked without taking his eyes away from Aoife.

"You obviously feel the need to get yourself hurt."

The centurion glared at him daringly. "You threaten the soldiers of Caesar and Pompey?"

"Not at all," he replied. "I am only offering advice. They are yours."

"Mine? You will leave such beauty behind and not attempt to fight for it? Absurd! You cannot be a man at all," he laughed in his face and reached for Aoife's leg.

"Choose!" Scathach called out, though her voice boomed loud enough for nearly the entire camp to hear her. All eyes shifted to her. She seemed to go red with anger. Phaedrus had never seen this happen. He was just as alarmed as the centurion. Perhaps the hatred she had built up extended no further than here, he thought. But the display of reddened features surely caused the centurion to reconsider momentarily.

He collected himself quickly. "Choose? What choices do I have?

There is beauty or more beauty before me. Either of you will suite me. What if I choose you both?" he chortled.

"Choose the five men you would like to bury this night," she told him.

He continued to smile, though his teeth were yellow and rotted. "Why would you threaten such a worthless fight? These men are battle soldiers. Any one of them will kill a woman, or even a child for that matter, but I rather like the looks of you and would enjoy your company much more while you are alive. You're not much good to me dead," he said sadly as if giving her an ultimatum.

"Then how do you recommend we settle this?" she asked.

"How about we kill your friends here, the mercenaries?" he looked deadly at them. "And then we take you?"

While Piladius withdrew slightly, Phaedrus never balked. "Which ten would you like *me* to attempt?" he asked without loosing his composure.

"You would challenge ten of my best against you...alone?"

He looked about him. "Choose," he said dryly, "so that I may seek employment within. Choose or move aside, my good man," he teased.

Now the centurion was taken aback. "You are not much to look at. I will enjoy their bodies into the early morning hours before I cut off their heads and cast them to the wilds of the forests. And your corpse will be stinking in the mud long before I am done with them," he threatened.

"Sire," Piladius suddenly, though nearly sheepishly, spoke out. "You do understand the consequences, I trust?"

"Consequences?" he ushered.

"If this Greek mercenary fights and kills ten of your men, we all go free and without interruption, because you are a man of honor. If you allow the woman to fight and she kills five of your men, we all go free and without interruption, because, again, you are a man of honor. But, if you kill the Greek, the women will take up arms against you and fight you, even though they may die in the process," he said looking around at the sex-hungry eyes of the garrison. "You will lose the flesh that taunts your lusty desires. Regrettably, sire, I see only one way to resolve this issue."

"What would that be?" he asked, tempted.

"Simply allow us to pass."

He laughed openly, haughtily. "What makes you think I will do that?

There is nothing in it for my men or me. What if I decide to kill you all and have it done with?"

"That is not an option, sire," Piladius chimed. "You see, we will all fight then and that will leave your legion in a mess. I say that only because I know how well my friends fight."

"There is not much more of a choice," the centurion gleamed. He sensed to have won either cause.

"Oh, there is, sire. There is life. You can choose to keep your own life. You see, I know of Pompey though I have only heard tidings of Caesar along my way. But I know that if you allow these women to fight against *battle-ready* soldiers and your soldiers lose, you will have to answer for it. And when Caesar and Pompey hear that soldiers in winter quarters died particularly at the hands of a single woman or two women, for that matter, they will want more than retribution from my friend's head and mine. I believe they will probably take your head as well—all the way back to Rome so they can hang it on your wife's doorstep. Either way, you will pay the price for loosing men foolishly. And especially when there is a major war in Gaul."

"Pass!" he shouted. "And don't come this way again. I won't be as kind," he shouted as he turned and burst through the ranks of his men.

They moved off without further comment.

"That was quite a piece of work!" Aoife claimed when they were far enough away. "You have quite a gift with words, my friend."

He was sweating profusely, though the evening winds were cold. His hands were shaking and his heart beat loudly in his chest. "I was lucky," he said nodding his head in reflection. A moment later they were crossing the bridge into the city of Vindobona.

The city was a hub of workers and businesses, lawmakers and bureaucrats. Roman soldiers stood everywhere, watching, listening. Courts had been established in huge stone buildings with carved figurines guarding entrances and on alcoves and on the tops of roofs. Pillars stood thirty and forty feet tall in front of the buildings showing the architectural talent of the local artists. And there were commoners and travelers looking for work and other mercenaries among the populace. The smell of cooked food filled the streets as well as the occasional scent of wine and ale from several of the local taverns. The interior housed many families as cries filtered into the early evening hours from babies and smaller children. Older children played in the muddy streets with sticks and balls, laughing and hitting the ball back and forth to each other, keeping it away from the younger ones trying to capture it. In the midst of the clamor of noises, they found a stable capable of housing their horses and baggage. Afterward they retired to a tavern where they took up a quick meal of stew and bread, then purchased rooms for the rest of the evening.

"If you want," Aoife addressed Piladius. "You can spend the night with me," she teased.

While the invitation seemed palatable, he declined her services and went straight to his writing. The jolting conversation against the Roman centurion earlier was enough to keep him busy all night. Phaedrus, on the other hand, remained at the table drinking what the locals called a flagon of ale. "I would remain indoors tonight, Aoife," he informed her. "There are many soldiers here who wouldn't mind losing their head for a night against your skin."

She looked at him with surprise. "I'm flattered, Phaedrus. I honestly didn't know you worried about me at all."

"I worry for us all. Your sister worries for you. I intend to see your sister through this journey, Aoife. And I will stop at nothing to see she makes it to wherever she is going," he smiled curtly.

"Would you care to keep my company? Just to make sure I don't wander off?"

"No. I think I'll gather some information and get some rest myself," he finished.

She scoffed at him and turned away, leaving him alone at the table.

It wasn't long before he was approached.

"Kind sir," an elderly commoner said as he sat beside him. "Are your women for hire? Or are they your personal slaves?"

"They are neither," he replied stiffly. "They are warriors."

"Come now. With all that beauty and the way they are shaped? Surely you must own them?"

Phaedrus flipped the cover of the flagon, a design so the flies would stay out of the ale, and took a deep drink. "Sir, no one owns them."

He looked perplexed, though his beard and shaggy, matted hair gave little of his features away. "Then they are for hire or for capture," he stated.

"If you think you can capture them and, or, hire them, you are mistaken. They would just as soon kill you as look at you. Believe me, they are beauty beyond belief, but they are the most fearsome warriors I have ever met."

"Are they looking at fighting with the Roman soldiers there," he shifted his gaze to the outdoors where a small band of Roman soldiers stood guard. "You know, in the war with the Celts?"

It appeared then the old one might have information he was looking for. And he was giving it freely. "That was our initial intension, but we are undecided. There was a guard who met us when we first arrived. He was not pleasant and I believe his only desire was to ravage the women and continue on his ignorant way."

"Hmmm," the old fellow sighed. "A big fellow or a small, skinny kind of man?"

"A big fellow, I'd say."

"That would be Arnasticus, Caius Trebonius' personal centurion. Trebonius has moved west with two legions and all the horse, leaving that lot to guard the city. A terrible lot, if I have ever seen one. Best to leave him alone."

"Is there any news of the war in Gaul?" he asked.

"Not much. Gergovia seems to have special interests by both sides. It has been visited twice: once by the Arvernian and once by Caesar. Word has it that they are all moving to Avaricum. Caesar has already passed the rivers Loire and the Allier twice. They are pushing north into the Bituriges country and are seemingly recruiting the Aedui for support. What a lovely bunch they are! They tend to go with whoever is winning."

"How many Roman soldiers are committed to the war?"

Caesar has taken the ninth, tenth and the thirteenth legions with him. They were hard pressed to move in winter quarters, but Caesar was determined."

"You know a lot for a commoner," Phaedrus commented.

"I'm not just a commoner. I may look like one, but looks are deceiving.

I'm actually a hired scout. I am a Celt, but I need the money to survive and I will go anywhere to get it. I have followed the lot located on the west side of the city for a long time. We are waiting for Trebonius to return so we can push off to continue the war with the Parthian king. It appears a pre-engagement with Orodes II last year proved fatal for us."

"I understand. I wish you well, my friend," he said and lifted his cup once again.

"Whatever you do," the elder moved closer, his breath was sour. "Stay clear of Arnasticus. If you need assistance go to Marcus Suvellius at the west gate," he advised quietly. "And keep your eyes on those beauties up there," he shifted his green-gray eyes to the ceiling and the rooms above.

"I will—and thank you."

No sooner did the old fellow stand to leave when a heavy rush of feet stampeded above them. In the next moment Scathach cast a loud yell, one that Phaedrus had heard before. All eyes shifted to the ceiling, waiting for the rafters to cave in as the building trembled slightly from her cry. He knew she was in the midst of a fight, perhaps for her life. He jumped to his feet and started for the stairs to assist her. A second yell came from Aoife as she joined in the fight. Phaedrus had to move quickly if he was going to be of any help. Neither woman had a weapon for they were all stored in the stable with the animals. This meant that Scathach and Aoife were using only their hands and feet to defend themselves though he knew their skill was exceptional. It was only two more leaps to the top step and he would be there to get them away safely, but he was suddenly cast to the floor from hands grabbing him behind and thrusting him forward. He never had a chance to join them. With his body held to the floor by an unknown force of men behind him, he turned his head to watch as both Scathach and Aoife danced in a wild frenzy. Their arms and legs lashed out dangerously, hitting and kicking everything in sight. Gathering all his strength, he gave one last effort to free himself from his captors. A moment later it all went black.

"Phaedrus! Wake up!" the harsh, yet familiar voice screamed. It was followed by a bowl of water splashing against his face. He woke instantly and shook off the residue. "Yes, yes, there you are."

Phaedrus tried to move but the chains kept his arms and legs restrained to the cold wall of stone. "Where are they?" he asked though it sounded more like a curse. The cell itself was cold yet musty and dank in odor.

"Oh, don't fret, my good man. They are safe. A bit bruised, but safe none-the-less. You however, are not in such safety. You have been a hard adversary to keep up with."

Phaedrus wiped the water from his eyes to clear his vision by raising his shoulder to his face. The chains allowed for this much movement at least. When he looked back out the old man who had provided him with information on the war was standing to his front, but at a good distance. "Who are you?" he asked.

The older man smiled. "Oh...now we want to know my name. Last night all you cared for was information on battles and numbers of men and where Caesar was and who was guarding this city. Now you want to know my name? You are a funny fellow, Phaedrus."

"Your name!" Phaedrus spit out.

"When I am ready!" he shot back. "First, I have some questions for you. Where are your supplies?"

"My what?"

"Your supplies! Where are your horse and baggage?"

"Why? What purpose do you need that information? Surely you would have been watching my every move from the moment I stepped into this city. You go find them."

He moved closer and whispered. "I did watch you, and I did see where you left them, but they are gone. Where did you move them?"

Piladius, Phaedrus thought to himself. What a good man he is to have this day, he considered. He must have escaped and stole off with the horses and supplies. Though the matter of if he left the city out of fear or if he was hiding until he could come for them was completely unknown. Surely he would wait for the right moment, Phaedrus thought. But now he was in no position to bargain with the old man. He had no idea what to tell him. And if he were tortured, which was most common on occasions such as this, he would have absolutely no idea where to start for it too would be a lie. He had to think of something fast.

"Where!" the old man demanded, his breath was still sour and his teeth were stained yellow.

"You have stolen them!" Phaedrus challenged. "You knew who I was the moment I arrived, watched where I put my horses and supplies and you stole them. Now you're testing me to see if I know where you've put them," he said intentionally loud—loud enough for the guard at the entrance to overhear. If ever there was a time for security for ones life, this was it. Let the guard hear as much of the conversation so when the time comes for answers, the guard's word will be taken into consideration.

"You lie!" the other reported. "You have moved them secretly and I want to know where."

"What importance is my baggage to you? You have the women. Why do you want the baggage too?"

The other lowered his voice and turned about briefly. "Are you that naïve, Phaedrus? You were sent on a mission from Nero. He has been captain at sea for the last year and knew you could not be trusted to carry out his orders, though he knew you would find the women. He sent a second expedition to locate you and kill you just to make sure you carried out his wishes. You have failed. Now it is up to me to return the stone to Nero and bring back your head to prove that all is done."

"This is all about a stone? A stone!"

"Oh, it's not just a stone, Phaedrus. You have no idea what it can do."

"So why do you take it back to Nero? Why not keep it for yourself?"

"Because I have no use for information such as it possesses. The reward for returning it is a thousand times more than the stone is worth to me. And you, of course, are worthless. You don't even know what side you're on anymore. You almost had me near the Carpathian Mountains, my good man. You killed more than half the men in my company in that brief encounter. Three more died in route to this place from their hands and arms being severed by your swinging pugil stick. A fine weapon that. Did you make it yourself?"

Phaedrus smiled. Then it disappeared. "What is your intent?" he asked dryly.

"You already know, assassin. You failed, now you pay the price. I just need a little more information before I finish this business."

"You never told me your name," Phaedrus quickly changed the subject. He knew what would come next if he didn't. The women were probably close by. He had to figure a way to escape. He was positive they were already working on that too. If Piladius had not run from the city in fear, he too would be lurking in shadows trying to find a way to help. For now, he had to keep the old man's mind busy with other things than the taking of his head—and trust that the others were working just as diligently to escape.

"Why is it so important to you?" the old man asked.

He squinted dangerously. "Because if I don't kill you before this is over, I will hunt you down and ensure everyone knows your name when it hangs on a pole below your head."

He laughed haughtily. "You are not in much of a position to do anything, my good fellow. Of all things you should be begging for your own life. Remember, it is your head that will go with me to Nero when I return to Rome."

"Yes, yes, but will you deny me your name?"

"Will you deny me the location of your supplies?"

It was going to be a stalemate. Neither would give the other any information. He just had to trust that Piladius was working on something to help him get away. "No," he replied.

The old man walked to him deliberately and slapped him hard across his face. The blow forced his head to turn to one side and a stinging pain erupted that sent his mind reeling in anger. "Tell me!" he demanded. "I won't play with you for long, Phaedrus. You are a good assassin, but your loyalty is something to be desired. Now, tell me or I'll take my aggression elsewhere."

Phaedrus knew where he was going with that. The women would be brought to him and tortured before his very eyes until he gave up the answers. That would not do. He had to think of something else to gain time.

"Old man!" he started. "I don't know where the supplies are."

"You dare to take me for a fool!"

"No," he stalled. "I really don't know where the supplies are. We had a fourth with us, a scholar. He's quick witted and sly and he can read and write in many languages. We carried him along only to assist in breaking the language barrier between nations as we moved. I often thought of him as a thief and one not to be trusted. I am guessing that he saw you coming for me and took the opportunity to steal the supplies for himself."

"Guard!" the old man called immediately.

The guard stepped into the stockade room and waited.

"Send in…"

A loud voice cut him off. "Who dares to use my stockade for personal use?"

"Arnasticus," the old man greeted him. "I am on Roman business."

The big fellow stood before him with closed fists on his hips. "What business would Rome have that I cannot be informed prior…" he stopped short and looked at Phaedrus whose heart sank. "You!" he looked squarely at him then scanned the room for the two women. "What is this?" he directed at the old man. His right jaw was slightly swollen, Phaedrus noticed. The tooth must be extremely sore today. Not a good day to get him mad, he considered.

"A thief and an assassin," the old man answered. "I am to take his supplies and his head back to Nero in Rome. Do not cross me Arnasticus or you too will answer to Nero."

"You dare threaten me, old man?"

"You dare to interfere with official business?" the old man replied, undaunted by the fierceness in the other's personage.

"What can this mercenary possibly have done to warrant this kind of treatment? Surely, he came here freely and looking for work as a hired hand for Rome. Unless…" he teased, knowing how beautiful the women were.

"Do not question it, Arnasticus. The women mean nothing to me and they have nothing to do with it. They are merely vessels for which he has plotted his work. We need only the supplies and his head and we will be on our way. The women are yours if you want them."

The sound of keeping the women pleased him, but he was also curious—as most Romans are when there is booty to be taken. "What sort of supplies does he carry?" Arnasticus asked.

"We will get nowhere here, Arnasticus. Come," he said and led the big fellow away from the cell. "Let us discuss this elsewhere."

Phaedrus praised the day as he watched them leave. This perhaps gave him the time he needed to plan his escape. He needed the time and he desperately needed a plan, but he also needed help. He knew the moment his empty cell was discovered Arnasticus, his men and the old man with his mercenaries would be after him. He would have to gather the women and together they would have to move day and night to stay ahead of them. But the first thing he had to do was get out the chains. He studied them carefully. Each of them was new and the stockade itself was recently built. It was probably put up the day they made camp. It would be a wonder to discover if he was the first prisoner ever held captive inside. First he pulled on the chains then he attempted to jolt them free. He even tried to kick them free from the wall, but it would budge at all. He nearly gave up. His ankles started to bleed from the iron rings and his wrists were bruised. He knew the steel would hold him forever. There was no escape without a key to unlock him. All he could do was make an attempt to trick the sentry. "Guard!" he called out.

The soldier stood in the doorway and peered inside. "Keep quite!" he shouted back.

"You have to help me. The iron has cut into my feet and wrists," he said truthfully.

The guard looked and saw this, but paid no heed to his cries. "It'll have to wait," he replied.

The guard was young and perhaps a little stupid from the looks of him, Phaedrus thought. This was probably the only post Arnasticus could trust him to watch for his eyes seemed slightly crossed and his mouth was a little crooked on the right side. "You have to help me," he pleaded. "If Arnasticus returns and discovers you have let me bleed like this he will make you pay for it. Do you want to be punished from that man?" he attempted.

The guard shook his head but couldn't quite comprehend what Phaedrus was telling him. Phaedrus realized that talking to the guard would have no effect what so ever. He would have to trick him into actually getting close enough so he could kill him and use whatever means to get himself free.

"Look!" Phaedrus said in desperation. "You have to stop this bleeding," he pleaded a second time. Then his heart sank again as another figure stood in the doorway, his sword pulled and ready for action. There was no way he would escape now, he thought.

"What is this?" the second asked in a gruff, unnatural voice. Phaedrus thought he recognized it, but couldn't quite place it. In a sense, his hopes raised.

"He bleeds," the first told him.

"Go check him. I'll stand guard," the second ordered.

As the guard stepped out of sight and into the cell the second guard stepped forward and with a rapid thrust of his sword cut the man straight though his chest from his back.

Phaedrus looked up in surprise. "Piladius!" he whispered. "Good man!" he was ecstatic. He never would have suspected the scholar to change into a soldier's clothing and come for him in such a way. "Quickly, get the keys."

Piladius stood there momentarily. He was stunned. He had never killed another man before—at least not face to face, or directly by his own hand. He slightly recalled the arrow being loosed from his bow. It wasn't the same thing. A sword being forced through the flesh of another human didn't have the same effect. Just knowing that his sword went straight through the soldier's body and skimming bones to come out the other end made him gag. The thought of it all nearly made him vomit right there, but he realized that the situation was more drastic and his getting sick would be the last thing he needed at this time. He held it in, if only by sheer force of will. After it passed he drew his attention to Phaedrus who stood there waiting to be released.

A few moments later Phaedrus was dressed in the dead guard's clothing and both he and Piladius stepped from the cell into the sunlight. "Where are they?" Phaedrus asked in the next instant.

"Second from the left," Piladius answered and pointed. "They are together, but there are more guards around them. They put up a great fight and I don't really think they expected to get captured. Aoife went really mad, but Scathach is completely insane about the incident. I believe they were ready to die in their endeavor to get away," he told him.

"Oh, I believe you. I have seen that look many times. Are they well?"

SCATHACH

"Ummm…" Piladius stammered. "They are healthy, if that answers your question."

"What have they done?"

"Let's just get them free."

"What have they done?" he demanded this time.

"They have been raped, Phaedrus…repeatedly."

Phaedrus' mind went blank. It was a great insult to him. "I'll kill them!" he threatened.

"They are too many. Trust that they will overpower you. We have to be tricky about this if we are to save them. They are tied naked to wooden tables inside and the soldiers are charging admission to touch and rape them. Scathach still fights them with all her strength, but Aoife has given herself up for dead and lets her mind go to another place. The raping has no effect on her any longer. She lies waiting for the next without care."

"Do you have the horses and the supplies?"

"They are standing ready as we speak."

"Good. We have to get inside. What is the best approach?"

Piladius had already thought this through. "We pay handsomely for them."

"We pay to have them released?"

"No. We show that we are interested in buying in to the raping and coerce the Romans on guard inside the cell. When they are gathered round, we kill them and make for the trees behind the stockade. We will have to be fast, but we can do it. After that, the rest is up to you."

"Well done, Piladius."

"Halt!" one of the guards sounded when they neared. "State your business."

He peered over the guard's shoulder at the five who kept looking inside, laughing and pointing. Beyond that he couldn't see a thing. Under his breath he answered. "I understand you have gorgeous women inside?"

The guard harrumphed. "They used to be. The one is a fearsome wench. It took seven of us to get her down. She killed three soldiers in the process. The other killed another but went down a bit easier. If they didn't

133

fight us so much we wouldn't have had to hit them so hard. A few weeks from now they'll be good as new," he chuckled. "Are you interested?"

"How much?" Phaedrus asked, though he wanted to rip off his head right then.

"How much do you have?"

"I'm not playing that game, my good fellow. Let me see the merchandise up close."

The guard faltered slightly. "I don't even know you. How do I know you'll pay anything?"

Phaedrus looked sternly at him. "I'm a Roman soldier. I always pay my debts."

The other was taken aback and didn't quite know how to respond. Besides, Phaedrus' chest started to rise and fall in anger, though he tried hard to keep himself under control. "Come with me," the guard told them.

The first sight of them nearly made his eyes fill with tears as he observed both women stretched out on wooden tables. They were like sacrifices to the gods ready for the final killing blow to the heart. There was a strong odor of life-blood and the stench of unclean sex that permeated the chill morning air. He gazed at them once more. They shivered in the coldness. Suddenly the tears turned to anger and then hate. But to save them he would have to master his emotions and concentrate on winning this situation over. "They are worthless. I will not pay for that," he said and pointed to Scathach who suddenly recognized his voice and looked up, perhaps for the first time, through swollen eyes. They had beaten her silly. There were bruises everywhere on her milk white body. Phaedrus shook his head to show her that his plan of rescue was afoot and continued as if she had never noticed him. "Is she wounded?" he asked of Scathach whose thighs were covered in a bloody mess. At this he worried.

"No, she is of her time. There are some things that even Rome cannot stop," he laughed and the five soldiers with him joined in. Piladius was standing at the entrance watching for anyone else who might be interest to see what was going on inside. The sickening feeling kept emerging to his throat, but he kept it all down.

Aoife never moved. She was ignorant of anything or anyone in the room. She lay there with her puffed eyes staring out at nothing; her legs spread far apart and male fluids gleaming from her belly and thighs. There were bruises on both breasts and all down her left side, perhaps with a broken rib or two, and her left cheek was blue and yellow. Both eyes were slits from being hit repeatedly. It sickened him to see this. He knew if they were capable of getting up, the six soldiers standing there would have no chance of survival. Even in the condition the women were in at the time.

"They are beyond use!" Phaedrus complained. "You've completely and deliberately wasted them on those beasts out there!" he nearly shouted, but kept his voice low enough not to draw attention.

"They are still good for the purpose," the guard told him with a hinting smile. "And just to prove it I'll only ask half the price I normally charge," he offered. "For a fellow soldier, you understand?"

Piladius listened and watched and looked and observed and guarded and his mind was numb with knowing what was happening and trying not to know at the same time. He couldn't stand watching them any longer; naked, unable to protect themselves, unable to defend themselves from the vicious animals that came for them with their evil Roman coins. His stomach heaved and he held his mouth, though he fought it long enough to commit to the final act. He had finally had enough. "I can do it," he said, though no one knew he was talking to himself. He had never been this repulsed his entire life. Though he had heard stories of women and children being raped and beaten and murdered for no reason, he had never witnessed the result of such atrocity as that which was before him. He moved from the entrance and drew his sword.

Phaedrus knew what would happen next. Piladius' eyes glazed over and he saw nothing but black. The soldiers inside were not ready for him. While most of the men in the legion who camped without had beaten the women senseless, the soldiers inside must have thought Piladius had come along to show a little swordplay. This wouldn't dim the measure of male satisfaction. In fact, they gloated to see he would even dare to attempt this with the women in their condition. They were about to praise him for his heartiness to consider it. The Roman soldiers surely thought he was among the bravest of their group. They moved aside for him to get a better view of the women. Phaedrus backed away and drew his blade as well.

Piladius never gave his actions a second thought. With as swift and powerful a blow as he could deliver, he swung the weapon sideways and severed the nearest guards head completely off. It rolled to the corner and blinked rapidly, the brain still trying to figure it all out. The body however, stood then stumbled slowly and collapsed. It twitched for a long time.

The leader fell back against the wall in shock. This was completely unexpected. As he sat there, Phaedrus sliced his sword across the chest of the guard nearest him then cut back only to see the guard fall with his entrails dangling from the soldier's open palms. Piladius brought down the next with a quick stab to his heart. While the bones splintered and cracked under the pressure of the blade, he ignored the sounds and forced the blade home. Phaedrus wasted no time in taking out the remaining two soldiers who stood around trying to put it all together. When it was over, only the leader was alive. He sat shaking silently in the corner. Tears flowed from his eyes.

Scathach was released and lay there only for a moment. In the next instant she was on her feet. Without delay she walked to Piladius, ripped the sword from his hand, approached the leader and without hesitation shoved the point through his left eye. She stopped only when the blade hit the back wall. He died instantly.

Piladius vomited.

"We have to go, now!" Phaedrus hurried. "There is no time to delay."

"Aoife will not make it. She has shut herself off," Scathach told him.

"I will carry her, but we must go quickly," he said almost in a panic. "More will be coming here soon. I know Arnasticus and the old man will be returning as well. If we are caught, we are all dead," he told her with utmost urgency.

"I will help you," Piladius said as he wiped his mouth, went to Aoife's side and started lifting her from the table.

"Quickly, the mantles," Phaedrus said to Scathach. She bent and stole a mantle and brooch from two of the guards. She wrapped one around herself and one around Aoife to cover their bodies. A moment later they exited the stockade and dashed straight for the thickets behind. Phaedrus carried Aoife in his arms while Piladius kept watch at his back. No one had been watching, but they knew it wouldn't be long before someone discovered what had happened.

CHAPTER X

A loud trumpet sounded behind them followed by the clamor of a hundred orders being issued to every Roman soldier in every direction. They would assemble according to rank and title and form columns for inspection: the *sagitarii* with their bows and the *mattiarii* with javelins and the *lancearii* with their pikes and the mounted *cataphracti*. They would form echelons about their scorpions and their catapults or *ballistarii* as they are called. The pennants will fly and all will be ready for battle in a short period. And there was no time for wasting. It would take only a few minutes to gather and then they would be underway, most of them never knowing what the reason, yet following the orders of seniors based on a misled sense of duty or honor. Most of the soldiers had enlisted in this army as a career move, collecting booty from the raids on villages and kingdoms of the Celts. It was a good way to make a living, provided you could kill your adversary no matter their race, creed, religion, age or gender. Men, women and children were slaughtered and mutilated all the way from Cisalpine Gaul to Germania and east as far as Galatia in Asia Minor. And as they gathered and collected their supplies Phaedrus realized they would know nothing of what was actually going on. It was blind obedience without doubt. But Phaedrus knew. They were after him. And the Romans would waste no time. They would kill him without ever attempting to negotiate. So long as the baggage was visible, they would eliminate each of them without discussion. The baggage was no longer an asset. It was a liability—a liability that would cost them their lives.

Phaedrus and the small group moved along without delay. There could be no time for resting, no time for repairing wounds or hunting food or eating by fires. Being part of the Roman Empire in previous years as an assassin allowed him the knowledge of how news travels across the land. In times past, information could be transported hundreds of miles in less than a day and only by use of voice. He knew they would have to be beyond that range to feel safe. That safety, he knew, was a long way off. His insight and military tactics would be an advantage, but not necessarily against the tumultuous.

"Which way?" Piladius was lost. They were riding double, holding the women in front of them so they wouldn't fall as they moved. Both were nearly dead, but there was no place to hide so they could recover. The scanty forests were not enough to keep them hidden for very long. They had to continue west. Bucephalus and Khutalk trailed along with the two packhorses Mahendra had given them. Piladius was unable to think clearly.

"The best thing to do is to find a way back to the north side of the river. They will expect us to move south away from the populations that thrive along the Danuvius. Soldiers will be waiting for us in every village from here to Brigantium (Bregenz), of that you can be certain. But we also need the water. It will guide us to our destination and it will also keep us alive until we get to the Arvernian," he said and took the lead.

With new direction, Phaedrus pushed them long into the day. Before the sun had set, they switched horses and let Bucephalus and Khutalk take the weight for a time. While they had food in the packhorses, they never stopped long enough to eat. Distance was what they were counting on to survive.

The snows had melted enough to leave the sodden earth in a cold mush and the river swelled too high to cross without a bridge. Phaedrus kept to the wooded areas the entire time, coming to the river only to scout out new avenues of approach to cross. It was late in the afternoon of the second day when they found one capable of passage, though the bridge was worn with age. It barely looked safe enough for a man to cross never mind an animal with baggage. Yet the attempt was successful and they continued their journey on the north bank hoping the Romans would press further south. At this point, overcome with fatigue and hunger, both Piladius and Phaedrus agreed to a stop for rest. If soldiers were following this close behind there wouldn't be a chance anyway. Surely they had half a day's lead on them.

They pulled Scathach and Aoife from the horses and wrapped them in warm clothing before laying them near a low fire. Piladius, though more familiar with scholarly duties, insisted on tending to the wounds. He had read and transcribed several journals on the practice of modern medicine, particularly herbs and salves to treat and cure ailments. Without the availability of such items however, he made use of several things found in their baggage. Among them…the stone!

"Phaedrus!" he called when he found it.

The assassin looked but didn't know what to tell him. Curiosity wanted him to take it and attempt to discover the great mystery. Another part of him told him not to betray the trust Scathach had surely bestowed upon him. "Put it back," he decided.

"But…it's the stone! We can use it to see what becomes of us!"

Scathach stirred. It must have been talk of the stone. It was this stone that got her in this situation to begin with. It was this stone that caused her village to be destroyed and her father to be killed and her friends to be murdered and beheaded. The stone also got her and her sister, Aoife, beaten and raped and nearly killed. For a moment he wanted to take it in his hands and throw it into the river where it would never be found again. But there was something about the stone that required Scathach to keep it near, something that made her keep it above all other treasures she possessed. Perhaps too, it was her father's wish that she should keep it always.

"Put it back, Piladius. We will find out what becomes of us soon enough. There is a lot that can change before we find the end of our road, my friend."

Reluctantly, Piladius returned it to the sack where it was hidden and brought out the herbs Scathach had always kept with her to use for wounds. It was not uncommon for her warriors to be injured on their journeys into battle. For once it would be used on the leader of the female fighters.

After their wounds and bruises had been treated, Piladius sat and rested. He was exhausted as was Phaedrus who lay comfortably wrapped in his heavy mantle. The night was chilled, but the serious coldness of winter seemed to have passed for the season. Spring would be along soon and the warmth would return. That was something to look forward to.

Piladius looked up at the stars as he relaxed. "Do you wonder that there is anything out there?" he asked absently.

Phaedrus followed his gaze. "Not really. I never think about it. I don't know why anyone would. You would never reach it from here."

Piladius chuckled. "I realize that, but to wonder if…"

"I'm sorry my friend. I live in a world where there are only choices: good ones and bad ones."

"And this one?" he asked of their current situation.

"Ahhh…this one," he pondered. "It was a good choice and a bad one. Good, because we are doing the right thing. Bad, because we are constantly being tracked by the hounds of Nero."

"Will it ever end?" Piladius asked casually.

"Hard to say. I thought for sure her two friends' death would have convinced him that the stone was missing and that Scathach was dead for certain, but now I don't know. He has sent an assassin to kill the assassin. That has me a little bothered, but it's not necessarily surprising."

Piladius thought for a moment. "It's similar to Suren's situation, isn't it?" he conjectured.

"I suppose," Phaedrus replied. "He won't be coming back from this journey you know. He is going to meet his death."

"Why would he do that?"

It was Phaedrus who took the time to think. It was hard to explain, but he made the attempt. "The same reason you came back to save us from the Roman stockade. You think about it over and over until you realize it is the right thing to do. After you rationalize the reasons for doing such a thing you know you have to commit to it even if it costs your life. That was a wonderful and unselfish thing you did back there, my friend. To be honest, a blood brother would not have been as brave in that kind of situation. You are to be commended. Had you run off and kept to yourself we would have perished."

Piladius flushed slightly. "Yes, but they would have come after me sooner or later. It's the stone they want. They would have hunted me down until they found me. Then they would take the stone and kill me just the same. Either way, I was doomed to be a hunted man," he said though he seemed to glow in his premonition. "But how does that reflect to Mahendra. He is one of the finest fighters in any land. Why should he commit himself to death?"

"Because he has rationalized it out. He will return to Orodes II and he will fight every one of his soldiers even though the odds will be against him. He will kill a thousand men, but there will be one who strikes a lucky blow that will kill him. He has already committed himself to the task. And his memory will be lost forever. It is men like you, Piladius, who must keep his name alive. Write it down for all ages to remember. And make him the glorious man you know him to be."

"But what if, by some luck of the gods, he lives?"

"Well," Phaedrus thought with a hint of surprise. "That would be something."

"Yes, it would. It kind of brings us back to my original question doesn't it? Do you think there's anything out there?"

Phaedrus looked at him hard. "You are quite profound, my fine scholar." He took another gaze. "I'm sure something, either real or imaginary, could exist there," he surmised.

With that he let it rest. Both stared up at the stars for a long time, drifting between reality and imagination before finally falling into a deep, well-needed sleep.

Something startled Bucephalus and Phaedrus snapped awake immediately, his hands resting on his pugil. An instant later, sharp blades locked in place at both ends as he crouched in the foggy mist. He was ready for anything. "Piladius," he whispered. The other didn't stir. He was snoring soundly. "Piladius!" he whispered more urgently. This time he moved.

Somehow the training over the past several weeks had made an impact on Piladius. Normally, at a time like this, he would refute the rudeness by barking obscenities or complaining that he needed more time to rest. This time however, he lifted his head and looked without for danger before ever speaking a word. His hands slowly reached for the bow he knew lay beside him. It was always at his side. Phaedrus had told him that the weapon was his wife and he would sleep with it for the rest of his life. He had paid attention. While on his back, he lodged an arrow against the gut-string and waited silently for a signal from Phaedrus. Whomever was out there surely expected them to be asleep, they were certain.

Khutalk suddenly spooked and bolted. The other horses followed. A figure emerged from the mist with a broadsword high above his head. He was covered in hair, obviously a barbarian of the Germanian population, and his dark eyes warned that he intended to kill anything that got in his way.

"Protect Scathach!" Phaedrus ordered then stood to meet the large figure.

Piladius came up to one knee and locked the arrow beside his right ear while he searched for the next to come from the mist. It happened almost immediately. He let loose the arrow. It flew straight and true, as he was taught to do, striking the man in his upper chest. The man went down with a lot of grumbling noises gurgling from his throat. The next arrow was lodged and ready. Phaedrus went to work. The pugil spun like a spinster's wheel, cutting and severing body parts in all directions. There must have been a dozen more coming at them from all around. Piladius let the next fly and the next, hitting his target both times.

Scathach stirred in her repose. She knew there was danger about her. Her natural instinct was to fight back, yet she lacked the strength to assist. Her flesh tensed and her skin seemed to expand and grow red. It was uncommon for this to happen yet it did. Her inner-anger must have reached a point of extreme fierceness. You could see she wanted to stand and assist, kill everyone and anything that came for them. Yet the strength was not there. Still, she struggled.

"Keep her down," Phaedrus kept his eyes on everything at once.

Piladius never hesitated. In the past he would have already been too late, according to Phaedrus. He was punished with lashings from the back of a sword each time he failed to perform a command immediately. He threw himself at her and calmed her as much as he could verbally while keeping the next arrow waiting for another target to come into sight. Again, he didn't have to wait long. He let it fly. Three more men went down in front of Phaedrus. And another worked his way out of the fog to find him. Then a sound caught them all by surprise.

"Phaedrus!" the voice rang out of the grayness.

"They know you!" Piladius cautioned.

"It is he," Phaedrus replied knowing it was the old man who had chained him to the wall of the stockade.

"Who is he?"

Phaedrus shrugged. "He hasn't given me his name. But I must admit he is persistent."

"Come, my young assassin. Let these games cease. I know now that I cannot come to you in such a way. I thought for a moment that the mist might give my men a chance to have you, but I see you have been expecting something of this nature to occur. Shall we speak?" he offered.

"Enter, but come alone. If I see another foot land anywhere near I will hack it off and shove it down your throat after I open it with my blade."

The other chuckled slightly. "I believe you would. I will come alone," he said and stepped into sight. It was the old man. Though he wasn't old any longer. He was more middle-aged and attired in the garb of a Roman diplomat.

"Marcus Junius Brutus!" Phaedrus spit and stood to meet the general. "I should have suspected long before now. Has it been that long?"

"I thought for sure my voice would have given it all away. I was glad that it didn't. I don't like to be known away from Rome. Soldiers of the trade just don't seem to understand."

"On the contrary, sire. I do," Phaedrus replied.

"Who is he?" Piladius asked while keeping his eyes open for more movement.

"Marcus Brutus," Phaedrus informed him. "Roman general and serpent of the devil. He managed, somehow, to trace his family line back to the Brutus who had driven out the last King of Rome, Tarquin the Proud. He claims that prophesy has led him to this destination. I say he is nothing more than a liar and a thief."

"Come, come, now. I am not here to collect more names than I already have. A seat on the senate or perhaps the emperor's thrown, maybe, but not another name of insignificance. Please...just tell me where the stone is and I will be on my way. It appears you have more important things to tend to," he said with a cast of his eyes at the two women lying beside the smoking, but otherwise dead fire.

"How many do you have left?" Phaedrus asked.

"How many have you killed?" he returned.

Phaedrus looked around him. "Maybe fifteen."

Brutus counted in his head. "Thirteen more. But I'd really like to keep them. They aren't much for brains, but their strength is unsurpassed."

"Not much of a team if you ask me," Phaedrus hinted.

"They aren't much with weapons either. But trust me, you don't want them to get their bare hands on you. I've seen them take down forest deer without a weapon of any sort and carry the carcass a league or two just to bring it to his friends to cut open and eat."

"I'll keep that in mind. So..." he tried to keep the general busy. "Why the secrecy? Why so far from Rome?"

"The stone, my good fellow."

"You have no intension of bringing it back to Nero, do you?"

"Well, actually no. The story sounded good at first, but to tell the truth, I want the stone for myself."

Phaedrus settled a bit. "I thought as much. Though it wouldn't have surprised me to know that another assassin was sent to kill the assassin. It's been done many times in the past. Kill the man who did the killing and eventually nobody knows anything about it, anywhere. It's almost as though it never happened. By the time it gets back to Rome the entire incident was a misconception and an accident occurred causing the death of an unknown."

"You're learning, Phaedrus. Perhaps you should return by my side and consider a seat at the Senate?"

"I haven't the stomach for it."

"Well then, what can I offer for the stone? Gold...? Silver...? An estate with land as far as the eye can see? I cannot simply allow you to continue on your way without achieving my goal. I have to make some sort of attempt to get it. After all, I did travel this far."

Phaedrus did not hesitate. "It's not mine to give."

"Oh, don't trifle with me. I don't care who it belongs to, just deliver it and I will be on my way. You can take your friends and your miserable life and go where you please."

"I will do that anyway."

"I thought you might speak as such. That is why I took this opportunity to set a few *sagitarii* in place. The moment I turn to leave, they will launch their missiles at your sleeping warriors there," he pointed. "Now what say you, my good man? Do I get the stone?"

Phaedrus didn't know what to think. It was a good trick, one that he would have thought to do, but was more worried about saving all their lives instead of leading them into more trouble. It was Piladius who took up the conversation however.

"I say it's going to be hard to see the future with an arrow hanging from your left eye," Piladius informed him as he turned his bow and set an aim for the general's eye.

"You would let the women die just to keep me from getting the stone?" he nearly laughed at the thought of it.

"No, sire," Piladius smiled as he spoke. "I merely state that I am, regardless of who you attempt to kill with your arrows, going to shoot you in your left eye. No matter what happens here today, you are dead. If you turn to leave, I will shoot you. If you bark an order to some unknown killer hiding in the mist, I *will* kill you. You see, sire, you *are* going to die this day. And it will be this arrow here that ends your life. Now, how many stones do you think it will take to see that future?" he laughed now.

Phaedrus was stunned. Would the scholar do it? Was he insane? There was nothing to negotiate here. The deed would be done the moment the general moved to do anything. If that happened, they would all die. Not much reasoning there. Unless, he figured, Brutus would balk and take his life back to Rome. But that was not likely. He had come too far to turn back empty-handed. There had to be some conclusion to this endeavor however. Where was the reasoning? Where was the planning? Where was the strategy? What tactic was Piladius employing to force Brutus into succumbing to the obvious stalemate? There was only one conclusion, he ventured. Someone would die.

"What foolishness is this? You would let your women die for a lousy stone?" Brutus stalled, though he was uncertain how to proceed.

Piladius was undaunted. "Who said anything about women dying? I merely said you would die. There is no one else to consider in this move, sire. There is only one fact that you have to understand. That is the fact that you are going to die. Do you have any last words you would like to say before I send you on your way, sire?" he asked with all the decency and respect he could form in his nearly shaking voice. He had never been confronted in such a way. He had never threatened a man with his own life. This was all completely new to him, but he had made a decision and now he stood behind it. If he had to murder this general for no reason other than protecting the life of his friends, he was willing to do so.

"You do realize that the moment you send that shaft into my body, you too will be dead?"

"Sire, I would expect nothing less from such an honorable man."

"You dare mock me!" he bellowed in anger.

"You dare to threaten me!" Piladius bellowed back and stood, keeping the arrow pointed directly at the eye. "One last chance, pig!" he was furious. "What words do you take with you to your gods?"

"Wait!" Scathach lifted her head, though it took all her strength. The swelling of her flesh had gone, the redness of her skin turned pale, sickly.

To some relief Brutus accepted her interference. "Speak woman!" he said hurriedly.

In short gasps for air to fill her bruised chest she asked. "What does the general want from the stone?"

The question took him by surprise. He didn't know what he wanted from the stone. He knew that the stone was said to give insight to events of the future. But other than that there was nothing he really wanted of the stone. To form a simple answer, he replied. "To see what becomes of me. To see what becomes of Rome."

She coughed. "And if I give you these things, you will return to Rome?"

That was a hard decision. The stone, he knew, could provide him with all the insight of Roman secrecy. He could be at the forefront of every major law and every major seat in the entire Empire. Everyone would be calling upon him for answers and all he would have to do is call upon the stone to see what really happens. But, there was also the possibility that he could become Emperor. If that were the case, he could rule it all: make his own laws, charge his own seats to be filled, select his own consuls, magistrates and triumvirs. He would command all the army and all his generals. All would be his to command as he pleased. But he had to make sure he became Emperor. With that much power at hand, he would be unstoppable. He would be the wealthiest man in the world. Yes, that was what he had to know. And if the stone could not foretell his ascension to the Emperor's throne, he would find the way to force the position into his hands by mischievous deeds. Yes, that was what he must know.

He thought for a moment and considered her offer carefully. "If you give me the answer to three questions, I will return without further harassment," he countered.

"Send your men away immediately," she ordered him.

"What about this one," he directed to Piladius who held him in his sights.

"He will allow you to go," she breathed with a wavering finger of negation towards Piladius. The scholar lowered his weapon.

"I will return," Brutus told her then sharply turned away and faded into the mist.

"Scathach!" Piladius was at her side, looking at her wince in pain. Her eyes were slits behind swollen lids. She could barely see, he knew. The bruises must surely hurt but she fought it long enough to sit up. She grimaced every inch of the way.

"How is Aoife?" she asked quickly.

"I'm not sure," Piladius answered. "She hasn't moved since we escaped."

"Scathach?" Phaedrus joined them, yet he kept his eyes on the area around them. "Are you sure you want to do this? What if it is some sort of trick?"

"It is no trick, Phaedrus. I can hear it in his voice. He is more desperate for answers the stone may possess than he is in the stone itself. If I give him the answers he wants he will leave."

"But what if the stone gives him the wrong answers?" Piladius asked.

"Then," she winced. "I will give him the answers he wants to hear."

"What if he tricks you after you give him the answers and he tries to steal the stone from you?" Phaedrus thought.

She had the answer long before he asked. "I will kill him instantly."

Again Piladius asked. "Are you up to this Scathach? You are completely, mentally and physically weak."

"What choice do I have? Get the stone and my pouch of herbs."

There really was no choice, both men surmised. Without her assistance to aid Brutus in his search for answers, they were all dead. Obviously, Brutus had had enough respect to know that many more lives would be lost to include possibly his own and made the right decision. If it all went as planned, each would be going his own way without mishap. But there was always a chance that something could go wrong, and Phaedrus would be ready for it if it did.

It wasn't long before Brutus returned. Beside him were two huge escorts. "They will accompany me," he told them when they were visible. "If there is treachery afoot, I am assured safety by their presence."

"Trust that we will honor our word. But they may stay just the same," Phaedrus told him.

They helped Scathach to sit comfortably then lit another fire to get her warm. Brutus seated himself opposite her and waited until everything was ready. While the fire was being made ready, Piladius went for the scattered horses. They had bolted to the southeast and wouldn't have gone too far, he knew. After several minutes he returned and took the stone to Scathach along with her herbs.

"Is that it?" Brutus asked incredulous. "It doesn't look like much."

"It isn't supposed to. It was never intended to be an icon to marvel at. Remember this," she told him and though her eyes were slits they opened enough for him to see the seriousness in her deadly gaze. "This is only a piece of the whole. There are two others just like it. It is said that if they are all gathered in the same place and laid together in the monolith that was intended for their eternal rest, that all things would be revealed to mankind. All that is known and unknown to life and how it came to be would be unveiled. The mysteries of all living creatures would no longer be a mystery. That is why they have been scattered across the lands in every direction."

"Is that possible?" he was amazed. "Why wouldn't we want to know such great mysteries?"

"Because we are a curious people," she told him. "If you take the curiosity away, there is no reason for argument. Everything will become fact and there will be no possible chance for imagination to exist. If there is no imagination to fill the mind with wonders, we will cease to exist."

"How can that be?" Brutus insisted. "That's impossible."

"Not really. If you knew yesterday that you were going to die if you followed us today, would you have followed us?"

He thought for a short spell. "No. That's absurd! I would have stayed away and lived."

"Of course you would," she replied. "So why did you follow us today?"

He grinned. "To get the stone," he answered stoically.

"So you were *curious* to see the stone work?"

"I suppose," he answered.

"So you can only imagine what the stone will reveal to you because you are curious?"

"I suppose," he repeated.

"But if you knew you were going to die you never would have made the attempt. Is that correct?"

"Of course. I would have stayed away."

"You have just proven my point. If there is no curiosity and no imagination there is nothing to live for. You would survive only out of self-preservation to exist. And even that would not be much worth living for. Everything would be known. If you knew that the home you were about to build was going to be destroyed in a year, would you build it?"

"Of course not. I'd go elsewhere."

"And what if the place you went belonged to a relative who was going to die the day after you met him. Would you go there?"

"Of course not. I'd go elsewhere."

"So why go anywhere at all? It seems that you are destined to understand what happens next, no matter where you go or what you do.

The point is…you cease to exist because you already know what is going to happen no matter where you go or what you do."

"I think I understand," he said. "If I tell you the sun is brown, you will argue with me because we are not fully sure what the color is. But if the stones were set together we would know everything as a fact. We could no longer argue about the sun's color. We could no longer use our imagination to make our dreams come true. Rome would become useless because we will know what happens to it long before it occurs. Therefore nothing would be done at all because we would know what happens. If that were true, we would never build it to begin with." He paused for a brief moment in thought.

"That's right. You're beginning to understand fully. Now…do you want to know?"

"Just the answer to three questions. That's all I wish to know. After that you may keep the stone and go your way. I promise not to interfere. But no tricks!"

"What do you wish to know of the future?" she asked him.

"What becomes of Rome? What becomes of me? And what becomes of my family?"

She smiled, as if knowing this is what he would ask. "Come closer," she told him. He did as instructed. She took up his hands in hers, the stone between them. They were callous. Much more than she would have thought a general's hands should be. He was a worker as much as he was a general obviously. "Close your eyes," she instructed. He obeyed.

She reached into the pouch and removed a pinch of seeds from the calyxes flower and threw them into the fire. When the smoke filtered into the air she breathed it in deeply, relaxed then studied the stone before her. Concentrating on the series of lines etched across the middle, she moved her eyes up and down between each set. Her vision began to fade and new shapes took form. There was great secrecy about this man, she saw. He wanted power beyond anything imaginable. He was there among the senate and did greet another, victorious from the war in Gaul, on his return; Caesar she knew. A strong influence among the people of Rome he would attempt to become King, Emperor, not just dictator. And his ascension to the thrown would be unanimous throughout for both people and politics love him greatly. Brutus, she could see, would be there beside him, guiding him to more victories across the nations of the west. Together they would become two of the most prominent adversaries in the known world. Nations would come to him with precious gifts of gold and silver and gems and all that they owned just to gain his favor. Kings would give away their beautiful daughters as hostages to gain his favor. Yes, all the nations of the world would bow before these two men. Rome, she saw, would flourish for many centuries mostly due to the insight and meticulous detail of politics these two men harness to keep Rome above all other nations. Caesar would be a great king, she could see. And yet, there is something familiar about them both, she saw, something in their blood. But then there she stood, watching it all at a distance. Something interfered with her vision, something she had done. It wasn't right, but it happened regardless. A moment later she was driven from the images by a harsh shaking. When her vision cleared, Piladius stood above her.

"Scathach!" he called urgently. "Stop!"

She looked up and saw Brutus staring at her bemused. "What did you see?" he asked.

There was no time to think. She threw out the answers as quickly as she could, just to be done with it. Just to…see it all destroyed. "You are Emperor!" she exclaimed. "But first, there is something you must do," she said in a hush. "There is one who is in Gaul. He is as you are, a general of a great and powerful army. He will return to Rome in victory over that nation. You must not allow him to talk of his success among the people of the group there."

"The senate? Why not?"

"Because he seeks the throne for himself and will destroy all of Rome if he does. That is why you and an accomplice must plot to end his life before he is allowed to talk to the people. This I have seen, Brutus. Rome does not survive unless you are seated at the throne as King and Emperor. This you must do with all secrecy," she told him in a lie. She didn't know why, but she couldn't resist. There was something pushing her to tell this great untruth.

"And your family will continue to rule long after the days of your death. You will have two sons and they will become great men," she continued her inveracity. Still she pushed on, telling him the fabricated canard as though it were what she really saw. He glowed at her details. Even if it were false, he could see some truth in what she said. His family was of a strong and noble stock already. What more could Rome benefit than to have his lineage succeed far into history?

"Yes, yes, I can see that," he was satisfied. "But why must Caesar die?"

"If that is his name, you must kill him," she said. "If you fail, you will never see the throne, nor will your sons ever be born, nor will Rome ever flourish beyond the southern borders of Gaul."

"Truly, there must be another way. Cannot I send him into exile?"

She looked at him through the slits of her eyes. "He will return with his army, those loyal only to him, and destroy you. No. You must kill him! The people of Rome demand it. You will see," she told him then let her head slump in exhaustion.

Phaedrus was suddenly at her side, watching in all directions for an unseen enemy to come rushing in for the stone or their lives. Nothing moved aside of Brutus who stood, satisfied and smiling, though they knew he seemed a bit tense about killing Caesar. Still, for the safety of Rome, he would surely do as Scathach advised.

"You have your answers," Piladius told him as he helped Phaedrus lay Scathach back down on the warm furs. "Let us keep this simple. Take your men and go."

The thought of being Emperor overwhelmed him. His eyes glassed over with the glorious thought of all that power, all that wealth. He would do it, he knew. He would plot to kill Caesar and assume the throne for himself. And the people would love him, as it was foretold. "Yes," he said to everyone in general. "I will make an excellent King and Emperor. And I will do as I have been told," he said and turned without looking back. "I take my leave. May our paths never cross again," he said in parting. Just as he was about to disappear he turned back to Phaedrus. "I will tell Nero you are dead and that the stone is still missing," he assured him. Phaedrus nodded understanding and approval before tending to Scathach.

"Scathach!" Phaedrus whispered. "What have you done?"

She stirred and attempted to open her eyes. After a moment she replied. "I have told him a great lie, one that will cost Rome dearly."

"Why would you do such a thing?" Piladius asked as he contemplated the ramifications of her confession. If it were all a lie, she has altered the future before it occurs. No one will benefit from what was to be. All events regarding Rome would be the result of her intervention. Again he asked. "Why, Scathach?"

Phaedrus looked at him. "Ask her father."

"He is dead!"

"Exactly. Why does she care what becomes of Rome? Anything she can do to Rome will never pay for the life of her father in her mind. I'm not saying she has done the right thing, but restitution has been made if only this once," Phaedrus told him.

"But she has altered history by telling a lie."

"It is not history until it has passed. History will only be made when the act of killing Caesar is fulfilled."

Piladius thought for a moment. "Then Caesar's death may not happen in such a way?"

"That is correct. He may die in the battle with the Celts. Gaul may swallow his name forever and Brutus will never know what the truth will be."

Piladius was slightly relieved. "But," he thought again. "She can look into the stone and tell us now what becomes of Brutus, can't she?"

"I suppose," Phaedrus answered. "When she is stronger we will ask."

The sound or horses galloping away sounded through the mist. They were certain that it was safe for the moment. Yet they knew Arnasticus, Trebonius' centurion would not give up the hunt. Surely he would follow them into Gaul.

CHAPTER XI

The thick fog had lifted by midmorning from the heat of the new day's sun leaving the land visible ahead. It seemed early for the season but the weather presented a comfortable ride west as the small group pushed on through the woodlands, following old dirt paths and easy foot routes through the trees. Hills and valleys were numerous, making it difficult to see dangers ahead, but the copse of fir hid them well enough. Aoife had not come awake yet, but they hoped she would force herself to overcome this gross misfortune soon. Death would come for her if she didn't pull herself out. Piladius still rode with her in his arms as they went. Scathach rode in front of Phaedrus though she stirred now and then for short periods of time before slumping back into a deep sleep. Their wounds appeared to have healed some. Scathach's eyes were not as swollen and the bruises on her ribs had turned a pale yellow. The split in her lip, where she was punched at least once, was tender but healing well. Still, both were in bad condition from possible internal injuries and a good rest was needed.

Four more days passed before Aoife finally stirred and came back to them. A clinging memory pressed the corners of her mind and she was furious at what she was forced to do against her will, especially by a people she detested. The first thing she did was throw Piladius from the horse and turn the steed against him, ready to end his life. If not for Phaedrus and Scathach jumping in the way with Khutalk the deed would have been done. She twisted the animal about, nearly toppling the horse over in the angry move then jumped to the ground herself. Her legs nearly gave way, but her hatred kept her steady long enough to start searching for food. They realized that she hadn't eaten in nearly a week. She was famished.

"Aoife," Scathach called to her softly. She knew what she was going through, but she also knew she had to put it behind her; move on. The deed was done. If restitution were due, she would find it and make it so. Scathach had come fully awake only the day before. Though she could probably ride alone, she chose to ride double with Phaedrus only because she knew she could fade off and fall. Phaedrus would keep that from happening. Other than that, she felt better.

"What, sister!" she was extremely sour to everyone. She found the sack of dried meat and ripped a slice from within and devoured it.

"We cannot delay. There are soldiers following."

She looked the way she had come. "And we're moving away from them? Turn about and kill them, sister!"

"They are too many, Aoife. We will not win," she was sympathetic.

"I'll do it myself," she swore and mounted, though her mind became dizzy.

Piladius stood beside her and swung his arm up long enough to catch her waist and pull her from the horse. "You will die for no reason!" he told her.

"Why do you care?" she stammered. Her head was swooning and they could see her eyes rolling in her head. She was going to go down again. Piladius was holding her when she finally did.

It was afternoon when she came back to them. "Stop!" she shouted and leaped from Bucephalus. "I need a bath," she screamed and searched everywhere at once for water. She could still feel the man-seed on her belly and thighs, though Piladius took great pains to cleanse her when the opportunity presented itself. He knew she would feel the filth still on her body. Yet the thought of the deed made her feel dirty and cheap and sick and she smelled terribly. She may have liked to play and have sex with almost any male, but the choice of who and when was always hers. And she always cleaned afterwards. No one took advantage of her unwillingly. It was an outrage! And she had to wash it away: cleanse her entire body of the evil deed.

"The river is slightly to our south," Phaedrus told her. "But we have to be careful. There may be soldiers waiting there for us. We cannot be seen, Aoife."

"I don't care," she replied, not really listening to anything besides the directions to the river. She turned and started to walk. Keeping their eyes open, the others followed.

The river continued to swell from the melting snows and the water was extremely cold, though they each washed thoroughly. The frigid water nearly froze their bodies, but they came completely awake after it was done.

"Where are we going?" Aoife asked calmly.

"We are moving to the west. The Arvernian is there."

"Arvernian? Who is he?"

They tried to sum it all in short description, but the events of the past several days were explained in detail. Aoife hadn't realized she missed so much during that time.

"So, we are going to kill Romans?" Aoife finally asked with a bit of satisfaction.

"If we get there in time. The battle has been ongoing for a while. If we can find our way to Vercingetorix he will welcome our skills. And you can kill as many Romans as you wish," Scathach told her.

That night they camped beside a low fire and slept comfortably. No dreams came to them in their sleep and they woke fresh. Before the sun rose they were moving again, pushing further west and following the wide river. By early morning they had reached Regincum (Regensburg) where the Danuvius turns slightly southwest. The oppidum was well fortified but foreigners were not welcomed, they discovered. Too many barbarians, Romans and mercenaries had taken advantage of the goodwill they offered, often stealing supplies and killing the men and raping the women. Children were of no consequence either. Anyone who wanted into the city now was either known or asked to leave.

"Cross the river there," said the guard at the gate as he pointed to a narrow bridge built of heavy trees cut from the deep of the forest and dragged to the Danuvius. "Continue to the southwest and you will find Manching. There you can seek comfort. They are not as worried about their safety as we are," he told them from behind a pair of thick wooden gates.

Without further confrontation they continued forth, crossing the river and moving through the lanes and paths taken time and again to get to Manching. By early evening the city was in sight. A wall of stone perhaps six feet tall ran for nearly four miles of which the oppidum was contained. Like Pannonia the city was alive with music and art. Yet it also possessed Greek influence in architecture with tall stone pillars holding up large structures of great importance: their library and their senate buildings. There were thousands of people here who worked in shops and on farms. Trading had found its way into the mix, they could see. Golden coins were minted here also. It was a wonderful city. But most importantly, the inhabitants were all Celts. And even better than that, they were sympathizers for the Arvernian. Phaedrus realized that they had come to the right place.

A guard met them at the entrance. Not only was the wall guarded with armed men, it was fortified with barriers of heavy brush and brambles and thickets that would tear a man's limbs from his body if he attempted a false entry. In the midst of these were wild hounds, hungry and mean as any beast from hell. Behind these, and at staggered intervals, were Celtic warriors who repeatedly teased the hounds into a horrific frenzy. If an enemy were lucky enough to make it through the brush and the insane hounds, he would have another time of it trying to escape the pikes and spears of the Celtic watchmen. The army, according to the guard, was nearly five thousand strong.

"I will announce your arrival to his majesty," said the guard as he turned and walked away. Another Celt took his place, watching them sternly.

He returned several moments later with a young lad at his side. "The king wishes you to join him in the dining hall. The boy will take your horses and see that they are well fed and cleaned. Your baggage will be stored with the horses," he informed them.

"My regards for your utmost concern," Phaedrus told him. "Would you be as kind to lead us to the location?"

"Follow me," the guard announced formally.

The hall was a spacious room filled with men of all sizes. The men of Gaul were tall of body, their skin moist and white. Their hair was blond by nature but one could see that they color it to keep it so. And they possessed an odd style of hairdressing as they tended to smear their thick, shaggy hair with lime water and pull it back to the top of their head and over the neck to produce something of a horse's mane. One could easily mistake them for wood-demons. And there were other men here whose tall body and muscular physique possessed hair that was fiery red, similar to Scathach's and Aoife's. These were obviously of the Germanic tribes who come from the north; Suebi, Phaedrus recalled. To make themselves look even taller they combed their reddish hair sideways and tied it in a knot on the very crown. Oddly, each man sitting at the circular table setting owned a mustache that covered his entire mouth, though the sides of his cheeks had been shaved clean; nobles, Phaedrus knew. But they were warriors just the same. Each wore a torc of twisted gold about his neck and several of them wore golden corslets to protect the upper torso. They were feasting on wild pig and fish baked in salt and vinegar. And there was bread in baskets set evenly atop the table every third man. All conversation stopped when they entered.

As is the custom, all who come are invited to partake of the feast. And those who are not known at the feast are considered equal until the feast is ended. Additional chairs were set for the company and they sat silently, looking throughout the crowd of men whose eyes could see the beauty of the women, yet the scars of their recent defeat. A moment later they went back to their feast. When they were certain the chief had begun to eat, the small company joined in.

As the basket was passed, purposely, Phaedrus noticed the meat. Before Aoife could reach for it he whispered. "Do not touch the thigh,"

"Why?" she asked. "It is the best part of the pig."

He smiled. "If you want to live, you will leave it alone. The thigh is for the king or the king's hero. None other shall have that piece of meat. If you do, you invite single battle with the hero and most times it is to the death."

"Then I will kill him," she commented.

"I think you probably could, but you have not fully recovered from your injuries. The chances of failure are increased. Please, Aoife, don't make this the end of our journey. Simply take another piece or none at all," he advised though he smiled as he delighted in the presentation to show that he enjoyed the offered meal. She took a slice of the shoulder in disgust and threw it on her bronze plate. All of them left the thigh alone.

A bard, Piladius noticed, sat alone eating what scraps the nobles threw aside. He was considered the parasite of the feast for he would sing his praises before the assembly, reciting deeds of great valor and honor about the chief or the chief's hero and receiving acclaim for his knowledge of the remembered events by being allowed to join in the meal.

When the feast was finished and the food and wine finally brushed away or rinsed from their thick mustaches, they turned their attention back to their guests. The chief was first to address them. He was as broad as he was tall and extremely muscular. An embroidered shirt of bright colors covered his torso and a mantle of checkered design was fastened to his shoulder with a brooch. His hair was blood red, but long as a lion's mane and curly. Standing before the assembly and looking directly at Phaedrus he asked, "What brings you to me?"

"We seek to aid the Arvernian," Phaedrus answered calmly.

"So you are mercenaries looking for work?" Most laughed at the thought of them being mercenaries because the women were of such beauty. Surely they could not fight.

"No," Phaedrus replied without insult.

"Then why would you seek out the Arvernian?"

"To assist," he began. "We require no payment. We want only to assist in the destruction of the Roman army and when this is completed, we will leave. That is all."

The chief shook his head in disbelief. "You require no payment? What kind of fools are you? Your women will be killed in the first battle."

Piladius stood. "Sire, do you have any idea who these women are?" he asked.

He looked closely then shook his head. "No." Everyone laughed.

"Sire, shall we put it to a test?" Phaedrus interrupted.

"Ahhh, there it is. I do enjoy a test," the chief answered.

"Your best!" Phaedrus called out.

"My worst will do," the chief responded with satisfaction and a brief chuckle.

"Yes, but if she beats your best, you can be assured she will defeat any of your men. If she wins against your worst, you will claim it as luck and attempt another."

The chief thought for a moment. "You are right." He turned about and looked at all in attendance. "You," he pointed to the nearest man. "You will fight her."

"Me?" the barbaric monolith questioned. "I will squash her too easily. Let someone of less stature tackle her."

"Yes, yes, I see. We don't want to clean up the mess after you are done." He turned to another less huge than the first. "You," he said.

"Sire, I cannot fight with women."

"Surely you are not afraid of a woman?"

The man hefted his chest two sizes and stood. "I am afraid of nothing! I just don't understand why such beauty has to be wasted," he commented with a smile. "A woman such as this should be washing my feet and scavenging for corn, not fighting."

The words from his mouth brought fire to Scathach's brain and she suddenly went red with anger. She wasn't tied down to a table any longer and had full use of her arms and legs. Her eyes were no longer swollen. Though her muscles were stiff from being beaten and bruised, she knew she could kill this man.

"Sire!" another shouted at the distraction of Scathach's physical change. Oddly, her flesh began to expand and swell from her anger.

"You!" the chief exclaimed as he saw the transformation. "You live!"

"Sire?" the man who had been chosen to fight backed away slightly. "What is this?"

The chief looked at Scathach then at Phaedrus, Piladius and Aoife in turn. "My apologies great warrior," he directed at Scathach. Stories have reach far and wide of your success in battle. We have heard that your village was destroyed by the tenth legion of Rome before they were transferred to Caesar in Gaul. I am truly humbled."

"The pleasure is ours," Piladius answered. "But we require rest and healing from our journey so that we may move on and meet with Vercingetorix."

Now it was the hero who stood: the king's hero. He was larger than all the others and his face was cratered and scarred from many battles. Wounds and battle-scars lashed his forearms to his shoulders in crisscross cuts in his flesh and there were places where chunks of skin were cut from his body and healed over time. It had the appearance of being a puzzle that was put together haphazardly. Like most of the others, his torso was also covered in a golden corslet with a mantle tied over one shoulder by a brooch. His hair was in disarray, dirty and shaggy though spiked to give the countenance of a fearsome creature. His skin was leathery. He walked beyond the chief and challenged her. "I have no knowledge of such a warrior. If you care to heal and rest, you may do so after you do battle with me," he said though the smell of alcohol fumed the air about him. The wine had done its work well during the meal.

Scathach moved forward from the table and came directly to him, unarmed. The moment she took a striking position in front of him he drew a knife and attempted to slice a backhand across her neck. He never had the chance to continue. In one swift move, Scathach forced his arm to continue the motion then bent low and swept her foot across the floor, kicking his feet out from under him. He fell on his back with a loud crack, the air careening from his lungs like a blow with an iron hammer to his chest. He gasped and sucked for air. The knife fell to the floor beside him. She stepped over his heaving body and stepped up to the table where his meal was still sitting on his plate. She lifted the thigh into the air, turned to show her defiance and took a hefty bite from the fattest part of the meat. The gathering cheered with laughter and toasts of wine.

"I am Ambiorix," said the chief. "And I will help you to get to the Arvernian."

"What about this one?" Scathach asked him.

"He will be fine. Leave him," he said and led them away and down the long hall.

They were set up with sleeping quarters and a place to wash and relax. Slaves were given to them to assist in all their needs. Piladius however, took advantage of speaking with the men of the tribe and remained behind to drink and listen to the music and watch the dancing that took place as the others left the dining hall.

"How is the war with Caesar? Is there any news?" he asked of anyone who would answer.

"It doesn't look good," Cruibne replied. He was a rather slender warrior of the Atuatuci tribe with a colorful shirt that was covered by a striped mantle. A bronze brooch held it over his right shoulder. His eyes were dark brown, his brows bushy and deep red. He had a hearty laugh, but several teeth were missing and most of the others were rotten. "Caesar is moving thousands of men to the northwest and along the coastline to the sea. There are two legions in Gergovia (Gergovie) and two more legions are moving to Avaricum (Bourges). The last word we received told that Vercingetorix was being forced to cross the Loire River in search of aid and assistance from the Aedui tribe."

"How many are going to help him from this city?"

The big fellow looked at him with a glare. "We will stay until Rome comes to us."

"What if Rome doesn't come?" Piladius asked.

"It will come."

"How can you be certain? Why can't you help Vercingetorix where he needs you most?"

"Because of Ambiorix."

"What of him?" Piladius asked.

Cruibne looked at him sideways. "You have no idea, my good fellow," he said. Then his eyes got very big. "Bard!" he shouted.

The music stopped and the dancers looked out in fright, fearing that something had gone wrong. It wasn't uncommon for one of the wenches to be gathered in a barbarian's arms and carried off to be used in any evil manner he chose. Some were even killed for the sport of it. They relaxed when the elder stood from his corner and approached the summons.

"Yes," he answered meekly from the center of the dining hall. He was of medium size yet thin. His hair was long and gray, flowing to meet the length of his beard. His eyes were steel gray with specks of brown and his lips seemed to mumble as he moved. A pair of wrinkled hands shook nervously. He was frail, they could see.

"This young man knows not why Caesar will seek out Ambiorix. Will you explain?"

"A chair for the wise?" the old one asked.

"A chair!" Cruibne called out and one was produced immediately from a slave standing by.

"Ambiorix," the old one started his praises. "The gods are with him, for he is of the brightest star that shines in the winter/spring sky. His people, the Eburones, are strong against the will of Caesar and constantly engage him in battle. They shall be victorious in their pursuit for they have already destroyed a great legion and continue to push them back to the hell they have come from…"

"Enough!" another cried out. "I have heard enough. Bring the women back out to dance for me!" he shouted. The bard stopped, picked up the chair and retreated to his corner. The music began even louder than before.

"So there is a greater fighting force waiting for Ambiorix to return?" Piladius asked.

"No. In fact he is probably the last of the Eburones tribe to be alive," Cruibne whispered darkly. "I barely escaped with my life alongside him. Together we fled to this city. I tell you here and now, the Eburones shall never see their land again, for they are gone from us, forever. The Treverians tendered great promise of land and great wealth to Ambiorix to ambuscade the Romans of the Fourteenth Legion. And it was an easy matter because Ambiorix was favored greatly by Caesar. But Caesar's lieutenants, Sabinus and Cotta, have met their death in battle against Ambiorix—through trickery and deceit. And Caesar himself has set the world on fire with the head of Ambiorix."

"So, Ambiorix is a Treverian?" Piladius asked as the music fill the room to a heavy climax of dancing and cheering.

"No. He was the chief of the Eburones, hired by the Treverians. Because of his ambush and murder of Subinus and Lucius Cotta, Caesar has proclaimed that all will die for what Ambiorix has done. Tens of thousands of Nervians have already died and tens of thousands of Atuatuci have been taken prisoner. Anyone who offers Ambiorix assistance is destined to perish under Caesar's mighty army. Ambiorix barely made it away with his own life, being tracked to the forests and marshes and nearly caught several times. He managed to find me scavenging the woods for food and together we took flight to make it here. At his arrival he forced a way to gain trust and confidence in the people and formed this army from those mercenaries and hostages who have escaped the western war. We believe Caesar will find out that he is here and come for him. That is why we have no desire to go to the war when we know it will eventually come here to us. And we will be ready."

"We cannot wait that long. It may never come to pass and our wait would be for naught. I don't know why they push so hard, but the women warriors are determined to move further west. It is as if they seek some sort of vision from this Vercingetorix. I am baffled by it all," Piladius told him.

"Then I say we let them rest and recover while you and I take advantage of the wine and women while we can," Cruibne said as he drank deeply and pushed out his empty cup for a refill, which came almost immediately.

In their private quarters, Scathach and Aoife received the best medical treatment they had ever encountered. The physician, Osmiach, was well versed in the art of medicine. He had more containers and vials of herbs and salves and healing mixtures than either of them had ever seen before. And he had complete knowledge of each item he used. The Druids had taught him, he told them as he prepared a concoction of spices. They drank it without question. By morning they were both feeling much better. Soon they would depart for Gaul. And then they would find Vercingetorix. But they still needed time to recover.

CHAPTER XII

Another week went by and the weather turned warmer, flowers began to spring up in the fields, in gardens and along roadsides. The mood of the people seemed to bloom as well. Another harsh winter had passed, taking minimal life with it. Now it was time for replanting the fields and repairing damaged buildings and preparing the senate for decisions on the war. The army would train hard every day and the children of the city would attend open-air classrooms. And as they would train and learn, so would Scathach and Aoife.

Osmiach met them in the dining hall and greeted them. "You look well, today," he said as he grabbed a slice of fruit. "You will be ready to depart soon, I can see."

"Yes," Scathach told him as she consumed a bit of cheese and milk, though it tasted different from what she was used to.

"I have watched you train these past several days, while the others were out preparing for battle. You keep to your own and I can see why," he told her. "You are exceptionally gifted."

"We don't want to be bothered, nor interrupted," Aoife told him.

He was a middle-aged man with graying marks in his dark-brown hair. His green eyes were alert and quizzical, yet always searching around him as if someone waited in dark corners for him to be caught unaware. His nose was long and narrow and his face was naked of beard and mustache. Even his hair was kept short and neat on his head, unlike the shaggy unkempt hair of the warriors. He smiled at them and took another slice of melon into his mouth. "There is something I must tell you," he said though he didn't look up. He chewed the fruit nervously.

They both looked at him and waited for several seconds. "Well…get on with it Osmiach," said Scathach.

"You cannot go to Gaul," he said calmly.

They both laughed. "Why not, physician?" Aoife asked in continued laughter.

"I do not recommend it," he said then.

Scathach put down the food and drink. "We have come a long way for this. My destiny lies to the north and to the west. The only thing in the west is the war with Caesar and Vercingetorix. That is where I will go," she told him.

"And where will you go after that?" he asked.

She hadn't really thought about it. Everything, so far, had led to the war and no further. It was a strange sort of question, but one that she knew she should have an answer for. Quickly, she replied, "North."

"It will take you a long time, you know."

"That is acceptable," Scathach allowed.

"Not when you are with child," he said calmly, though extremely nervous.

"What!" Scathach was up out of her seat. "That is not true," she warned.

Osmiach stood, ready for retreat if he had to. "No, Scathach. You are not with child, Aoife is."

"How dare you!" Aoife jumped over the table and darted for the physician. Scathach was behind her trying to catch up. In a single leap Aoife managed to trap Osmiach into a corner of the room and cast him to the polished stone floor with the front of his shirt gathered in her fist. Her other hand was ready to beat him senseless. "I told you not to tell!" she yelled.

"Aoife!" Scathach caught her and held her swinging hand back. "Let him be!" she screamed at her sister. The sound penetrated the hall, reverberating off the long walls and fell silent in the outdoors. Birds scattered at the trembling sound and men training in the open fields halted for a second. When silence continued, they returned to their lessons.

"I will kill him, just like I will kill every Roman who ever comes near me! They will pay for this," she yelled out, then suddenly burst into tears.

"Aoife, come with me," Scathach said softly, grabbing her by the shoulders in comfort.

She let her hand drop and released the shirt then stood, wiping her eyes as she did. It wasn't right, she thought to herself. It wasn't supposed to be this way. Nothing was going to stop her from continuing on this journey. And she would kill every Roman soldier she met as payment for such a disposition.

Reluctantly, she followed Scathach through the halls of the chief's home, which was more castle-like than contemporary home. There were thirty bedrooms, four lavatories, four eateries, two dining halls and three large bathing areas. The home also contained a private location for Osmiach to tend to his practice. At the end of the hall she stopped and opened the door to her quarters. "We have to talk," she told Aoife.

"There is nothing to say," Aoife told her as she entered and jumped onto the bed.

"Yes, there is. You are with child. You cannot commit to battle in such a condition."

"Sister, you will not stop me."

"Stopping you is not my intent. But you must take care that the line of your blood is not lost, even if it is the Roman seed that grows within you."

At that Aoife scoured. "I will kill them! And when I am finished with them, I will raise this bastard child and kill it too!" she threatened.

"Aoife! It is your blood too!" she scolded, though it came out in a deadly whisper.

"I will not have it, Scathach. I will not keep it!"

"You are talking nonsense! For the sake of your father, you must keep the bloodline strong," she told her.

"I will, Scathach, but it will be a child from a man of my choosing." She stood from the bed and stomped to the door. "What would you do, Scathach?" she asked then opened the door and departed, leaving her sister alone with her thoughts.

After that Aoife tended to her own business during the day and night as did Scathach. For the most part it was as if they were back in Pannonia:

except Aoife wasn't pregnant at the time. Now that she was, it bothered Scathach all the time. She constantly faulted in her training—loosing concentration and falling from the rope of feats or practicing her *kiai* and loosing the force of her voice in the middle of the lesson. She attempted to juggle to keep her mind busy, but found that seven apples were all she could keep in the air at one time and it became tiring. Phaedrus spent as much time with her as possible to assist in keeping her skills sharp. He was an excellent opponent to train with, she realized. He even managed to help her carve her own pugil in the same manner as his and attach a pair of steel blades on each end, as she saw Phaedrus do. She was pleased with her efforts. But now she began to train in a different way with this new weapon. Such a deadly thing, she surmised. She couldn't understand why anyone with a brain would ever get close to one of these while it was swinging in the air. But she trained hard and never gave the thought another chance to return.

Aoife managed to train on her own with the help of several volunteers who found training with a woman fascinating. Though she taught them with barely a stitch of clothing on her back, they seemed to understand quickly that she was there for training only. The first time one of them attempted to try something unfavorable, she cut off his little finger and gave it back to him. Osmiach found himself busier than before. Yet, Aoife trained even harder than ever, determined if not desperate for retribution. The seed growing inside her reminded her constantly of how much she despised the Romans and how much she wanted to kill them. Occasionally, she would take it out on the men who trained with her and injure one of them on purpose. They tended to keep their distance, yet they came anyway, if just to see her muscular body sweat and gleam in the sunlight. She actually started to grow an audience. And she started to like it.

Piladius remained with Osmiach learning new methods of healing and assisting with the wounded that Aoife tended to send their way. He learned much of the medicine and herbs that were contained in the little space given by Ambiorix to Osmiach and they spent a great deal of their time talking of travels and things of the world. Both, it appeared, were interested in politics and philosophy while keeping their mind on those things that are real, such as wounded soldiers and sickly remedies. And Cruibne confronted him often, asking questions about Scathach and her training methods. Without her permission he secretly spied on her while she practiced and found it fascinated, though he made Piladius promise never to tell.

And then there was Ambiorix. He was seen only twice in the days they had spent in Manching. Most of his time was preoccupied with his council on the war, keeping abreast of the situation with Vercingetorix, and getting advice from his generals. His time was also absorbed by the numerous new laws that continued to emerge from his senate due to an increase in the city's population. More structures, homes and public buildings were being built in and around the oppidum. More farmers had settled in the area. The farmers offered their services to plant crops and provide their benefactors with payment of sixty percent of their earnings and twenty percent of the entire crop. Taxes collected from these farmers cost another fifteen percent of their earnings. Ambiorix, for the most part, was both benefactor and tax recipient.

In the times that they saw Ambiorix he was reserved and sheltered, kept guarded by several of his biggest and strongest, though Scathach maintained a non-confrontational meal of the thigh each time they ate together in the dining hall. The king's hero never attempted to debaucher her reward for defeating him. He, in fact, gave up his chair entirely and sat beside Cruibne. The hero's chair remained vacant until the women warriors had departed the city. Only then was it reclaimed, though tested in single combat several times afterward.

But Scathach had her doubts about Ambiorix. She sensed a strong mistrust of him and perhaps a tendency to portend a mischievous smile when he listened to events during the evening meals. He smirked of hidden thoughts and great secrecy. There was a hint of corruption and personal agenda during conversations with his nobles and his generals. While Scathach took notice, the men around him seemed oblivious to his intensions—whether good or evil. It was no wonder Caesar wanted his head on a pole to march around with in the city of Rome. He was a likely candidate for treason in any kingdom, including his own.

Yet Ambiorix was a powerful speaker, she soon learned. His orations to the multitude, especially his army, provided words of encouragement and victory. His speeches demonstrated his power and foresight by his telling of the successful encounter—treachery—over the Fourteenth Legion. Of course he never mentioned the fact that his tribe was completely destroyed and removed from the face of the earth by Caesar's remaining legions. He may be the only Eburones tribe member left to tell the story at all. In that case, he could speak whatever he wished on the matter without the possibility of argument or debate. Regardless, his army cheered him each time he spoke of battle and success, each man banging his sword against his decorated shield. Scathach knew however, that most of them had never met a legion of Roman soldiers, had never fought in a battle at all. And many, she knew, would die very easily. While they were fierce fighters, they would literally throw away their lives for the belief of a single word. And that word was Ambiorix.

The weather had warmed, though still chilly during the mornings, and the air cast fresh odors of spring foliage. It was a pleasant smell and Scathach breathed deeply. It reminded her of her own village when the tribe would start to plant their corn for the season. It grew taller with each year. But there were flowers and fruits and berries that she had gathered for different occasions: some for healing, others for pleasure, still others for eating. It would be time for her people to move across the Turan and into the Sayan Mountains for their ceremonies, she remembered. Arieoles and Oseida are there now, she suddenly recalled. It wasn't that long ago that she buried them in the sacred *kurgan*. They were good warriors, she reminisced. But all life comes to an end, she knew. It was just a matter of how one chooses to live that distinguishes them in the minds of others. Yet the bitter memory of her father's death and the destruction of her own village quickly brought her dreaming to an end. She knew then that she had to move along. A great deal of time had been wasted here. She had regained her strength and her fighting skills had returned, perhaps even better than before.

"Phaedrus," she said as he escorted her back to her quarters. "We have to leave."

He smiled. "I know. I've sensed it for some time. I've just been waiting for you to make the decision."

She thought for a moment in silence. "What about Aoife?"

"Aoife can decide on her own. The child she carries is hers."

"Yes, but this is a dangerous journey. That child may be all that is left of my family."

He stopped short in the dirt path. "It is still not your life. Life is a precious thing, Scathach, but if you cannot live that life the way you want, then that life is useless. You are nothing more than a puppet connected by strings and someone else is always pulling them. Decisions are made every day, some good and some bad. It is your intension that makes the difference. If you intend to see this to the end, you must push on at all cost. If not, then you should turn around and go back to your old village and rebuild it, live out your days in happiness," he told her.

She thought long as she looked at him. After a while she asked. "What is your intension?"

He was silent. Somehow he had trapped himself. He didn't know what his intension was at this point. He was sent to kill her and return to Nero in Rome with her head and the stone. He failed because he made a decision to assist them along their journey to the west. Beyond that there was no other intension. But he knew also that he could not play a fool and stand there looking at her without an answer. With a need for urgency he dropped his sack of weapons, grasped her by the shoulders and kissed her on the lips. When it was done, he expected her to strike him and he waited, dreadfully, for it to come. Instead, she turned away and continued to walk on, leaving him behind, without speaking.

They had gathered again in the dining hall for the evening meal, eating to the sounds of a harpist plucking his strings lightly from the corner of the room where the bard usually sits. He wasn't present this evening, the small group noted. Perhaps they only kept one parasite on duty during meals, Scathach considered. She ignored it and went back to eating slices of salted pork and bread. Nothing had been said about the kiss along the road and nothing further was said about Aoife's decision to travel. The matter was closed and destiny would play its hand when the time came, she figured. Nevertheless, the dining hall was full of blond and redheaded warriors feasting on a great meal, the mixture of chattering voices and soft harp music cascading throughout the room. But then the door burst open and a worried messenger marched forth.

"Sire!" he raised his right fist to this chest in salute. He was sent from Vercingetorix.

"What is it," Ambiorix was slightly annoyed by the distraction, but curious just the same.

"Caesar," he tried to catch his breath. "Caesar is gathering his forces for a final blow against Vercingetorix."

"Where?" Ambiorix stood and silenced the entire room instantly.

"They have pushed him across the Loire River. When he sent me hither, he was seeking assistance from the Aedui through ambassadors. He has burned the bridges that cross the Loire and last I saw, Caesar was biding his time, taking all the plunder and corn and grain from the city of Avaricum. Caesar began a terrible siege on Avaricum that lasted twenty-seven days. Even in the incessant rain, two-wheeled towers, eighty feet high, and ramps, three hundred and thirty feet long, over which they could be rolled into place, as well as a high siege terrace, were constructed. This they pushed to the walls of Avaricum. We managed to set this on fire and thus threw pitch and tallow onto the apparatus to keep flames high and the Romans away, but by morning they managed to extinguish the flame. And with the morning came a terrible storm with heavy rain. We were forced to take shelter. That was when Caesar attacked us. We were taken completely by surprise. The Romans, exasperated at the length and difficulty of the siege, massacred all within the city and took everything of value no matter what. We were over forty thousand strong inside the walls, sire. Neither old men nor women nor children were spared. Perhaps eight hundred of us managed to escape to Vercingetorix who is still waiting on the east bank of the river. Caesar is gathering more soldiers to his army and will attack again, we are certain. We must assist the Arvernian I tell you," he pleaded. "Vercingetorix has delayed them all he can. He has burned every field with which to gather food and killed every beast he could not bring along to keep his own men fed and he has torched every city so that the Romans could use nothing that was left behind. But they have survived and are now beginning their preparations for a large battle. The skirmishes we have engaged them in, have done nothing more than make them angry. We must do something soon, sire!" he begged.

"We will," Ambiorix nearly laughed. "We will wait for Rome to come to us."

"But sire, they will all die! Families will be killed and our brothers will be lost. Vercingetorix will not have a chance to fight. Surely you are going to assist him?" he asked, his eyes wide and round and looking for approval in his plight.

"Assist? Of course not…Rome will be at our front gates soon enough. While he marches his troops across the wilderness to achieve our city, he will tire and grow weak with hunger and sickness. Then we will destroy him and his great army. He will not win against our forces," he bragged with a chuckle in his hefty voice and the men cheered him. A salute of raised cups went to the air and they toasted to the ovation. Only the small group of travelers took the matter to great concern. Their hopes lie with Vercingetorix and they needed to be there beside him, fighting the Romans, not with cowards who know nothing of battle.

Scathach had heard enough. "How long?" she stood and asked. All eyes turned to her. The room fell silent again.

"How long?" the messenger asked in return, confused.

"How long will it take to get there?"

He understood. "If we push hard we can be there in four days, but there will be little rest," he told her. "The mountain passes are clear, but the travel is rocky in places and treacherous for the horses."

"We will leave in the morning," she told him. He beamed with delight.

"You will do no such thing!" commanded Ambiorix.

The messenger shied away, slightly.

"I will do as I please," she told him casually though she cast a deadly, even glare at him to test him. "Please show me the man you would use to stop me. If you wish to hide behind your walls of stone and wait for Rome to come to your doorstep that is your decision, but I will not wait for him. I have seen his army fight many times in my life. They will cast huge boulders into your walls and knock them down with little to no effort. Then they will burn the dead bramble that you think will protect you because there are barbs in the branches. But look closely warriors. The branches are nothing more than dead wood and they will burn quickly. Your barbs will be useless. Then Caesar will fire his missiles at your hounds and your men and completely destroy half your army before he even attempts to march to the gates to see what is left for his men to pick from. I haven't even mentioned their horses. Now, do you still wait here?"

The room was as quiet as a burial mound on *Sahmain*. Finally the hall erupted in protest, nearly every man proclaiming his opinion of what should or should not be done. Ambiorix stood in the middle of it, dumbfounded. He had not counted on this sort of reaction. At all times he had maintained the order and discipline of the warriors and his army. In a matter of seconds the entire gathering of nobles who govern the welfare of the city and the high-ranking officers of his army were up in arms. A fight started at the end of the table where a dagger was drawn and one of them fell. While all eyes looked to see who it was, they continued their debauchery of the war with the Celts and what should be done.

Ambiorix went completely mad. "Enough!" he shouted as loud as he could. "Desist!" he bellowed.

The hall calmed, though after a few seconds.

"You!" he pointed to Scathach. "You have brought this upon us. We know where our defenses are and how to withhold the enemy who seeks our city. You belittle us to think that you could possibly be right in all things. You are a stranger and you are wrong! You know nothing of this city and its potential to destroy our enemies. Go from us! Leave us!" he told her harshly. After this he turned to see whom it was who had fallen. Without comment he inspected the body of Tullinus, one of his lieutenants and then departed the hall, leaving everyone else to watch after him.

When he was gone from them the messenger turned back to Scathach. "A woman? Of all you who stand here with the knowledge of war between Rome and your brothers, you choose not to fight at their side. But a woman who is not of your city heeds the call. I am shamed by your insight," he said to them.

A knife flew into the air and struck him in the middle of his chest. He fell gasping for life, twitching and writhing on the floor until it ended.

Their attention came back to Scathach and all waited to see what she would do.

"I would have been surprised if you allowed him to leave without his head on a pole," she said smartly. "I would have done the deed myself if I were one of you."

They grunted acceptance and sat back down silently, running the entire event through their minds. There were decisions that really had to be made. Perhaps the city wasn't as protected as they had thought. The woman warrior had pointed out weakness in their defenses that should be looked into instantly. Maybe they should build another wall outside the current wall for added protection and establish fresher brambles of thorns to keep the walls protected should the enemy scale the walls. No matter, they had to come up with a plan to protect themselves. But whatever it was, Scathach and her small group would have no say in the matter. She was ordered to leave by Ambiorix and no matter how strong she was and how much talent she possessed in combat they would do as he ordered and be gone from the city by night.

"Come," she said to her sister and the others. "I cannot stomach the sight of them!"

Within the hour they were on their horses headed beyond the outer gates and moving west. It was a relief to be gone from them. If not for the fact that Scathach and Aoife required time to recover from the raping and beatings, they would have been well on their way long before now. The guards saluted them in passing, acknowledging them with a slight bow of their head and wishing them well on their journey. Several of them had watched Aoife many times during her practices. She recognized the one with his missing little finger and nodded her head in respect for his efforts as she passed. He smiled wanly in return.

"Wait!" a voice shouted out to them from behind.

They turned about, but not in alarm.

Two horses rode up to them with a packhorse trailing. "We want to come along."

"Cruibne!" Piladius smiled. "Osmiach!" he claimed and grasped forearms which was the custom of their greeting.

"Why?" Scathach asked. "Are you not worried that your king will have you tortured for treason?" she asked them.

"He will not know we are gone until morning. By that time he will not care," Cruibne told her. "Will you allow us to ride along?"

"You are welcome," Phaedrus told him.

"That is good then," he replied. "Besides, I am from the Atuatuci tribe and have traveled this land many times, though mostly to the northwest. Still, I know the area and I also know where to find the Arvernian."

"I see your point," Scathach said in welcome. "It will be good to have you along. But what about you?" she asked Osmiach. "You will most surely be missed."

"Regrettably, I will be. But I would rather be a party to those who seek to fight for what is right than hide in dark corners waiting. Ambiorix will curse me, but he will survive long enough to find another to replace me. I on the other hand would rather travel with you," he offered.

"Then you too are welcome," she offered.

CHAPTER XIII

The messenger had told them the truth. The way west was extremely mountainous and rocky. While the Turanian horses were well suited for the travel, the drafts, or working horses used by Cruibne and Osmiach, were not. On the first day out the packhorse they brought from the city of Manching had caught its foot between two sharp rocks jutting out of the ground and twisted it in a way that shattered the fetlock, sending the bone splintering through the skin. The poor beast howled in pain and lay down instantly. Without her iron hammer to ram into the front of the stallion's skull to destroy it, she resorted to using a blunt, heavy boulder that she had to hold in two hands. She had to strike three times before the animal finally stopped shuddering and fighting for its life. What other choice did she have? The poor animal would only suffer greatly if she had not done the deed. With the weight of the extra supplies the two remaining packhorses had to slow slightly and rest more often. But that was nothing compared to the problems that started for Aoife.

On the afternoon of the second day they had reached the end of the Danuvius River and gained the heavily wooded lands leading to the Rhenus (Rhine) River that Cruibne knew they would have to cross. Almost two miles short of the river Aoife doubled over in pain. Instantly, eyes shot out for danger lurking behind tall fir and brush thick enough to hide a thousand wild animals. Nothing else occurred, but Aoife still cried out in anguish.

"What is it?" Scathach was beside her, still mounted, still looking for danger.

Tears were in her eyes. "I don't know. It just hurts," she said in gut wrenching pain.

"Osmiach!" she called to the physician. It was the second time she was glad he was along with them on the journey. "Look after her," she said as she leaped onward and took a tour of the area briefly to ensure there was nothing out there that had caused this to happen suddenly. She returned moments later, satisfied that whatever it was belonged to Aoife and not from an outside source. "What did you find?" she asked on arrival.

Phaedrus pulled her to the side while Piladius helped Osmiach lift Aoife from Bucephalus and place her on the warm hides they had taken along the trip. Blood was smeared down her thighs and she had gone dreadfully pale in the face.

"What is it?" she asked though there was a hint of warning in her voice.

"Scathach," Phaedrus tried to calm her. "Aoife lost the child," he said softly.

"What?"

"The baby…it's gone. She has lost her child."

With a goatskin of water poured onto a cloth, Piladius and Osmiach cleaned her carefully; cautious not to seem offensive or to give her the impression they were repeating what the Romans had done to her in Vindobona. In her state of mind it could easily be seen as such. While Osmiach did most of the cleaning, Piladius kept his eyes on hers and spoke softly of things he had written in his journal. To keep the story consistent, he removed the small ledger from its place in his shirt and opened to a page he thought would suit her to hear:

"The coliseum is packed daily, but not for the gladiatorial fights or the fate of the prisoners who mostly die. They come for Aoife, the woman warrior who has demonstrated the skill and art of combat beyond any woman they have ever seen. At the corner of the arena she stands, her fiery hair gleaming in the glowing sunlight. Her nakedness arouses the audience for she is truly a Goddess in the flesh with a sword in one hand and a spear in the other. Her muscles flex as she bends to meet her opponent and she dislodges him from his horse while at a full gallop and brings him to his knees before her. Appeasing the crowd for their condemnation or their forgiveness, she reaches

out to them, looking for approval. Satisfied with the result of the multitude she releases
him of further tasks and did, in that moment, take unto her roof the head of another
warrior. It was not hate nor was it of personal gratification, but of honor and dedication.
She too would have given her head honorably had she lost. But such a warrior is this
woman who would do this deed and still give praise to her foe regardless of race or region.
She is to be commended for her actions and her extraordinary skill. She has made a
name for herself in the arena. The bets and antis have more than tripled since her
participation, I have witnessed. And I too have found the excitement in watching her
fight…"

He stopped suddenly. He hadn't realized that he began to make more
personal remarks than ones of historical value. Women were not subject
to finding him alluring or enticing. Most would scoff at his attempt to
seduce them with philosophical words of seduction. It wasn't what they
wanted. Women wanted to be grabbed with spontaneity and ravaged with
lustful groans of ecstasy that tended to last only a few moments then
move on to the next man or the next rest period. That wasn't for him. He
wanted to love and be loved for who he was and what he was. Surely there
was a woman out there for him. Maybe not these women, though they
gave him a feverish groin on occasion, but surely there was a woman out
there who wanted to be loved purely for the sake of being in love. And
while he had the gift of word, he would wait for that woman to come into
his life. Beautiful as Scathach and Aoife were, he could resist them for as
long as it would take to find the right one for him.

In his absent thoughts, he hadn't noticed Aoife staring up at him.
Though her face and even her lips were still pale, she smiled. "You were
watching?" she said softly.

He flushed slightly. "Yes, I watched nearly every day after I trained
with Phaedrus. And I wrote it down each time," he told her. "And
Mahendra came as well, on occasion," he added to draw direct attention
away from himself. Then he turned about to Osmiach. "Will she be well?"
he asked.

"She should really get some rest, but I will leave it up to her. If she feels
she can make the journey, I will permit it," he said.

"I have no other choice. I will not be left behind. This situation only saves me the trouble of killing it when it would have gotten older. And I would have killed it, just because it was of Roman blood. Now I can concentrate on the rest of them," she said and sat up, though weakly. She grimaced as she moved, but she forced herself to stand and mount.

"Aoife," Scathach stopped her briefly. "Are you sure you can do this?"

Aoife didn't answer. She turned Bucephalus about and rode west ahead of them. Not long afterwards they came to the Rhenus.

"Which way?" Phaedrus asked Cruibne.

"We go south until we find a place safe enough to cross. Then we continue west," he told them and moved in that direction. An hour later they found a suitable bridge and made the crossover.

"How much longer now?" Scathach asked. She disliked not knowing the location of her travels. Had she been moving across the Turan she would know exactly where she was because she had traveled there so many times. Relying on information from an outsider, such as Cruibne was, caused her to travel more cautiously and ask questions more frequently. On top of that, Aoife seemed to become agitated and bent to the withers more often to ease the pain in her middle. Scathach worried for her.

"Another day or so we should come within the territory of the Sequani," Cruibne told them.

"Who are they?" Aoife asked him. She remained in constant pain but pressed forth ignoring it as more a nuisance than a condition.

"They are a simple people who mainly keep to themselves anymore. My brother married a woman of their village many years ago and managed to raise five young boys and a daughter with her. Three of them were lost to the war with Caesar six years past. His oldest serves as Ovate to the Druids in Carnutes…"

"I know of them…the Druids!" Piladius interjected with exaggerated animation. It was as if a piece of knowledge he had learned was triggered into existence and the flood of books he had studied over the years had come back as a long lost memory. Over the past year, he was practically thrust into the life of a hunter and now a killer of men, rarely getting the opportunity to read and study and perform any of the traditional scholarly duties he was used to. Any more, he was as much a barbarian as the rest of them. But he knew the best part of his life was spent learning and understanding other cultures and languages through philosophy and poetry and politics. The knowledge of Druids, he recalled, was a complete mystery to all. Yet it was one of the most fascinating religious topics in most kingdoms.

"Yes, well…" Cruibne raised his bushy brows in mild concern. "The youngest son and the daughter are still living in the territory, last I heard."

"Is it a good place to stop and rest before pushing on?" Phaedrus asked, thinking of Aoife's situation.

"We could," he said in relief. Somehow they knew he wanted to see his brother again, and yet they knew if there was not time for it he would have continued on without stopping at all, nor would he have asked in his own behalf. It was obvious he was dedicated to the task ahead.

They camped under a starlit sky and a low, warming fire that night. They gathered close together in their warm fur blankets, Phaedrus a little closer than normal to Scathach, Piladius noticed. There was no discussion, only personal thoughts throughout the evening. A lot has happened in the past several months and each took a long time to reflect. Life had changed so. Though the days became longer with the coming of spring and soon summer, they went to sleep early, hoping to rise before the light greeted them with a new day and move on to the Sequani. There would be news of the war there, they knew. Without ever speaking a word, they each knew what questions would be asked upon arrival. Foremost would be the location of Caesar.

By noon of the next day they had reached the territory of the Sequani and followed the directions to the home of Susterix, the brother of Cruibne. The town was less populated than Cruibne remembered, but then again the war had depleted the number by several thousand. It was the Aedui who had caused this death. It was the Aedui who, after many years of self-righteous politics, decided to adopt the laws and standards of Rome. The Sequani went to war with them over the ownership of lands and people and laws and Rome backed the Aedui to the point of nearly obliterating the Sequani from the planet. Since that time the Aedui have chosen a position that suits them best for the moment, depending on which side is winning.

The home was small, but roomy enough for them to be comfortable. There was a warm fire in the hearth where a cooking pot oozed of a meat stew similar to the meals Scathach and Aoife were used to preparing and eating in their own village. Susterix welcomed them and introduced his family as they exchanged greetings. They could have been twins—only twenty years apart—Piladius thought as he noticed a smile of several missing teeth and most of the others rotted. He was much, much older and his brow was extremely bushy and deep dark red with touches of gray, his hair shaggy and tangled. Yet he overlooked appearances and accepted the welcome with gratitude. The next few hours were spent in reminiscent times from all parties over hot, herbal broth and a good portion of the stew. Oddly, Aoife began to feel better.

Before the afternoon was swept away, they had learned dreadfully that Avaricum had surely fallen to Roman soldiers fifteen days earlier and that both armies had moved south toward Gergovia and the country of the Arverni, mirroring each other's campsite alongside the Allier River. But it was only after Caesar had secured ten thousand infantry and all the cavalry belonging to the Aedui that this was done. It was now the fifth day before the calends of April and Vercingetorix was no closer to gathering the states under his command and combining the strength of all Gaul against Roman influence. Yet he conducted ambuscades and skirmishes along the way to keep their minds sharp and alert at all times while securing what little hostages he could from neighboring states. The Roman army began to grow weary of this sort of fighting, losing their vigor and endurance to control all of Gaul, though seeking every opportunity to plunder and gather booty from most Celtic towns they were allowed to eviscerate along the way.

"How do we find them?" Cruibne asked.

Susterix looked about as if spying not to be overheard by unwelcome ears. "You won't have to find them. They will return. This I can promise," he said in a gloating laugh.

"How can you be certain? This is the second time we've been told Caesar will be coming to us. What makes you so positive?" Scathach asked incredulously.

"Because the Aedui are a bitter, spiteful people. They consider themselves above all others as the keepers of all Gaul. They will give you everything they have and offer more, but the moment you turn your back to go away they take it back and claim they have recovered it from robbers. There is treachery even among the treacherous," he told them. "While the Roman army and the Aeduan infantry move south to the Arverni territory and the town of Gergovia, which is nearly impossible to penetrate because it is built high upon the mountain, Convictolanis, assigned supreme authority as magistrate by Caesar himself just eight days ago, plots to gain support of the Aedui and the outside states to prepare for war based on a self-sense of freedom for all Gaul. The plot is afoot even as I speak to you. Trust that it will not be long before they return."

"And where will they come to?" Phaedrus asked.

"I am positive they will come back by the Avaricum direction and cross the Loire. Then they will send ambassadors to meet with Convictolanis to decide what steps to take next," he conjectured. "In case you are wondering about my intelligence to such matters, I suppose I should tell you I have a very close friend in Litavicus, for he is the one so bribed by the Arverni to begin such rumors as to set the state of Aedui against Caesar. And though we hunt often in the valley between here and there, I know he is not smart enough to know how to plot such a trap of people. Convictolanis' trust in him is extremely overrated. Trust then that I know him and that once Caesar has discovered by what means he issues his threat of war they will come running back to the territory of the Aedui."

It was quite the summation, Phaedrus thought to himself. Even Cruibne nodded understanding. "But what of Vercingetorix?" Cruibne asked his brother.

"Ah…he will send ambassadors to Convictolanis as well. And as I am told, by Litavicus, will be assigned to make allegiance to the Aedui as a complete power over all Gaul. But this too, will not come to pass, for I have heard of the strength and power of the Arvernian. Even in his own land he was cast out only to return stronger and powerful enough to put to death those who had banished him from his homeland. He will not swear allegiance to them now or ever. But if his gods permit, he will attempt to rule all of Gaul himself. And I cannot blame him, to say the truth."

Scathach was slightly confused. "But they all fight Romans, do they not?"

"It depends on which side is winning. What good would it do the state if Caesar wins and you are against him? What good would it do the state if Vercingetorix wins and you are against him? Either way, the state wins so long as it chooses to fight for the winning side."

"But who is to know which side is the winning side?"

"There are ways," he told her. "First, if you are in battle and you find yourself in an overwhelming situation where death is eminent, you rip from your right shoulder all cloth and show the naked flesh. This instantly tells a Roman soldier that you are of the peace and do not fight in any battle. Though lately this has been used as deception and the Roman soldiers have butchered many who were truly of a peaceful nation. Just the same, it has worked in the past. Once you have determined which side is winning, you choose your next employment: Rome or Gaul, and fight for them. It is that simple."

"The citizens of Gaul are that fickle?" Scathach asked. "Do they not have honor?"

"My dear lady," he laughed. "I, like my brother here, am from Germania. We strongly believe in honor and courage and commitment and dedication. But these men of Gaul believe in their all-powerful Druids. They are the driving force behind all that takes place, though they stay separate from state matters and confine themselves to the knowledge of trees and stars and the movement of the earth and the rotation of the sun and the moon. They hold sacrifices of people and animals and all nature of things that we Germanians consider absurd. Yet the Celtic tribes of Gaul believe in them wholeheartedly. With that much strength in the belief of Druids, no one would threaten to dislodge the center focus of their entire society. If you can live to fight another day, why loose your life meaninglessly. While you would cast your life away because of honor and courage, they would show cowardice to preserve their miserable existence. It is just that simple," he told them with a shake of his head.

When all was said on the war with Caesar, Cruibne decided to spend some of his time in private with his brother. Susterix enjoyed the company.

"You travel with women now?" Susterix asked feeling a bit out of place.

"You have no idea who these women are, Susterix," he commented with an edge of danger in his voice.

"Are they really that good?"

"At fighting, yes. Better than any three, maybe four, men put together."

"I have not heard of them before," Susterix told him.

"We have traveled far, but the women and the two men even farther."

"Where do you go from here?"

Cruibne scratched his bushy mustache. "To fight is all I know. I'm not sure they know where to go from there."

Susterix thought for a moment. "Cruibne, my son is almost ready for manhood. I cannot teach him the ways of fighting. He doesn't listen to me. If I tell you of a place, would you go there and settle, then send word for my son to join you?"

Cruibne looked at the hearth in thought. Where was this going? Why would he want Cruibne to take his son? "I suppose, but why are you doing this?"

"I want the warrior to teach him."

"Scathach?" he asked in amazement. "She is the best fighter I have ever seen, anywhere. I'm sure she will do it if I ask her, but why do you want your son trained by a warrior?"

"Because times are harsh here in Gaul. If he doesn't become trained, he will become dead."

Cruibne understood then. It was true. Anyone living in these lands had better be a fighter or at least have knowledge of how to fight. It was the only way to make Susterix feel better. "I will do my best."

"Good, then there is an island far north of here that our father loved greatly. The fishing is greater than any place I've ever been and the land more fertile than any I've ever stepped on, though it is rocky in most places. Father called it the island of *Eilean a' Cheo...*"

"The Isle of the Mist!" Cruibne smiled. "I had forgotten about that place. Father only mentioned it when I was a young boy."

"I've been there, Cruibne. It's a wonderful, peaceful place, though occasionally they get visits by nomad tribes from the upper Pict region. But still, it is a place you should consider if you need to live in a place that you can enjoy for the rest of your life."

"I will give it serious consideration," he told him. "I'm not positive what the women have in mind. If they ask, I will recommend it and send for your son."

"Thank you, my brother," Susterix said and grabbed his forearm in gratitude.

Meanwhile, Aoife rested, under the direct orders of Osmiach. Piladius spent the rest of the day writing what he had heard and what he had seen. Scathach and Phaedrus wandered off into the forest to work on more training techniques. She still had not mastered her new weapon. Against the legions of Rome, it would prove a very valuable item to have, she considered. And in the hands of a master, as Phaedrus was surely one, it could be devastating to any opponent. But as they neared the patch of thick trees, she turned quickly, catching him off his guard and trapped him with her arms around his body. While he wanted to shake her off by catching her legs in his and tripping her, he let her complete her endeavor. Expecting to be thrown to the ground, he waited to absorb the impact. It never came. Yet what happened next was more surprising than anything he ever expected. She kissed him.

They looked at each other for a long moment, as if wondering what to do next. He could have done anything in that moment and it would have seemed natural to her. And in spite of his respect for her as a warrior, his inner sexuality was aroused by her unexplained effectual display. He had broken the ice before by kissing her without her permission. Nothing was said about it afterwards. Now it was she who kissed him and it felt different, awkward and sort of out of character for Scathach, though he couldn't complain. He had seen her naked before, but that was in training. He didn't have the same reaction this time. In the next instant, he tore open her shirt and threw her, though carefully, to the ground, removing her clothing and tossing them to the side. It was more an act of the beast, he thought later, though there were no regrets from either of them. They smiled and it was as if they gave great thanks to each other for performing a service rather than the sanctity of making love with a wife or a woman about to be married. There was more animal instinct involved on both parts than that of a relationship. Yet when they had set up to train later that day, they both realized that their relationship had taken a step further. Neither was sure what to make of it. For now, they were inclined to let it be and concentrate on the matter at hand; training. Though they were extremely tired shortly after starting their battle lessons.

Aoife was feeling much better when they returned and Osmiach along with Piladius welcomed them back. Phaedrus walked in first, his hair and his shirt disheveled. Scathach was in the same shape. There was an odd feeling of betrayal about them, they sensed and when they put it all together they realized what had occurred. Aoife was instantly jealous. She wanted the Greek to herself, had always wanted him. There was no way Scathach would ever give herself up for the likes of him. Sure, he was slightly handsome and extremely muscular for his size, but her taste for men was far superior. Eventually, she knew he would have given in to her and taken her the way she always wanted. But she also knew she shouldn't make a scene since she was not in her own home. Yet she still had to say something.

"Did we have a nice day?" she said with a wry smile.

Everyone looked at Aoife, knowing now what she knew and attempted to do; ruin the moment.

Scathach didn't care. It was a matter of tension and stress relief. Fine! She played the life-game, but it was with a man of her choosing, not one that would take her involuntarily. And they both were rewarded for it in the fact that they continued their plans to train without speaking of it once. "I had a wonderful day," she commented with an airy tone that simply drove Aoife mad. She had done that once before, a long time ago. It was with Torak about four years back, when they were still very young. Aoife, even then, played the life-game, as it was called, with many boys her age and Torak was one of them. But Torak had eyes for Scathach and as he performed the life-game with Aoife all he could think about was her sister, Scathach. And in the final moment of ecstasy Torak called out Scathach's name rather than Aoife's. She beat him senseless. Just knowing that boys, and now men, wanted Scathach more than they did Aoife drove her insane. And when Scathach heard of the incident with

Torak, she claimed that same innocent airy tone that she did a moment ago. But that was okay with Aoife for now as she thought back in reflection. Torak's brother, Joshuba, was much more the man Torak ever was, she surmised. And he loved her for the woman she was. She sat back and harrumphed, looking out the window. She would have him yet, she knew. Somehow, somewhere, she would have the Greek in her arms, she swore silently. Piladius and Osmiach grinned to each other and ignored the flush yet guilty expression on Phaedrus' face.

The morning brought more news of the war in that Caesar had sustained small skirmishes with Vercingetorix at Gergovia and was now of the impression that he had lowered their esteem enough to depart the area and go back to the Aedui. Susterix was right after all; the war was returning.

After a quick meal of leftover stew Cruibne bade his brother farewell then joined the others who were already packed and ready for the move west.

They had managed the small path between the Rhone River and Mount Jura which was barely enough room for one of them to travel at a time. Eventually, they found a bridge capable of crossing and moved out into the open plains that were already overgrown with tall grasses. Small animals scurried out of their way and Piladius managed to kill a few rabbits with his bow, keeping up with his practices. Scathach was glad to see that. But this time he was forced to cleaning it himself. While he complained about the ripping of the fur away from the meat, he was glad when it was done. Rolling it in a wet cloth, slightly salted, he placed it with the other foodstuffs in the sack and knew they would cook it later on.

Later in the afternoon they made their first contact with a garrison of Roman soldiers who had been camped just east of Augustodunum. This small town lies just thirty miles from the Loire where they had hoped to pick up the trail of Vercingetorix and perhaps join him. But just as they saw the garrison, a centurion of the first watch saw them and sent a patrol to inquire of their business in this somewhat remote area.

"Halt!" the centurion ordered. He was slightly pudgy and round in his dirty, chubby face. He seemed more lethargic and put out by having to travel across the space to question them, but he went about it as professionally as he could. "State your business," he commanded, somewhat haughtily.

"We have no business," Phaedrus answered, attempting to avoid a confrontation, at least until they could tell numbers from what they could see of the camp.

"Then move along to where you came from. There is nothing you need in this direction," he told them.

"I have not traveled this far to return without my just award," Aoife told him sarcastically. "Now if you would be as kind to move your fat carcass from my path, I would like to pass."

"How dare you!" he shouted and raised a hand to order the escort to restrain them and bring them into the camp, but Scathach was already in motion, regardless of the number in their party. In an instant, she went completely red with anger and performed the salmon leap from her horse. Her sword came out from its place at her side and sliced across the air in mid-motion and severed the plump centurion's head from his shoulders. The others retreated slightly, but thought better than their run away from a woman and returned in the next moment only to be cut to pieces by Aoife and Phaedrus together. The last was returning to gather the assistance of others, screaming as he went, when Piladius strung an arrow and let it go, striking the soldier in the middle of the back of his neck. The Roman fell to the earth and twitched forever, the arrow lodged deeply in his spine. On seeing this within the camp, the alarm went up. While they were not many, they surely thought they could overcome the five who approach them, especially since two of them were women.

Scathach regained Khutalk and sprang forth to catch up to the rest who continued to press down on the camp. Aoife was first to strike, surprising them at how fast and accurate she was with her sword. Scathach joined her and keeping her mind filled with all that Mahendra had taught her started with her *kiai* sending her scream out so loudly that everyone, including her own company had to block their ears. It so surprised the Romans that she managed to kill five of them before they realized what had happened. She instantly joined Aoife in dispatching ten more with barely a struggle. They were not as trained as she would have suspected.

Several *sagitarii* from the camp had sent a foray of missiles into the midst of the fight in an attempt to force them to withdraw, but Phaedrus was too busy to move away and continued to slice at everything that moved for him with his pugil. The army garrison fell, man upon man, as they came within reach of his weapon. Not one arrow, not one sword ever came near Phaedrus. He danced among the Roman army like a magician performing tricks for a king, striking awe in all who were able to watch just before they fell. Piladius remained behind with Osmiach keeping an eye out for troop movement along the flank and protecting the rear from ambuscade. Cruibne went directly forward and attacked the *sagitarii* who had gathered in a small triangular formation to launch their arrows. By the time he had dispatched them he had taken two arrows in the upper shoulder, but never stopped fighting until the last archer was dead. When this was accomplished he withdrew the shafts from his flesh and went to assist the others who by that time had already secured the entire camp.

"Are there any more?" Scathach slapped one of the survivors hard across his face.

"You have killed them all. You...a woman!"

"Scathach?" Phaedrus was beside her. She was still red with anger.

"I want them all dead!" she threatened, though her voice had softened. "All of them!" She was furious. Perhaps the rape was more than she could handle, even though she appeared to have recovered from the ordeal. Perhaps it was seeing them close up and killing them that triggered her sense of complete destruction. She didn't wait for the soldier to answer any further. She thrust her sword into his chest and twisted it until the bones crunched under the pressure and went to the next. "How many?" she asked.

"Warrior...we were left behind by Labienus to guard the baggage and to wait for his return from the north. We were only forty men, a physician and a lieutenant whom you have killed," he said and pointed to a body among the dead.

He was young, she noticed, perhaps one of the new recruits who really knew nothing of battle or war. The hair had not even matured enough to grow on his face, the blond fuzz glowing in the sunlight. "Leave!" she told him.

He was stunned. "Leave?" he asked.

"Return to Rome and never come back here. If I ever see your face again I will kill you first and foremost of any and all who would be around you. Do you understand me?" she swore.

He nodded nervously. Phaedrus relaxed. Osmiach smiled in satisfaction. Aoife however, withdrew her knife and cut his throat. Osmiach turned away and gagged while Piladius turned with him and walked away, not willing to see the young boy struggle to hold on to the rest of his fading life.

"You didn't have to do that," Phaedrus said to her as he passed. "Let's leave!" he told them.

"What about the baggage?" Cruibne asked.

"Burn it. Keep what we can find that will benefit us along the way, but burn the rest," Phaedrus answered sourly.

Among them, they shared over a thousand Roman sesteri, scattered the goats, pigs and cattle across the lands and burned all the remaining baggage along with the bodies rotting in the sun. By early evening, they were moving onward to the west in search of Caesar.

"If this is the best they can do..." Aoife shook her head at the ease of winning the fight.

"It was only a small portion of their number, Aoife," Phaedrus assured her. "You will think differently when you encounter them within their legions. Remember, I have fought beside them for a long, long time as an assassin. They taught me much."

Several miles away, near a slow running stream, they made camp. As they settled in they looked to the east and watched the last flickers of a fire burn out above the trees on the horizon. Over a low fire of their own, they cooked the rabbit that Piladius had killed and cleaned earlier then lie down silently to dream. Somehow, they each knew that the war had found them.

CHAPTER XIV

A cold rain woke them in the early morning hours. It started as a slight drizzle and by the time they had gathered their belongings became a torrential downpour. Reluctantly, they were forced to take cover among the largest trees they could find until it passed. Sometime during mid afternoon the black clouds broke and the sun peaked out enough to tell them it was safe to continue on. Fortunately, it was only a few miles ride before they found the fortified settlement of Bibracte. Because of the state of emergent matters taking place within the confines, the entire oppidum was a hush of secrecy and mischief. Emissaries from both armies had sought out Convictolanis who had gathered here with his senate to vote on which side they should support in the war and to solicit this support through bribery and promise. Again, it seemed as though the Aedui would be on the winning side.

They used the coins they had confiscated from their recent battle against the Roman army to purchase quarters and set up their horses in a farmer's stable rather than the common stables of the knights and nobles who were sent to confer with Convictolanis. Most of their baggage they kept with them in their quarters. They purchased meals and new clothes to wear, feeling out of place in their current dress. It was only a matter of time before they would hear of the whereabouts of Vercingetorix and they would join him. But there was so much conversation in the way of choosing sides. According to Scathach and her small group, there really was no side to choose from. Caesar would perish with his entire Roman army. That was their goal; that was their intent. What other side was there? But listening to the people gathered here brought cause for alarm. They were indeed treacherous. The Celts, they realized, could not be trusted. It was almost the same situation Mahendra was walking into with the Parthian king. There was no one to trust. Friend or foe could kill him and no one would question the reason. The same applied here. If the Celts did not come together in this, they would surely lose, Scathach knew, no matter what side they were on.

In the dining hall of the place they had purchased quarters, Piladius sat with Osmiach searching among the crowd for travelers like themselves. There were many and they were all drinking heavily of the Bibracte ale. And they were of various tongues, he noticed. He understood most of them, though he had to pay closer attention to grasp the location of their dialect. He was satisfied that he had not forgotten his art in speaking, or understanding, many languages. But then he heard something familiar. Actually, it was someone whose voice he recognized. He sat straight up, stiff in his back like a cock searching for a hen, and scanned the room in every direction.

"What is it, Piladius," Osmiach asked though he didn't seem alarmed.

"I know that voice," he said.

Osmiach laughed. "There are lots of voices."

"No, no...there!" he stopped looking, pointed and stood. "Vlad!" he called out.

An older man, thin and slightly balding turned to him and stared. After several seconds of searching his mind for recollection, his features shifted, brightening. "Can it be?" he questioned then smiled. "By the gods!" he exclaimed and stood to meet him. "Piladius, my boy!" they embraced.

"It has been a long time, Vlad," Piladius commented while still shaking the man's forearm sternly. "How have you been?"

"I've been better. I finally got to where I can see a bit of the profits,"

"Bad year?" Piladius questioned, excited to see a familiar face among the rabble.

"No, a good one. Last year was terrible."

"Sorry, I didn't know. What happened?"

The elder looked at him in surprise. His features shifted again, this time more solemn. "You haven't heard then?"

Piladius was still smiling, still glad to see his old friend, Vlad. Of all the traders his father had carried along, Vlad was perhaps the one he enjoyed most. He had several sons of his own, but couldn't seem to teach them the art of bartering. Eventually, he attempted to have Piladius teach them in the ways of a scholar, to educate them at least. That didn't seem to work out either. But he always treated Piladius with a lot more respect than everyone else did in the caravan of traders and always seemed to go out of his way to say hello at least once, sometimes twice, daily. Somehow he must have realized the loneliness Piladius experienced on his long travels across the many trading routes and felt a bit of the solitude also for his sons never confided in him—not even with a lowly good morning. He always made a point to simply stop by Piladius' cart. But now he maintained a slightly worried look.

"Heard?" Piladius asked shaking his head.

"The attack. Two years ago. Right after you left the caravan," he said, attempting to give some hint of knowledge Piladius should have of the event.

"I don't know of anything. What are you talking about?" he asked though he continued to smile ignorantly.

"Your father, Aram. The Xiongnu…they returned after those savages departed, taking you with them. They realized that Aram had lied to them and…"

"Father? They killed my father!"

Vlad lowered his head and tried to stare away from him, embarrassed perhaps for surviving when the taskmaster did not. He didn't realize the younger man had no knowledge of the attack. Two years had passed and never did he hear a word about what had happened. All this time he thought his father was performing his skill well across the continent. He was hoping to meet him again someday, even if he had to seek him out alone: to show him what kind of man he had turned out to be. And then to find out like this…

"I don't know what to tell you, Piladius. I lost my entire family. I only lived because I was away from the camp, gathering water after we replaced the wheel on my wagon. My sons were too lazy to get it for me so as usual I did the chore myself. Regrettably, they were all dead by the time I returned."

"Did my father suffer?"

"I'm sure it was quick. They took every head in the caravan with them. When they departed, they had left the bodies scattered everywhere for the wilds of the forests. I gathered them together and after several hours, burned the remains. I thought it was the right thing to do. I'm sorry lad. I wish we could have met again on better roads."

"What about their wares? Did they take those also?" Piladius asked, remembering several items he thought he would like to have from the back of his father's wagon.

"Gone…horse, cart and baggage," Vlad told him. "The Xiongnu took all of it."

Depressed, Piladius shook his head. "I'm glad you made it safely, Vlad. But why are you here?" He had to change the subject. The news of his father's death hurt, but he wasn't going to dwell on it to the point of embarrassing himself in front of this lot. His father would want him to move on, he knew.

"The war…" he said and sighed complaint. "After I departed the caravan I moved back to the sea where we always start our journey. I signed on as a hand until I saved enough money to buy my own wagon and begin again. We were trading fine just north of here when that convict—as we call him—the new magistrate took control of all trade wagons and supplies for the purpose of carrying provisions and arms to whomever. I just bought that wagon too! That's why I'm here. I can't go anywhere until I raise enough money to buy another wagon so I can begin trading again. And I can't buy a wagon because the magistrate has taken them all as property of the state. There's no telling how long I'll have to wait here."

"Why can't you leave?"

"On what?"

"They took the horse too?"

"They took everything! That's why most of these men are here. And they've got families as well. They're stranded!"

"I'm sorry, my friend. You're more than welcome to join us," he said and pointed to the table where Osmiach watched the conversation.

"Ah…my boy. I would enjoy that greatly, but I cannot. I must go my own way now. The days of Aram are gone from me as a long lost memory and I could not stand to see any more sorrow in my life. Your father was a good man to me and treated my family extremely fair, more so, I suspect, than others. It is great to see you, but I must turn away from your offer, though I do admit, you have changed a great deal. You are much broader in shoulder and perhaps a little taller. Where are your scholarly robes now?" he chuckled slightly.

Piladius smiled at the other's observance of his stature. "They too are a long lost memory. I try to keep to my studies when I can, but I have become quite a good hunter and, regrettably, I have killed."

"You! Piladius, son of Aram! I don't believe it. How can that be?" he laughed with a roar, but understood the need to protect ones self in times such as these.

"Rome!" he answered sourly. "I have found a new family."

Vlad looked at him carefully. "In the Sarmatian women?"

"They have taught me much, Vlad. And to be honest, I am grateful. I know now that I can make it on my own if I have to."

"Then I am glad for you."

The door opened and three men walked in, directly to Vlad. "We have found one, but we must leave now and the cost is double," the one in the middle said in a whisper.

He looked to Piladius sadly. "I must go. I may not get another chance. They have found a wagon to take us back to the sea. I will not be back this way again. I can see why your father stayed away all these years," he smiled at Aram's insight all those years ago when he scoffed at the thought of trading with Celts. Had Vlad known what life was like here and how the state works against its people, he never would have come himself. But hearing of the new lands progressing into bigger cities always draws the hungry trader. It was more trap than treasure, Vlad concluded.

"May luck be with you in your travels, my friend," Piladius told him and embraced the older man once more. He turned then and walked back to his table. Osmiach remained quiet when he arrived.

It was night when they finally got news that Vercingetorix was camped nearby. Scouts and spies were everywhere. Through the secret chains of messengers scattered throughout Bibracte, they were finally informed as to the exact location. But they would have to be escorted. Going to Vercingetorix alone would only bring disaster.

Early in the morning, long before light came forth they gathered their things and moved quietly away from the oppidum. The guards thought it of no consequence since travelers were moving in and out all the time. A small group like this with two of them being women would pose no threat to anyone. They passed without confrontation and made haste for the wooded lands slightly southwest near the Loire River. When they were within sight, a trumpet-like sound from a *caryx* echoed through the valley and they stopped where they were until someone came out to greet them.

"State your business," said a very tall man of excessive muscle. He was naked from the waist up and his stomach rippled like water along a riverbank. His biceps were the size of tree trunks and flexed with every word he spoke, daring any of them to attempt trickery. Aoife's eyes were wide with delight. Scathach was leery, though she thought she had seen him somewhere before. An escort of seven men accompanied him. Each of them wore a helmet of bronze with designs impressed around the brim. One had a pair of horns protruding from the side, making him look cattle-like.

"They seek the Arvernian," announced the messenger who had delivered them here.

"On what matter?" he asked, keeping his eyes alert and watching all around them for signs of foul play.

"We wish to join him," Phaedrus said and moved slightly forward. "We have battled Romans every step of the way, from the Black Sea to the lands of Gaul. We cannot defeat them all unless we are united with the Arvernian."

The huge man laughed. "Women?" he laughed openly. "What good are they in battle?"

Aoife's delighted smile went away. No one speaks of a Sarmatian warrior in that tone. And Scathach was of the same opinion. Without regard for anyone about her, she stretched forward, pulled out her pugil—with the blades kept inside—and swung at the big figure waiting for a response on his horse. He was taken by surprise at the quick attempt, but then she burst forward, slamming Khutalk into his horse and jumped behind him. Her sword suddenly tightened at his throat. A second later the blades extended on both ends of the pugil daring his escort to try to remove her. "You have difficulty with women among you?" Scathach asked.

"Sarmatian warriors?" he asked though he swallowed hard.

"Very good. Perhaps now we can meet the Arvernian?" she asked.

"We have heard of you. You'll have to forgive my rudeness, but women as beautiful as you do not seem the type for battle."

"And what type of woman is right for battle?" she asked him.

"There is only one woman who is right for battle. She is the mother of all women warriors. She has been the Celtic Goddess that all young women seek to become when they reach the age. But none have ever compared."

"And this goddess' name?"

He harrumphed. "Why…Scathach of course."

She released him and jumped to the ground. "Where have you heard this name?"

"My dear woman, it is a name known throughout all Gaul. Scathach is the name of the one true goddess who shall be feared by all in battle. Everyone knows her name here. Why do you ask?"

She delayed answering. Could her father have known this name before he gave it to her just before she departed? She understood that the name came to him in a dream…perhaps not. But then, Mahendra had said that she would be known as '*she who strikes fear*'. Could he have known as well? She became confused. "We must see the Arvernian," she told him then.

"Then follow me and I will lead you to him."

She mounted Khutalk and followed through the thick woods until they came into a large campsite where thousands of men had pitched shelters of whatever materials they had available; clothes, furs, blankets, shrubs. Small fires had been lit every thirty paces or so and around these men gathered to cook their meat and talk of heroes. When Scathach and

Aoife entered the camp a scream of excitement went out for there were no women among them and the only ones who ever came into the camp were used as whores before they were sent back to the towns they had been taken from. But whoever found these beauties had surely paid a good price and the men knew it. They clapped and whistled and cheered as they passed through the campsite. While Phaedrus and Piladius grew angry, Scathach and Aoife became slightly worried. Were these barbarians any better than the Romans who had taken advantage of them in Vindobona? Not likely, they both thought, though they did not speak of it, ever. Osmiach and Cruibne followed without ever knowing there was a growing tension in all their stomachs.

When they reached the tent where Vercingetorix was quartered, they left their horse and baggage then entered. Though the women kept their swords at their side, Phaedrus and Scathach both entered with a pugil in their hands, using them more as a staff than portraying them as a weapon. "Sir," the large fellow interrupted the other's conversation with his generals. It had become an end of day ritual for him to consult with all his generals since the war was no longer in his favor. Keeping informed of all troop movement and the whereabouts of all scout and spy activities and locations was essential in planning his next move.

"What is it?" he asked and turned to see who it was that had interrupted him. When he spotted Scathach and Aoife, he smiled. The obvious came to their minds and Scathach, as much as she wanted to join and assist him in his endeavor to conquer the Roman armies invading Gaul, nearly ran to him and cut off his head. "Leave me," he said at once to his senior officers. They departed without speaking a word, though each spied the women in passing. "What have you brought me this time?" his eyes beamed with pleasure and he absently licked his lips.

"Sire," he brought the other's attention to him before he could embarrass himself. "They are Sarmatian warriors and they wish to join us in our fight," he said, hoping he would understand.

"Fight? These women wish to fight? How can such beauty," and he stood and walked to them, around them, studying them both. "How can such beauty be cast to the foul ways of war? There are so many other ways a woman can be made of good use…" and he ran the back of his hand across Aoife's cheek.

Scathach went red and her flesh began to swell. Piladius and Phaedrus knew what would happen next. Before it did, Piladius, for all his guts and honor, stood past them and spoke out. "Sire! Please," he pleaded. "They have traveled a long way to meet with you. If your worship wishes them for other amusement than that for which they have come, I must inform him that these women will surely die this night."

Vercingetorix was as large as the man who had brought them into the camp. His hair was blonde and had natural curls that kept his aging features boyish, though his body was most definitely that of a grown man. His eyes were solid blue and piercing, his nose long and straight like that of Phaedrus. His brows were not as bushy as those of the Celts they had seen along the way, but he was one of them nonetheless. His hands were huge and strong, callused and rough from years of fighting Romans. He looked at Piladius unconcerned, unafraid.

"Why will they die?"

"Sire," he spoke rapidly, before he lost his nerve. "They have been taken advantage of by Roman soldiers and they have killed many of them in retribution. For your worship to speak of them in such a fashion as they have already been subjected, I fear they will take your worship's head and those of every man here, just for thinking of them in that manner. They will then take on your worship's entire army from within the camp's center. While the numbers of your men may make them weary, and eventually cause their death, I fear most of your army will be laid waste and the battle for Gaul ended long before you ever see another Roman soldier," he said as diplomatically as he could.

Vercingetorix looked at the tall man who had led them here. "Who are these people and why have you brought them to me?" he shouted, angry now that his thought of being pleased by a beautiful woman was destroyed, and then also by the insolence of the adjudicating speaker.

"Sir, they are Sarmatian warriors. I know not their names, but trust them to be an asset for our side, sir. I have seen them fight," he said with experience.

"Women?" he screamed. "Fighting with our men?"

It was Aoife who stood forward then, though she spoke to Scathach and Phaedrus rather than to Vercingetorix. "This is the man we came to fight for? This is the man who we thought was king of Gaul, and the man who could bring us just reward for our troubles against the Romans. Sister! He is no more the swine we roast at our *kurgan* festival in the Sayan. I say we leave now, sister! We would have more success on our own," she said then spit on the ground.

"How dare you!" Vercingetorix stepped forward and without waiting for her to turn about, slapped Aoife across her face, sending her to the dirt. She was back on her feet instantly.

Scathach and Phaedrus were both in motion, crouching and moving to find space.

"Guards!" Vercingetorix hollered, though they were already moving from behind and in front of them. "Lucterius!" he called to the tall, muscular man who had brought them hither.

Lucterius backed away and Vercingetorix squinted with alarm. Was he suddenly traitor? Why was he backing away? Was this a trap? Surely not from Lucterius…he was the most trusted soldier in his entire army. So why would he move away?

Three guards burst forth into the entrance with spears pointed at them while four more came from the place where Vercingetorix was holding conference with his generals. Each held his spear at an angle ready to pierce their chest and find a warm heart. Vercingetorix moved away. "Take them and kill them all!" he ordered. "Lucterius! You stay with me!" he barked.

Five more soldiers came into the tent with swords and the three already at the entrance were pressing down on them. There was no room for pugils inside, not without hitting Aoife and Piladius and Cruibne and Osmiach, they realized.

"Scathach!" Phaedrus called to her.

She already knew. If they were going to live they would need more room and the only way to do that was… "Lay down," she ordered them quickly, ready to strike. A split second later the blades snapped from the ends of the pugil. The four without pugils fell to the earth and lay with their eyes watching for a slashing weapon above their head.

"Wait!" Vercingetorix bellowed as loudly as he could. All motion stopped in an instant and all eyes went to him.

"What did you call her?" he asked Phaedrus, his eyes round and searching.

"I called her by her name...Scathach!" he said with an impending tone.

Vercingetorix looked to Lucterius who smiled knowingly. "Can it be?" he asked his most trusted man in the entire kingdom.

"I don't know about her name, sir, but she has a talent that I have never seen in any woman. If they can kill Roman soldiers as quickly as they nearly took my head, I am willing to have them on my side."

"But...women? Fighting alongside our men? There will be mutinous times, Lucterius. Look at them!"

Scathach took a step forward, determined. Vercingetorix put up his hand to her. "No. Not your ability to fight, warrior...your beauty. My men will see you as an idol of lust. Have I not just done the same? It was not my intention to insult you, but your beauty exceeds that which our sore eyes are used to seeing, yet long for. Please forgive my harsh approach, I meant no insult to you. Pleasures of the flesh are not common for any of my men," he said sadly, knowing that most of the wives and families and loved ones had been killed or were taken as slaves or traded to other states as hostage.

They relaxed their arms and those on the ground stood and brushed themselves off. "Our desire was only to join your forces and assist in killing Caesar and his army."

"Why do you have such hate for them?" he sensed.

"Because they have destroyed my village and have taken our father Brona, his head, as trophy to their city in Rome as proof of victory over the Sarmatian warriors." Scathach told him.

"I can see your reasons. But they are many while we are few. I cannot gather the states to commit to me. They fear the results of revolt because they have no vision of future. Therefore they hide and offer good tidings, but support us not. I fear I am alone in this, with only a few thousand of my countrymen to aid in the battle. It is uncommon for outsiders to offer help in this matter." He smiled in gratitude and welcomed them to sit around a table where his generals had been talking with him earlier. With a swishing hand in the air, he dismissed the guards around the room.

After much discussion of the war and the tactics employed to get them to this point, it was decided that the small group would remain with Lucterius. Being of exceptional skill in horsemanship they would be better suited as mounted cavalry for short skirmishes to keep the Romans away from food supplies and from foraging in the forests along their routes. Most of the cities in the area had already been burned, the grain and corn collected and stored in wagons to feed the army and the remainder burned or thrown into the river. Livestock was either confiscated or killed so the Romans would have nothing to eat, setting their sights on deprivation and starvation to make them weak—though this had not stopped them as yet. Without the support of the Aedui however, it all seemed impossible, not because the Aedui were great fighters, but because the states believed that the Aedui were the breaking point in the war. All else had practically been destroyed. That was why they came to this place. And Caesar too was nearby with his entire army, waiting for them.

CHAPTER XV

Negotiations were unsuccessful in Bibracte and Vercingetorix could feel his grip on the war loosening. He was losing control of his men as well and more of them deserted daily, frightened by the lack of support and the fact that they had gained nothing in the war as of yet. He had already lost several hundred of them in Gergovia for the same reason. The only way to defeat Caesar was for Gaul to unite completely and that wasn't happening fast enough. Though non-participants of war, the Druids too had declined to add support whether through divine sacrifice or through verbal praise of encouragement for fellow countrymen. The states were reluctant to release more hostages to him. They had refused him arms and now they had refused him horse. What he had was all he would get. The only option available at this point was to force an all out battle between Caesar and that of all Gaul. He was thrust into a decision he didn't want to make without the backing of the states yet he knew was necessary for all of them. One way or the other it would have to end.

After five weeks in camp, they became restless. Scouts and spies came and went constantly. Irritation and annoyance was common among the men and fights broke out more often, sometimes resulting in the death of one or more of them. But they had learned in this time that the northern legions under Labienus had moved back to the south and were bordering Agendicum, a city belonging to the Senones. Caesar with his two legions had crossed the Allier then moved north along the Loire and had mirrored Vercingetorix's army, harassing them with short attacks of missiles and cavalry, though Emporedirix had led similar skirmishes for Vercingetorix on the east side of the river to keep the Romans from pushing forth. Two more legions were observed moving in from the east, most likely with Arnasticus in their midst, and seeking to join their commander, Caius Trebonius, who had also moved in from the north with Labienus. Still, Convictolanis and the Aedui refused to support him and time was growing short. Vercingetorix realized this and called for his staff to join him in his quarters.

Lucterius, it was determined, would send small units to plead their cause to the ends of Gaul in a final attempt to secure their support. Together there would be fifteen thousand cavalry on this march. Scathach, Aoife, Phaedrus, Piladius, Cruibne, and Osmiach would join Lucterius. The others would be broken down by rank and sent in different directions. They were given another three weeks to return. They had set their place to meet at a place called Alesia, which was some fifty miles northeast of where they had been camped. This place, Vercingetorix told them in the meeting, will determine the fate of us all in Gaul. Upon receiving these orders, Vercingetorix departed his quarters and gathered his troops about him.

"Countrymen...brothers!" he shouted. "Tomorrow we march to Alesia!"

It was as if a great thunder roared from the clear, open sky as the mass of warriors cheered in a sigh of relief. To them it was war or peace and they knew peace had not come to them yet. And without peace there was nothing else but war and it was best to get it done with. Though Scathach was already of the assumption that Celts loved to argue and fight no matter what the occasion, even among their own.

Before daylight, the cavalry moved out in their various assigned directions. The instructions for each party were clear: they would return in three weeks time to meet at Alesia with as many infantry and cavalry as possible. By then there was great hope that all of Gaul would be ready to help and if so, win!

The days started out well, with sunshine greeting them each day and only scattered thunderstorms and showers on occasion. Not once had they seen a sign of Roman movement, though they had passed twenty or so towns that were burned to the ground and double that in the number of villages that were completely destroyed. The populations had moved to the larger cities and it was harder to coerce them into believing that Gaul could win the war against the multitude of Roman soldiers and the skill they possessed in battle. But there were those who had been ready for them to arrive, waiting for the right time to revolt and take up the challenge to join Vercingetorix. By the time three weeks had passed the fifteen thousand cavalry managed to collect close to a hundred and fifty thousand countrymen to join them. From the ends of Gaul they marched to Alesia.

Alesia, one of the most beautiful of all the cities in Gaul, was fortified by double walls of brick and mortar and reinforced by timbers cemented into the breastworks already in place. Ramparts had been built of the earth and made for viewing and planning strategies in the coming battle. The gates had been reinforced for intrusion by battering rams while pitch and tallow were prepared and kept in constant supply along the walls and at the parapets. And behind the walls of the great city, Vercingetorix waited with his hundred thousand men. The elderly and the women and children had given themselves up just two weeks earlier. For lack of food they sought out the Romans for help, but rather found themselves turned away to starve or return to the city. Many refused either and died along the walls to the once great city. Vercingetorix felt for them in their time of need, but he knew this was his time. He had enough food to supply his army for one month prior to achieving the city before they would have to venture forth and gather provisions from the other states. That was before Caesar came along and surrounded them with deadly trenches and traps and ambuscade. But if the employment of his cavalry were successful, there would be no need to venture forth except to join them in defeating Caesar. Knowing the end of the third week was up he kept the entire army alert and ready for battle at a moment's notice.

On the evening of the last day, Lucterius had met his first obstruction since setting out for recruits. And he was not the only one to be confronted by it. Litavicus joined him at the edge of the trench where they studied it together.

"I've been here for two days," Litavicus told him. "It completely encircles the entire city for ten miles. They have forked spikes hidden everywhere in the sides and along the bottom. And if you succeed in crossing this trench there is another on the other side of it that they have filled with water. Both are fifteen paces wide and nearly impossible to cross."

"Where is Caesar?" Lucterius asked him.

Litavicus pointed. "Out there, laughing at us. We have lost two hundred horse and three times that in men on our first attempt last night on the north side. They have sealed themselves inside the circle and have decided to wait until Vercingetorix starves his men into surrender. That is why we have been trying to break through the barricades."

"How far has anyone made it?" Lucterius asked.

"One scout has made it back to us, but barely. I will take you to him."

Even though there seemed to be dark days ahead, Lucterius was surprised to see the number of men who had been gathered to support Vercingetorix. His eyes sparkled in the moonlight at the sight of them huddled around fires, waiting for any word from the men trapped inside the city. Litavicus led him to a location where a physician was busy at work removing limbs from those who had been injured in last night's attempt. Disease had set into the wounds and he hacked away like a mad man to remove it quickly. The victim screamed mercilessly just before passing out from the serious amount of pain he had to endure. Once the limb was removed, another Celt cauterized the severed opening with a flat sheet of iron that stunk of burned human flesh, causing those close by to gag in response.

"Here," said Litavicus.

Lucterius walked to the young warrior. He smiled despite his missing forearm. "Litavicus says you have been to the city?"

"I tried, sir," he responded. He couldn't have been more than sixteen years old.

"Tell me what you saw there."

"I had to crawl into the first trench on the outer banks of their defenses. It is perhaps fifteen paces wide and the walls are studded with spikes of wood. After crossing this there is another of equal distance, only this one is filled with water. I was forced to swim through this trench to the other side. Upon reaching the bank of the inner circle I was forced to find my way around traps covered in branches where they had dug holes into the earth and planted stakes on the bottom for our men to fall into. After this they have secured *stimuli* to blocks of wood where the iron barbs face outward, digging into our feet or that of our horse. Beyond this is another trench of forked branches that leads to a palisaded rampart perhaps twenty or thirty hands high with a breastwork of earth studded with more forked branches. I had to twist and turn to get by these safely. Once around this, I found that towers had been erected every four hundred paces of which twenty or so Romans stood watch. Hundreds of other Romans huddled around these towers and in the general vicinity. In the middle of the night, I crossed this line hoping to see the end of their devices to keep us away, but discovered even more dangers. On the other side of the rampart there are three more trenches of which the middle one is again filled with water. I believe it could be approximately a thousand paces between the trench filled with water and the last trench leading to the city. This is where the remaining Roman soldiers wait for us. There are thousands of them scattered in every direction. The final trench I estimate to be about twenty paces wide. It too is filled with forked branches, sir."

All this time Lucterius listened and imagined the difficulty anyone would have forging the defenses of the Roman army. Caesar had planned his maneuver well, though in three week's time it was amazing what he had accomplished. "Tell me," he said after considering the entire story. "How did you manage to get all the way back here, without continuing on into the city?"

He looked to Litavicus, then back to Lucterius. "I made it to the wall, sir. But I did not know the name of my commander. The warriors at the gates did not know my senior officer by his name when I gave it. Therefore they mistook me for a spy and sent a volley of arrows at my body. They pierced my arm with a missile from atop the city wall. I ran away as fast as I could and just barely made it here with my life," he said, though it was evident he was not angry.

"You have served your brothers well," he said and patted him hard on the shoulder. The impact made the younger man wince, but he accepted the thanks and smiled just the same.

G. H. LAUZIERE

"What do you think?" asked Litavicus.

Lucterius shook his head in contemplation. "I don't know. How many have returned?"

"You are the last. Most of the others returned yesterday and some last night."

"We have to get word to Vercingetorix inside the city. We can't get to the walls without running into the pits or getting cut down by *sagitarii* mounted on top of those towers. We can't get our horse beyond the trenches unless we release the water and clear a path to the rampart...." There was too much to consider and he continued to weigh it all as he spoke, yet the more he considered the situation, the more he shook his head at the dangers involved. Caesar was truly a great strategist in this endeavor. But the Celts would pull it together. They had to. "Gather the others. We will meet at midnight to discuss our pursuit."

While Lucterius met with Litavicus, Scathach pulled Phaedrus aside. She had been quiet the last couple of weeks and kept to herself. There were plenty of things for them all to do in order to acquire the support of the outside states, but she was absent from them often: sometimes in the morning, sometimes in the early evening. Returning to the place where they were to meet after three week's time allowed her the opportunity to speak with him freely, now that all the warriors of Gaul had been collected for a final revolt.

"Phaedrus," she said as they sat alone beside a low cooking fire. "I am with child," she told him dryly.

Nothing more was said. Complete silence followed her statement. It might as well have been told on top of the highest mountain or beneath the deepest sea. While she knew he had heard her, the words may as well have fallen on deaf ears. The warm night air blew in light breezes, rustling the leaves and thin branches of the surrounding trees. The moon cast dark shadows over the land and distant voices could be heard singing traditional Celtic songs of worship and praise.

"The choice is yours," he finally answered. She understood. He had given her his blessing to commit to battle or give it up and move away from the war to have the child. But there was never any doubt between them as to the father of the child. They had played the life-game only once. And this was the result of that communion.

"What of your sister?" he asked after several moments went by in silence.

"I have been thinking of exactly that," she answered. "She will not be pleased. I will tell her when I return to the camp," Scathach told him. "I only wanted to hear your objections before I did so."

It was after midnight when Lucterius came back to them. His meeting with the Celtic chiefs had unified a plan to assist the Arvernian. When the strategy was laid out everyone understood and prepared immediately. The attack would come soon and there was much earth and wood to be gathered. Every soldier, to include the wounded, was required to pick his share of wood, stone and earth to throw into the trench while a second crew forged the first and drained the second of its waters into the fields. Alternate trenches had already been made to take the water away from the site so it would not fill in the first trench. And it would have to be done quickly. At his command they would attack beyond this and attempt the rampart. The noise of the attack, he suggested, has to be so significant that Vercingetorix will come to assist from inside the city. It is the only way he will know the attack is coming. Together we will unite to confuse our enemy and bring an end of this siege.

"You whore!" Aoife swore at her after Lucterius left and they had a moment alone. "How dare you do this to me?" She looked at Phaedrus then. "It should have been mine!" she screamed.

"Aoife," he tried to console her. "You are beautiful, but you are not the woman I wanted. Scathach has always been the one. You have to know that."

"I don't have to know anything. Scathach has always been first. Scathach has always led the important battles. Scathach was always first in father's eyes. Always it was Scathach for everything. I just knew that I would be the first to have a child."

"But you almost did have a child," he told her. "And you were angry about it."

"Yes! But the child was from the blood of a pig! I wanted a child of my own from my own man of choosing."

"Aoife," Scathach said as softly as she could. "You have had many opportunities. You've played the life-game so many times before. I thought long ago that you would have a child before me."

"I guess that didn't happen! Did it, sister!" she scoffed and stomped away angrily. "And stay away from me! Both of you!" she shouted before she was out of sight.

When the bridge of stone, earth and wood was made ready, the *caryx* sounded and the water was suddenly let loose from the second trench. The moment it began to recede, an alarm went up from the Roman soldiers assigned to watch it. Fires ignited in every direction for better viewing and shadows ran hither from within the confines of the circles searching for the breach. At that moment Scathach discovered that there were twenty bridges formed along the outer circle by the Celts and all finished at the same time. With the earthen works in place, they now waited for the final signal, the loud blowing of the *caryx*, before initiating the attack. At the great sound of the trumpet-like horn, a yell went out over the land from a hundred and fifty thousand voices that woke the city and claimed triumph for all of Gaul. The infantry pushed ahead and broke the first two circles. But then it was Rome who woke up and the beast that lay sleeping soundly on the palisade and high above in the towers slung its mighty tail out at the Celts and nearly paralyzed them with her biting teeth.

Scathach had seen battles before. She had fought many brave warriors and beaten each of them. She had seen blood, drawn blood and tasted blood. She had seen men on chariots and on horse and on foot and never took the time to look into their eyes or their hearts as they went to their death. To her, battle was a way of life. You fight and you die. There was nothing else. But atop her golden, Turanian horse, Khutalk, she watched thousands march to their death in a matter of minutes. If the soul of a man had a place to go and one could watch it leave the body as a flash of light in that final moment the sky would have rained daylight over them all in that fight. The Celtic archers, of which there were nearly thirty thousand, sprayed a shower of missiles at the towers and along the palisaded rampart. Each fired exactly seven times as the infantry moved across the trenches and broke forth on the open land leading to the rampart. A hundred more fell victim to the holes dug into the earth, impaling themselves on the stakes and a hundred after them fell prey to the *stimuli*. The towers above the rampart then came to life and Roman missiles flew into the air in a shower that no one could possibly have lived through. But bodies lifted themselves from the ground and stood above those who had fallen to their death to push on in force. Once they were again on their way, Lucterius commanded the cavalry to follow. Never, in her life, had Scathach ever seen a war such as this. Fierce, fast and furious, the Celts ran to their deaths without any regard for their life. And while thousands died, not one of them came in contact with the enemy. This was not a war, she realized. There is no honor in throwing yourself in front of an arrow without knowing who let it fly. At this she was furious and she went red with anger.

Lucterius brushed passed her. "Attack!" he shouted and forty thousand horses moved for the trenches. Among them were Aoife, Phaedrus, Cruibne and Scathach.

Another *caryx* sounded inside the city and a cheer went up as Vercingetorix came forth with his cavalry from the gates of the city. He was followed by several thousand infantry, each yelling as he went forth. They skirted the first trench with minor losses, but found the second more difficult with the number of missiles being cast at them. Not only did the arrows fly from the *sagitarii* but the catapults and the scorpions too came to life, battering them with a relentless hail of missiles, pitch, tallow and large balls of fire. And then there were the *lancearii* who waited on the other side of the bank with their spears aimed and ready. When the horses neared the bank, they cast these at the Arvernian and drove him away long before he ever made land. Vercingetorix realized the attempt was failing, but he would not allow for failure. There was no other time to make preparations. It had to be done now. He screamed at them to push on and turned to lead them fast enough to drive across and make land among the hail of spears and arrows and fire. The attack then went on foot.

Scathach lost track of the others among those moving into battle. The rampart was impassable but the multitude ran and pushed and fought to reach it. It was strongly fortified and the enemy hailed them with everything they had and the number of Celts on the attack fell drastically.

Still not one enemy was in sight, and yet the bodies fell everywhere. She was lost to an invisible army, though her anger and determination forced her to push on. She could feel the heat of her body prickling on her flesh as it grew redder, her inner-rage building. Still, there was no enemy to fight. Mahendra had given her all these skills and she ran them all through her mind: the juggling, the balance on the rope, the breathing, the pole, the stretching and bending and all the ironwork. All of it was used as lessons to prepare for this moment. And now that she was here, none of it was of any use! Useless! Then it happened....

From the middle of the open land between the palisaded rampart and the outer circles, Lucterius fell. A missile had struck him in the throat and he disappeared among the number of bodies that continued to fall. A moment later, the inevitable came.

"Retreat!" a voice sounded from behind them. "Retreat!" he screamed again and thousands fell back to the trenches and into the woods beyond.

Vercingetorix, upon hearing this call, took flight and led his cavalry back into the city, but with a great loss of his own men.

Scathach raced for the trench and crossed the bridge of earthwork where she stopped, turned and waited at the edge of the forest for those in her party. Oddly, she feared for them. But that was not the only thing she feared. Looking back at the devastation displayed on the open land where the flames of the Roman fires burned brightly, were thousands upon thousands of Celts. Everywhere there was death. And among them were those who were dying or seriously wounded. They screamed for help while archers from high atop the towers picked them off one at a time in a counting game. She could hear them laughing each time they struck another and killed him while he tried to crawl away to freedom. And then they started to pick off those who tried to flee beyond the trenches and escape into for forest.

"Scathach," a whisper fell upon her ear. "We have to move back. They can still get us from here," Phaedrus told her. She could sense the disappointment and fear that fell heavily on his heart as well. This was her whole reason for coming here: to fight beside the Arvernian, to kill the Roman legions, to rid the world of Caesar. Now that it was over, there was nothing left to do. The battle was lost. They had thrown their lives away for no reason. The worst, she realized, is that the number of Celts against the Roman soldiers were far superior. It should have been an easy matter to conquer them. But Caesar's plan had worked. And now he had won. The Celts marched away, saddened by it all, back to their homes. There would be no more chances.

Suddenly Scathach folded her head to her chest and cried.

CHAPTER XVI

The tears continued to flow for a long time. It was over, done. The entire battle lasted less than two hours and it was finished. By the thousands, the Celts departed with their baggage and their horse and their personal belongings and moved back to their homes in the far corners of Gaul. They had lost.

The sun rose on the horizon and she watched steadily onward across the opaque battlefield. On the palisaded rampart she finally saw him…the man she had waited so long to see. With his hair shimmering in the new sunlight, he marched up and down the rampart mounted on his white stallion and wearing a bright red mantle. The rays of sunlight beat upon his golden corslet sending flashes of brilliant light out over the land for all to see. He had won and now he mocked them by his supreme presence. It was all Scathach could do to keep her from releasing an arrow from this distance, but for what purpose? It was finished.

The soft summer breezes blew from the west, off the ocean that lay hundreds of miles away and the scent of death and decay had already taken to the air. She watched as buzzards claimed the fields to pick at the flesh of the dead while half a dozen wolves had moved over the trenches to join them in the great feast. On the rampart, the Romans had gathered their dead and collected them together in one place. No one went to remove the Celts. There were too many of them and the hazards displayed over the trenches and the lands were still there. The dead would remain for the wilds to clean and carry away…or to rot, stinking in the earth.

"It is a terrible sight," said a man beside her. She had seen him twice since she had come here. The first time was in conference with Vercingetorix just before leaving to gather the infantry three weeks ago and then last night on the battlefield beside Lucterius. Emporedirix climbed from his horse and came beside her to look out over the trenches. He was tall and strong. His very nature showed he was bred for politics. He carried his mantle over his forearm, his corslet loose and ready to be removed. His helmet of bronze was tilted back from his brow and his hands were folded over his chest. She looked at him…carefully. There was something familiar about him, but she couldn't tell exactly what.

"This is not what I expected to see," she told him and brought her eyes back to the sight of the battlefield.

"Nor I, dear woman. It is a pity I didn't get to see you fight," he attempted to smile, but it didn't happen. "I have heard great things about you and your talent as a warrior."

"I only wish I could have used them on him," she pointed to the figure of Caesar moving along the palisade, barking orders to his senior officers.

"I fear we have lost it all," he said and then a tear fell from his eye as well.

Scathach looked at him, saddened by it all. She had come so far to be here. He removed his helmet and let his hair fall, long and curly, while he wiped the sweat from his forehead. Then he lowered his head and said a lowly prayer for the lifeless forms cast away before him while the tears continued to flow. He had given up, she could see. He was finished. He was….

"You!" Scathach nearly frightened him.

"What?" he asked snapping his head up. He searched about dangerously.

"I have seen you…in my…my," she couldn't tell him. No one was supposed to know about the stone. But here he was. Her vision had come true in a flash of recognition.

"What are you talking about, woman?" he was nervous.

"I have seen this in a vision," she told him.

"In a dream?" he asked.

She gave it a moment. "Yes. In this exact place."

"Then you knew we would loose?" he asked.

She was apprehensive of his slight accusation, but she replied. "No. I simply saw you in my vision and your appearance told me that you had given in, given it all up. And now I know why," she said as she glanced about the land. "I didn't know who you were, just that there was a great pain that made you appear so," she told him.

He relaxed and followed the suns reflection across the field. "It is a sad day. I don't know what will become of us now. We are lost to Rome," he announced.

"It doesn't have to be that way," she told him.

"What choices do we have? There is no possible way to gather what is left of this country to fight against that," he said indicating the number of their enemy on the rampart.

She thought for a time, though in anger at the thought of Rome winning anything. "I will avenge my father's death," she told him.

"I didn't know," he replied. "I am sorry for your loss."

Then she thought of it. "I will move north of here and gather my own army," she said. "One that will destroy him."

"That will be a difficult task, even for you Scathach. But I am afraid that I will have to answer for much of this."

"How can you be certain?"

He wiped the tears that had fallen on his cheek. "Caesar had chosen me long ago as an aide…an ambassador to Rome. He trusted me and I gave him much of what he wanted to see and hear, though many times they were lies to keep me in his favor. But I will tell you this. If you are the Scathach that we Celts have come to know as the greatest warrior goddess, I will send my countrymen to find you in the north. For the sake of Gaul, you must promise to train them and return them to their homeland in order to defeat these tyrants of Rome. We must beat them back and take what rightfully belongs to us."

The thought of it made sense. There was no possible way to gather the men of Gaul to go into battle now. They were defeated and their pride had been taken from them without ever striking an enemy. They were forced to return home and wait for Rome's decision on their fate: Roman law, Roman taxes and Roman politics. They would become a submissive people and Rome would squash their dreams. Scathach wasn't about to let that happen. Not while she was alive and possessed the means by which change could happen.

"Send them," she said with an edge of defiance in her voice. "Tell them to find me, Scathach...*she who strikes fear*, and I will train them. But tell them also, that I will only take those whose hearts are true, for if they are not, they will not see me."

He looked at her. She meant every word. A flash of hope claimed his youthful features and he sent a smile to her. "I will do so," he said. Then he turned away and rode off, leaving her to watch over the dead.

In the fourth hour of the day a cheer went out from the interior of the rampart as a *caryx* sounded from within the city walls. It rang loud and clear over the silence of the battlefield. And in a brief moment of sadness beyond the outer trench, hundreds of Celts watched from the thick of the forest as Vercingetorix walked through the gates, crossed the trenches unharmed, knelt before Caesar and surrendered the city of Alesia. The war in Gaul was now complete. There was no reason to stay.

Scathach climbed on top of Khutalk and turned him back to the campsite. When she arrived she found her party sitting around the last of a smoldering fire. None of them spoke, their thoughts dismal and their hopes gone. Their eyes were cast down in despair. Aoife sat distant from them all. Upon her arrival, Aoife turned her head to the deepest parts of the wood.

"We are leaving," Scathach told them.

"Where?" Piladius asked. "It is done. Can we return to your old village, now?"

"It is gone, Piladius," she said.

He looked at her for a long time. She actually called him Piladius and meant to speak his name as such. She didn't call him Ploppus or dolt, or simpleton. She had called him by his name and it clung to the air with a dint of respect. "Where to?" he asked with more interest.

She looked at them all. Osmiach seemed not to care where they went. He too was filled with disappointment and trepidation. Perhaps he would have been better off waiting in Manching for the Romans to come there. He absently wondered if it would have made a difference. Cruibne seemed oblivious yet interested to join her no matter. His shoulder, with constant help from Osmiach over the weeks, managed to heal well from the two arrows that had found him. Aoife never turned around. And then there was Phaedrus. He had put so much time and effort into getting them here. It was all lost and his eyes showed his distress of the situation. Where would they all go now that could make a difference to anyone?

"North!" she told them. Cruibne suddenly came to life.

"How far?" he asked.

"Far enough that I can avoid the sights of this and start again. I want an army of my own: to train, to form and mold into my own design."

He smiled. "Scathach…would you be interested in an island? Perhaps an island to yourself?"

"An island?" she asked.

"Yes. It is north of here and quite far, but it is a wonderful place. My father told me of it long ago. I didn't want to say anything, but my brother, Susterix, has asked that we go there when we were finished here and later send for his son. I think it would be to our advantage," he told her.

She gave it some thought. "What is this place called?"

"My father called it *Eilean a' Cheo*. It is known as the Isle of the Mist."

She smiled. "It sounds like the perfect place. Isle of the Mist," she thought openly. "We will go there," she told him. While everyone seemed interested in pursuing the destiny of Scathach, and perhaps finding a place engulfed in peace, Aoife scoffed and turned her back. She had grown to despise Scathach and Phaedrus. But not knowing where else to go and being so far from anything she was accustomed, she had no choice than to follow. But she would change that someday, she figured. She would make them all pay for this….

A year had passed since they left the village just northwest of the Black Sea, a village that was no longer. The Dnieper region was lost to stories of myth and legend. While there was always hope that some of the Roxolani tribe had survived the Roman desecration, Piladius realized that perhaps they were gone from all time unless he wrote it down. And while he wrote and traveled north, following Cruibne's direction, the reality of never seeing his books again struck him. He had buried them behind Scathach's home in the hope that he would someday return and get them back. The further they pushed across the land, the more he knew that day would never come: the knowledge from years of study, the lessons in language and art and poetry gone forever. His only possessions were Homer's Iliad, Plato's *Republic* and a short book of poetry, all of which were now stored in baggage with the supply horses. For the longest time he carried the Iliad with him in his shirt. It was odd that he now left it among the other items he kept with the baggage, as if it meant nothing when for the longest time it meant everything to him. His life now was one of the hunter and the warrior, though he maintained his ability to think rationally and write about it daily. Of all the disappointments in his life, the only regret he had lately was that he had not shown Scathach the way Phaedrus had taught him to mount his horse in quick battle assembly. The spear still hung on the side of the packhorse, though no one ever asked what the hook was for. Perhaps no one ever would. Someday, he thought again, he would show them all. He would have made a grand display at the Greek games, he considered. And in reflection, he thought about the Celts and the short battle they had just encountered. Was it really any different from the Iliad?

As they gathered the last of their things and mounted their horse, Piladius looked out one last time. Out there, over the trenches lay Lucterius, poor…poor Lucterius. His dreams were of great wonders for the people of Gaul and he firmly believed in Vercingetorix. Perhaps the Celts will come together again someday, he thought. As the sight passed from his eyes he spoke softly on a breath of quiet air, "Hector…poor, poor Hector."

"What?" Phaedrus asked. He was close enough to overhear.

"From my book," he told him, though absently looked to the rampart where the Romans began vacating the palisade.

"I know of him. The son of King Priam," Phaedrus said coldly, as if he thought of it too.

"You have read the Iliad?"

"No," he replied. "I heard the story from a teller in the market square when I was a young boy. I never forgot it though."

"It is one of your finest hours," Piladius commented, addressing the way in which Achilles was defeated.

"We Greeks are remarkable…I must admit," he said in a chortle.

Understanding the need for humor in times such as these, Piladius laughed. "Yes…you would know."

The way north was an easy matter while following the Sequanna (Seine) River until they reached the coast. In the harbor town of the Caletes they found the people alive with much celebration. The Druids had called upon the god Lhugnasa in thanks for a fertile crop this year and made sacrifice to a large bull in one the selected fields. One of them had prepared a sacred knife blessed with the bough of mistletoe before it was thrust into the heart of the great beast and then burned. And while the people danced and drank heavily about the fire, the small group searched for a way to cross the sea to the land beyond. It was difficult. There were no boats large enough to carry baggage, persons and horses that hadn't already been used by Roman forces in previous years that were smashed or burned after use. Local fishing vessels were too small and many feared even to attempt passage to the other side.

"How far is it?" Cruibne asked.

"Round about twenty leagues," replied an old man fishing at the docks.

"Are there any other ships that come here?"

He looked up and out at the open sea. It was quiet and calm, the water slapping against the shore in short wisps that teased and tickled the tiny rocks gathered there. "Quite often, actually. I'm surprised there's none here now. I've been here most of the season and the docks were full of traders and merchants coming and going all the time. You just wait awhile, they'll be along," he said casually.

"Is it safe to wait with my friends by the docks, there?" he asked the old man.

"Safe as anywhere. We don't usually see much trouble here, even as active a harbor that it is. Oh…you'll see the occasional scuffle in the tavern or the local whore who doesn't get paid, but they're a good sort here," he told them honestly. "Oh, yes…" he continued as the memory struck him. "Stay clear of the Blue Whale," he advised.

"What is that, my good man?" Cruibne asked and searched behind him for the location.

"There is a man who goes there. His name is unknown to anyone, but he is always looking for prey."

"For prey?" Cruibne pressed.

"Yes. I have seen him. He's not a big fellow to speak of but fast and eager to kill at the drop of a coin. He'll take your bet and your head in the same exchange just for the laugh. A trickster he is. Beware of him. His game is simple. He is a sailor from over the seas who claims no land as his own. He boasts of great adventures and large sea monsters. From the ends of the world he says he has sailed and been shipwrecked, sunk and burned and still a survivor of the vast oceans. But he claims one thing that no other has in his possession. And he challenges anyone to take it from him. Like the man before him, the weapon has passed on from one owner to the next, each challenging for the right of ownership. The game almost always results in death. I tell you this only so you will stay away."

"What sort of weapon do they challenge for?"

He looked up with sharp, steel-gray eyes. His beard fell to his chest and his bulbous nose was sun-baked and blistered from the many years of sitting by the sea. "It is a spear."

"A spear? That's the weapon?"

"Not just a spear, my young fellow. A special spear."

"What can be so special about a spear?" Cruibne sat beside him to hear the story.

Scathach and the others watched from afar as Cruibne and the old man talked together. She needed a good bath, she considered. It had been a long time since she could relax long enough to enjoy one without worrying about an arrow coming out of the air and killing her while she cleaned herself. Reaching into the sack on the back of her packhorse she removed the bowl Oseida had made for her long ago. While it was only a bowl to the unknowing, Scathach knew it was the head of Bracus severed and cleaned and painted and shaped into a bowl only for her to use. It was a great gift. And she thought then of old times between Oseida and Rwan. They were good friends. It all seemed like a lifetime ago.

"The spear," the old man started while Scathach went to the water and scooped some into the bowl. "The spear is no ordinary weapon. It is made from the spine of the Beluga fish."

"The Beluga fish?"

"A whale, my good fellow. Do you know nothing of the sea?"

"This is my first sight of it," he said looking out at the vastness of the expanse. "But I have heard stories."

"This spear is made from the spine of the Beluga. Its appearance is like that of any other spear except that it has sharp barbs that cannot be touched by the naked hand. One must cover their palms or it must be cast, as it most times is, with the foot, for the barbs will surely cut your hands to pieces. The difficult and most extreme effect of the spear is that of its impact. Once lodged in the body of an opponent, the barbs extend themselves, almost in self-defense, causing everything inside the body to be torn asunder when withdrawn. This usually leaves the victim dead," he finished.

"I will tell the others of this. I thank you for your time and I will take your advice. We shall keep our sights open for the next ship," he said, stood and bid him a good day.

The water was indeed refreshing and though it was masked with salt, they each cleaned themselves regardless. Aoife bathed alone, away from the others. As during the entire journey from Alesia, she remained separate, seldom speaking to anyone and commenting only when asked a direct question. She slept away from the evening fires they made and ate meals away from the camp, usually from meat she killed herself. Her mood had become sour and she snapped more often when decisions needed to be made. Yet she espied Phaedrus often, watching him, taunting him in fleshy tantalizing hints, though still jealous that the child Scathach carried was not hers to have.

They were impressed by the story of the whale spear and though he promised the old man he would keep them from that location, the story fascinated Scathach so much so that she had to see it for herself. After getting directions, the small group skirted an alley beside the harbor docks on the north side and found the Blue Whale among the shops and buildings used to store goods taken off the ships when they arrived and put aside for later transport to bordering states and various destinations along the coast.

The Blue Whale smelled of old ale and stale wine. Most of the inhabitants were already drunk by the time they entered. They sang, in bad harmony, songs of the sea while playing a stone game on a board Scathach had never seen before. They looked up at the small group when they entered long enough to tell they were no threat then went about their own business singing and playing. The company, except for Aoife who remained at the docks, took several chairs at a table close to the door and sat waiting, searching the room for the serving girl. A heavy-set man, balding at the forehead and crown, finally approached them. A towel draped his shoulder and an old, stained apron covered his front.

"Whatcha need?" he asked, but not as polite as they would have suspected.

"Drinks all around," Phaedrus told him and removed a gold coin from his purse. The balding man stared at him for a second then turned about and went for the drinks. A moment later he was back with their order. He took the coin, looked at it for several seconds, bit it with his yellow teeth and harrumphed.

"Gold is gold. No matter where it comes from, right?" he asked them in a grin and shoved the coin in his pocket.

"Sure," Phaedrus replied and took a deep drink of his ale.

"Has anyone seen it?" Scathach asked as each continued to search the room while trying not to make it look too obvious.

"Nothing," each replied separately.

"Perhaps the old man lied," Cruibne told them.

"No matter," Phaedrus answered. "We needed this break anyway. We haven't had a good moment to relax and enjoy the drink of the gods for a long time."

"Drink of the gods?" Piladius laughed at him. "Honey is the sweetness of the gods and wine is the drink they prefer above all. Why would you put ale in front of that?"

Phaedrus laughed. "For the conversation, my friend. I just wanted to let you all know that it tastes good and we should enjoy it."

Cruibne held his cup to the air in salute and called out for a refill as he drained the liquid. It wasn't long before they all had another in front of them. Phaedrus was right. While sweet wine may have been the drink of the gods, the ale in this harbor truly possessed a taste worthy of praise.

The afternoon was swept away in laughter and merriment. Perhaps it was the attitude of the people in the tavern or the fact that they didn't have to fight anyone to keep the drinks coming. So long as they had money the ale came quickly. They even managed to purchase drinks for several of the local men who cheered them on every time they laughed at something. The winner of the stone game was given several free drinks and he saluted them each time he drained the cup. They laughed and told stories of old days, both good and bad. They toasted to the dead and they toasted to the living. Soon, Phaedrus and Piladius joined in song, teaching the locals something from the Greek tablatures. Cruibne attempted a poor rendition of the Germanic tribal song he had learned when he was young, but forgot the words and never found a pitch to hold on to. He was booed with laughter and pointing fingers, but it was all taken in stride. It was a great time and they enjoyed every moment of their stay. It was a shame they would have to leave. This place seemed an entirely different world than they were used to, a place where nothing mattered so long as there was fun and laughter and drink to wash it all down.

But Scathach didn't partake of the ale. She had a hunch that the old man wasn't lying. Old men don't lie to strangers without reason. No. He had told them because he wanted them to find this place. Strangers along the peer looking for a ship to cross the sea and they don't want to know what the Beluga spear is about? Rubbish! The old man surely had told the truth. And while there was much celebrating around her, she smiled and laughed and watched and waited. As the hours passed she kept her eye on the door waiting for the mysterious man to walk in.

Before the sun set Aoife came through the door. All eyes turned to her as she stood there alone and looking as beautiful as ever in the fading light. A cheer of excitement went up and she smiled, flattered at their approval, but looked immediately to Scathach. "A ship! Coming into the harbor," she told her.

As she said this, the laughter died down and everyone booed her interruption. They realized that Phaedrus and Piladius and Cruibne would have to leave. But most of all, they realized that Scathach would leave as well. They had been watching her since she entered. Rare was it for someone of such beauty to walk through those doors. And even more rare was for it to occur twice in one day, as Aoife was every bit a goddess as Scathach, especially to the man who has been drinking all day. As long as her companions were drinking and having fun, they would stay long into the night while the locals stared at Scathach, waiting for them all to pass out. Then the lucky man among them would take her for himself. It wouldn't be long, they figured. But that wasn't going to happen now, even though their thoughts were running wild with the idea. As they booed the interruption, the old man from the docks slipped in slightly behind Aoife and worked his way to a chair in the far corner of the tavern. He held a white staff in his hands and leaned heavily on it as he moved. The tavern mumbled its way into silence.

"What?" Phaedrus stammered. "Where's the laughter?" he shouted loudly, still enjoying himself. His hand flew into the air in agitation. "Come on, somebody sing!" he shouted and started one of his own songs from his childhood. Piladius laughed and joined him.

Cruibne too wanted to have fun. It had been a long time since he laughed like this. He spotted the fisherman and stood. Perhaps the old man would enjoy a drink and some song, he thought.

As he neared the far corner a local put a quick, but hidden, hand up to stop him. "Leave him alone," he said in warning. Cruibne ignored him. He had spoken with the old man at the docks earlier. There was nothing to worry about here. He pushed by with a smile plastered on his face.

"Old man!" he nearly shouted and all eyes went to him. Several shook their heads and those who possessed hidden knowledge turned away. Scathach sensed something bad was about to happen yet she didn't know what to do. There was something about the old man that bothered her, something about him that wasn't quite right.

"Cruibne!" she screamed before he got to close to him. The building shuddered at the resonance of her fierce voice. Nearly everyone put their hands to their ears in pain…everyone except the old man. He sat in the corner, alone, watching her. And she watched him.

"Scathach!" he shouted back. "What are you doing, woman? I just wanted to say hello to the old man," Cruibne complained as he shook his head to clear it.

Scathach was up and moving, though extremely cautious. No one attempted to stop her. Cruibne remained where he was until she got to him. "Go back to the others," she ordered. It was the first time she had spoke to him in such a way and it frightened him, slightly. Knowing what he did about Sarmatian warriors, he obeyed without further comment. When he was back sitting beside Phaedrus, she turned to the old man.

"It would 'ave been fast, y' know," the old man said with a grin under his thick mustache and beard. While he appeared old, his voice, she noticed, seemed much younger.

"Is this the way you trick them into dying?" she questioned.

"It's only a game, lass. Are ye willing t' play?"

She smiled dangerously. "A game?" she surmised. She looked at him thoroughly. While it was breezy by the docks, he was heavily clothed for the season, a hat and gloves on his hands…. Gloves! she noticed. She forced her eyes to the floor where the point of the staff was digging into the wood. "Nice staff," she commented.

"Only one of its kind," he replied. "Wanna play?" he pried.

"And what does the winner get?"

"Why…me *Gae Bulga*," he told her. "If y' win…y' git t' take er home," he said.

"Ah…the Beluga fish…" she commented as she studied it. "I have heard the story. An odd piece," she commented as she continued to watch it. The gloves he wore kept the pointed barbs away from his skin. Just getting hit by any part of it would leave scars on the flesh, she knew. And looking at the point she found double-edges to the blades, though they too were made from the bone of the Beluga. The entire weapon was carved from the spine and now she marveled at the thought of owning such a treasure.

"Not much time, lass. Do y' pass or play?" he teased. He could see she wanted it. It was in her eyes. Like so many before her, he could tell she wanted it. His nose twitched with excitement.

"What weapon do I get to use against you?"

"Are y' really 'tempting t' give it a go, lass?"

"Name the weapon," she glared at him.

"Sword!" he shouted.

"My sword against your spear?" she asked, though that suited her just fine. She was more than willing to do the job with a sword.

"No, lass. I too shall fight with a sword. The *Gae Bulga* is the prize," he told her, laid the spear aside and stood facing her. Out from behind his shirt came a magnificent sword. Another prize for the winner, she thought. It was all of fifty thumbs long and one hand wide at the hilt. It was similar in size to the one she had made under Mahendra's instruction. She watched it for a long time, measuring the weight of it in her mind. As she watched it, she attempted to place the land where the steel had come from. But that was not necessary. He was glad to fill her in.

"The *Asi*," he said and showed her the keen edge as he rubbed a gloved thumb over the blade. Not as dirty as the black iron o' the Anupa," he said looking at hers hanging from her waist. "*Ukku* steel," he continued. "Very sharp...very dangerous," he smiled and took his gaze from the blade and brought his attention back to Scathach.

Phaedrus and Piladius hadn't noticed what was taking place, but that was a good thing. In their condition, they would surely perish in this endeavor, she realized.

"So, you know your weapons," she smiled in return. "Hindu steel is obviously the best. But do you know how to use it as well as you use your mouth to tell others about it?" she continued to smile and it annoyed him slightly.

"Y' won't be thinking that with y' guts hanging on th' floor, lass. A terrible thing, too, for a young, pretty lass like y'self."

"The prize," she repeated. "Do you wish to die without it, or shall I leave you here to tell the tale of how a woman took it from you when I am gone with it?"

The smile disappeared. "Let it be, lass. Don't bother with this," he warned a final time.

"I've decided I want it for myself now," she said and pulled her sword from its place at her side. "And I'll take the sword as well when I'm finished."

"Y' no match for me, lass. Let it be an go y' way. I do n' want t' harm y' beauty."

"No, but you were willing to kill my friends just for the laugh."

He looked to where the others were watching him. Though they appeared not to be too worried about what was taking place. "They would 'ave put up a good fight, lass. But that's what men a' for," he drawled. "Fightin's not f' the likes o' you, lass. I say…let it be."

"Are you a coward now?" she asked. "Perhaps I should just take them both now and tell the world what a fuss you put up about a woman taking your weapons from you," she teased and he grew angry.

Fast as lightning he swung the blade across, splitting the air in two with a sharp whistling sound. Scathach bent back just in time to avoid the blade, but just barely. She came back with a stance to parry the next swing, but he continued to swing around and came back low, chopping at her ankles. She jumped out of the way again. He was good, she realized. But he had not impressed her yet. She teased him further. "Is that it? This is what I've had to worry for all day?"

"You will die!" he forced and he went completely mad. In the blink of an eye his disguise disappeared, his wig fell to the floor, his bulbous nose thrown beside it. The heavy garments went away revealing a chest of solid muscle that sweat profusely of his hate. His gloves came off and fell in the pile beside him. "Now let us see," he told her.

Somehow she worried. He went completely insane. His disguise was well put together to keep him hidden from unsuspecting travelers, but now his rage had taken him to a new level. She would have to be careful, though she knew he would be no match for her.

Her training with Mahendra came back twofold and she breathed in deeply, waiting the next attempt. It came almost immediately, but not in a direct assault. He slashed to the left then to the right. Then he chopped down from high above his head. Scathach parried the swing to the left and the swing to the right. But when he chopped down at her, the blades crashed against each other in a mighty blow that sent chards of steel flying everywhere. He had broken her sword, snapping it in two at the middle. He smiled and relaxed his stance.

"Y' should 'ave taken my advice, lass. Now y' weapon is n' good. What say ye?" he asked.

Scathach went red with anger. To think about all the time she had spent in making that sword: the incessant banging and heating and cooling and sharpening and banging again. Day after day she hammered the steel into a weapon befitting of her own design and skill. She began to swell with rage and she looked at him with a bitter taste in her mouth. It was as if Caesar stood in front of her. Above all other things, she would kill him no matter what. "Now," she said with a deadly tone. "Now you no longer have the option to live and tell this tale to others who wander into the harbor. Now I will take your weapon from you and kill you with it," she told him.

For an instant he balked, wondering how that would happen. She had no weapon, no chance for stopping him from taking her head. And he meant to have her head now. But the notion that she could possibly consider taking his weapon and kill him with it, struck a note of caution. Regardless, he realized he would have to finish this. He swung as hard as he could to lop off her head.

Scathach bent like a reed in the wind and watched the blade sail over her chest. He realized his mistake when she came back up and kicked him in his right shoulder, forcing the sword out of the way. His right side now lay unprotected and she spun around and kicked his feet out from under him with her other foot. The move was so fast that he barely got the chance to regain his balance before the ground was snatched out from under him and he was sent to the floor with a loud thud. The impact made everyone wince. The wood cracked beneath his weight. The air was instantly taken from his lungs and he gasped for a breath while struggling to get to his feet at the same time. It was too late. Scathach put a foot to his already heaving chest and drove his ribs to the floor. They cracked loudly and his eyes shot up in his head in agonizing pain. He screamed out then. The sword was taken from him without resistance. A moment later she stood over him with the blade high in the air, ready to take his head. He reached up to stop her, beg her, to plead for his life. She wouldn't have it. He had taken something of importance from her, like the Romans who had taken her father and her body and her friends. He would not live for that reason.

As she poised to strike off his head Phaedrus called out. "Scathach!" and broke her stride. "Do not do it," he pleaded. "He is not worth it. There is more honor in allowing him to live, though I know what he has done."

Her anger was still there. She could taste it. He will die, she said to herself. He deserves to die, she repeated in her mind.

"Scathach!" he called again, breaking her concentration. "Let it be!" It was more a command than a request and she turned on him.

"How dare you!" she threatened. It was the first time she had ever spoke to him in such a manner. Somehow, from that moment on, things would never be the same between them.

The fighter gathered his breath while Phaedrus attempted to convince Scathach to yield. In the time she had kept her weapon from ending his life, he reached to the side and grabbed the *Gae Bulga* with his bare hands, though his chest cracked and crunched as he turned to move. Blood instantly shot out from his palms as he held it. His intent was to end Scathach's life and recover his weapons. But that wasn't to be. She saw him grab it. In the beat of a fly's wing she took his hand off at the forearm. He screamed in pain. The *Gae Bulga* was won. She watched it fall to the floor as the fighter grasped his arm to stop the bleeding. He cried out again. Scathach ignored him. He had tested her and she had won. The prize was hers. And the *Asi* sword was hers as well.

CHAPTER XVII

The ship coming into the harbor was a Galician merchant vessel used for both fishing and trading of goods along the coast. It was large enough to carry all their supplies and horses and much more. After an hour of deliberation between the captain and Phaedrus, they secured a position aboard her, but at a cost twice the normal rate because one; they would have to go out of their way to make the port and two; women were not allowed on board. It was difficult to convince the captain that the women were the mightiest warriors ever known. It wasn't until Scathach approached them with the *Gae Bulga* in her gloved hand that he gave in and accepted payment terms.

"She truly has beaten him?" the captain asked incredulously. "It's not possible. He is very wise and extremely tricky. He would never have given it up, especially to a woman. She must be a great fighter to have won such a prize."

"My good captain, she is by far the most incredible woman you will ever see in battle. And I have watched your crew eyeing her as they pass. I would advise them to stay away. The man who owned the great spear no longer has an arm and his chest is all but caved in. Not only did she take his spear, she also took his sword—immediately after she used it to remove his arm," he said and pointed to the new blade hanging at her side.

The captain looked and marveled at the craftsmanship. "I will tell them. They have all heard the tale of the great Beluga spear. They know that whoever possesses this weapon is a great fighter. If the woman has taken it from him, then they will surely leave her be."

"What time do we depart?" Phaedrus asked.

"We leave at first light," he told him. "Have everything ready or you will be left behind. But there is one more thing: the women travel below deck. It is a curse to have them above deck and my men will not sail if they see them."

"Agreed," Phaedrus replied and turned to Scathach. "We will be ready to leave."

Long before dawn they gathered at the docks and waited for the captain to usher them aboard. While they patiently waited to make payment and permission was granted, the crew kept their eyes feasted on the women. Though there was some slight grievance and a few negative remarks about them coming aboard, they made sail almost immediately. The galley was silent with crewmembers running about tying ropes and preparing masts to catch the right winds while ten sets of oars churned in the morning tide. Water lapped lazily against the hull and the ship tilted in motion with the slow, rolling waves as it moved out of the harbor and into the open sea. The horses became uneasy and snorted in agitation. They were comforted with encouraging voices and soft humming to keep their minds busy. It was only twenty leagues to the next shore. Perhaps if the winds were good they would make it there before nightfall. If not, they could be here till morning. The horses would have to endure.

The weather was fair for sea travel and the winds picked up the further out they sailed. Phaedrus and Cruibne went topside several times to keep them informed as to their distance, but it never seemed like they were getting any closer. By night, and under the light of oil lamps set every several feet, they heard the call of land off to their port bow. The captain gave the order to drop anchor and they waited until morning to be let off and carried inland to the shore. In the dark, they chanced the possibility of hitting rocks or getting caught on a sandbar rendering the galley inoperable. Captain Mino wouldn't risk the hazard.

By morning, they reached the shore with the use of three smaller boats—two of which made three trips between horses and baggage.

When it was finished, Mino pulled up anchor and sailed away. The land rose up to greet them. But for how long was that greeting extended?

They moved unimpeded among the territories of the Regni and the Atrebates. There were many farms and smaller towns they passed without stopping so much as to ask for a drink of water. The people looked at them with indifference. By mid afternoon they managed to cross the Tamesis (Thames) River and pushed further north until they came to the Ouse River where they stopped and made camp for the night. There was very little conversation between them. This journey was completely new to everyone. They took in every view and kept it in their minds. This is the trip that hundreds will have to make to find them and they would all have to know the way individually. Though they traveled quickly across the land no one approached them. Somehow they kept their eyes open and their ears sharp for caution against a surprise attack from Roman soldiers they feared were hiding among the tall trees and thick brush. Nothing ever came for them.

While the weather was warm in the day, the evenings were still a little cold, even for the summer season. They were prompted to wear warmer clothing than they normally would have worn at this time of year, but none of them minded it. Though it was chilly at night, they would rather spend it bundled up by a warm fire than tossing and turning in the dreaded heat they normally found in the south and had no control over.

"How much further?" Scathach asked Cruibne. He was the one leading this expedition. He was the only one who knew where his father said the island lay and where Susterix said to go. If not, they were surely wasting a lot of time. But they trusted that he was cognizant of where the island might be.

"Another seven to ten days," he replied and noticed the exasperation in Piladius' sigh. "When I was younger my father told me it took a month to get there with my older brother tagging along. But we are all adults and we can move much faster. I give it close to eight days and we should see the coastline to the Isle of the Mist," he said.

Eight days, they each thought to themselves.

Each morning they woke, bathed, ate and moved along. After six days they had passed through the regions of the Brigantes the Selgovae the

Damnonii and the Votadini, though they tended to keep to the east and close to the shores of the ocean. But then they met the Caledones where they were stopped. They were being watched from every direction: in the trees, among the bush, along the path, behind the rocks.

"I remember them," Cruibne told them. "Father told us they are one of two things. They can be your friend and they will help you, or they can be your enemy and they will not stop until you have gone or you are dead," he said.

Scathach looked at them when they peered out from their obvious hiding places. They were rather small in size and not much in the way of muscle. They each held a bow or a spear and most noticeable of all…they painted their naked flesh in blue, their hair wild and frenzied. "What do you recommend?" Scathach asked.

"I say we march by and keep to ourselves. Say nothing at all," Phaedrus told her, trying to keep them from a battle. While the Caledones could be seen moving about the wooded land, there was no telling how many they were. If they had come in numbers, it could be hazardous.

"No!" Cruibne warned. "We must approach them and speak with them."

"Who knows their language?" Aoife finally spoke her first sentence since she reached shore. Until now, she had remained silent.

They looked to Piladius.

He backed away slightly. "Don't look at me," he told them. "I am familiar with languages in the south, but I know nothing of these people. I didn't even know they existed never mind try to speak their language."

"Oh, come," said Osmiach speaking up. "There's nothing to it," he said and stood bravely to the front and walked a short ways ahead. "Hello, there…" he called out and waved an empty hand in the air.

Nothing happened. The Pict, as they knew them to be, shuffled from one location to the next trying to confuse them. Streaks of blue dashed about in streams of light. Most of them had woad designs painted on their backs or on their chest of their native totem, Piladius discovered.

After several seconds without a response, he turned and came back to them. When he arrived, one of the Pict tribesmen moved from his hiding place among the tall trees and approached to stand within several paces from them. "What you seek here?" he asked in a clear voice.

There was surprise in all their faces to see that they understood the same language, though broken. Scathach stepped forward. The moment she did, the Pict moved back. "Woman no speak!" he shouted and took a stance to cast his weapon at her if she approached any further.

Cruibne and Phaedrus both stood forward, slightly in front of Scathach. "The woman is a warrior," Phaedrus told him. "We seek the Isle of the Mist," he told him.

"Why you go there?" he asked with caution.

"To live," Cruibne answered. "To train warriors and to live in peace…if you will have us," he finished.

"You no seek war with Pict? You no fight to take our land?" he asked.

Scathach spoke up. "No, we seek only to live in peace," she answered him.

The Pict held his ears and shrieked loudly. "Woman no speak! Woman no speak!" he shouted as he held his ears tightly.

She stepped back in disgust and let Phaedrus and Cruibne carry on the conversation. They would have to get used to a woman sooner or later, but for now it would have to be later. She remained silent as she stood beside Aoife and waited.

"The woman speaks the truth," Phaedrus told him. "We only seek the island. We wish you no harm and we will leave you alone."

"You no want to harm Pict?" he asked though still skeptical.

"No!" he answered.

"You wait here," he said and went away. It was nearly an hour before he returned. The small group was sitting in the tall grass resting and relaxing under the warm sun when he broke through the edge of trees and approached. Scathach had taken the time to juggle seven stones while she waited. Piladius attempted the trick, but managed only three at a time and did a very poor job at it. Aoife laughed and joked at him each time he spilled them on the ground. He shrugged her off and turned his back to her. Regardless of his ability, Scathach urged him to push on with the task. He kept at it until the Pict arrived.

"You go," he said with a pointing finger to the northwest. "Island there," he turned his head in the same direction. "King say you take five with you."

"Five?" Phaedrus spoke.

"King want eyes on you all times. You go, but you take five."

Cruibne joined Phaedrus. "My father never mentioned this, but then again, he only traveled with my brother when he came. It must be the women that bother them. Let them come and then we can figure out what to do with them later."

"We will take five," Phaedrus told him, if just to be on their way without a fight.

They traveled another day but the skies turned dark and gray. A heavy storm moved from the western horizon, out where the sea meets the rocky shore, and lit the sky with flashes of brilliant light every several seconds. They watched it move onto the land and then the rain fell. The five Pict tribesmen fled for the cover of the tallest trees. It was a good decision, though Scathach and the others were just a little late. The rain hit them hard. Between the horrific cracks of lightning, thunder boomed over the land and rolled loud enough to shake the ground. Then large drops of water fell from the sky and pelted them hard. There were tiny pieces of ice amidst the raindrops that stung their flesh, whipping them mercilessly as they searched for shelter. The horses bolted for cover and everyone followed until the storm had passed. When it was done, they came out from hiding and continued on across the soggy land, shaking the wetness from their hair and clothing. Later that day they found themselves moving along in some of the tallest grasses they had ever seen. Almost immediately the senior Pict put up his spear in the air and stopped them short.

"Perilous glen," he told them. "Very much dangerous," he continued and threw an ear out across the area listening for any sounds. At the sight of his intense concentration, everyone followed his lead and listened for what might be hiding among the secret places in the glen. The grasses grew much higher the further they went and before long they were as tall as the travelers who pushed across. Scathach and the others climbed onto their horses and rode above the grass to get a better view.

"There," Scathach told them with a pointing hand in a direction directly north of their position. "It opens up there," she said and waited for the leader to continue on. He halted and didn't move. "There," she said again, as if he hadn't heard her. Still he remained where he was.

She climbed from her horse and approached him.

Phaedrus stopped her. "I don't believe they will listen to you. Remember, 'women no speak'?" he said with a hint of laughter. "You will have to earn their respect to talk before they will either listen to you or answer you. I will tell them," he told her.

When Phaedrus approached them, the leader put up a hand. "Danger!" he warned.

"Where?" Phaedrus asked and drew his knife.

The day went silent, the air pristine.

"Phaedrus...Scathach," Aoife called out. "Something moves through the tall grass from the west," she said and they all turned in that direction.

The blades of grass bent under the pressure of the hungry beast that came for them. By its pretentious approach Scathach could tell it was angry and perhaps ravenously hungry. Were they entering a private area? Did they interrupt the natural order of creatures that live on this land? No, she realized. This was just a simple beast that hunted prey as much as they hunted animals to eat and survive. And they would have to kill it before it kills them. She reached to the packhorse and withdrew her pugil.

"Get back," she said and took a position to the right of them, facing the impending monster that now thudded across the land. It snorted and growled and thumped the earth louder and louder with every footfall. The others drew weapons just to feel safe even though they were comfortable Scathach could handle the situation on her own. But could she?

It was only feet from her and she could now see the blades of grass bending to reach her. She bent low and snapped the blades in place. Whatever it was would be cut to pieces. But it all happened too fast. The wild pig ripped through the grass and sprang for her faster than anything she had ever seen. She barely got the chance to swing her pugil before the beast jumped for her throat, breaking the pugil in two. Scathach was thrown to the ground. In a flash, the wild beast turned on her to skewer her with its four-inch tusks and fill her full of puncture wounds before ending her life and dragging her home for a prize. But those around her were armed and ready. The first to react, oddly, was Piladius. In the time they had used to assess the situation and prepare for the creature, he had lodged an arrow across his bow and sat on his horse waiting for it. When the beast broke through the tall grass and he saw that Scathach was brushed aside and now in danger, he let the arrow fly true. It struck the beast in the shoulder. A terrible howl followed the impact though it continued to hunt Scathach down.

She was caught off balance by the impact. With the arrow sticking out from its shoulder, it pressed down on her and would have killed her in seconds had it not been for Aoife who now performed the Salmon leap and flipped forward from the withers of Bucephalus and sliced down as hard as she could on the head of the wild pig. The beast went down almost instantly. For the longest time it twitched and yapped its jaws thinking it had won, though it died several minutes later.

Scathach looked at Aoife. "Thank you sister," she said in gratitude.

Aoife stood over the beast and returned the look at Scathach. She remained silent, but turned to gaze at Phaedrus, waiting for recognition. When he didn't speak, she turned away and went back to her horse. Someday, she thought to herself.

"Are there any more of those?" Scathach asked the leader of the Pict tribesmen. She threw her pugil to the side. It was snapped in two. She would have to make another some day, but this one was no longer of use.

The man looked at her in astonishment. "Woman fight!" he said, amazed. "Woman speak," he allowed with a bow of his head in honor or gratitude, whichever they were willing to accept.

"Are there any more of them?" she asked again.

"Yes," he replied. "Sometimes to ten or more. We must hurry. Others come for the dead," he said as he looked at the carcass. Quick as a flash the other four tribesmen forced two spears down the throat of the beast until they protruded from the other end and lifted it from the ground onto their shoulders, though they struggled slightly with the effort. "We go," one of them said as they moved along rapidly.

They found themselves at a distance of two leagues before the tall grass reduced itself to a normal height. They listened carefully as they pressed along, waiting for more beasts to come for them. None showed, though they could hear the angry squeal of several others behind them searching frantically for the meal they were denied.

"I don't ever remember my father telling me of that," Cruibne said when he felt safe enough to relax.

"It has been a long time, Cruibne," Phaedrus told him. "Much has changed, I'm sure," he finished.

Yet the more they pushed on, the harder the land became. They suddenly found themselves walking over large rock formations. Boulders suddenly jutted from the earth in various places, huge and impending and in some cases mountainous. Trees became slightly scarce and were collected more in copses of several spouting fir here and there. By the time they made camp, it was completely dark.

As they built a fire they could smell the salty sea close by and feel the breeze rise off the ocean swells. They could have pushed on to the shore, but it was one of the tribesmen who called for them to stop. He was worried about sea monsters attacking in the middle of the night.

"Best to be safe," he told them as he found a comfortable place to set camp. At their own fire, he cut the beast they had caught earlier and disemboweled it, throwing the guts southeast or downwind from the camp. He quickly prepared a spit from one of the spears still run through the beast and shared the meal with all of them when it was done. The meat was delicious and they devoured it in minutes though much of it was left over by the time they were finished. They would leave the rest for the animals of the wild when they departed in the morning.

That night the Pict spoke openly to Aoife and Scathach, telling them of the land and the people. While they had managed the perilous glen, they were told that one of the most formidable hindrances of getting to this place was the land they called 'the plain of ill luck' just west of the tall grass and beyond the mountains close to the sea. Those who attempt the cross from that place usually turn back immediately, they told the tale. The blades of grass, when touched by anything, fold up and create a defense by showing sharp edges that cut into the feet or ankles. Predators rarely make it through alive. Those smart enough to know what they are doing prepare for this encounter or they simply go around. But the way around can be just as dangerous for there are cliff walls to the west and mountains to the east. While the easiest way to cross is directly through the plain of ill luck, most skirt this and follow the coast until they find a better place to land. Most of the time they cannot do this unless they come from the far south for the northern shores are too dangerous and the waves too high to reach land.

When the stories were finished they lay back to sleep. The Pict slept on the hard ground using only a mantle they had taken along to keep them warm during the chilly nights. They pushed out the bigger fire they had made to cook the pig and threw the carcass into the wilds to keep predators away from them while they slept. Though they fell asleep almost immediately, they knew that the end of their journey would come with the new day. Under a low warming fire, they rested for the last time in the territory of the Pict people.

When daylight woke to greet them, the small band of travelers found Scathach at the edge of a great cliff looking across at the Isle of the Mist.

"How do I get there," said Scathach still looking out at the island where large mountains rose to the sky and into the clouds in the distance. The peaks were not visible from where she stood, the gray, misty clouds covering them in a thick blanket.

"I don't know," Phaedrus replied as he looked on with her. There was a strange feeling of mystery about the view.

She turned and waited for the leader of the Pict tribesmen to approach. He smiled with his rotted teeth at the sight. "You like?" he asked.

"I don't know. How do I get there?" she asked him.

"Boat. We go north along coast. Get boat to take," he answered.

"Is there a boat large enough to get us all across this water?"

"Not all," he told her. "One go and boat come back. One more go and boat come back. Horse will have to stay here," he said.

"What!" Aoife was angry. "My horse stays here?" she asked with a red face.

"Boat no big enough!" he told her. "Boat no big enough. Must wait for large boat come take horse," he told her in his broken Celtic language.

"I'm not leaving him Skitatsya!" she warned.

"Aoife! We will do what we have to do to get there. If that means leaving the horses until later, we will leave them. And my name, for the last time, is Scathach. Do not call me by my other name!" she said though she tried to keep her voice under control.

"Why? Isn't your old name good enough? It's the name Father gave you when you were born, isn't it? Why do you get a different name? Why not me?" she was suddenly sour, and angry and full of hate.

"I won't discuss it, Aoife. Father died because of my old name and now my new name is about to catch us in more trouble. That's why we are here. Remember? Let's leave it alone and work on getting to the island."

"What if I don't want to go?" Aoife stalled.

Scathach looked at her. "Where would you go, Aoife? What would you do? Who else do you know well enough to trust here?"

Aoife looked at them all, including the Picts. None of them were someone that she could trust for anything. She really didn't know them, even though she had traveled with them for nearly a year. She turned back to her sister. "I won't fight with you Scathach. Besides, look at you. Your belly is starting to bulge with Phaedrus' child inside you. You make one mistake too many and you'll lose it like I lost mine," she said sarcastically.

"No, Aoife. There is a difference between this child and the one that you had. I want this one. And I'll keep this one," she said in a low, dark tone.

"You bitch!" Aoife slammed at her. "How dare you!"

"Aoife…" Scathach tried.

Aoife turned away. "When we get to the island, you go your way and I'll go mine. Do not bother me after we arrive there, sister, or I *will* fight you and I *will* kill you!" she threatened.

"You would harm your own sister, Aoife?" Scathach asked her.

Aoife turned back to look at her, eye to eye. After several silent seconds she answered. "Don't come looking for me until you are ready to die," she warned for the last time, pulled Bucephalus by his lead and walked north ahead of them all.

Scathach looked out one more time over the sea. Another island, smaller by the looks of it, just southwest of the Isle of the Mist stood quiet in the waves that beat against its shores. "What island is that?" she asked to break her attention from Aoife's abrupt departure.

"Island of Druids," the Pict described. "Most come same way you come, but not many stay. Come, we go now," he informed as he watched Aoife getting far ahead without stopping.

They walked for most of the day following the shoreline of cliffs and ridges. Occasional mountains rose off to the southeast and there were bogs and moors they had to stay clear of. By mid-afternoon they found the place where they could cross. The distance was perhaps a thousand yards from one shore to the other and the waterway calm and passable. There they found two fishing boats tied to a boulder of limestone jutting out of the sand on the beach. As the land leveled off to meet the shoreline the way became easier. Phaedrus and Piladius were first to cross, then the women. The horses were left to wait with two of the tribesmen while the rest made their way to the Island of the Mist with the baggage. When they were all on the shore, the Pict leader approached Scathach.

"We go back, now. We bring you to Island of Mist, now we go."

"When will you return?" she asked. "And what about our horses?"

"We come back," he stopped and counted on his fingers. "Four days. We bring horse then. You come see," he said and attempted to smile, turned and took his boat back to the other side.

They waited for him to reach the far shore before they realized that they were completely on their own with no transportation back to the other side. None of them had ever been here before. There was no way of telling which way to go. And there was no telling what to expect of the land or the animals that dwelled on the island. But they were soon to find out for this was now their home.

"Do we take the woods?" Scathach asked them.

It was Aoife who spoke up first. "I'm following the shoreline. I saw the place I want to stay at when we looked at the island from the other side." Without hesitation, or waiting for anyone else, she picked up what belonged to her and started along the shore heading west.

"Well?" Piladius asked, wondering what to do next.

"We'll follow and see where it takes us," Scathach told them, grabbed her things and followed. "Besides, Aoife is right, there is an excellent view of everything that comes to the island from that place."

The beach lasted for a few hundred yards before it became a marsh of reeds that eventually turned into a musty forest of ferns and mosses and even heather. Small animals stared at them from hiding places among the fallen branches of conifer and larch trees wondering who the new creatures were that moved on two legs. A red deer spied their approach then bolted to the thicker part of the forest to avoid them.

"At least we know that there is something to eat," Phaedrus said positively to them.

The land seemed to fall beneath them as they found their route back to the shore and stood among the cliffs overlooking the sea. The view was breathtaking, though frightening. A wrong move in the wrong direction and one could easily fall to their death below. The path became narrow and they were forced to walk one behind the other to continue. Then the land spread out again coming to the shore. At the point of the island the sea sat perhaps twenty-five feet below its rocky edge.

"Here," Aoife told them. "This is where I will live." She dropped her baggage and sat, looking out at the sea and the smaller island to the west.

Scathach didn't want to fight any longer. "I will continue on until I find a suitable place for myself. I will be along the shoreline as well, if you need to find me."

It was another quarter mile of jagged, rocky cliffs that allowed them to walk in single file only. One wrong step and death would greet them quickly. After four more miles of steady grass and beach areas, they found the place where Scathach would build her new home. Oddly enough, someone had been there before and built a strange bridge giving access to the location, though they never discovered the maker.

"Is it safe?" Phaedrus asked as he stepped toward the bridge.

The moment his foot touched the edge the bridge rose up and tossed him off.

"By the gods!" shouted Cruibne. "I've never seen such a thing."

"Nor I!" Piladius joined his assertion.

Phaedrus picked himself up and came back to the bridge. It was oddly built—level on the one end with a rise in the middle and leveling off again on the far end. He studied it closely. Beneath the bridge was a short drop of about twenty feet where water snakes had coiled up in a sleepless nest. Hundreds slithered in and out of the small cracks from the shore to the sea and back. "Don't want to fall in that," he surmised and the others looked over his shoulder.

"So, how do we cross?" Piladius ask.

Scathach stood back and watched without speaking. She had never seen nor heard of such a bridge and it fascinated her. Those coming to train from her would surely have to meet this test along with all the other obstacles they had encountered in this northern country. If one can make it to this location and cross this bridge, he will surely be eligible for training by Scathach, she considered. But for now, even she had to figure out the way to cross.

"No mortal could have made this," Cruibne told her when she came to inspect the bridge. "Should we continue on and try another location?"

"No," she told him. "This is the perfect place to stay. He who can cross here is certainly granted permission to live here and train here. And I *will* cross it, Cruibne…I will."

Like Phaedrus, Scathach put a foot to the edge of the bridge and the bridge lifted up to throw her back. She was too fast for it. Before it could catch her and hold her to toss her, she withdrew her foot and stood as the bridge rose high into the air while the other end dipped down toward the dreadful pit of snakes.

"If you fall in Scathach, I'm not sure you're going to live. And I'm more positive that I won't be jumping in to assist you this time," Piladius told her, though he smiled sincerely.

"Don't worry my little scholar. You should be working on the thought process of how this works instead of telling me what you won't be doing," she replied a little irritated.

"Well," he walked closer and looked at the way in which the bridge was built. "No matter what you do it's going to sway in the middle. If you can jump to the middle I'm pretty sure you can stand there for a while and contemplate jumping past the other side before it dips down and spills you into the nest down there," he pointed.

"That's not an option, Piladius."

"Yes, but if you are fast enough, you could make it."

He was right. There was a possibility that if she could jump to the middle of the bridge she could jump again to the other side before the bridge lowered itself.

"Stand back," Scathach told them and took several steps from the bridge. With great effort she ran to the edge and performed her salmon leap that sent her into the air. The bridge rose up to stop her but she was too high. She landed in the center and realized that she had done it, but the bridge began to buckle in the middle and prepared to throw her off to the side. She froze for a moment but caught herself and leaped again to barely make the other side. When she landed, she was out of breath and frightened, though she appeared angry and frustrated more than anything else.

"Nice!" Phaedrus said. "How about the rest of us?" he asked.

"You'll have to figure that out on your own," she told them in a tease. She really didn't know how they were going to get over. None of them knew how to leap like the salmon up stream, hovering in the air for a long time before falling back to the rushing water.

"I have it!" Piladius shouted.

"What is it, man?" Osmiach asked though he was more perturbed at the whole affair. This was a game for everyone except him and he never was good at games.

"Backwards!" Piladius told them. "If you try to cross it forward you get thrown off. If you walk in the direction…wait…" he said and called to Scathach. "Put your foot on the edge of the bridge and be ready to step away quickly," he told her.

She did as he suggested and the bridge rose up to throw her backward. The bridge didn't lower itself the way it did when she put her foot on the other end.

"I believe that's it," he told them and to try his theory he turned with his back to the bridge, stepped backward and put his foot on the edge waiting for it to rise up and throw him off. It did nothing of the kind. "I knew it!" he shouted. He put the rest of his weight on the bridge with his back to Scathach. Step by step he slowly made his way to the middle of the bridge and over the hump then down the other side until he hit land. With a swift step back from the bridge he let out a quick sigh of relief. He sat on the ground and put his head in his hands exasperated. "I can't believe I just did that."

"You did well, my sharp scholar," Scathach told him. "Now the others," she said and turned about. The land was hers and she would build her home here, she knew. It was the perfect place. "We will tell no one of this," she said as they began to cross. "Those who come to this place will have to earn the right to be here," she finished, as she looked to the shore where she would build her home.

CHAPTER XVIII

Over the next three days they spent nearly every moment building a fortress from the materials around them: stone, stick, mud, earth, reed, thatch…everything they could find. The process was long and arduous but they managed. Sore muscles, aching backs, cuts and bruises scarred them all, but they worked hard to complete the building Scathach envisioned, though much more time was needed to accomplish the task. On the fourth day they walked back to the shore where they had arrived. There, they met Aoife who was already waiting. She was dirty and disheveled, her hair matted and crusted in earth and bramble. The dirt under her fingernails and the smudges of grime smeared across her face and arms gave them caution. She obviously had not faired well over the past three days alone.

"Aoife," Scathach approached her.

"I just want my horse!" she said sourly. She walked away, closer to the beach.

"Let me try," Piladius told her.

Piladius walked slowly and stood behind her as she continued to look across the way to the other side where her horse would soon be coming. "She really cares about you, Aoife. Is there anything I can do to help you?" he asked calmly.

"Yes," she said softly and turned to him. "You can leave me alone!"

"Aoife," he tried.

Out of nowhere, she slapped him across the face as Scathach had done so many times before. It wasn't right. He was no longer the little scholar who wouldn't fight back. He had hunted and he had killed and he had worked hard to get here, just as they all had done. He didn't deserve this. He stepped close so she couldn't strike him in a full swing—this at least he remembered from training with Phaedrus in Pannonia—and slapped her back, if only lightly.

Aoife took offense and stepped back. A knife found its way to her hand and Piladius knew it would end this time. All that he had worked for to accomplish even the smallest tasks would come to a halt with a knife in his throat because he cared for a woman who didn't care for anything or anyone but herself.

It was Scathach who saved him. "Aoife!" she shouted and the earth nearly vibrated at the sound. It was enough to make her look and time enough for Piladius to move out of the way.

"Do it and we will end it all right here!" she warned.

Aoife turned back to the sea, ignoring them all. The knife went away.

The Picts had returned as they said they would. It was a larger boat that had taken them this time. The horses were brought over by twos along with chariots and extra horses and extra people.

"What is all this?" Scathach asked them.

"You train fight," the leader had told her. "We come to learn fight, and you teach."

"You go to her?" Aoife asked, though it was more an attack on the Picts.

The Pict looked at Aoife. "You train too?" he asked.

Aoife wasn't ready for that, but she stood erect and answered. "Yes. I train none but the best."

He looked between them.

"We will both teach them," Scathach answered.

With the last ship came something even more unexpected. A fair-haired man of exceeding muscle and height claimed the shore and stood looking at them. "Cochar," he greeted when he caught sight of Cruibne.

He looked familiar, but Cruibne did not know him. "Do I know you?" Cruibne asked.

"I suppose so," he smiled and put out his arms to show the length and breadth of himself. "Do you not see father in my eyes, at least?" he said as he moved closer.

"Hagar…? Hagar Cruibne?" he shouted and smiled and ran to him. Both hugged and shook forearms and cheered their greeting.

All who watched smiled at the reunion, whoever he was, and Aoife began preening herself, to meet the handsome newcomer.

"Cochar?" Scathach asked when they were finished and both approached to meet them all. "Your name is Cochar?"

"I go by Cruibne," he said as if ashamed of his first name.

"It's a fine name," Piladius said. "I didn't know you had more than one," he laughed openly.

"And who is with you," Aoife asked as she moved to them and studied the tall fellow. She suddenly adopted a coquettish attitude and inclined her head to look up through her lashes.

"This is my nephew Hagar," Cruibne said with a proud smile, though they were about the same age. "He was sent to learn with the Druids in Carnutes many years ago, but I'm sure there is a story to hear when we discover why he is here," he told them and Hagar nodded in fact.

"Let us go, then," Scathach offered. "There is much to accomplish."

Over the next several months, things changed between them all. Scathach's pregnancy caused her moods to sway almost every moment and she became angry at the slightest errors in training. Her home was built to her specifications and large enough for her and several others to live comfortably, but not for the Picts or any newcomer who did not know the way to the fortress she had built. There were other buildings built for them on the other side of the bridge where the trees had been cut down and the land leveled to settle the growing numbers. And they lived there without argument. As soon as the homes were built, they began warrior training and the new army that Scathach had hoped to make quickly came together. Soon there would be enough of them to go back to Gaul and move southward to Rome.

Cochar Cruibne caught up on the latest with his nephew, Hagar, only to discover that Caesar had massacred nearly every Druid in Carnutes.

Hagar barely escaped with his life. Caesar adopted a 'death to all Druids' policy realizing that once the Celts knew that their mighty Druids could be destroyed, so could they. And it worked. Hagar was on his way to the island of the Druids when he caught word of a man named Cruibne on *Eilean a' Cheo* or as they called it, the Isle of the Mist. He just had to see for himself.

Then the child came. It was a girl. And Osmiach was there to assist in the near-fatal birth. Complications arose from the breech baby and Osmiach, with his excessive knowledge of medicine, saved both mother and daughter. Phaedrus named her Uathach and Scathach accepted the name with satisfaction. But two months later she was pregnant again: this time with twins.

Aoife became angry to the point of rebellion almost every time she heard Scathach's name or the name of her daughter Uathach or the fact that Scathach was pregnant again. Aoife, though still beautiful, tried and tried to get pregnant herself, to fulfill her life and bring equality between her and her sister. It simply wasn't meant to be. Much as she tried she could not give birth to a child. Had the Romans done this dreadful thing to her? Did the child she lost a year ago take all possibilities of ever having another child? It angered her more and more and she began to take it out on the army that she now controlled and taught day after day. Then her wickedness took on another alteration when Bucephalus became sick. She spent every moment with him though it did no good. Shortly after he died. Aoife was crushed. She suddenly hated everyone. To relieve some of the stress and anxiety she portrayed to her army, she was given two of his offspring that had been raised from a mare in Gaul as a present. Both stallions were as beautiful as Bucephalus himself, perhaps stronger. These, she accepted and trained herself yet remained hostile to everyone around her regardless of the gift. Piladius had heard of the bad luck and approached her. He immediately noticed her change in attitude and confronted her only to be slapped for the last time, ever. When he stood from the ground, he looked at her coldly, his mouth bleeding, and said. "From this day forward you will not see me on this island ever again." At that moment he went directly to the beach and took the first boat further west to the island adjacent to the Isle of the Mist. He took not a single item that belonged to him. The book he had incessantly wrote in about their adventures and even the Iliad remained behind. The Druids there accepted him without hesitation. Much as Scathach tried, she could not convince him to return. The only regret he kept with him was that he never got to show her how to mount his horse from the hook in the spear that Phaedrus had made for him. So many times he tried to achieve that point. Disappointed, he let it go and sailed away to learn from the Druids. He promised never to return.

Aoife was not one to give in either. Perhaps it was Phaedrus, she considered over time. Was he the only man who could bring a child to them? She would have to trick him, she knew. With that idea, she called one of her soldiers, a Pict who had some knowledge of herbs and spices and the like, and made him deliver a concoction to make her sleep better at night. The mixture was taken purposely to Phaedrus who unknowingly drank it while hunting alone in the forest. The animals, he knew, liked the view off the ledge of the cliffs on the western shore where they ate freely of the tall grasses that grow there and he followed their trail. Aoife followed close behind and when she saw that he was delirious with sleep she tricked him to lay down with her. Believing it to be Scathach, he gave in to the warmth of lust and desire and performed the life-game with Aoife. When it was done and the potion wore off he was furious.

"What have you done!" he shouted at her. "Why have you done this dreadful thing to me?" He staggered and drew his knife. Aoife bent and dodged left and right, smiling as she went. It was a good game and Phaedrus was an excellent opponent, though he remained under the influence of the drug, causing him to attack clumsily.

"Come for me, Greek. Show Aoife what you're made of," she teased and laughed.

He would kill her for such trickery. "You are the work of evil!" he bellowed and stepped forward to cut her throat. She pivoted and he missed. In the middle of the swing he tripped and staggered to the edge of the cliff. He struggled for his balance—a trait he had always been accustomed—however, the drug was so overwhelming and his brain in such a spell that he slipped and fell to his death on the rocks far below. While Aoife was sorry he had to die, she was also happy now. Scathach had lost her husband, her lover and the father of her children. All the way home, she laughed and giggled and screamed out with joy at what she had done. Now she too would have a child of the famous Greek, Phaedrus. And she would show it to Scathach when the time was right. But she never realized the cost of such betrayal for the seed of Phaedrus never grew inside her.

When he failed to return that evening, Scathach sent out a party to find him. They returned two days later with his broken bones. Scathach fell apart, but held herself together long enough to overcome her sorrow and grief. A great funeral was prepared, of which Aoife was invited to attend, and a *kurgan* was built for her husband. An iron hammer was made special for the occasion and with it, she shattered the skull of his favorite horse and buried it beside him along with everything else that was his. Most precious of all went his pugil, the deadliest weapon she had ever learned to use. After this was done, Scathach became the fiercest woman ever to live. All dreaded her, yet they came from everywhere to find her and learn from her.

Word spread from region to region and soon there were hundreds who came to seek out Scathach. She became known as the 'Shadowy One' among islanders who came to learn, though *she who strikes fear* remained a constant title as well. But there were many who never made it to the island at all, becoming lost in the mires and bogs or died crossing the plain of ill luck or the perilous glen that was known to swallow a man's life whole. Those who made it were regarded as earning merit to be taught by Scathach. And she did so with earnest and patience.

But there were others who had come to join Aoife as well. Growing tension between them rose to a paramount as the armies began toiling against each other on occasion. As the months passed, they scheduled games with each other's army, if only to break the stress and tension they felt towards each other. There were distance games with foot races and chariot, and accuracy games with spear and arrow and games of technique using the sword, and balance techniques on the rope of feats, though Scathach and Aoife never participated in any event. Yet while they never participated, they each had their favorite. Aoife always had the best chariot and charioteer in her favor. None could beat him though many desperately tried. To some degree, it made those less fortunate better in a short period of time.

Cruibne learned well over time and, as Scathach became absorbed in motherly duties, took on the responsibility of training the remaining army. She made him general over all others and he shined at her approval to earn such a title. He became gatekeeper to her fortress and took pride in inviting those who could pass the test of the tilting bridge. His nephew, Montagne, sent by Susterix, joined his brother Hagar two months after he arrived. They spent all their time together, learning the art of fighting. Later that year, it was decided that Scathach would only train those who could cross the bridge to her fortress. Too many had come to gain instruction and the masses were overwhelming. There was no time for her to teach them all. Now, only those capable of gaining access to her home across the bridge would be allowed to train personally with Scathach. To that degree, many lost their lives in the pit of snakes, their bodies washed out to sea or eaten by the inhabitants of the pit itself. Those who made it, either by luck or wit, became her greatest.

But after her sons were born she immediately took an interest in their training, though Uathach seemed to catch on extraordinarily fast for her age. While her sons, Cuar and Cette, studied each day, Uathach became more adept in trickery and treachery as an art. Lies and deceit became every day occurrences with her and she was good at it. Even at her young age she was a beautiful girl. Men would be calling for her long before she turned twelve, Scathach knew. And her daughter possessed Aoife's attitude toward men as she watched them train in the morning with utter fascination. It worried Scathach, but she also knew that none would attempt anything with her daughter for fear that she would kill them. And she would kill them.

It was seven years since the birth of her daughter and the way of life for Scathach and Aoife became a myriad of new fighting techniques for a myriad of men across the world. It was decided that the battle for Gaul would have to resume and the armies would have to come together if only for that one cause. It may have been the only thing both Aoife and Scathach agreed upon in a long, long time. Caesar would have to die. They would have to end the aggression of the Roman army and push them back to their own country. There was talk among the army that Caesar planned to push further north, as far as the country of the Picts. That was too close to them, they knew. Something would have to be done soon. Word had it that he was on his last trip to Rome to secure more legions for the attempt.

And that was the unexpected fatal blow Scathach had given, yet never realized she had done so.

Though the winters on the Isle of the Mist were extreme, far more so than those of the Dnieper region of her old home, the spring and summer seasons were perfect. On the ides of March, during the planting season, as most of the southern part of the island was now inhabited by families who had come to stay, Scathach reached up and took down the stone. A long time had slipped by before she looked to the stone for any reason. A strange feeling was with her when she decided this and she became absorbed with a need to know from the object of her father's obsession. Something in the world had changed and somehow she knew she was the cause.

Between the lines she looked. They faded and changed into a vision, blurry and hard to see. Like looking underwater, she fought to clear the vision in her eyes, but the opaque shadows moved about unseen. There was something terribly wrong, she knew. The vision suddenly changed again and the view was clearer. Then the faces burst forth in recognition.

"Brutus!" she whispered dangerously. "You've done it!" She wanted to scream out with joy, but held it in. She watched, as the vision became a prominent picture of clarity. "Yes…" she said openly. "Stab it into his cold, icy heart!"

Caesar, she watched, entered the meeting of the Senate in Pompey's theater and sat upon his seat. Brutus entered shortly after and walked to him slowly, a brother who was just as true to Rome as anyone. Everyone approached Caesar, the most powerful of men in all Rome. Bending low to his knee, they each kissed his ring in welcome: a hero, a commander and a great leader. And then there was a change, for there was Marcus Junius Brutus and beside him his conspirator, Gaius Cassius Longinus. Without a word, he looked into Caesar's eyes with all the adoration of a great king, a great leader and a brother. Then his vision clouded and his mind cleared with the knowledge of what he had to do. Without further hesitation, he thrust his sharp blade into Caesar's heart. With him came Longinus, his knife shoved clean to the hilt into Caesar's chest. Repeatedly, they stabbed Caesar while he fought to gain control and push back his attackers. There was nothing he could do to stop them. At the last, he lay at the foot of Pompey's statue covered in his blood, his life slowly going from him. With the last of his breath, he looked up at Brutus in question. "Even you, lad?" he asked of the sudden betrayal then lay still on the cold stone floor.

"It is done!" Scathach yelled and the entire building shook.

She ran from the fortress and down to the shore just before the bridge. In a hoarse, raspy voice, she screamed. "Caesar is dead!"

Cruibne came to her. "Scathach," he whispered. "How can you know this?"

"Trust me, Cruibne," she said. "I have seen his death."

A month later, news arrived from Gaul that Caesar was, in fact, dead, murdered by the design of the Senate and most particularly by the hand of Brutus. Her plan had worked, but to what extent? She had seen the vision from the stone as one of prosperity and fortune for Rome under Caesar's control. All the kingdoms of the world would come to him and offer hostages and fortunes to become an ally. And Brutus was beside him in all his actions, powerful and glorious. Now, it was completely changed. What lay ahead for Brutus was unknown. Would he become emperor, now that Caesar was dead? She had lied and told him so out of treachery. How much of the world would be changed by her interference? Something told her she would find out through the stone when the time was right. It was the stone, after all, that gave insight to the disastrous betrayal of Caesar and the false claim for Brutus to succeed as emperor. But would it come to be?

When the news broke out over the island, the soldiers came together. "What do we do?" they asked of both Scathach and Aoife. The answer was simple.

"Continue to train and learn to be the warriors you came here to become," Scathach told them. "But since Caesar is dead and Rome no longer claims a design on us, there is always a chance that Rome may change its opinion and come anyway. It may not be today or tomorrow, and it may not be for several years, but Rome may change its mind. To that end, we must be ready. And that is why we will continue to train. However," she continued, to add finality to the meeting. "We will require the training to last one year only. At that time, you will be sent back to your country to do your country proud and live honorably. And you will seek out and send your best to find me and I will teach them to become great warriors as you will become."

At this they cheered and threw their hands into the air. At the edge of nighttime, a large fire was started at the shore in celebration and a great feast was prepared for everyone. All had come to eat, including the soldiers from Aoife's camp.

While the army of both Scathach and Aoife joined together, the feelings each had for the other never changed. At the celebration, Osmiach, who was designated orator and judge for all events during the games of competition because of his indifference to either side, was chosen to lay down the laws during such festivals. At all occasions of celebration it was declared that each soldier was of equal talent and skill. Depending on the soldier involved Scathach or Aoife handled any grievance or violation of this rule personally. Death by the hand of their trainer was usually the result of the disobedient. The rows of heads along the seashore was a constant reminder to them of their fate should they forget this one simple rule.

But Aoife still despised the fact that Scathach was capable of bearing children while she was denied the chance. Bitterness stole her soul and she gave in to spite and greed. Everything Scathach had gained, she wanted. While her physical appearance was exceedingly beautiful, the blackness of her heart made her an ugly crone to those who could see through her flesh. And this hatred made her train harder than ever before. She wanted it all and she was willing to sacrifice everything to get it.

It was nearly a year later that Scathach developed an ill feeling in her stomach. Something else had changed in the world and she could sense it. She immediately went to the stone and removed it from its special place. As she had done so many times before, she studied the lines and moved her eyes up and down until they faded and a vision came into view. The sight was dark and only the soft glow of a single lamp gave enough light to see in the small space. When her eyes could see clearly she found she was again with Brutus. Had he summoned her to this place? How was that possible, she wondered? The feeling changed, oddly, for somehow she actually felt as if she had physically come to him in the night, if only by her shadow. Perhaps it was her ghost that had come to him, she thought. No matter, she was there with him in this hour and she felt as though she had been squeezed through a dark forbidding tunnel to get here. It was not right, she felt. This was not supposed to be happening. She realized that her interference had caused this rip in history, a tear in the fabric of events to be now undone by her sense of pride and hate of Caesar and what the Romans had done to her village and to her body so long ago. There was no way to make it right. All she could do was watch and see what would become of him. She was no longer allowed to interfere for she wasn't really there and yet she *was* there.

He looked at her, this ghost from his past. "You come at my final hour?" he asked. "Have you not betrayed me enough?" he continued, though sadly.

She didn't know what to say. He was devastated. Misery claimed his pale features. So much grief had found him. His loss was much greater than any man she had ever known, though she was certain Mahendra's grief could compare. "I have no words for you," she told him. "I cannot interfere any further."

"Did you not foresee Marcus Antonius in your precious stone? Did you not foresee the great fear in Rome at the death of Caesar under my hand? I am outcast! Now I wander the land in search for a home, in search for a life, and always at the end of a sword. I have formed a new army and even that is lost to me. There is nothing more. Did you not foresee this! Tell me, witch!" he shouted.

"Brutus," she said softly, almost solemnly. "My hate and my fear have done this great injustice to you. I tell you now what I truly saw in the stone that day. Caesar was to become a great man. The people of Rome would have made him king, their first emperor. Great things were to come of Rome under his rule and you, Marcus Junius Brutus, were to rule at his side as his most trusted friend. All this, I have taken from you—I have taken from the entire world. Yet, I cannot bring it back for it is not within my power to undo what I have done."

His voice softened. "Alas, my fine witch, I too am guilty of greed for I saw myself as Caesar and it overtook my mind with a deep lust to rule over all of Rome. Had I only listened to my heart…" he said and bent his head low. Then he looked back up at her apparition. "Now my time has come, woman warrior. You have played a grand game and have become victor over all Rome, no matter what may come from this day. You alone have undone a great kingdom without ever raising your sword. You have severed the vital limb of a great country with as much as a single word. That is a great deed, and I salute you as a soldier," he said. "Your company has been welcome this night, Scathach. I will seek you out in the next life," he finished. And with that she was thrust back to the place in her house where she was gazing at the stone. It was done. Her malicious lie had completed its course in history. She vowed never to deceive another through the stone.

A month later, she learned that Brutus had taken his own life in battle.

CHAPTER XIX

With the news of Caesar's death and now that of Brutus, his murderer, there wasn't much left for her to fight for, unless Rome continued to seek prosperity in the northern territories. But that could be many years away and under a completely different ruler. Perhaps it would be a whole lifetime, she considered. Yet with this bit of information, and the sudden decline in Roman interest for the northern territories, she dismissed most of her army to return to their homelands. Hagar was among those who decided to return to his home. With him went his younger brother, Montagne. It was a sad farewell, but after several years of living away from Susterix they realized the time to return had come at last. Many, of course, stayed on to train regardless of Caesar's death. These, she discovered, became greater fighters yet. But even though the war in Gaul was complete and Caesar was dead, Aoife continued her hate and disregard for Scathach, almost as much as she hated the Romans. There was constant fighting between them though the battles were won and lost by their most skillful warriors. The number of heads hanging on poles by the shore became a significant landmark for those undertaking the responsibility of their own actions. While there remained a great number of fighters who were willing to take up the challenge for Scathach, Aoife continued to rival her with her charioteer who surpassed everyone on the island, though he never challenged Aoife or Scathach directly. And most precious of all besides her charioteer, were the horses that pulled him to victory each time he fought. They were Chrysaor and Pygmalion, the prize stallions of Bucephalus. Aoife chose their names herself. Told to her in a story by one of her soldiers, Chrysaor was the name of the horse that rose from the blood of Medusa, the snake-headed witch. It was said that if you looked into her eyes, you were instantly turned to stone. Chrysaor had the same effect—one look into his eyes paralyzed you with stunning curiosity. Pygmalion was named appropriately for his hatred of women. Aoife could never approach him. In fact, the stallion went mad whenever any woman was nearby, but she marveled at his great strength and ability, giving life and meaning to Bucephalus. And year after year they grew stronger and more prominent throughout the distant lands in the tales of the women warriors who trained men on the island. While Aoife gloated in her achievements, sending messages to Scathach almost daily of the number of new arrivals to her army, Scathach maintained her silent reverence for the quality of her own army as opposed to their number. She knew that it would all change some day. She could feel it.

Another seven years had passed before Scathach received a visit from an outsider—someone she had been waiting to see for a long, long time. She had trained many men to fight though Cruibne became her benefactor for success due to his skill and technique over the years. Fine tuning a soldier was her direct responsibility—if she was available and then only if he was able to withstand her terrible methods. She had distanced herself from everyone around her, including her daughter, Uathach. And then there was Osmiach her faithful physician and Cruibne her most trusted companion. They too had felt the change in her. It started with the death of Phaedrus and slowly progressed to the solitude she now shared with her twin sons, Cuar and Cette. Her time was completely absorbed with them. They were to be her greatest achievement ever and she refused to accept anything less than perfection. She was hard on them always. They learned the *kiai* by the time they were four years old and while they lacked the ferocity of voice, their battle screams could pierce your brain through your ears like a wounded animal calling for help in its final hour. They were juggling five apples at the age of six and by the time they were ten shot bow equally as well as most of the men who came here. They were proficient on the rope of feats and both possessed exceptional balance. But the stranger who walked to the bridge that day was someone she had been waiting for, someone she had seen in the stone a long time ago.

The stone, she thought to herself then. Was it the stone that created the life she led on the Isle of the Mist? Was it the stone that had forced her so far from her homeland at the northern Black Sea? And now this young boy has come to find her. Had it been that long that she saw his vision in the stone? She used the stone more often now, but only when the graduating student was able to ask her the questions his heart sought to know. And each time she looked, the vision of this fine young boy came to her in the midst of the answers the others looked for in their own future. Now she would discover why, for the time of his coming had arrived.

"I seek the Dun Scaith," said the stranger on the far shore.

"It is on that island there," said a young Pict boy whose brother was chosen to live among the soldiers who train. "On the Isle of the Mist," he said with a smile. "Are you going to learn too?" he asked, almost excited.

"I will try," he replied.

"You're not very tall. You might have trouble," he said.

"I've made it this far, lad, and nothing has eaten me yet," he returned the smile. "Is there a boat nearby?"

"Down there," the boy pointed to the north along the shore. "A man will show you."

"Many thanks my fine boy," he said and pushed on until he saw the boat just ahead.

"You're rather small for this, lad. Are you sure you wish to train here?" the boat-master questioned.

"If you cherish your job and wish to see another day on this sea, I recommend you take me to that place without further insult," the stranger said though his face seemed to glow in a strange feverish color. The boat-master obeyed and never spoke to him again, fearful of him.

On the Isle of the Mist he followed the path that nearly everyone took to gain access to the fortresses of Aoife and Scathach. But he knew not which direction to take when he came to the fork in the road. Aoife's fortress was well built and fortified with her army standing watch on every corner and some who stood watch in the woods and among the branches of the highest trees. He ignored their silent observations and studied the land and the fortress built out toward the point of the island for a long time before he decided to push on. Following the trail that leads to the cliff's edge going to Scathach's fortress he met another man passing him in the opposite direction. The stranger, a cook's servant who was sent to gather herbs from the forest was forced from the path to allow the stranger to pass.

"Kind sir," said the cook's servant, realizing the other was a warrior by his dress and the weapons he carried on his back, though he looked very young. The path was too narrow to allow them both to go by at the same time. "Would you be as kind to hand me my basket upon passing," he asked as he smiled and without further word climbed down below the cliff to hang there until the stranger passed. When he was by, the cook's servant climbed back to the road while the stranger turned about and handed him his basket.

"Is this the way to Dun Scaith?" the stranger asked him.

The cook's servant raised his eyebrows. "You don't want to learn from the sister?"

"The sister?" he questioned.

"Aoife… She is harder on her soldiers, but easier to train with. Scathach's fortress…Dun Scaith they call it now, that's a tough lot. If you're lucky you might see *she who strikes fear* but only during the games. Not too many get to train with that one. She is entirely too hard on her warriors. She spends most of her time with her two sons in the mountains," he looked beyond and up to the high tops off in the distance. The peaks were buried under the misty clouds.

"She is the one I seek," he told him.

"A shame," he said shaking his head. "Follow the path there," he pointed. "It will lead you to the village of her soldiers. You can get more information from them on where she can be found," he droned then turned away and mumbled to himself as he walked down the narrow path.

"Many thanks," the stranger said and moved along, though he was sure the other didn't hear him.

At the bottom of the hill where the coast meets again with the shoreline, he spotted the row of huts. The chunk of metal against wood was heard in the background as Scathach's army trained somewhere distant, their battle screams reverberating over the water within the inlet. Across the field there were others gathered in groups watching their teachers show new methods of fighting with weapons while others showed how to fight with nothing but hands and feet. Other students were off in smaller groups still, talking of home and battles and lands and kings and things such as that. Then, by the shore, there sat another small group. The students there wore a familiar dress unlike those of the Pict students or the students of the eastern countries. They were students from his home in Ireland.

"You there," he called out and moved to them.

"Who is it that calls?" one of them asked and looked up to see a familiar pattern of dress, but one whose squares were of a different color. "By the...can it be!" he shouted.

"Ferdiad!" the stranger shouted and moved for him, hugging and kiss him in welcome. "And you, Naoise, and Ainnle and you Ardan, you have all come to learn with the warrior queen?" he asked them. The others returned the introduction and smiled, shaking his forearm in greeting and exchanging kisses of greeting.

"You have come to see the Scathach?" Ferdiad asked him.

"Yes. Do you know where I can find her?"

"Most definitely," he answered and pointed out beyond the shoreline to a bridge leading to her fortress that sat by itself on a small strip of land. "She lives in there."

"Can I get there?" he asked.

"Oh, yes," he replied in a tease. "But first you must tell us of our homeland. What news do you have?"

Together they sat about the stones and he told them what they wished to hear of their country. When he was finished, he told them the story of his journey to find Scathach. "Forgall sent me to find this place with Conall Cearnach and Laegaire Buadach, the 'Battle Winner'." They recognized the names immediately and listened more closely. "I spoke with Emer, my wife to be, and she has told me of Forgall's trick to deceive me. Forgall hopes I will never return to marry his daughter. His thoughts were to have me killed by the legends of the plain of ill luck or the glen of perils so that Emer can marry another—any other besides me, in fact. However, both Conall and Laegaire have returned to Ireland without me. During our trip there came upon them a terrible dream that neither could resist. Both returned without ever seeing this place. I alone have made it, and I will find this Scathach if I have to die in the attempt. I will not be denied," he warned.

"We came here in a small group and that was hard enough," said Ainnle. "How could you possibly make that journey alone?"

He puffed his chest slightly. "I was astray and fairly ignorant of the way, but I saw a terrible great beast coming towards me. It watched me everywhere I moved and it followed me, though slightly ahead. Whatever way I went, so went the beast, and then it stopped and turned its side to me. I instantly made a grand leap and was on his back, racing through the forests and the plains and the marshes. I dared not guide him for fear that he would turn on me and devour my flesh, so for four days he ran freely until we came to the boundary of the place where men live. There he stopped again and rested. Below us were lads rowing in a small loch and they looked up and began to laugh at me riding such a horrible beast. So I simply leaped off and bade it farewell. It never tried to harm me. I walked toward them through a deep valley where I found a large house. There, a comely young girl welcomed me. And she knew me by name!" he said in surprise. "She claims she is the foster child of Wulfkin, the Saxon, when I went to his home to learn sweet speech from him a long time ago. Though I remember the visit with Wulfkin, I do not remember the child. After a good meal of meat and drink I was introduced to a man called Eochu and we talked of this place. Eochu told me of the plain of ill luck. He said that on the near side of the plain the feet of men would stick fast and on the far side every blade of grass would rise and hold them fast on its points, cutting them and ripping the flesh down to the bone. So he gave me a wheel and bade me to follow its track across the one half of the plain. And then he gave me an apple and told me to throw it and follow the way it went until I reached the end of the plain. Then he told me of the perilous glen and instructed me to follow the only path that would take me through to safety. Though I have heard many could not make it, I found it easy to cross."

They cheered him and laughed at the ease with which he talked of his adventure, even if most of it seemed a little stretched. Yet that was his way.

"You are surely gifted," Ferdiad told him. "You have not changed much from when you were Cullin's hound," he laughed openly. The others joined him.

"That was long ago, my brother," Cuchulain said and laughed as well.

After another hour of stories from Ireland, they were happy at last and willing to send him on his way, seeing that he was eager to meet the Shadowy One. "Have you been there?" Cuchulain asked each of them.

"No," Ardan replied. "We do not know the way."

"How can you not know the way? It's right there," he said pointing to the bridge.

They each looked to the bridge then back to Cuchulain. "We don't dare. It's too dangerous," Naoise told him. "Besides, I have a greater desire to see Ireland again soon."

"If I must cross that bridge to see her, then that is the way in which I will go," Cuchulain said and stood. With his weapons on his back he started for the bridge.

Ferdiad grabbed his arm and stopped him. "My brother," he said softly. "Many a king's son has got his death there. Beware!" he warned, though a smile pressed the corner of his lips.

"A young boy is coming to the bridge, Scathach," Cruibne told her. He was standing guard at the gate when he saw Cuchulain approaching.

"A boy?" she asked without looking. She didn't need to. She had seen him long ago.

"A boy," he confirmed. "But he is dressed as a warrior and carries his weapons upon his back as such. He is new here," Cruibne informed her. "He may have crossed the western mountains with all their raving beasts and the dragon's lair, but he still has to cross that bridge," he sneered.

"Does he come alone?"

"Quite alone."

As the youth walked to the end of the bridge, she smiled in recognition. Yes, the vision in the stone had come true again. He was exactly as she remembered him in the stone. "We will wait to see if he can win this obstacle to assess his worthiness to train with us," she told him.

As they waited, the youth came to the bridge and examined it thoroughly. After a moment he turned back to see his friends staring at him and urging him to take his first step. He sensed trickery. While they were his countrymen, there was always a good joke on the one who would fall for such tricks. He refused to be made fun of. To everyone's surprise, he sat and built a small fire from the wood he found nearby. Then he rested.

"He cannot cross!" Cruibne shouted victoriously.

Scathach looked out from her gate. "No. He is resting, saving his strength."

"Mother?" a voice called from within her spacious home.

Scathach looked up and saw Uathach watching the young man from a window high up. "What is it?" she answered.

"That young man...who is he?" she gestured to Cuchulain who sat by his fire.

"A visitor," she answered.

"He's very handsome," Uathach said. She was all of sixteen and ready as all maidens are for marriage, though no one dared to ask for fear of Cruibne. He would surely kill the first to attempt such a quest. And Scathach would be next to contend with for such a query. As painful as it was for the warriors not to be able to touch or feel her, Uathach was tasked with serving them their evening meal. To tease them further she would flaunt her miraculously gorgeous features before them at the dinner table and then taunt them with her maturing yet seductive voice as she went about her chores.

"Watch him closely," Scathach told Cruibne. "I am going back to the mountains."

"How long should I wait?"

"It is your choice. He may not make the attempt until the morning greets us. He may not make the attempt at all. When he is ready, he will try," she assured him.

"You seem positive about this one," he commented.

"I have seen this one," she replied.

He looked at her. "Where have you seen him?"

"A long time ago in a far away place," she answered.

"Your daughter has a fancy for him I see," he said bitterly as he stared up at her. For a long time he had his hopes on earning the chance to ask her to marry him, but thought better of it each time. He had been with Scathach for many years and she had taught him how to fight better than anyone he had ever known. Though he was competent in his abilities, he was not overconfident. Uathach was a beautiful woman and one worth losing his life for, but he was also old enough to be her father. How could he ruin his relationship with Scathach in such a way? Harder still, how could he get Uathach to ever look at him the way he looked at her, always? For so long he had held back his desires. Only Osmiach knew of his feelings for Uathach, promising never to speak a word of it to anyone. But now there was a new man to contend with. No other warrior would ever cross him because he knew that Cruibne would kill him, and quickly. Somehow, he felt it would be different this time.

"Yes. I do believe you are right," she said with a slight smile, though it was covered by squinted, daring eyes.

"I will wait," he said reluctantly as he watched Scathach move away. Her erect posture and her slow gait gave him the impression she had mastered everything around her. The very earth was hers to command. She had grown over the years, but her skill had never faltered, nor had her beauty. While her ability to fight and train became twofold in strength and endurance, her appearance was still the most radiant. And when there were new techniques developed, as time and experience often present these changes, she mastered each in a very short time, while even the most skillful took several weeks. Simply gazing at her very personage demanded respect. When she was out of sight, he turned back to the young boy sitting at his fire.

"Oh, he's darling," Uathach was beside him.

His hands gripped the gate menacingly. "He's only a boy," he said sourly.

"And I'm only a girl," she fluttered her lashes at him. "But look at his muscle, Cruibne. He's a grand one," she concluded.

"It's hard enough keeping this lot away from you, Uathach. Now this one is on the menu and you have your eye on him as well. It's going to cost him his head."

She looked sternly at him. "You touch one hair on his golden head and I'll see yours on a pole hanging over my doorstep!" she threatened.

He smiled then. "You have your mother's sense of humor," he noted.

"And my aunt's as well," she replied flirtingly with a quick sway of her hips and a toss of her long strawberry hair.

Cruibne grew angry. Conversations with her ended in resentment constantly. "He still has to cross that," he pointed at the bridge below, giving the subject a sense of finality.

"He will make it. I can tell. It's there in his determined eyes," she answered then turned from him and walked back to the home closing the door behind her with a slam. Cruibne turned back to the bridge. The boy sat unmoving, his eyes suddenly closed.

As the afternoon came to an end, Cruibne gave in and left the gate. The lad would have to wait for morning to try the bridge, he figured. Only a fool would attempt to cross in the night.

Without further delay he went to the barracks where his warriors were preparing for the evening meal. He knew Uathach would be preparing as well. Shortly after they would meet in the dining hall. Without him there, the soldiers would take advantage of her generosity, though none would dare touch her. His presence dominated all ill thoughts of lust and procreation.

Cuchulain's eyes snapped open while there was daylight left in the sky. The bridge stood before him, mocking, daring. He approached it with caution. Surely there was some sort of strange magic here, he considered. His companions were too eager for him to test it. Without noticing, the small group of boys who had watched him moved closer across the lawn and down to the shoreline just behind him. "Go ahead," they urged him.

He ignored them, but continued regardless. He had come so far to get here. There was no going back without achieving what he had come here to get. He put a solid foot on the end of the bridge to test his weight. It immediately rose up and tossed him backwards to the ground. "Whoa!" he said as he climbed to his feet. He went back again. At the edge, he looked down into the pit below. It was a good distance down there. He knew if he fell in it was over. Nowhere was there a way to get out of that, especially with the number of snakes and other crustaceous life squirming about, not to mention the number of bones and skulls that had been picked clean. But he knew there had to be a way to cross. The distance was too far to jump completely over, but it might be possible to take three or four giant steps, he thought to himself. After several deep breaths he took a good step onto the bridge careful not to fall into the pit, but it bent to the middle again, curled and tossed him back to the ground.

A larger crowd gathered about him. They laughed hysterically, teasing him, urging him to try again. Many hoped he would make it, though others cared less if he fell into the pit and died. So many had tried before him and found themselves scrambling to claim the rocky edges with their fingers bleeding from the sharp jagged rocks and their flesh ripped from their body trying to escape the biting snakes and other vicious creatures lurking below. This young boy would be no different.

Their laughing angered him, but he ignored it as best he could and concentrated on the bridge. There had to be a way to cross this obstacle, he knew.

The noise outside caught Uathach's attention and she came back to the window to watch. The crowd grew bigger yet and she marveled at the strength and determination in the youth's features, though there was a sudden and drastic change in his appearance.

Again, he approached the bridge and thought for a long moment. It was possible to get there in two jumps if he could only manage to reach that far, he considered. But the distance was great and he was such a short warrior to make the attempt. Without waiting any longer, he shot out and leaped onto the bridge. He landed short of the center that would allow him to leap again to the other side. It buckled and fought him like a great beast and he hung on as hard as he could, fighting to keep it from tossing him into the pit. A moment later he picked himself up off the grass. The gathering laughed uncontrollably.

He was angry and his madness changed his features. His flesh turned red—red like Scathach's flesh would turn when she too was angry—and there was a great heat about him, like that of a fire. Then he puffed his cheeks and bellowed his muscular chest. Win or lose he would conquer this bridge. He stammered forward with swift intent. All the determination he could muster fell upon his brow and he knew that this attempt would either kill him or he would finally get across.

Uathach watched the transformation and realized that there could be danger for him if he could not control his emotions to conquer the bridge. She had to help. "Like a salmon," she called from her window.

He looked up to her, barely hearing her words from that distance. Her beauty caught his eye and he calmed slightly though the voices laughing in the background brought his anger back to his heart and the temperature around him grew hotter.

"You must leap into the air like the salmon," she told him again.

He heard her, yet didn't understand what she meant. He gazed back to the window. Her hand was waving in the air like a salmon swimming upstream, taking several seconds in the air before landing back into the water. He suddenly understood. "Leap into the air like the salmon to gather as much distance as possible," he whispered to himself. Without waiting he tested all his equipment to see that it was secure to his body and leaped again, only this time he clung to the air like his javelin and landed directly in the center of the bridge. Before it could fold to spit him off, he bent and leaped again before the other side of the bridge could rise up and bring him back down. When it was done, he was standing on the other bank looking at the gate to Scathach's fortress. Uathach cheered and ran downstairs and out the front door.

Those gathered on the other side cheered him and there was great celebrating when he walked to the gate with his spear in his hand. With the force of ten men he thrust the point of his weapon into the door so far that half the shaft went through the wood. At that, Uathach opened it to see him standing there. He was the comeliest man she had ever seen, though his height was slightly shorter than hers. His eyes caught hers and held her. She breathed deeply, steadily while her heart beat loudly in her chest. His golden hair was curled to his shoulders and his flesh was the sight of perfection. His muscles flexed on the shaft of his spear and she watched his chest heave with sudden annoyance. But he studied her like a fine piece of jewelry one might find in Athens or Greece or even in China. His position softened slightly.

"Are you the Shadowy One?" he asked her.

She giggled at his stupidity. "Do I look that old?" she returned.

"They say there is no age to the warrior queen."

"So, I'm a queen?" she teased, flirtingly.

His temper flared and he pushed the door in slightly to look around the area. "Are you the Scathach?" he demanded, his tone more commanding.

"No," she said shortly, giving up the charade.

"Then where can I find her?" He was growing impatient.

Uathach became disgruntled. "You have to earn the right to see her. I will tell her you are here and she will come for you," Uathach told him sharply. "But what is your name, handsome warrior?" she flirted again.

He stopped searching the land around the home and brought his attention back to her. "I am Rhiayu and I seek Scathach. Tell her that I have come. I shall wait here," he told her.

She laughed openly. "You will die of hunger if you wait there, strange man. She could be days from returning here. You will seek out Cruibne. He will offer you a place to stay and food to eat. While you wait, you can train with the others who have made it across the bridge. They train each day with Cruibne."

He looked across the way where several warriors exited the barracks and were working their way to the dining hall. "You tell the Scathach that I am here. And you tell her also that I will not be denied," he told her shortly, pulled the spear from the door and departed to find Cruibne.

"So you have made it," Cruibne greeted him, though he was not pleased.

"I was told to find the one called Cruibne," Cuchulain replied.

"I am he. You are welcome. Since you have crossed the bridge, you are allowed to train with those gathered here," Cruibne told him.

"I will train with the Scathach," he told Cruibne with a steadfast tone.

Cruibne laughed at him. "You will train with me first!" his features suddenly changed.

"You are not the Shadowy One. Why would I train with you?"

Cruibne became slightly irritated, but then he saw Uathach coming from the house. She had changed into something more revealing than normal. A low-cut tunic she had weaved herself came just above her knee and low enough to show the cleavage of her bosoms. He flushed at the sight and stepped in front of her. "Where do you think you are going?" he asked angrily.

She knew he would be mad. "I am performing my chore as dictated by mother," she told him in a snappish tone. "I see you have met Rhiayu," she commented casually.

"Mother?" Cuchulain questioned.

"Yes. My mother is Scathach," she smiled mockingly and stepped by to enter the hall. It was instantly silent when she went inside. Cruibne knew he had better get inside also. "You," he said to Cuchulain as he passed. "Get yourself a chair and eat with the rest. Then get plenty of sleep for we train early."

Cruibne was right. The morning did come early. The sun had not broken through the trees to meet them when Cruibne walked into the barracks yelling and screaming for them to get up. Everyone rose and went outside, relieved themselves in the nearby pit dug the day before, buried the refuse and came back to meet with Cruibne. They instantly started exercises, then weapons training and techniques of fighting. Cuchulain had no difficulties with any of it. In fact, he was superior to most of them already. By the early afternoon he was bored with the training and approached Cruibne.

"Where is the Scathach?" he asked.

"You're an eager one I admit. But you still have to pass my test first," he told him.

"Your tests so far have bored me. Only the warrior queen can teach me what I need to know."

"We shall see, young warrior. When she returns from the mountains, you will have the chance to speak with her. Until then, you are mine. Do you understand that?"

He looked at Cruibne. He was several inches taller, but not as broad nor did he seem to possess as much strength. His teeth were rotted and his hair was constantly in a state of disarray. Rhiayu wondered how anyone could train so many warriors when he could barely keep himself clean and neat. Appearances, obviously, didn't matter when teaching someone to fight for their life. "I will give you that much time, teacher. But I will not be denied."

"Don't worry. You will have your chance," Cruibne grinned, though there was much sarcasm in the look.

For three more days Rhiayu worked on technique, balance, battle yells and fighting. He was taught to work with iron and to make his own sword from the bellows of the smith who seemed to have an endless supply of raw materials. Where the smith got them no one knew, but he always produced the steel to be worked. Then he cut his own branch from a tree of his choice with which to make his own spear. He learned the basics of medicine from Osmiach, testing special combinations of herbs found on the island and those imported from various other lands. And while all this took time to achieve, Cuchulain became impatient. This was women's work. There was nothing he had learned here that he hadn't done in his homeland. He was above all this. Three days had passed and he was no closer to seeing the Shadowy One than he was the day he got here. Would she ever show, he wondered? Did she exist at all? Uathach had said she was her daughter. Perhaps he should question her. Besides, he knew she liked him. Surely she would give him good advice. She purposely came to him during each evening meal and teased him, whispering teasing pleasures into his ear and rubbing her flesh against his arm while she reached to refill his flagon of wine. And Cruibne watched him each time she did this. His face became hot and his temper flared every time she pressed against the young warrior. He had had enough of it, but what could he do? There really was nothing. And while she verbally molested his ears with her taunting, suggestive hints, he concentrated on getting to Scathach.

After a quick lunch of meat and corn, he departed the barracks and went to the house just off the inlet. At the front door, he knocked loudly.

"Who is it?" Uathach called from inside, though he heard several feet shuffle toward the door and then the drapes were pulled slightly aside to allow faces to peer out the windows at him. The house, it appeared, was infested with young women who cleaned and sewed and embroidered and numerous other things.

"It is I, Rhiayu, and I have come to find Scathach. I refuse to wait any longer!"

Uathach opened the door and stepped outside. "Come with me," she instructed.

Several paces beyond the house she stopped and looked up to the cold, mysterious mountains. "There," she pointed. "That's where you will find her. She will be sitting among the branches of a Yew watching my two brothers in training. As you performed the magical leap of the salmon to win over the bridge, so you must do it again to gain access into the tree. There you must hold your sword to her and demand your right to be trained. Can you do this?" she asked, though she seemed distraught. She realized that if Scathach trained him she would most likely not see him again.

"I understand. But that is all I have to do?" he asked as if a trick were under foot.

"Unless she chooses to fight you…yes."

Without waiting, he departed for the hills and further into the mountains. The way was rough with sharp rocks and winding, twisting paths. Determined, he pressed to get closer to the mountains. After nearly two hours of searching he saw the Yew. Beneath it Cuar and Cette were juggling stones while balancing on a rope tied from one rock to another. The woman was high up in the crest of the Yew busy with stitching a piece of clothing that had been torn.

He looked at her for a long time before moving forward. She was the Scathach and she was one of the most beautiful women he had ever seen. He could clearly see where Uathach got her beauty. But how could a woman of such magnificent beauty also be such a great warrior, such a great teacher? Surely this woman was not the Scathach he sought. Yet, Uathach had told him she would be up in the Yew and there she sat. He knew he would have to be cautious, regardless of how her beauty attracted him.

He crept forward, silent as the rising moon. With a great leap, like he had done to cross the bridge, he bound for the Yew, reached the top branches and released his sword, pointing it at her heart.

She was motionless, unconcerned, but continued her stitching uninterrupted.

"Death hangs over you this day. You are the Scathach?" he asked, though it was obvious his question demanded answers.

"I am," she replied undaunted.

"Then I demand that you teach me."

"And who are you that I should cower in fear?"

"I am Rhiayu," he replied. "And I will not be denied further," he pressed the point of his sword to her chest.

She put down the knitting and looked up for the first time. "I have been expecting you Cuchulain," she told him casually.

"You know my name?" he was shocked, but his stance remained steady.

"I have known you longer than you have been alive. I have been waiting for you."

"So you will teach me?" he asked, never removing the sword from between her breasts for fear that she would strike him from the tree and finish him.

"You have been trained well, I have seen this. There is a story of a young man named Rhiayu who was caught outside the party of Cullin's home. Cullin's hound attacked him. The animal was set on the property to keep all intruders away. It was said that only an army with enough strength could get by the animal, but you, alone, had taken the beast down and killed him. Cullin was distraught at the loss of such a great dog and you, with such loyalty and honor, chose to stay on as his watchdog until another could be trained to replace the one you had killed. That is quite admirable," she spoke. "So what say you now, hound of Cullin?"

"I demand that you finish my training," he ordered.

"Then I will tell you this, Cuchulain. Whatever three things you can ask of me in one breath, I will grant to you. But if you fail, you will leave me and seek my assistance no further."

"Agreed," he said then thought briefly. Knowing of the legend of the Scathach and the skills she possessed, he asked in sequence. "I request a thorough training in arms, a dowry for my marriage to Emer and a prophesy of my future," he said in a single breath.

"It will be done, hound of Cullin. Now go from me and seek out my daughter, Uathach. She has an interest in you. Otherwise you would never have found me."

Without further delay, he jumped down from the tree and faced Cuar and Cette who had been watching silently from below.

"You have great strength, warrior," Cuar told him, amazed that the shorter man could leap that high. "I could not have done that. Perhaps we will be friends," he finished.

"If I have the time," Cuchulain replied with a final look up at the Yew where Scathach stood watching him.

CHAPTER XX

Over the next few weeks Cuchulain trained with Scathach and her sons at the foot of the mountains to the northwest. Like her sons, Cuchulain started with breathing exercises, though he bored quickly of this. Then he learned to juggle, though he knew no reason for such nonsense. That was before she put him on the rope of feats and made him perform the task. While he could juggle three apples easily, he struggled to do it while balancing on the rope. Yet he could balance easily on the rope without juggling anything. In fact, he was excellent on the rope of feats until he was instructed to juggle. It wasn't long before he mastered both his balance and his juggling. He then moved on to five apples and then six and then seven. In no time he was performing extraordinary feats on the rope with apples being tossed into the air and never having more than one apple in his hand at one time. Then she worked him with pugils against her sons, each taking a turn after the other was knocked off. Cuchulain was never bested at this lesson, lasting the entire time on the rope while Cuar and Cette exchanged places many times. And they were comparatively equal in size in strength, she noted. Then he was instructed in ironwork. His sword was molded by his own hand, as was his spear, sharp and straight. And, as Scathach had suspected, he was already exceptionally skilled at both. His javelin however, was the stronger of the two. And he possessed superior skills in the art of his *kiai*, though the force of his yell was not nearly the strength of Scathach's. Not surprising, he had surpassed all the tests she had initiated for him. Yes, he would be the greatest warrior she had ever trained. The one who had trained him before his visit here had done a superb job of preparing him. All that was left was some fine-tuning from Scathach. But then came Aoife.

"I hear you have a new student?" Aoife said casually on a random visit to the fortress. She was escorted by her charioteer and her two best horses, though Pygmalion stomped his right foot menacingly into the earth at the sight of them.

"I do," Scathach answered without further comment. She knew Aoife would question her until she had all the answers she wanted. She remained evasive as possible.

"They say he is exceptionally gifted."

"He is a warrior, Aoife. Here to learn like the rest."

"Then why are you training him and not toothless Cruibne?"

"Because this one has crossed the bridge and found his way to the mountain and my tree. He has earned the right to be trained by me. But why such an interest in this one?" she asked back.

Aoife looked about, trying to catch a glimpse of the new arrival among those walking about. He was elsewhere. "I heard he was very good at virtually everything."

"I wouldn't know. I train him only to fight. Those who want to learn how to play the life game go to you. After what he has learned here, I don't see him working his way towards your camp any time soon," she said though she smiled in a mocking sort of way.

Aoife was not taunted by the comment. "Where is he?"

"Why?"

"I am told he is very handsome as well."

"You are told a lot for someone who has no idea who comes or goes in my fortress, Aoife. Perhaps, you should live with me and we could train him together?"

Aoife laughed. "Not likely sister. We would kill each other."

"Perhaps you are right. Let's call this even and be done with it," Scathach suggested.

"Even? Not with you. It will never be even."

"Oh, yes," Scathach said in remembrance and with a taste of sarcasm. "It will only be even when you have a child."

"Who told you such a thing?" Aoife was aghast. "It's a vicious lie!"

"Who told you so much about my new student?" Scathach returned, nearly gloating.

Aoife looked to the house where several drapes had been moved aside to allow those within to peek out at them while they conversed. "She is a sly one, that," Aoife said with a gleam in her eye.

"She takes after us both." Scathach told her.

"More than you know, sister," Aoife shot back. It was a verbal battle, as was most common between them.

"Do you think?"

"You know she sleeps with him every night, don't you?" Aoife told her.

Scathach didn't know, but played along as if she did. "She is of age. She can choose any man she wishes."

"Sure she can, but with your best student? He creeps up to her bed through her window every evening just to have his way with her," she pressed hoping to anger Scathach. It had no affect.

"He is engaged, Aoife. When he is finished his training, he will return to his homeland and take a wife of his own. Uathach will mean nothing to him. And she, for whatever it is worth, will gain the experience she needs to trust no man, no matter how good looking he is, or how strong he is, or what he says to get his way. And she will be leery of the next, knowing how to handle his trickery to perform the life game. Much as it may pain her, she will learn one of the hardest lessons in life."

"She will learn to hate you, Scathach."

Scathach thought for a moment. Looking into her sister's eyes, she said. "Sometimes hate is all we have to keep us together."

Aoife looked at her through squinted eyes. "Sometimes you can be so right." Without further comment she made her way back to her chariot and stormed off with her escort trailing.

After she was gone, Uathach came out from the house. "Was that Aoife," she asked knowing full well it was.

"You are sleeping with Rhiayu?"

"Who told you?" Uathach was suddenly worried.

"Do not lie. I don't really care who you sleep with, but remember this,

Uathach, he will leave someday and you will be alone. He will return to Ireland and marry another."

"Not if he chooses to stay here with me," Uathach commented coldly.

"Mark my words, Uathach," she called after her. "He is a man of principal, though his morals are much to be desired. Trust that he will leave when the time is right."

"I will do no such thing," Uathach replied and entered the house.

"Scathach?" Cruibne joined her.

"What is it?" she replied though hesitantly.

He took his time. "Ferdiad and his friends have requested a reading," he told her.

"Have they earned it?" she asked him.

"They have each passed all the tests and they are scheduled to leave soon. Ferdiad, in particular, requests one for himself. The others are more hesitant to know. They believe fate can be altered so long as they don't break the fabric of the world of knowledge to see it before it happens. Ferdiad is not so reluctant."

"Send him to me tomorrow and I will tell him."

"And the others?"

"Tell them there is no future for those who choose not to see," she said and turned away. There would be no more discussion on the subject. Obediently, he would send Ferdiad to see her in the morning.

Scathach went back to the mountains. When she got there Cuchulain and Cette were practicing with pugils on the rope of feats. Cette didn't last long. Cuar took his place only moments after they started. Shortly after, Cuar was back on the ground. Cuchulain was smiling at the ease with which he could knock them down. While he probably would have become bored with the lessons, he was getting better because he practiced them in a game-like style. It made the lessons go by much faster. And they were much more interesting. But then he spotted Scathach walking up the hill and took on a serious sense of concentration, letting Cette strike him a few times before dislodging him from the rope.

"Leave!" she said to Cette when he stood and brushed himself off.

Cuchulain noticed the change in her. "Am I to go as well?" he asked.

"No!" she replied. She looked to Cuar and repeated to Cette. "Leave, both of you!"

Cuchulain knew something was wrong. And by the sounds of Scathach's voice, which nearly hurt his ears, he pretty well guessed it had something to do with him and Uathach.

When the boys were out of sight she returned her attention to Cuchulain who was still on the rope of feats. She bent, picked up the pugil Cette had dropped and in one leap bound on the rope with him. He shifted his balance to adjust for the additional weight.

"You have been extremely busy, hound of Cullin," she commented darkly as she took up the stick and examined both ends. There were no defects.

He didn't know how to respond. He was sure she knew about the late night visits to her daughter's bed. And he was sure that the reason for this separation from her sons was to discuss the matter. But knowing of Scathach he also knew he had to be ready for anything. After all, she *was* the Scathach. There is no human emotion in the woman warrior who trains on the Isle of the Mist, someone had told him long ago. 'Never trust that she will be your friend. She is teacher only,' he was warned. His instincts were right. With a quick slash to the right she brought the weapon down and connected with the bottom of Cuchulain's pugil as he attempted to protect himself. She smiled at his anticipation. Yes, he was good. But she was better.

"What are your intentions?" she asked him while both sticks remained connected. There was pressure applied to the connection to gain an edge to the balance they both sought on the rope.

"I have no intentions, Scathach. I am here to learn and return to my homeland," he answered.

"And Uathach?" she asked, but then she twisted the stick and brought the left end crashing down on his shoulder. He wasn't fast enough to block it and he went reeling to the ground. He stood rubbing the place where he was hit. "Back up," she ordered him.

He bent and lifted the pugil. A moment later he was back on the rope in front of her. "I don't know what you want from me, warrior queen," he said and took up a battle stance.

Scathach recognized the ploy. He would attempt to dislodge her the way she had dislodged him. It was the student teaching the teacher all over again. She remembered doing the same to Mahendra many years ago. Cuchulain was quick at all things, one of the fastest learners she had ever seen. And he retained everything he had learned. He was handsome and sharp and bright and eager, she could tell. And she knew him like she knew herself. He would try to catch her at her own game.

He did. He swung down on the right and she blocked the strike. When he came back with the left she bent low on the rope, lifted her leg and kicked him in the stomach. He went back to the ground.

Gasping for a good breath of air into his lungs he paused and looked at her. A strange glow appeared about his hair and Scathach sensed a pressing heat around her. He was getting angry, she knew. That was good. That was what she wanted. His flesh finally turned red with anger and he leaped back to the rope. "You won't do that again, warrior," he threatened.

"I'll ask you again…what are you intentions?"

"And I'll tell you again…I have no intentions," he replied.

This time he swung first. She blocked. He swung back to the left. She blocked. He swung back to the right and halfway there he stopped and threw out a fist that hit Scathach in the face. Blood instantly fell from her lip, but before she could fall she flipped backward in the air—following the motion of the blow—regained her balance, swung her pugil in a figure eight movement and hit him twice, once on the leg and once on top of his head. He winced in pain and went completely mad. Like a wild, crazed beast, he swung and swung, hitting Scathach's pugil over and over as she blocked his futile efforts to get her. When he failed, he threw down the pugil and came for her with his bare hands. She threw hers down as well. Both of them were angry. Both had gone mad. Both had turned red in their flesh. The heat from their anger was intense. Anyone standing nearby would be sweating profusely. The only difference was that Scathach could control her emotions, but for how long? They held to each other. Neither could remove the other from the rope. She was taller by perhaps a foot, but he possessed much more mass and muscle. They were evenly matched. But how long would it last?

Scathach finally released him and stepped back, away from his reaching, grasping hands.

"Stop!" she shouted and he lowered his head, grabbing his ears in pain.

"I will kill you!" he shouted back while shaking his head clear.

"You will do no such thing. You will explain why you have come here."

He brought his hands down from his ears. "Explain why I have come?" he reiterated, slightly confused. "I have come to learn from you. I have to be the greatest warrior in the whole world. And none but you can teach me," he replied.

"So, what is your intention?" she asked again.

"To learn," he replied sharply then calmed as he realized what she wanted from him.

"And my daughter?"

"She has seduced me with her words, warrior queen," he said embarrassed now.

"She has much of my sister's wickedness about her. It is not entirely your fault. Go now. Clean yourself then return to your barracks. Leave my daughter be. She is ignorant of men and their needs."

Without question, he slipped by her and left the mountain. Neither had won, neither had given anything up. Both were satisfied to know the reason for his coming here was genuine. More than anything, he was glad she held no grudges against him for sleeping with Uathach. Surely a lesser warrior would have committed himself to kill him for such acts against his daughter.

It was time for dinner when Cuchulain returned to the camp and washed. He joined the others who were already sitting at the long tables ready to eat. Ferdiad and Ainnle sat across from him and Naoise sat beside him. Cuar and Cette, he noticed, didn't eat with the rest. They ate separately inside the house across the way. Private meals were always prepared for them away from the others for fear that one of the trainees would poison them.

"We leave tomorrow," Ferdiad told him.

"I will be sad to see you go," Cuchulain replied.

"We wish you well after we are gone," Naoise said. "There is word that you are by far the greatest warrior here."

Cuchulain smiled at the comment. "I was great before I came. I am even greater now that I am here, and I will be the greatest by the time I leave."

"Not many get to train with Scathach," Ferdiad told him.

"So I am told. I must admit it is difficult work, but extremely rewarding."

"I wish I had your talent," Ardan stepped in behind him and sat to his other side. "I was just overhearing the conversation," he added with a smile in greeting. "Did Ferdiad tell you he was getting the *imbas forasnai*?"

Cuchulain stared at him. "The what?"

"The *imbas forasnai*, a reading from the Light of Foresight. They say she can see into your future through some sort of rock or stone or something," Ardan informed him.

"I'm sorry my brother but I don't understand what you are saying."

Ferdiad cleared his throat. "Before a student graduates from this place, the last thing they learn is the leap of the salmon. That is why we are eating in this room tonight. We have finally learned to cross the bridge that has barred our way for so long. For someone like me, and these bloody blokes here, it is taught at the end of our stay. And as a final departing gift, Scathach offers a reading of our future through the *imbas forasnai*. But not everyone accepts this gift. I will accept, but the others have refused."

"So what will she tell you?" Cuchulain asked him. He was intrigued.

"I don't know. I have to wait until tomorrow. I was told she would call for me."

"Do you really think she can see into the future?" Cuchulain persisted.

"And much, much more. Will I see you tonight?" Uathach whispered over his shoulder. Her long strawberry hair fell across his face and smelled of Primrose. Her flesh was soft against his cheek.

Cruibne watched her from his chair at the head table overlooking the entire room. With him sat eight others who were considered teachers among the warriors. Osmiach too, sat there beside him. Cruibne grew slightly jealous.

"We are finished you and I," Cuchulain explained to her, remembering his recent encounter with Scathach.

"Finished?" she questioned. "I thought we were just beginning," she teased in a flirting tone then put a hand over his shoulder and pinched his bicep slightly.

He grabbed her hand though she pulled it back, leaving him to hold only to her little finger. Without realizing his strength, he twisted it back and away from his body. "I said we are finished!"

She screamed out in pain and the entire room went silent as she fell to the floor holding her broken finger. Tears welled in her eyes as she held it against her chest, the pain growing and her cries escalating throughout the room.

Cruibne was on his feet. This was his chance. He would have the warrior's head for this. He had warned her that her flirting would cost him his head and now she would see for herself. It was only a matter of time before he would get the chance and here it was.

"On your feet!" he ordered Cuchulain at the end of his sword.

"You are angry. Go away before you get hurt," Cuchulain told him.

Ferdiad's eyes widened in horror. "Cuchulain? Do you know who speaks to you?"

"I know who is there and I am telling him to go away before someone gets injured."

Cruibne had been the commander of Scathach's army for many years. He was considered her most trusted companion in the entire fortress. Lives were lost on many occasions here on the Isle of the Mist and this one would be no exception. Just because he was being trained by Scathach personally did not affect Cruibne's decision to fight the young warrior. If he was that afraid to lose his life he never should have come here in the first place. Besides, Scathach trained Cruibne to fight as well. Who was to say the other was better? The insolence of Cuchulain's tone made him insane. "Get outside. We will finish this now!" he ordered. There was a haunting, sinking groan throughout the room as Cruibne stepped away and walked to the exit. "I will meet you out front," he said in parting.

"Cuchulain…he is the most skilled teacher here. He will kill you," Naoise warned. "What will you do?"

"I will face him. He is not much to beat," Cuchulain commented casually.

"How can you be so sure? He has trained so many. I am worried about this one," Ferdiad shoved in. "Why not stay and apologize to the girl?"

"Apologize?" Cuchulain's voice rose in anger. "She caused the injury herself. Let her apologize!"

Osmiach arrived and lifted Uathach from the floor. Keeping her finger elevated he escorted her from the room. They listened to her sobbing long after she left the building. The attention was now drawn back to Rhiayu.

"So what will you do?" Ainnle asked him quietly.

He shoved his bowl of food across the table in anger. "I will face him and I will kill him. And if I fail...he will kill me."

Ferdiad stepped up. "Are you willing to face that? What about Emer? What about Ireland? This is a long trip to make only to die, Cuchulain. Are you willing to risk it?"

"My brother," he looked longingly into Ferdiad's eyes. Ireland was reflected in the vision, his homeland, his blood and his life. "Tis a greater thing to die in honor than to die a coward, never knowing what could have been," he told him.

They let him go.

"Choose!" Cruibne told him in the fading hour of the day. The edge of night was upon them and the darkness grew every second that passed. The sun was long over the edge of the great sea, the last flickers of light dragging the tide out as it went.

"Javelin and buckler!" Cuchulain answered.

Torches were lit outside for all to observe the confrontation. They knew it would be to the death. One way or the other, one of their heads would be set on a pole at the seashore.

"So be it," Cruibne replied and ordered the weapons to be delivered to them both. "Thirty paces apart," he commanded.

Cuchulain studied the horizon and the distance. "Forty," he negotiated.

"That's quite a distance, young hound of Cullin. Can a dog throw that far?" he laughed at him openly.

Cruibne was perhaps ten years older and obviously more experienced, but Cuchulain possessed extraordinary talent and strength. Though his height was considerably shorter, his mass made up for the deficiency. "Ask me that when you are pulling my javelin from your chest, teacher," he returned.

When they had reached their distance apart, a sword was brought forth and thrust into the earth between them. When it was done the winner would recover the weapon and take the other's head. Yet, at this point, no one could determine the outcome. Those who knew Cruibne were well aware of his skill and would most likely side with him against the newcomer. But there was so much talk of the hound of Cullin, that no one dared wager against him.

"Whenever you are ready," Cruibne called to him with a smile.

Cuchulain was exceptionally gifted here. He had performed this feat many, many times before. The best way to win against your opponent is to allow him to throw his javelin first and then beat him with speed. "Begging your pardon, teacher. I offer you the chance to strike first," he replied casually, confidently.

Cruibne obliged him with a cunning smile. The young man would die and lose his head much faster than anticipated, he thought. An event such as this could repeat itself for hours if the contenders were good. And Cruibne knew the young warrior would be an excellent match for him.

But he wasn't ready for what happened next.

"I am obliged to you for your kindness," Cruibne said and put one foot behind him and arched his back for the first throw. "Let us be done with this!" he said and threw his javelin high into the air to make the distance of forty paces.

Cuchulain didn't waste a second. The moment Cruibne arched his back and aimed for him, he launched his own javelin with all the strength and power in his soul, letting if fly fast and hard and straight—straight for Cruibne's chest. There was no arch. There was no height. It was blinding speed aimed directly for Cruibne. Cruibne let down his guard to watch the projection of his own missile. By the time he realized what had happened in that split moment it was already too late. He barely saw the one coming for him against the fading light. By the time he remembered to bring up his buckler to protect himself it was over. The shaft of Cuchulain's javelin struck him through his heart. He fell instantly. The buckler he carried was useless. He never had the opportunity to raise it in defense. The hound of Cullin had killed him.

No one cheered. No one cried. No one said anything, as Cruibne— teacher, friend and companion—lay dead on the ground. Yet no one said anything to Cuchulain either. The air was completely silent. Even the northern breezes that blow from the mountains in the distance seemed to stop for a moment of silence in remembrance of the faithful, dutiful Cruibne.

Scathach stood silent at her doorstep. She had been watching the entire time. The challenge had been issued and she would not stop it regardless of who won or lost. It was the way of the warrior. Cruibne had been with her for fourteen years. They had shared many laughs and tears over the years. They had wagered many times on the warriors who attempted to cross the bridge, losing their favorite sword or their favorite spear to the other each time they lost. He was there when her daughter was born and again when her sons were born. He took on the responsibility of training her warriors when she was unable to because of her pregnancy. And he continued to train them long after Phaedrus died and she withdrew to the mountains because of her loss. Yes, Cruibne was a great friend. He was more like a brother. And it was all taken from her in the blink of an eye. He was a fine warrior and teacher, she knew. And she would repay him by building a *kurgan* for his body and that of his horse and belongings, though his head would remain at the beach for all to see. For that she was saddened. It would always be a reminder to her of his unerring loyalty and his honesty and his friendship. And it would also be a reminder to her for not stepping in to dissolve the conflict before it ever got started. But she had sensed his bitterness toward Rhiayu the day he arrived. Perhaps this was best, she considered.

Cuchulain saw her watching him from the steps of the house. What had he done? Out of the rushing sound of his blood in his ears, he realized he had done a terrible thing. But what was done was done, regardless of how he felt inside. He was committed to finishing the task. That was the way of all warriors, he knew. He walked forward and withdrew the sword from the earth and approached Cruibne's lifeless form. Not knowing the man personally made the task easier, yet he knew that many around him, watching him, felt otherwise. He had taken something dear from them. And he realized his error. Like so many years ago, he would have to replace what was taken until another teacher could be found to take his place permanently. Without further hesitation he dropped his buckler to the ground, lifted Cruibne's head slightly by the hair and severed the head from the body in a single blow. He was thankful for the sharp edge of the blade to do the job swiftly. When he was done he released the sword, letting it fall to the ground. He turned about and looked at everyone staring at him, unspeaking, unmoving. He turned again. This time he walked to the house and looked at the warrior queen.

Osmiach joined her at the door. Uathach was quieted and resting inside. She had no idea what had occurred out across the yard. "What has happened?" Osmiach questioned in horror as he watched Cuchulain walking toward them with Cruibne's head in his hand.

"Cruibne has lost," she commented dryly, sadly. Her throat constricted slightly.

"I wish it were otherwise, m' lady," Cuchulain said to her and offered up the head. "As great a man as he must have been, I, the victor, request the warrior queen to speak of what deed be done to him now," he said.

She wasn't expecting his offer. "He was a good commander, Cuchulain, and you have slain him nobly fair. I so grant that his head shall be buried with his body in a ceremonial *kurgan*," she declared.

"So it shall be," he replied and bowed his head low.

"But now, hound of Cullin, I am without a commander. I have no general for my army. What will you offer for this void?"

He was expecting this. It wasn't long ago that he had been in this same position. "I give you one year as your general. But I also require you to continue to tutor me as your student."

"I accept your proposal, Cuchulain. You are indeed a noble warrior," she added. Then she turned to look out over the field where everyone stood waiting, watching. "Prepare the *kurgan*!" she commanded in a tone loud enough for all to hear.

CHAPTER XXI

It was mid morning when Ferdiad got his chance to meet with Scathach for the first time. He was impressed. Her beauty surpassed even the greatest stories of her appearance. She wore a long dress, tightly fitted to her body that fell to her bare feet. Her long dark-red hair flowed down her back. It was silky smooth and shimmered as it moved in the light. While most of the people cared little for the way they looked or smelled, she obviously took pride in keeping herself neat and cleaned at all times.

"So you have come to see if you have a future?" Scathach asked him at the front door.

"Yes, Scathach. I am troubled by what you may find, but I am more curious to know."

She studied him. He was a young man of perhaps twenty years and fair to look upon. His brows were thick and bushy for his age and his eyes big and brown. His nose was more bulbous than those of the Greeks or the Romans, she noted. She sensed his curiosity in his posture. While he was tall he was slightly shorter than she, but broader in the shoulders. His walk seemed clumsy and awkward. She could see why he had trouble getting across the bridge to her fortress. A few more months of learning to balance properly would solve that problem. But he was leaving and that would never come to be, she realized. "Come inside," she invited.

He followed her to a private room that was rather dark for the time of day. Candles were lit around the room where the flames flickered steadily. The air seemed thick and he breathed heavily. Two chairs were set in the middle of the space where a stone circle had been prepared in the open floor where peat moss burned on the open earth, sending puffs of smoke into the already thick air. "Sit," she ordered then went to the place where she kept the stone. She removed it and brought it with her to her chair and sat opposite him.

"It's hard to breathe," he said, nervously.

"Relax," she told him. "Let the healing properties fill your body through your lungs." Beside her was a small bowl. It was the same bowl Oseida had made for her many years before from the skull of Bracus. It was filled with herbs that she now tossed freely into the burning embers of peat. More smoke filtered into the air. The room suddenly became very warm to him.

She looked between the lines of the stone. The vision faded and brought forth a new one. Here, she saw him. Ferdiad, champion of the Men of Domnu—she saw him return to Ireland, happy to be home at last. It is a great land and he loves the people there as they too love him. He is a hero among many and strong and brave. But his time is short, she sees, for there is trouble. She watches as the Men of Domnu join a massive army with him among them. This queen, she observes, Medb she is called, sends Ferdiad out against… She forced herself to withdraw from the stone.

"What have you seen?" Ferdiad questioned.

She straightened in her seat and looked at him silently.

"Please," he begged. "I must know."

She would not deny him. "Your time is short young Ferdiad. I have seen your return to your homeland. Your life is very good for a time. There is much love and laughter between you and your friends and your family. But your countrymen join arms with the Queen of Connaught. She forces you to do battle against another."

"And…?" he asked.

She waited, unsure if she should continue.

"Am I victorious? Am I to remain a champion of Domnu?"

"You do not win, I'm afraid."

"I lose? I die? That's it? All this time learning to fight and it does me no good?"

She put up a hand to stop him and her face took on a look of sternness. "Your training here," she informed him, "enables you to withstand the fighting for a period of four straight days, young Ferdiad. Do not doubt that your time here enables you to last so long. There will be many who do not last even an hour."

"And who is it that I must fight and lose my life against?"

Now she had trouble. Should she lie? Should she betray him the truth? She had done that once before and paid the price for such a lie. The world will never know the worth of Caesar and Brutus. No, she realized, she could not keep the truth from him. "You die at the hand of Cuchulain," she told him. Yet she never told him the method with which it would occur. That was something she had to discover herself for the *Gae Bulga* was involved.

"What, my closest friend from childhood? My brother? Surely there has been some mistake?" he pried, alarmed at such a conclusion.

"There is no mistake Ferdiad. What the stone tells me is the truth. I wish it could be different, but I refuse to tell an untruth to you. You sought to know your future and now you have it. You must leave and carry out your life as you would regardless of what you know here. The information you gain here is yours for the telling. You may speak of it to your countrymen or you may keep it to yourself as a secret. But either way, you will find yourself fighting against Cuchulain, your friend and brother. And you will lose, I'm afraid," she said then stood. "The time has come for you to go," she told him quickly and escorted him from the room.

Silently, mortified by her revelation, he departed her house. He never spoke a word of what occurred inside that smoke filled room to anyone.

By mid afternoon she was back at the foot of the mountains observing and correcting Cuchulain and her sons. They were sloppy. Their efforts were substandard and she grew angry with each of them. "Cuar," she came to him and grabbed the sword from his hand. Of all the weapons she had ever used in her life, the sword was perhaps her best. She liked the way it sailed across the air, cutting a rift in the fabric of life before it heals itself long enough for her to swing again. The air never bleeds, but put a man in front of her and some of the most gruesome things will be seen. It whistled as she spun it back and forth—or did the air scream as she cut it?

"You cannot jab at your opponent as if you are poking a stick into his gut. You have to thrust the keen blade fully into him or you will do nothing but make him angry enough to come back and kill you. Do you understand?" she said as she hammered the sword-edge full to the hilt into the makeshift body they used for practice.

"Yes, mother," he replied and attempted the same. He finally got it through.

Cuchulain watched and listened. He was extremely impressed by the warrior queen. She was more than he had thought her to be before he arrived. They had said she possessed beauty beyond any women, even Emer, and he was not disappointed. They said she was by far the most skilled warrior in the world. And again he was not disappointed. But why did she do this thing? Why did she train so many—and always men? And then he thought to himself…what would he teach the young warriors who had come to learn from Cruibne. He himself was only a student and now he was required to teach. "Scathach?" he interrupted her correction of Cette who was doing equally as bad.

"Yes," she answered.

"What am I supposed to teach the others when I return to the camp? I am only a student."

The question was not hard. "Basics," she told him. "Do not attempt to show them the rope of feats for most are not ready for it. Do not show them the apple feat for their brains cannot handle the task of juggling anything but food into their mouths. Do not teach them the chariot wheel feat that you have learned here for they cannot grasp the concept. If you attempt it they will fail and leave before they are given a chance to learn anything. They believe they have come here to fight. They believe they are already the greatest warriors in the world. And we accept them as such for they do not know the difference. They soon learn who is better among them as the lessons continue. That is what makes them push harder. That is what makes them better soldiers. They eagerly strive to become the best. So you will teach them to fight. Educate them in hand to hand. Educate them in throwing the javelin. Teach them how to mold their own weapons. These are the things you will teach them. And if there are some who become extremely gifted, you will take them aside and teach them more. But never teach them something you have not mastered yourself."

He nodded. "I understand," he replied. "But what happens when one of them challenges the other to see who is better among them?"

The question was a good one. And there were those who did exactly that. But there was an easy solution to that matter. She walked to him and stood close to his face, bending slightly in the process. "They fight me first," she whispered.

He thought for a moment. Something forced him to ask the next question. While he probably would regret the answer he blurt it out anyway. "What if I challenge you?"

Oddly, at this she smiled. "I have been waiting for you to ask that," she replied. "Trust that it may come to be."

"And you will kill me?" he asked though he did not cower to know such a thing was possible.

"I have not seen it," she told him.

"So you already know what happens to me?"

"Some, but not all."

"Scathach!" Osmiach had claimed the bottom of the hill leading to the mountain range. "There is trouble," he gasped out of breath.

At the exact moment of his arrival a *caryx* sounded below at her fortress. There was indeed trouble. No one sounded the *caryx* unless a war was about to occur. And that meant that Aoife was nearby with her soldiers.

"Come," she said casually, not at all alarmed though her sons seemed a bit nervous. She led them back down the hill to the camp. Osmiach rested where he was to catch his breath.

The fortress was in utter turmoil. Her soldiers had collected themselves and their weapons and stood in formations on the opposite side of the bridge ready for Scathach to command them. Those who had passed the test by crossing the bridge on the north side of the fortress stood in three lines, ready as well. There had been bitter words between Aoife and Scathach many times in the past and many times they had settled their grievance by doing battle with their soldiers. This time it was completely different. On the opposite side of the bridge where the mass of her trained warriors had collected themselves, Aoife appeared with her chariot and perhaps three hundred of her own soldiers. She was dressed for battle, Scathach saw.

By the time Scathach was at the bridge a small skirmish broke out from the taunting of soldiers on both sides. When it was over, four of Scathach's warriors were dead and two of Aoife's.

No one noticed how Scathach crossed the bridge. She didn't jump nor did she leap into the air. She carried no weapon and wore no battle armor. Piladius had known how to cross the bridge without leaping. All who saw her on the other side of the bridge guessed that the bridge belonged to her and she had mastered it. For her there was no reason to leap. But as she walked, backward, she conversed with Cuchulain, giving him orders for her soldiers. No one noticed that she was walking backward. That was the trick Piladius had discovered seven years ago. And no one else ever knew except Osmiach and Cruibne. Not even her daughter or her sons knew how to cross.

Scathach approached Aoife.

"Who is the *kurgan* for?" Aoife asked, noticing the still-smoldering embers from the pile of wood that was burned on the new mound of earth the night before. Her charioteer was silent at her side holding her stallions still and quiet.

"Cruibne," she answered.

"Toothless Cruibne?" she laughed haughtily.

"He was a good man, Aoife."

"He was a fool! He never should have come here," Aoife told her.

"No, Aoife. The only fool here is me. That's because I allowed you to come along." She was extremely bitter this day. She knew Aoife would rub the death of Cochar Cruibne into the earth for as long as she could because she knew it perturbed her.

"Yes, well we may not have to deal with that for too much longer. Where is that new student of yours?" she asked as she searched the other side of the bridge.

"What business is he of yours?"

"He has injured one of my family," Aoife answered as she continued to spy across the bridge.

297

"You mean, my family? Uathach is no relation to you," Scathach pressed.

Aoife stood on her chariot looking slightly down at her. "She has my blood!"

"No, Aoife. Your blood is bitter and sour and deceitful and filled with treachery. You do not share the same blood."

"I demand payment for what was done to her, Scathach, and I will get it if it costs the lives of every man on this field," she bellowed.

"Your challenge is accepted. Choose the time and means by which you will lose," Scathach told her.

"Lose?" Aoife mocked. "The only thing…" She stopped. There he was. He was more handsome than Uathach had told her. She instantly dropped her mouth at the sight of his nakedness on the other side of the bridge. In the time she had spent discussing the matter with Scathach he had taken the opportunity to educate the army further. Each man undressed and screamed out in glory. But none were as impressive as Cuchulain. His body was so much broader and extremely filled with muscle from chest to foot. His golden locks, even from this distance, gleamed in the sunlight as they bounced off his shoulders. He yelled the loudest.

"Choose!" Scathach whispered menacingly though her voice was loud.

Aoife lost her concentration. The amazing features of Cuchulain had distracted her. She was forced to bring her attention back to Scathach. Her anger returned. "At the burn side of the field above my cliff," she told her. "We will settle this for all times, today," she said. And before she departed she looked down and said further. "I challenge my best against your Cuchulain. You may want to prepare another *kurgan* for when it is finished," she said then laughed and immediately had her charioteer turn about and prance her horses away. Her army followed closely behind her.

Performing her salmon leap, she was back on the other side of the bridge. "Rhiayu," she called. "Walk with me," she ordered.

When the army had departed, Cuchulain dressed and waited for Scathach to return. When she called out his name, he followed her as she led him into the house.

"What has she done?" Cuchulain asked her.

"She has issued a challenge against you for injuring my daughter. She wants payment for causing her such pain."

"And what have you said?" he asked.

"I have accepted. Now I have to explain what we will do," she said but first called out for one of the young girls who work inside the house. She came immediately, as if she were hiding just around the corner, and bowed her head before Scathach. "Send for Osmiach," she ordered the young girl. She obeyed.

In silence, they waited in the comfort of a soft couch until Osmiach came in. He was still winded from the long walk. The years had caught up with him. He wasn't able to get around as much as he used to when they first met. That was an entire lifetime ago, she realized. And as long as they had known each other, she never knew much about him. He remained to himself and was always quiet about his personal affairs. She would have to change that sometime soon, she figured.

"Yes, Scathach," he greeted at the entrance to the room.

"Aoife has issued a challenge against our young hero, Cuchulain. I am about to discuss our plan for winning such an event. Before I start, I would like you to prepare one of your special drinks for us. One that, let's say, lasts until the morning. That will give us enough strength and endurance to win over Aoife if the battle persists until that time," she told him.

He knew exactly what she wanted. Something was wrong and Scathach wanted Osmiach to concoct a potion strong enough to make Cuchulain sleep until the morning. By that time the battle would be finished and he would be spared any trickery Aoife may have planned to kill him. Why Scathach would protect such a man, especially after he killed her Cruibne, was beyond him, but she had her reasons and he would obey regardless of his personal opinion.

"I need no special drinks, Scathach," Cuchulain claimed. "I am strong enough to take on her entire army," he exhorted.

"Yes, but that may be what she has in mind. I offered her to choose the method by which the battle will be fought. Trust that there will be trickery involved. This special drink will enable you to surpass greater dangers than you have ever seen. It will give you more strength than you have ever known. You will be faster in mind and in body. That is the edge you will need to defeat her soldiers."

"Her soldiers?"

"Yes. You will battle against her soldiers. That is our way. None are allowed to fight against Aoife or myself personally. If that were possible, we would be engaged in battle daily from warriors across the world trying to make a claim for killing the greatest warriors that ever lived."

"And if I win?" he asked her.

"Then she will leave and go back to her fortress by the sea. And she will be as bitter as she has always been to me. But it wasn't always so," she continued. "We were great friends at one time. We were very close sisters. But she had a thing for the life-game that split our lives apart. She enjoyed ruining another's life by stealing the man from her bed, or killing a man because he would not sleep with her. It did strange things to her mind and she has been against me ever since."

"And what about you?" he asked her.

"What about me?"

"Are you not bitter toward her?"

She thought briefly. "I suppose over the years. I wish it were not so."

"Your drinks, Scathach," Osmiach interrupted as he handed each of them a cup.

"You will drink with me?" he asked of her.

"Yes," she answered, though she knew only one of the drinks was filled with the potion. "I will need my strength as well. This may be a long day," she said and finished it in one swallow.

The room swayed slightly and he felt dizzy. "Is it supposed to feel like this?" he asked.

"Let it fill your head, young warrior," she eased his sudden sense of uncontrollability.

"I cannot get up," he issued. He forced himself to sit forward on the couch. He couldn't get there. He suddenly closed his eyes and fell asleep. The drug worked quickly.

"How long?" she asked Osmiach.

"By my estimates, sometime during the morning."

"Good. Let him rest here. You keep a watch on him. I have to prepare the others for battle."

"Scathach?" he interrupted her departure. "Why have you decided to spare this one?"

"There are greater things in store for this one, Osmiach. Trust that I do this only because I know it is right."

"I have no reason to doubt you, Scathach, but he did kill our friend Cruibne. Does that loss mean nothing to you?"

"My dear Osmiach. It means a great deal to me. But you know better than anyone what happens when a challenge is issued here. One of them was doomed to die last night. This one just happens to be the victor."

"And yet you save him from another challenge?" he questioned.

She sensed his anguish. "There is trickery in this next battle, Osmiach. I prefer to engage Aoife on my terms and not hers, even though she has the choice of method."

"Then this day shall see you both in deceit. And she will want your head, Scathach," he warned. "She will not settle for a lesser hero than the one she intends to kill."

"That is the chance I am willing to take," she told him.

"And what if it is one of your own sons?" he asked, knowing the possibility.

She gave it some thought, but responded confidently. "If they accept the challenge, then I shall be honored, no matter the outcome."

"Scathach," he paused and looked at her as if giving medical advice. "We already know what the result of the outcome will be. Are you willing to settle for the loss of a son to your sister?"

She grew slightly angry. "If I have to, Osmiach," she replied then turned away before he could press the issue.

Realizing he had plenty of time before the young warrior woke, he decided to follow the others as they moved south in the direction of Aoife's fortress. In a field slightly east of the cliff that separated Aoife's lands from that of Scathach, they formed their soldiers in ranks. When Scathach arrived she was surprised to see what had been prepared for her. Aoife had planned it all in advance. She knew it would come to this. Uathach had probably told her how to plan it. She probably told Aoife every little secret about her own fortress. It was difficult to believe her daughter could be so mischievous. And to think she would betray her own brothers. Scathach approached the rope of feats and studied it at the approval of Aoife's gleaming eyes. Only three people in her entire camp knew how to perform on the rope. And one of them was sleeping comfortably on a couch of pillows.

"Shall we get started, sister," Aoife teased from her chariot. She stepped down and dismissed the charioteer while she went to a circle that had been deliberately made in the center of the western side of the rope. Her army had gathered on the southern slope of the field. Scathach retreated to the eastern side of the rope where a circle of equal distance had been prepared for her as well. Her army remained on the northern slope. No one was allowed to enter either circle or death would greet them instantly. Those were the rules and all would follow them.

When all was in place, Aoife called for her warriors. Three of them stepped forth, naked from the waist up and their flesh painted in black and brown colors. She smiled at their voraciousness to compete for her.

"Where are your warriors, Scathach?" she asked from her circle.

Scathach looked to her army. None of them knew what to do. None of them had ever seen such a thing. Then Cuar and Cette stepped forward. They were naked to the waist as well and painted in the traditional battle color of blue that the Picts had showed them years before. They walked forward until they stood beside their mother and just outside the circle.

Aoife laughed. "Ahhh, and where is your champion?" she asked slyly.

"Resting," Scathach answered.

"I hope he doesn't rest too long. It may be over and you will have lost. And I'd hate to see you lose your sons, Scathach. Surely your champion will come to protect them?" she gloated.

She was suddenly repulsive to watch and Scathach looked to her sons. "Do as you have been taught and you will be victorious."

"Mother," Cette called to her. "Where is Cuchulain? He is by far the more superior on the rope of feats."

"My dearest son," she said. "I have misjudged my own sister and did not foresee this treacherous event. I have put Cuchulain to sleep until the battle is over for fear that he would die as a result of Aoife's wickedness and deceit. Albeit that I have failed to keep you safe from her evil ways. But remember…you are by far the stronger and you are both exceptionally skilled compared to her warriors. You will beat them and return as heroes to my fortress."

"I will beat them, Mother," Cuar said bravely. He was the stronger of the twins and eager for any kind of battle. Without hesitation, he jumped onto the rope and withdrew his sword. Cette jumped on behind him, though he became tense with nervousness.

"Two against my three?" Aoife asked. "Surely you have another who is capable of performing for us today?" she prodded.

"Let us see what your three can do against my two before I decide to use my third."

"Perhaps your champion won't show at all," Aoife threw at her. Her smile widened.

Uathach suddenly came out from behind a tree. She had been watching the entire time and waited for the right moment to arrive on the battlefield. She deliberately walked and stood beside Aoife, though just outside the circle. Her finger was wrapped tightly in a splint that Osmiach had given her. She smirked her betrayal at her brothers and then again to her mother. She knew this day that she would never be allowed to return home. Dun Scaith would no longer be part of her life.

As wicked as she could, Scathach cast a word to her sister from the other side. "Aoife," she said and everyone could hear her. "I was wrong. She does have your blood in her."

Both Aoife and Uathach looked at each other for interpretation. Neither could figure it out.

CHAPTER XXII

His mind told him he had to wake and his body shook violently inside. His inner-anger forced him from an intended long sleep and brought him to consciousness with a start. He had been tricked, but why? He looked around the room, dizzy still from the potion. He stood and left the house and went outside to find someone, anyone.

The camp was deserted, as was the house. Training weapons littered the ground beside the clothes that the warriors had removed from their bodies. Everyone had departed the fortress. He had to find them. Surely they would need him. It bothered him to know that Scathach would drug him to keep him away from a battle. Was she frightened for his life? Did she fear he would take all the glory for himself? Was she threatened by his strength and courage? Why was he the only one left behind? It didn't make sense. He had to think.

A noise behind the house caught his attention and he ran there. Two of the girls were drinking something that they probably shouldn't be, and they were hiding it from him.

"What are you doing?" he asked them.

They were young, pert and extremely naïve. They giggled at the sight of him and snickered as the muscles in his chest flexed in anxiety.

"Well?" he demanded.

"We're drinking! Now go and leave us alone," the taller one said. They were both of dark hair and fair skin. Both wore a tunic and sandals. They were neat and clean and of full teeth as they giggled at him more. "Go," she told him again.

They were comfortable drinking behind the house. It was as if they had done this before when no one was around to correct them. But regardless of their idiosyncrasies, he knew he had to find the others. "Where did everyone go?" he asked.

They giggled some more and turned away to steal another swallow of the liquid.

He was getting nowhere. "I'll ask you one more time. If I don't get an answer, I'll put you both over my knee and paddle your hinds," he warned.

They gave in without confrontation. "They left."

"I know that. Where did they go?"

"We don't know," the other finally answered. Her voice was as soft as the air. "They crossed the bridge and that was the end of it," she replied, snatched the bottle from the other girl and took a quick sip in laughter.

Well, that was a start, he figured. He ran for the bridge and performed the salmon leap to gain the ground on the opposite side. There was no second or third try. He made it in one attempt. The blood was rushing through his veins as he ran with all his might toward Aoife's fortress. If the army crossed the bridge they would only move in that direction, he guessed.

Two miles later he heard the murmur of voices gathered in a field above the cliffs that separated the distance between Aoife and Scathach's lands. He had to go back almost two hundred yards to cross to the east to get to the field. When he did, he was just in time to see Cuar jump onto the rope. A moment later he watched as Cette claimed a position slightly behind his brother.

"Sons of Ilsuanach," Aoife called out loudly. "Kill them!" she ordered and the three warriors standing beside her, the sons of Ilsuanach, jumped onto the other end of the rope facing Cuar and Cette. Each had withdrawn a sharp sword with which to do battle.

Their mass and muscle outweighed both of her sons'. Their balance on the rope was far greater as well. Uathach had given Aoife enough information to allow her to train her best soldiers as Scathach had done.

But worse than that was the fact that Uathach knew only her brothers trained on the rope of feats. She did not realize that Cuchulain excelled on the rope also. It was as if she intended to see her brothers killed this day, no matter what. Scathach gave a heavy sigh as the warriors faced each other. Osmiach was right, she thought then. She would lose her sons to her sister and it will be over: all because she feared for the life of a stranger. Was he worth it, she asked herself?

A golden-haired figure crested the northern slope with a sword raised in the air. A muffled cheer went up from Scathach's army at the sight of him. Cuchulain ran with sweat in his eyes to meet with Cuar and Cette who smiled in great relief at his presence. Without a single word to anyone he leaped onto the rope in the lead position and stared at the first son of Ilsuanach.

"Now we are three against three," he told them and a steady glow grew from around him. The first son of Ilsuanach retreated slightly in alarm. Everyone watching saw the transformation of Cuchulain. He went mad. His body puffed and gathered air like a siphon and his flesh went completely red. His chest heaved and his arms swelled to almost double the size. Scathach marveled at the sight for this is the exact way in which she too went mad.

With blinding speed, Cuchulain unexpectedly bounced on the rope of feats causing all the others to lose their balance briefly—including Cuar and Cette. When his feet returned to the rope he swung his sword down and hacked a crater on the outer thigh of the first son. He cried out in pain and bent to look at the wound. Cuchulain didn't hesitate. He came full around and cut off his head. It went rolling toward Aoife. A gift for the treacherous, Cuchulain thought.

The second came for him. He was angered at the sight of his brother's murderer. He would avenge him, he thought.

Aoife was at the edge of her circle. "Kill him!" she commanded. "Kill him quickly," she screamed.

Scathach remained silent. Whatever happened would happen regardless of what she said.

"Die!" the second son said as he came for the Celt. He thrust his sword forward for a quick jab at his heart, retreated the blade when he missed and came around to the side to cut at him in the ribs. Cuchulain twisted to the side, allowing the sword to go by him, turned back and blocked the strike to his ribs. He smiled though the heat on the rope intensified.

"Die, I say!" repeated the son. Again, he hacked at Cuchulain who blocked each attempt.

"Kill him!" Aoife screamed again. She also marveled at the sight of Cuchulain. Yes, he was one of the most handsomest men she had ever seen, but she was not willing to lose a battle over his looks. She would see him dead before she gave in to Scathach. It would be finished today, no matter what, she knew.

The second son of Ilsuanach came down with his blade to chop into Cuchulain's head from above, but got thrown back by Cuchulain's foot in his chest. By luck, the sword of the third brother stuck him in the back and he fell to the ground writhing in agony. While the third watched his brother on the ground, rolling in pain in the tall grasses, he never saw Cuchulain leap from his place and land directly to his front, piercing him through his heart with a knife.

Aoife went insane. She had lost. She wasn't supposed to lose. Uathach had promised a victory on the rope of feats. Who was the treacherous here, she suddenly thought. She had to react. She had to win. She would win no matter how many men it took to get to Scathach. Today was it. This was her last chance to get her. She turned to her right. "Crufe...Bim...Blaicne," she called to the sons of Ess Enchenn. "Do not fail me!" she said to them and watched as they too claimed the rope of feats.

Cuchulain's rage was with him. His entire body glowed red and the heat was so intense that Cuar and Cette kept back from him.

Now the sons of Ess Enchenn were not to be fooled with. By far they were even greater than the sons of Ilsuanach. They were taller by perhaps a foot and a half and weighed about the same as Cuchulain. They were each agile and skilled and possessed a look of resentment. All three had round black eyes, soulless, deadly orbs that seemed to challenge death himself. Their flesh was not painted like the others though their hair was pulled up high in a mass of spikes atop their heads. It made them look even taller than they actually were. Their faces reminded Cuchulain of a blackbird waiting for the stench of death and decay to rise from the bodies below the rope before jumping down to devour the flesh of the sons of Ilsuanach. They twitched and skittered back and forth on the rope in very quick movements. Cuchulain knew it could be hazardous to confront them directly. He would have to be cautious of them, he knew.

Scathach remained silent, still, though her palms sweated slightly. Osmiach had joined her, but remained, as all others, outside the circle. "She tests them further," she told her physician.

"And she will continue throughout the day, Scathach. Your daughter has betrayed you both. I don't believe Aoife, as well as Uathach, knew that Cuchulain was so gifted on the rope of feats. I believe they both expected the win to be swift. I believe they expected you to lose everything this day—your sons and your champion," he commented stately. "Now that she has been beaten, she will be an even greater threat to you. She will not stop until she has won, you know?"

"And I cannot allow that," Scathach responded.

"I know," he smiled.

Crufe tested Cuchulain's weak side first and swung sharply left. Cuchulain caught the blade just before it hit his left calf muscle. Their eyes never left each other's face. Each smiled to the other, daringly. It was obvious Aoife had trained them personally. Crufe brought the sword up slightly, rubbing Cuchulain's blade as he went, listening to the crackling edge while looking for a weak spot to gain an advantage. There was none. Realizing this he attempted the right side of Cuchulain's body. Again the blade was stopped. There was no weak spot here either. Their smiles disappeared. The match, they declared silently, would be even and fair. They suddenly jousted blades back and forth in rapid succession, each striking and blocking the other's attempt. Both armies were engrossed with awe at the sight. This would not be a swift battle, they could see.

Again they jousted swords, back and forth, side to side, stinging the air with their whistling blades. Neither was injured. The blackbird eyes gleamed with excitement. It was no longer a practice, but a real battle for him.

"Be done with him!" Aoife screamed at her champion. "End this, now!" she shouted.

He ignored her, concentrating on the golden haired boy.

Cuchulain changed his stance and caught the other off guard. The slight distraction enabled Cuchulain to land a huge fist in the other's face, breaking his nose. Blood burst out instantly and Crufe brought his hand up to wipe the annoying, sticky warmth away from his mouth. Cuchulain took advantage and swung. Crufe blocked the attempt and laughed. His breath was foul. That gave him an idea. Scathach had taught him earlier: 'to gain an advantage one must use whatever forces are available.' And the breath was such a force. While Crufe was a good fighter he would not expect a foul odor to penetrate his thinking. He would reject the smell of another man's breath upon his face. While it might be a trick, it was more an insult and he would definitely retreat from it, Cuchulain knew. He had only to get close enough to employ the tactic.

Bim dodged back and forth and Blaicne followed his movements at the back of the rope. Any time there was an opening in the battle Bim would thrust his sword out in an attempt to catch the Celt when he wasn't looking. The chances were slim, though he tried. Each futile attempt was useless against the well-trained Cuchulain.

Blaicne stayed as far back on the rope as he could without falling off. His bird-like eyes and his attention drew to Cuar and Cette who watched, doggedly, from the other side. Blaicne could kill them easily, he saw. If Crufe can eliminate the huge Celt they would surely win the battle. He envisioned the heroes greeting back at Aoife's camp. There would be a grand feast of pig and ripe vegetables. There would be music and dancing and women and lots of wine. Yes, he liked women and wine. All he had to do was win this battle and it would all be his. Aoife would reward him with great gifts.

A sudden screech, like that of a falcon, claimed the air and Blaicne withdrew from his dreaming. Crufe had been injured by a miscalculating swing and the Celt had cut off his hand at the wrist. He now used his left had to parry the mighty swings the Celt issued to take him down. Then they clashed together and both held their swords across their chests, neither with an opportunity to strike the other at such a close distance. But then the Celt did something completely unexpected and opened his mouth as wide as he could. With all the air in his lungs, he bellowed a puff of hot, rancid gut-odor from the depths of his stomach and made Crufe turn his head away and back off instantly. It was all the Celt needed to bring his sword up and cut off the warrior's head. He fell dead to the ground in a terrible, shivering thud.

Bim's eyes went wild. This was not expected. He went completely mad. The Celt had killed his brother. He bellowed a single screeching yell and walked forward on the rope as if he walked on the battlefield. His balance was exceptional here. But he forwent the necessity to parry and thrust and block and trick and scream and kick and do all things to make his opponent falter and eventually fail. He came straight for him, swinging madly and chopping at everything in the way. Side to side he swung. It was as if he were cutting down the biggest tree in the forest. He resisted Aoife's screams to control himself and fight as he was trained. Bim saw nothing but the Celt who had killed his brother and he would avenge Crufe's death immediately.

Cuchulain couldn't wait any longer. The large bird-faced man was pushing him backward into the others who stood behind him. His trick against Crufe had worked, but this one wouldn't let him get that close ever. He had seen what happened and now he was mad with hate and murder. He was completely insane and Cuchulain knew he had to end this one's life quickly. He waited for the next swing. When it came he slid forward on the rope, bent as the sword went high above his head and chopped sideways with all his strength. Both legs were removed from under Bim and he fell in a twisting spin to the earth. On the way down, Cuchulain sliced sideways and removed his head while the body was still in motion.

Blaicne stared in horror. The huge Celt had killed his brothers and he was the weakest of the three. There would be no chance to kill the sons of Scathach as he had planned. Aoife had promised great rewards. She had promised he would play the life-game for as long as he desired. He would not see them, he realized then. He knew his life would be ended this day and it was a terrible revelation to experience before the actual event occurred. Should he wait for the Celt to come for him? Should he cower and jump from the rope in defeat? No, he destined. 'I will stand here and let the forces of life take me whole,' he said to himself. At this he let his sword slip beside him.

Cuchulain took his time, though he made a miraculous leap in the air, bound several feet toward the last son of Ess Enchenn and thrust his blade deeply into his chest. The young Blaicne shuddered under the impact, his round, black, horror-stricken eyes rolled into his skull and he fell to the ground beside his brothers.

Scathach was relieved though she showed no emotion.

Aoife was furious for she had just watched her greatest soldiers perish.

The army gathered on the northern slope erupted in cheering and celebration.

The army gathered on the southern slope went pale with worry. Aoife will take out this loss on every one of them. There would be no celebration at her fortress this evening.

But Aoife wasn't done. No. Not this day. Today was the day she would end this battle between she and Scathach for all times. "Scathach!" she screamed out above the cheering army.

Scathach put up a hand and called for silence among her soldiers.

"I challenge you!" Aoife shouted.

Both armies went completely silent. The air seemed to stop moving and even the leaves in the trees stopped rustling for a brief moment. The battlefield was a dead place in time. No one said a word. A ptarmigan took flight from the brush nearest Scathach, fearful of the silence of the open field, and an arrow took it down before it got away. Thinking it a trap to kill the warrior queen, archers were set at various hidden locations to take down any assassination attempt. Archers for Aoife were hidden in the brush as well. The reward would be taken back to the camp and eaten at a later time.

"Do you accept?" Aoife pried. She stepped out of her circle and moved several steps closer to the rope.

The three warriors on the rope of feats withdrew and moved to Scathach, waiting for her to answer.

Aoife turned to her charioteer and beckoned him with a waving hand. He came instantly and stopped beside her. She reached up and withdrew a magnificent sword from inside the chariot and her personal spear that was set beside it. Then she dismissed him.

"Come sister. Let this be finished today!" she called, teased. She put both sword point and spear into the earth at her feet. Years of anger and deceit and tricks and armies and fighting and training were bottled up inside her. There would be no more after today. She would finish this herself and be done with it forever.

Scathach would not fight her own sister. If only as a long lasting promise to her dead father, Brona, she would never fight against her own blood. She would just as soon walk over and bend to the ground and offer her head up for sacrifice as to fight Aoife. And she realized that Aoife would probably take it. And there was no one here capable of fighting against her. She was, by far, superior to any of them, including the Celt. The only person capable of beating Aoife was Scathach and she would refuse at all costs, including the lives of her entire fortress. She lowered her head, unsure how to respond. Should she accept the challenge and give herself up? Or should she walk away, a coward? She would lose her army then, she knew.

Cuchulain recognized the distress on her face. There was great pride in her and he knew she would give herself up to save her own sister's life. He couldn't let that happen. It was he, after all, who had prompted this battle. If he had not hurt the young girl they would not be standing on this field. Aoife would not be calling forth her sister in individual combat. It was his fault alone. He suddenly lifted his head and stepped in front of the warrior queen.

"As the warrior queen's champion," he said loudly. "I accept!"

The field stifled a cry of idiocy for the young Celt. Why, after fighting so hard to win against such warriors, would he throw his life away to a warrior as gifted and talented as Aoife? She would surely be the winner over any man, no matter how tall or how strong or how skilled. It was suicide, they knew. But it didn't matter. He had voiced his acceptance.

Aoife smiled. She would have him now. None could beat her in combat. She would have Cuchulain's head and mount it at the gate to her own fortress as a reminder to all who was the more powerful. Her dark green eyes reflected such glory and she leaped onto the rope.

"Cuchulain," Scathach said to him. "She is full of treachery. She will use everything she has against you to win."

"I know," he sensed. "But before I go, I would ask what things Aoife treasures most in life?"

Scathach was taken by surprise. "An odd question, young warrior. I suppose her charioteer and her horses and chariot are her most precious possessions," she answered.

The answer was acceptable. With that information, he ran to the rope of feats and jumped on, facing Aoife.

From her position on the rope she studied him. "You would have been a delight to sleep with," she said curtly. "Now choose how you will die," she finished.

He looked at her as well. She was exceedingly gorgeous, far more so than even young Uathach. Her eyes were big and her lashes long. Her hair was dark red like Scathach and her body was better built than that of the warrior queen. He could see the resemblance in their beauty, yet he had to admit Aoife had an edge on her. Her breasts were full and inviting, her thighs white as goat's milk. It would be hard to kill a woman as beautiful as she. But he would do what he had to in order to survive.

"I said choose," she shouted at him.

"Javelin," he announced, hoping to give himself time, and perhaps an edge.

"Spears," Aoife announced loudly and two ushers came to her, withdrew her spear from the earth and handed it to her.

Cuar ran to Cuchulain and handed him one also. "Good on you warrior," he wished him well.

They dodged back and forth, neither striking out, but testing the others reactions as well as balance. They were both very good. Aoife suddenly back away from him. An odd move, Cuchulain thought to himself. He followed her motion only to be stopped at the point of her spear. He studied it closely. It was sharp…extremely sharp, he saw. He looked into her crystal-like eyes and backed from her. There was trickery here, he could tell. When he moved off, she relaxed and he watched her. She was comfortable. She was confident. He became nervous. And then his nervousness turned to madness. His blood boiled in his veins and his flesh grew red again. His arms swelled and his chest heaved. The air around him grew hot. She watched the transformation with eager anticipation. This would be a good fight, she knew.

Cuchulain stepped forward, his spear pointed at her as she pointed hers at him. When the points of the spears touched Aoife made one of the quickest slices to the side, front and straight down that he had ever witnessed and found the point of his spear had been severed from the end. It lay on the ground near Crufe's body. Aoife's army cheered her ability to do such a thing. Yet he never let the loss interfere with his concentration or his ability to return the encounter. But was it enough? As quickly as she struck, so did he and he slammed the end of his spear against the rope to trip her balance enough so he could cut to the side with his weapon. She was caught in the middle of a step when he made his move and she nearly stumbled, but when his spear swung out to catch her she bent and let it sail over her head.

"You are very good," he told her softly.

"And so are you young hound of Cullin."

"So you know my name?" he asked.

"Uathach has told me. She has told me much about you. It's a shame you went to my sister first and not to me. We would have had a wonderful time you and me. You would have been my greatest, you know."

"Yes, but now I am Scathach's greatest," he shoved back at her.

She grew angry. "Not for long, dog!" she cursed him.

He brought his javelin up in a pugil stance and waited. It wasn't long before Aoife attacked him again. This time she severed the javelin in two pieces at the middle. He used both to fend her off as she continued to slice at the sticks he held. Chards and little pieces of wood flew in all directions as she cut and tore slivers and chunks off the ends, piece by piece until there wasn't much left for him to fight with. And just when she thought she would have him, he threw it away and reached in with both hands and grabbed her spear. Both held to it fast. His strength was powerful, but so was hers. She liked this much better and she smiled at him, blowing him a kiss. His anger increased.

With all his strength and balance, he pulled her to him and fell to the rope as he rolled over and flipped her in the process. She went willingly and before he could guess that she had fallen off or stumbled she was standing to his front and came back around with a full fist to his jaw. He shook off the blow with minor aggravation and threw the spear away. They would continue with bare hands, he decided.

While he expected this to be an advantage in his favor, he was wrong. She was just as strong as he. They grappled on the rope throwing each other from one side to the other, then throwing blows and kicks at each other yet never doing enough damage to consider a winner. The blows and kicks and pushing and shoving went on for some time. Neither would win here, though Cuchulain hoped he would gain time. It wasn't enough.

Suddenly they both stopped and retreated slightly to either end of the rope, their eyes watching, searching for trickery.

"Water!" Aoife suddenly called out. She was sweating profusely. It wasn't because she fought hard, but because Cuchulain's body heat had grown intense and the air around him sweltered with his fiery rage. It came instantly and she offered him what was left of hers. He graciously took it and drank it. "Away!" she ordered and the water disappeared.

She turned to him, tired of the delay and all the sweating and talk. "Let this be finished," she finally said and he realized she meant it this time. She had tested his strength and his skill and found him to be a worthy opponent but the time had come to end the battle and kill him. There would be no more time for delays or tricks or discussion. She had her fun, she had met the great Cuchulain and now he would pay for the years of grief Scathach had given Aoife. And he would pay with his life.

"Swords!" she called out and jumped to the rope.

Yes…this was it, he realized. Anything could happen here, he knew.

Cuar approached again and handed him a sword before disappearing beside Scathach. He tested the edges with his thumb and swung it in the air a few times, listening as the air whined under his rapid thrusts. Aoife did likewise. The sword felt comfortable in her hands. They were one with each other and she felt the power in her thrust. Her blade was true, sharp and straight. She would have him now, she knew.

It didn't take long. She said she would finish it and she meant every word. She walked deliberately to him with her sword carried on her shoulder. "One more dance, Cuchulain."

He stepped forward, waiting for anything.

It came almost immediately. She swung out and down and he caught it, blocked it from his head. She jumped into the air, flipped backward at the awe of her army and swung to the side. Again he caught it and blocked it. Then she chopped left and right several times while pouncing on the rope and shifting her weight to either side trying to catch him off balance. While the balance trick had no effect, he tired of defending himself from her rapid swinging left and right. He noticed, oddly, that she never tired as she continued to fight. Then she turned and ran to the other end. He thought he would have her. It was a false calculation. She ran to the tree where the rope was tied, jumped up, pushed off the trunk with her feet and flew in the other direction over his head. She landed with a good bounce on the rope behind him. He spun around to catch her and she swung.

A sharp *ching!* cried out, splitting the air like the call of a golden eagle. Cuchulain's sword was broken clean at the hilt. He no longer had a weapon to defend himself. Aoife was smiling wickedly at him. The end would come here, she saw. Cuchulain no longer had any defenses to stop her and she would finally win. The victory would be hers. Her smile broadened and she came for him.

Cuchulain panicked. He had to think quickly. But while he thought of such things, he already knew what he would do. In the art of woman trickery he turned his head to the west and called out with all his remaining strength. "Look! Aoife's charioteer and horses have fallen over the cliff!" he shouted.

It worked. She stopped, fearful for her charioteer, but more importantly for her horses, the offspring of Bucephalus. "No!" she cried out in horror.

It was enough to undo her. Like a bolt of lightning, he knocked the sword from her hands, reached forward and grabbed Aoife by her rather large breasts and threw her on his back like a sack. With all his strength, he leaped from the rope, carried her to Scathach's circle and threw her to the ground. She struggled to gain her footage, but he threw her back and put his knife to her throat.

"What trickery is this!" she demanded. "Release me!"

"Do you forfeit!" he yelled at her. The armies became distraught and edged closer. Scathach simply raised a hand and all remained where they stood until it was over.

Tears welled in her eyes, but she refused to give in. "Kill me!" she shouted out.

"As you wish," he accepted and raised the knife over her.

"Wait!" she shouted. "Wait…" she softened and her voice suddenly trembled. The tears began to fall. She knew she had lost. "I forfeit," she swallowed hard. She realized it was over. Cuchulain had won using a woman's trick to fool her. Her charioteer was still where she had left him. Her horses were still waiting to take her back to her fortress. It was all a good trick, she realized. "I grant you three things in exchange for my life," she offered.

Even in her worse moment, she was exceedingly beautiful. Of all the women he had ever met, her beauty caught his heart and his rage went from him instantly. He wanted nothing more than to hold her to him and caress her body. He pulled her from the ground. There would be no more tricks. No more lies. No more deceit.

He put his knife away. "You will give to Scathach fifty hostages from your army and never again threaten her fortress with words of war." She nodded in agreement. "You will lie with me at your fort this evening," he said secondly. Again, she nodded in agreement. "And lastly, you will bear me a son," he told her. Reluctantly, she nodded.

It was finished. The battle was over. Aoife had lost and for the last time. There would never again be a challenge for war between her and her sister Scathach.

"Aoife," Scathach whispered consolingly.

Aoife raised her hand to her, never looking over her shoulder to see her sister standing in her protected circle. "We are finished, Scathach. The only regret is that I now live to know I can never come for you again."

"Can we make a complete truce of this?" Scathach pleaded. "Can we become the sisters we once were?"

"No, Scathach. Never," she said and walked away.

She made good her promises and later that night, slept with Cuchulain.

CHAPTER XXIII

The morning brought a chill wind from the northern mountains and Scathach realized that the cold season would begin soon. There was still much to do, though. More room had to be made for the fifty hostages Aoife gave up to her. And more crops would have to be harvested to supply them all with food to eat for the next several months. She looked out across the sea, to the island just east of hers. The Isle of the Druids, she recalled. They will be celebrating Lugnasad soon, she knew. A great fire will issue forth from their small island and light up the eastern sky for the entire world to see—if it were looking. And she and all who dwell on her side of the island will watch it far into the night and celebrate as well. Piladius will be there, she realized. He had never returned. He had spoken his words in haste, but kept good his promise. She suddenly remembered that she too would keep good her promise. She went outside and welcomed the chill air. It felt good on her flesh, reminding her of her home in the Dnieper region. After a quick splash of water on her face from the rain-barrel beside her home, she went in search for Osmiach.

"Are you well, Scathach?" he asked immediately, thinking something was wrong.

"Yes, yes, Osmiach. I wanted only to speak with you," she said calmly, comfortingly.

"Oh," he eased. "About yesterday," he said and invited her into his small but roomy home. He prepared herbal broth to soothe her bones and bade her sit in one of his comfortable chairs. She did as she was instructed.

After all, he *was* her physician. He was kind and considerate, she realized. There was never a bad word said about anyone, ever, from him. Except for Aoife, that is. But that was obvious to everyone who lived on the island.

Taking a cup of broth for himself, he took a seat beside her. "So what ails you this day?" he asked her over the rim of his cup.

"You," she answered. "I want to know you today," she told him.

His gray eyes lit for a moment. What sort of trick was this, he considered afterwards? "You want to know me?" he finally asked.

"Osmiach," she leaned to him. "I have known you for sixteen years, but I know nothing about you. I thought I knew a great deal about Cruibne, but I knew very little about him. Now he is gone and I realize that I will never know who he really was. Remember if you will, that we did not know he had a first name until we came to this island, almost a year after I met him. Cochar was his name, Osmiach. Do you remember? And you knew him long before I came along. And then there was Phaedrus— poor, poor Phaedrus. Did you know he was an assassin sent out to kill me and my sister?"

"He was?" Osmiach asked in shock, his eyebrows lifting high on his forehead.

"Yes. But after watching us and studying us for several weeks, he learned to respect us as he would respect one of his own female warriors in Greece. And we learned to love each other." She lowered her head and looked into the cup where the liquid rolled back and forth inside. "I want to know who you are, Osmiach. Before you leave," she said.

"Leave?" he replied. "Am I going somewhere?"

"Not right away, I hope," she told him. "But someday, like all living things, you will have to leave this life. And before you go I wish to know who you really are. You have always been my friend, Osmiach. I have always trusted you. But I never got to know you and now I wish to change that. I made a promise to myself before yesterday's battle. I want to make good that promise."

He smiled and took another drink. Then he sat back in his chair and looked out through the small window beside the door, over and across the inlet to the mountains far away. "It has been a long time since I've thought about my childhood," he started. And long into the afternoon he told her of his life. She was grateful for the enlightenment of his family history and for the places he had traveled to learn and for the things he had done to make the world a better place through his use of medicine. And she was saddened by his misfortune for the loss of his wife and son to disease and suffering. He, in return, was delighted to find how much closer they had become after the conversation was ended.

But then it was time to go. Cuchulain would be returning soon. He had spent the night with Aoife as part of the winning bargain. Now it was time for him to return and fulfill his obligation to command her army. It was also time for him to continue to learn more fighting skills for his training was not quite complete. And above all, there was still something she had to know about him personally. In the vision of Ferdiad's *imbas forasnai* she had seen Cuchulain use the *Gae Bulga* against him. The weapon belonged to her. And the only way to take it was to defeat the owner. She needed to know how he achieved her most prized possession. Would he kill her and take it? Would he steal it from her? She needed to know, but she would not press him for an answer too quickly.

He left her bed shortly after the sun rose and dressed. Before she could wake he slipped out the door and departed her fort using the only path to get to Scathach's camp. The night was a good one, though long. Aoife was not only miraculous on the rope of feats, but also skilled in bed. There were things he learned there that are not done in his homeland, but things that he was sure to take back with him. And before he left the island, he would be sure to visit her fort again, if only to see his son. He was sure she would have his child.

It was quiet along the path leading to Scathach's camp, save for the sound of his footsteps as he walked. An osprey shot out from the cliff in search for prey, flying out and over the water to disappear far below. He watched it until it was gone from sight. The cliff-ledge was narrow. One mistake and he would slip to find death waiting for him at the bottom. There was only room for one on the path. He remembered that from the very first day he arrived, when the assistant to Aoife's cook was out gathering herbs. The man, out of respect, had let himself down so Cuchulain could pass. And when he had gone by, he turned back and handed him his basket of goods. Strangely, another passerby blocked the path as he came to the middle. The sheer rock on the right was too high to climb and the path too narrow for both to pass at the same time. One would have to give up the road.

"Oh, dear me," said the old, haggard woman. "Forgive my intrusion, but I didn't realize anyone would be traveling the path this hour of the day," she told him nervously.

She was bent with age and wrinkled. A mantle covered her curved back and shoulders as well as her head, keeping her face hidden from him. It didn't matter. By her short, skittish movements, he could tell she was extremely old and weathered. He didn't need to see her face to tell that. Her bare feet were leathery, her toes nearly stubs on the ends. Her knees seemed to shake with the pressure of her weight on them. She crept along steadily with the use of a wooden staff to keep her balance and the sight of him frightened her.

"Do not worry, m' lady. You may pass," he said with a smile. It wasn't right to make an old woman hang from the ledge of such a cliff while the warrior passed freely. Besides, he knew she would never be able to climb back up after he passed anyway. He would be kind, regardless of her features and give way to the old one.

Without delay he climbed down from the path and held to the ledge with his hands. The ocean roared as wave upon wave smashed against the foreboding rocks that seemed to call to him far below. "Please pass quickly," he asked, suddenly feeling open and unprotected.

She moved along steadily. When she came to the place where his hands held tight, she lifted her staff and smashed it down upon them.

"Die!" she screamed in her haggard voice. "You have killed the sons of Ess Enchenn and now you too must die!" she pierced the air with her shrill voice as she stabbed the ground with the end of her staff, trying to knock him from his hold. "Fall," she told him. "Into the terrible sea!"

Pain shot from his fingers to his brain and he nearly fell. The old woman had tricked him. His rage was suddenly upon him and he instantly went mad with fever. With all his strength, he leaped to the path like the salmon leaps upstream and pulled his sword from his belt.

"You are their mother?" he asked looking at her rather small, misshapen figure.

She pulled the mantle away from her face. It was a hideous sight. The bird-headed woman was surely the mother of the three he had killed the day before. Her opaque eyes blinked like shutters, hair was upon her face in places where men grew it. It was difficult to tell if she was a woman at all. She raised her staff to strike him again and dislodge him from the ledge, knock him to the sea below.

He wouldn't give her the opportunity. Without waiting he struck off her head with the edge of his sword and watched as the old woman fell to the sea, her frail, twisted body smashing against the cliff's rocky edge every inch of the way. She would never bother him again.

"You have been a while," Scathach told him when he finally made it to the fort.

He was slightly embarrassed. He had slept with her daughter and she said nothing. He had slept with her sister and she said nothing. While luck usually runs in threes, he knew there was no possible chance of sleeping with the warrior queen. She maintained her position as teacher at all times. And for that he would respect her, always.

"Yes," he replied and said nothing else. What could he say?

"Go to Osmiach," she told him then.

"Why?" he asked her.

She looked at his hands. They were bleeding at the knuckles. He hadn't noticed before now. By the time he had made it to the bridge of leaps his rage had gone from him. Only now did his hands start to sting from the salt in his sweat on the open wounds.

When he was done with Osmiach, he was given instructions to meet with Cuar and Cette at the base of the mountains. By early afternoon he joined them in their continued training. He was surprised to see chariots set up on the field before the Yew where Scathach sat watching. Cuar and Cette had just finished setting up decoys in the field as targets.

For the next few weeks they learned feats on the chariot as well as their normal training methods on the rope of feats and those of hand-to-hand. They juggled and threw their javelins and swung their swords for hours each day. And Scathach was there with them, teaching them with her physical skills as well as her verbal. Cuchulain was doubly impressed by her abilities. He realized that Aoife would have died on the rope of feats if she were forced to fight against the warrior queen.

A month later a visitor came to the bridge. He could not pass and Cuchulain laughed at the sight of him trying to cross. Each time he tried he was thrown back only to scramble to his feet in anger. Cuchulain laughed again.

"It wasn't so long ago that another was that angry," Scathach said calmly at his side.

He marveled at the sight. "Yes," he answered. "I remember it well."

"Do you think he will make it?" she asked him.

"No," Cuchulain answered her directly. "He has the passion, but lacks the strength."

She watched as a forth attempt to have the bridge failed. "Will you wager against me?" she asked. She had done this many, many times with Cruibne. It was such a good game to them.

"Wager?" he was baffled. "Against the Scathach?"

She continued to watch the young boy trying again to make the jump over. "Surely you are not afraid to wager against me?"

"My dagger," he said quickly. "That he does not make it. It was my father's dagger and his before him."

"I accept. And if I should lose," she said. "I will deliver my favorite sword."

"Agreed," he accepted the wager.

Again the young boy tried his best to make the bridge. Again the bridge tossed him back to the other side. His face was futile, desperate. He was not a warrior, Scathach knew. No. He was here with a message to deliver, she could tell, but a message to whom?

He made another attempt, his breathing harsh in his lungs. He was getting tired, but he would not give in. He leaped as far as he could and landed in the middle of the bridge. To her benefit, he was almost there. He had but one more leap and he would win the bridge. But then the bridge buckled and tossed him straight up. He came down and landed on his belly in the middle of the bridge and his air went from him. It buckled again and he came crashing down in the middle once more, still keeping a death-grip on the bridge as he slowly slipped off to hold desperately to the side for his very life. His eyes searched grievously for something solid to hold to. Nothing was there to save him.

"Why do you not go to him and save him?" Cuchulain asked her then, feeling the young boy's fear.

"Because I may not be there for him always. If he relies on others to save him, he will never be able to save himself."

"Surely there are other things in life that he can become where his life will not need to be saved...a scholar, for example...a physician," he shoved in then.

"And you are willing to wager your father's dagger on this one's life?" she tested him.

He laughed. "I misjudged you, Scathach. I will know better next time."

The boy was slipping from the edge. There was no more strength in him. His eyes were closing and he was giving in to certain death below where the snakes and other creatures waited to devour his flesh. They could see it in his features as he began to relax and let go. The panic was gone from him, his fight lost. His message would go undelivered and his worthless life would pass without knowing what kind of man he would grow to become. With the last of his gasping breath, he let go.

"Not that easily," Cuchulain said as he landed in the middle of the bridge, grasped him by his shaking hand and leaped to the other side of the bridge with the boy under his arm. "You give in too quickly, boy!" he scolded him.

"I thought I was dead," he whispered hoarsely.

"Not yet. Why would you do such a thing?" he asked of such idiocy.

"A message," he replied softly.

"A message? For who?"

The boy caught his breath. "A message for the one called Cuchulain."

Cuchulain looked across the bridge where Scathach stood watching them talk. Had she known that he was just a messenger? He suddenly studied the boy more closely. Yes, he figured it out. She knew. No weapons, no sack, no provisions for a long wait or to journey further. She knew he was here to deliver a message only. So why would she wager against the young boy with only a message to deliver?

"I am he," Cuchulain claimed.

The boy's eyes lit in relief. "You?" he asked so as not to be tricked again. "Aoife has sent me to find you."

"What does she want?"

"You have a child in her. She says it is a boy," he told him. Then with haste, as he was probably instructed, he bolted back for the path leading to Aoife's camp. She probably feared Cuchulain would kill the boy for telling him about the child and told him to dash away as quickly as he could.

When he looked back up, the boy was gone. He glanced back across the bridge. Scathach was gone as well.

CHAPTER XXIV

The winter came and went. It wasn't as cold as it usually is during the season, but there was enough snow to keep them inside for several days at a time. Even during this time, they continued training. There were many things they did indoors to occupy their time.

But as with all things it was time for Cuchulain to prepare for his departure from the Isle of the Mist. He had learned all that Scathach could teach him. He had worked hard and excelled where many had failed early. He had become her greatest student, her greatest warrior. And he held true to his convictions to watch after her gate and to train her army and command them in such a manner as she expected. And they came to respect him for his strength and courage and above all, his honor. And he was so young.

When the snow melted and the earth was again a marsh of cold slush, he stood at the gate watching the planting of the next season's corn. Imbolc was four weeks passed and they were late getting the earth prepared for the new crops. Nearly a year had passed he realized then. He was suddenly homesick for the mother country. Emer will be waiting for him, he knew. Forgall will be angry when he finds his plot to end the boy's life was unsuccessful. He smiled at the thought and worked his own plan for getting Forgall's daughter from him in his mind.

A footstep behind him caught his attention. He didn't need to turn around. He knew who would be standing there. "You have to go to her, you know," Scathach told him.

He waited for a time. Then he said. "Yes. She will have my son soon." He knew she spoke of Aoife. "And you have one out there as well, Scathach. Will you not go and see her?"

She stood beside him, watching the soldiers planting in the field beyond the bridge. She was taller, by far. "I worry that I will be denied before I get the chance," she replied.

"When I go there, I will ask for her," Cuchulain told her. "If she is forgiving, I will return and speak of it to you," he offered.

"That will be acceptable. It will save my grace," she added.

"Come," he said then. "Let us seek out Osmiach and steal the herbal broth that boils over his stove," he said with a sly smirk on his cherub face.

A month later, news came of Aoife's child…a son. It was time for Cuchulain to return and see her.

"Enter," she said casually to him from her bed, though her voice sounded irritated.

The fortress was cold and musty. Her soldiers were worn and gaunt, thin and seemingly hungry. Many gathered around fires to ease the coldness in their bones as they shivered. Most of them had gone from the island, he noticed. He didn't realize her loss at the rope of feats was so great. He had no idea what sort of impact it would have on her army. While Scathach's soldiers grew in number, Aoife's dwindled to a scarce twenty or thirty. And none of them trained very hard at all. The training areas were laid waste and the weapons had turned to rust. Many of them were broken and thrown into a pile in the corner of the abandoned courtyard. It was not at all what he expected to find. But then he saw the child, resting at Aoife's side. It was his child, he could tell.

"Are you not satisfied that you have a son?" she asked, though her speech was more an accusation than a warm greeting.

"There is still much hate in you, Aoife," he told her as he studied the baby.

"Please," she chided. "How could I possibly hate anyone or anything? Look!" she said and waved her hand in the air around her. "I have all this to thank you for. I have nothing to be hateful for at all!" she shrieked. The baby started crying.

"May I," he offered to take the child, to comfort it.

"Why not…it's yours isn't it?" She was alarmingly bitter.

"Will you not accept that you have been beaten?" he asked her. The baby quieted, his small fingers reached for his face, his thin lips trying to speak words he did not yet know to his father. "He is handsome," Cuchulain said before she could answer him.

She sat up in her bed and dismissed her chambermaids. They flew from the room in fright. Apparently, Cuchulain was not the only one she disliked at the moment. "Give him a name and leave!" she said to him.

He suddenly became distraught. He shouldn't have to be treated this way. He was the hero. He was the champion over her. "In my land," he said to her clearly. "We have a word that binds all things into a pact. And should that pact be broken for any reason, a curse so evil shall come upon him that will undo his life completely. And this I leave with you, Aoife, warrior queen of the southern army. That I place a *geasa* upon you this day, that you should take this ring," and he lifted his family ring from his thumb and gave it to her, "and give it to my son when he is of age to wear it. And you shall then send him to find me, his father, in my homeland. I charge that you never allow him to speak his name to no man, make way for no man and refuse combat to no man. For if you so break this *geasa* I place upon you, you will surely die a sufferable death," he warned her. Then he looked at the child. "I shall call my son by the name, Connla," he said and looked one more time to Aoife. She was still beautiful in his eyes. It was sad that it had to come to this, he thought to himself. But his wishes were upon her in the form of a *geasa* and he knew she would obey them.

"Go from me," she said bitterly and turned her head away.

When he returned to Scathach's fortress there was a message for him to meet with Scathach at the foot of the mountains where they always trained. Odd, however, was the fact that Cuar and Cette were eating inside the house when he received the message. Normally, they waited with Scathach for him to arrive. This time, he knew, it was different. And somehow that made him nervous. Still, he would do as he was commanded.

"Your son," she asked when he arrived. She was dressed for battle, he noticed. "What have you called him?"

He had no reason to mistrust her. "I have called him Connla," he told her.

She smiled. "A fine name come from the hound of Cullin," she told him. "Look," she said, as she too looked high above where the peaks disappeared into the thick clouds. "I have decided to name them after you," she told him.

"You lie," he said aghast, though he was honored at her suggestion.

"No, Cuchulain. You are by far the greatest champion I have ever known. It is only right that they be called by a name that is as strong and worthy. From this day they will be known as Cullin Mountains, to give honor to the hound of Cullin."

"I am deeply honored, Scathach. But I don't understand why you would do such a thing. Surely your sons have earned the right."

"Ahhh, yes. My sons shall become great men also, but they will never become the champion you have become, Cuchulain. No. Your name will remain in this place long into the future. Beyond even my time here," she said then. "Men will come here and learn to fight as you have. Some will die while others become great. But none will achieve what you have in such a short time."

"I thank you, Scathach, for your kind words and your exceptional skill to teach me."

She moved to him then. "But there is something else, as well," she added. "I realize that it is time for you to go and there are but two more things I must know before you leave. Come," she said and led him to a new path going through the mountains. The road was directly behind her Yew tree and was only visible to someone who knew where to find it. Suddenly they went down, deep into the earth. Cuchulain became nervous again, fearing she would trick him. But why would she do that? She has never tricked him before. But the voice of his friend came back to him sharply… 'Never trust that she will be your friend. She is teacher only,' he was told long ago. Was it true? Should he not trust her? Nonsense. There had to be a reason for her to take him to such a secret place.

The light went away and he was suddenly engulfed in black. He couldn't see his hand in front of his face. "Scathach," he called out to be sure she hadn't left him alone in the dark.

"Keep coming," she called to him just ahead. His fears subsided.

A moment later a green glowing light issued from somewhere ahead and he could just make out Scathach's shadow in front of him. "What is that?" he asked.

He sensed her pleasure. "A very secret place, Cuchulain. No one besides me has ever stepped foot here."

"Am I to be frightened?"

"No. There is nothing to fear here. But this is where I need to get my answers," she told him.

"Why couldn't you ask me at the Yew tree? I would have told you there," he responded.

"The answers I seek are within this mountain, Cuchulain. Do not worry. I did not bring you all this way to kill you."

For that he was relieved.

A strong odor suddenly stung his nostrils the closer he came to the greenish light. Yet now it changed to a greenish-blue hue up ahead. The smell of salt air joined it the further he went. When at last they arrived he found he was looking out at the ocean, but standing in a cave of sulfur springs whose bubbling, gaseous sprays sent the acidic odor to the air, filling the path with the horrible smell. Anyone not knowing what was below would surely be turned back by the scent, he thought.

He searched the space. The rocks and caves were a cacophony of rushing waves and wild ocean sprays. He could feel the tide pulling him out to sea even as he stood watching it. Then he turned to where Scathach stood waiting for him. There, beside her, he saw the *Gae Bulga*.

"What, by the Gods, is that?" he questioned miraculously. His eyes got extremely large. He was obviously impressed.

"I have had a vision," she started and he brought his attention to her as he had done in all her lessons. "In that vision you have used this weapon, hound of Cullin. But the weapon does not belong to you. It is mine. There is only one way to acquire such a weapon as this," she said and turned to gaze upon it herself. Yes. It was an awesome weapon, she knew. But before she would test him further, she would tell him about it. "Look closely, Cuchulain. It is unlike any weapon you will ever know. It is made from the spine of the Beluga fish. It is flexible and light to carry, but extremely dangerous."

He marveled at the spear. She told the truth. He had never seen such a weapon. "Is it magic?" he asked then.

She nearly laughed. "Almost," she answered.

"Can I hold it?" he asked.

"Not yet."

"Then why do you show it to me if I cannot hold it?"

"Because it would slice your hand to tiny shreds of flesh in an instant," she warned.

He looked closely at it. "Why would anyone possess a weapon that cannot be held?"

"I did not say it couldn't be held, Cuchulain. I only told you that it would tear your hand to tiny shreds if you tried."

"Then what good is it?" he asked.

"You will see, but first you must earn it."

"Earn it?" he was confused again.

Before he had time to think, she threw herself at him and held to both of his arms, twisting and turning him in different directions, trying to cast him into the sulfur pit. He fought her, but knew not why, frightened at her sudden change of attitude.

"What are you doing?" he asked in a shout, worried that one or both of them would fall into the sulfur and perish.

"I am winning," she said and nearly laughed at his stupidity.

He fought her with all his strength to keep from falling into the pits as it bubbled a gaseous, acidic odor into the air. "What are you winning?" he struggled, fumbled then caught his balance again.

"Against you," she too struggled, but it was expected. He was, after all, a man of great strength.

"I cannot allow that, Scathach," he said, though dreaded his conscious efforts to let down his guard. Would she kill him if he did?

They pushed each other back and forth, jumping over large pits of sulfur as they went. Neither got an edge over the other. Soon, their rage was upon them. Both swelled to nearly double their size in their arms and their flesh went completely red. Cuchulain feared for his life for he had never seen the Scathach transform into her massive mountain of muscle when her rage was upon her. His rage too, gave him the strength to compete evenly. It was all he could do to keep himself alive, he knew.

The fight went on for hours, tossing and spinning and throwing each other over the pits. They were evenly matched, but time was now the factor here. They were hot, full of rage, and they were parched from sucking in so much of the sulfuric fumes in the air. Neither wanted to give in to the other but what choice did they have. They had been fighting for such a long time. They sweat profusely and wiped the perspiration from their eyes only when they found a chance, otherwise it stung their eyes until they found another opportunity to try again.

Suddenly, Scathach slipped on a rock. She staggered forward while holding onto him. He stepped back and over one of the pits and stopped....

There was a heavy silence between them, though the bursting bubbles and the crashing waves outside reminded them that life was still around them.

"What say you now, Scathach?" Cuchulain asked, panting heavily as he spoke. He held her slightly, but safely, above the pit.

She never feared him. "This choice is yours to make, Cuchulain," she choked from being too close to the fumes. "You must either drop me to my death, or pull me from it. Either way, I have lost."

There was no thinking about it, he knew. He quickly drew her to him, up and over the sulfur pit that threatened to take her life. "Why would you do such a thing?" he asked of her.

"To know how it was done," she told him.

"To know how I would kill you?" he asked incredulously.

"No. To know how you would win the *Gae Bulga*," she replied. "The only way to get the *Gae Bulga* is to win it. In my vision, I see that you use the weapon to kill another from your country. But when I saw this vision, I realized that you would have to win it from me. That meant that you would either kill me for it, or I would lose it as I just have," she said.

"What now?" he asked as she saw him start to calm himself from his rage.

"Now, I teach you lastly how to use the weapon."

She walked to the spear and reached down below it and pulled up a glove, the glove she had taken with her from the harbor town of the Caletes where she had won the weapon herself. With the glove on her hand, she reached over and gathered the spear in her hand. It was good to feel its weight again.

"Is it hard to learn?" he asked her as she led him from the cave back to the Yew tree.

"It will take a little time, but it is not so difficult."

"Then before we start, may I ask for your second?"

"My second?" she asked, not comprehending what he wanted.

"You said there were two things you must know before I leave. What is the second?"

She looked down to the valley, in the place where her house would be sitting at the seashore. "Did you see my daughter?" she asked him.

"She has gone, Scathach. She stole off with Aoife's charioteer in the night after the battle and left the island. No one has heard from her sense. They say he took her back to his home in Uffington, a town of the Atrebates."

She studied the landscape. "Perhaps they will marry and have many children," she said hopefully.

"It is possible," he agreed with her.

The rest of the day was spent at the Yew tree. Of all the training he had undertaken at the camp of Scathach, this was the most difficult, yet rewarding. Before the morning light greeted the new day, he had learned how to cast the spear with the use of his bare feet and won the right to carry the *Gae Bulga*. And he did so proudly.

"Come to me at my house tonight," she told him then. "And I will tell you of your future, young warrior."

Was it completely over? Had he passed all the tests? Was he now ready to return to his home and face Forgall to demand his right to marry Emer? He had changed so much, he felt. Scathach had taught him well. Had a year gone by already, he wondered?

After a long and peaceful sleep, he went to meet Scathach and knocked on her door. She opened it herself. "Come in," she offered.

They moved to the room where stones circled a hole in the floor and peat embers smoked in the center. Two chairs faced each other over the embers and she bade him sit while she gathered the stone. Sitting across from him, she reached down, grabbed a handful of herbs from the skull of Bracus beside her chair and threw it into the fire. More smoke instantly filled the space. Then she took the stone close to her face and studied the lines. As always, they disappeared almost immediately and a vision of Cuchulain replaced them.

She watched as the multitude fought against him and he killed them all, and all for the sake of a brown bull. How foolish, she thought though the vision changed, shifted and pushed on. Ferdiad was there again and Cuchulain killed him with the *Gae Bulga*. The point of the weapon entered his belly full to the shaft and there it did split him open with the pointed barbs that had to have the flesh cut away from it to be removed. And then there was another, much younger and extremely skilled, as he was skilled—trained by a great warrior—Connla, she knew. He would seek out Cuchulain, his father. In Emain Macha he would find him and die by him. And the vision pushed forth again, leaving all this behind. She saw him again on the battlefield. A broken *geasa* by his own doing found him poisoned. His life, she saw, was ended on the seashore, tied to a boulder by his own hands so that they would fear him even after his death. It would be a glorious, but short life, she saw. But how was she to tell him what was in the vision?

She pulled herself out and looked at him watch her. He was full of youth and handsome to look at. Had she been of Aoife's heart she would have taken him to her own bed and slept with him. But that was not her way. There were more important things to accomplish in life.

"A glittering future lies before you, hound of Cullin," she started. "You alone will stand against the forces of Cruachan. I see that thousands will be put against you, but you will shatter their lives with your sword and your chariot and your great spear, reddening the earth with their blood. And you will marry the one in your heart. Emer, you call her. You have a son, Connla, who will find you also. Your life will be filled with those who will challenge you if only to test your skill against their own. Only mark my words as I say to you, Cuchulain, hound of Cullin, however short your time may be, the glory of your deeds shall live forever more!" she said.

"Do you see nothing more?" he asked, slightly disappointed.

"The rest of your future is what you make of it, young Cuchulain. I only see bits and pieces of your life in the stone. It does not show me all things in your life. You must make your own life," she told him.

"Then it is finished," he said, almost sadly. "Tomorrow I shall leave you and return to my own land. Know, Scathach, that I will never forget you," he said.

"Nor I, you," she returned.

"There is but one more thing to do before I leave, then," he told her and stood.

"What is that?" she was curious.

From under his belt he lifted his knife and looked at it closely. It was well made. His great grandfather had made it with his own hands and passed it down to his son, and then he to his son. Now it belonged to Cuchulain. "You have won this fairly, warrior queen," he said and delivered it to her.

"My wager?" she suspected and accepted the gift.

"I lost, if you will remember. But I need to know," he stopped and looked into her sharp eyes. "Would you have let the young boy die in that pit below the bridge?"

She squinted suspiciously. "I would not have wagered otherwise," she said, obviously knowing that he would not allow the young boy to die there.

"Then your wager was really against me, wasn't it?" he figured it out.

She smiled at him knowingly. "That makes us both winners," she answered.

CHAPTER XXV

On the morning that Cuchulain left there was great sorrow on the island. She watched him go from the bridge of leaps with a heavy heart. The soldiers too, bid him farewell as they gathered along the road to watch him pass. He had achieved what he had come here to accomplish, Scathach knew. And he had received a brief view of his future from the stone. Though much as she wanted to, she couldn't tell him that he would kill his own son in twelve years. It would ruin him for always. He would never be able to uphold his claim as a champion of the warrior queen, Scathach. No. It was best to let him go unknowing of what really lay ahead. It would be hard enough for him to know he would kill Ferdiad over a brown bull. She was actually surprised he didn't ask her his name before he departed. Perhaps he knew she would not tell him. He was perceptive, she knew.

But in the years to come, she had changed and so did the land and everything around her. Rome never came to claim the northern lands. The new emperor never threatened to move against them. The army dwindled daily and the quality of warrior diminished. She sensed the island pushing her away and she worried that there was no place for her to go. She had aged, but her beauty never failed her. Her sons had grown taller than she and they were full of muscle and great strength and courage. They were her teachers of the arts now. She suddenly found herself sought by title only and no longer teacher. She felt obsolete somehow.

A year after Cuchulain left, Khutalk died of old age. While he was crippled with age, she didn't have the heart to put him down, leaving him to graze in the tall grasses to the north. A herd of healthy horses snared him in the corner of a thicket and bludgeoned him to death with their hard hooves. She was sad to see him go and he was never replaced. She burned him in a silent, lonely ceremony at the beach beside her home. No one was allowed near.

After that day, she spent her mornings walking to the cliff ledge separating her sister's lands from hers and watched, when she was able, while Aoife trained young Connla. She worked him hard and without mercy, she saw. He was an animal to her and she made him subordinately mean in all things. He was rough and ill mannered, uncaring about anything or anyone and dirty. Only the wretched beasts that live in the forest surpassed his habits of cleanliness. And Aoife made him that way. Scathach could see the hate in his black eyes as he practiced with his sword and buckler and his spear. By the time he was eight years old he was superior to any man Scathach had ever known at that age. And he was frightening. She knew Aoife's reasoning behind her methods of training. She hated Cuchulain just as much as she hated Scathach. She taught her son to hate him as well. She would train him day after day, hour upon hour to kill his father when they meet. Should she go and tell Aoife that her son is defeated in the confrontation? Should she warn her that her efforts to train him were futile against such power that Cuchulain possesses. Aoife was obviously unaware of Cuchulain's skill as a warrior. She was underestimating his ability to kill anyone who gets in his way, including his own son. Should Scathach stop her?

No. Aoife would not listen if she tried. So, Scathach was inclined to sit high atop the cliff's ledge and watch the boy grow older and wilder and more dangerous with each day that passed. To her sorrow, she half expected to see Uathach return to visit some day. That day never came. Uathach was gone from her, perhaps forever.

But the time had come and she felt it in her blood. It was time to leave the island. There were terrible days ahead, she knew. But she would no longer be a part of it. She had aged so. She had lost her edge to fight like the giant she was so long ago. She could still bring fear into the hearts of men, but she was beyond her ability to fight like she should. For that reason, and for personal reasons, she chose to leave.

"Osmiach," she called on that brisk morning. Spring was in the air again and she could smell the freshness above the salty sea breezes.

He had aged as well, limping with arthritis as he moved. He now carried a staff to help him keep his balance. "Are you ill?" he was worried. He was always worried for her. He had learned to love her like a father and cared for her and her sons as if they were his own.

"No, my good friend," she said shallowly.

"What is it then?" he knew something was wrong.

"I must leave, Osmiach. My time here is finished."

He shook his head, understanding yet wishing it was not so. "I knew it would come some day," he told her. "I cannot come with you," he added, looking at himself and his condition.

"I know," she replied and looked deeply into his aging, yet loving eyes.

A teardrop fell to his cheek. "I will miss you, Scathach, warrior queen."

"And I, you, Osmiach, physician, friend…father," she put in lastly.

He smiled and leaned to her, holding her close with all his strength. It was the first time he had ever held her.

"What of your sons?" he asked then.

"That is what I wish for you to do. I cannot tell them for they will only follow me and stay on my heels like a calf to the cow. No. You must tell them that I am gone when you find the opportunity."

"Where will you go?"

"I cannot tell you, my friend. You too will seek me out if I do."

He nodded. "You are wise," he teased. "Ahhh, but I will miss you Skitatsya," he said and she looked at him with alarm.

"What did you call me?" she asked then.

He lowered his gaze. "I called you by the name your father gave you, child."

"Yes," she was shocked at his sudden knowledge. "But how did you know my name?"

"I have always known your name. Your father and I were very close friends," he told her then. "Before you left, he sent me a message to watch for you and join you if I could, to help you and guide you. While my own misfortunes were with me at the loss of my wife and son, you came to Manching and rescued me from my misery. I found a new reason to live and new reason to go on. But, regrettably, I never told you the truth about knowing your father, Brona. He was a good man, Skitatsya. I tell you this now because I know that if I don't I will never forgive myself for keeping the only lie I have ever held in my heart. Trust that I only had your safety and well being in mind when I chose to follow you the night you left Manching. And I have remained faithful to you since," he finished.

She instantly forgave him. It must have been a great secret that he kept with him for a long time, eating at him every time he saw her. It must have made him feel good to finally tell her, she knew. She smiled regardless of the timeless lie. After all, he was her physician. And what matter would it make otherwise. She was leaving. No one would ever know her real name when she was gone from here. Not after today, anyway.

"And what shall I tell your army?" he asked her.

She looked to Cullin Mountains and smiled while breathing deeply. "Tell them I have gone to the mountains to watch over them always."

He looked behind him and up to where she gazed. "Cullin Mountains," he said then.

With that she went to her house a final time and took only the items she needed for her trip, including the skull of Bracus that Oseida had made into a bowl and the only sword she had left, the *Asi* she had won from the tavern in the town of the Caletes. It was the sword that had shattered hers in the fight. She knew it would be a good weapon to have. But she would only have it for a short time. There was another she wished to give it to. Lastly, she took a staff with her to balance herself, but more importantly, a weapon should she need one.

She dressed in traveler's clothes, concealing her full identity and followed the narrow path to Aoife's camp. It was vacant of activity, a ghost house for the daring, she thought. After today, Aoife would probably live there alone, she surmised. She put it out of her mind and went to the shore. There would be a boat there, she knew. There was always a boat there. When she arrived, Aoife was saying a final farewell to her son Connla though he refused to acknowledge her presence. Somehow they became bitter enemies over the past few years. Neither really spoke a word to the other. There was so much hate built up in him, Scathach could see. But she wouldn't let that keep her from her task.

Before the boat departed for the far shore, she came up and jumped aboard. Nothing was said about her lateness to arrive. When they reached the far bank everyone departed, going in different directions. Connla was left on his own. He briefly looked back to the Isle of the Mist and waited, perhaps for his mother to call him back. She wasn't even there on the shore to see if he made it. Sadly, but eagerly, he turned, lifted his bow over his shoulder and began walking, alone.

Scathach absently caught up with him. "May I walk with you, stranger?" she asked, though she kept her eyes clear of his gaze. It was like breaking her horse Khutalk again. Never look the animal in the eyes for they will fear you are hiding something and stray from you. Keeping your eyes to the ground and away from the animal will give it more curiosity. Eventually, the animal will come to you of its own free will, she knew. Connla was no different.

When she didn't look up at him, he felt superior. Perhaps she would need his help, he figured. "There are dangers out here," he told her, though she thought his voice was slightly nervous.

She fell for his invite. "That is why I wish not to walk alone." She continued to watch the path to her front, never lifting her eyes.

He watched her steadily watching of the road. "You are welcome to join me," he told her. Then he noticed her steady, even gait. "You are very wise," he said then.

"And you are very kind, young warrior," she returned and kept her eyes averted. After several moments she continued. "Are you not Connla, son of Aoife the warrior queen?" she asked as if his name were a great thing.

It sounded good to his ears. He grinned as he repeated it in his own head. But then he became extremely serious. "I am not allowed to speak my name to any man," he answered sharply.

"Ahhh, but I am not a man," she told him cautiously.

He looked at her again. "No…I suppose you are not."

"Then you *are* the son of Aoife?" she asked again.

"Yes," he admitted. "She is my mother."

"And you are leaving?" Scathach pressed, though her eyes never looked at him.

"I am going to find my father," he informed her sourly, bitterly.

Scathach could sense his tension. "Is he not on the island with you?" she asked though she knew the answer already.

"No. He is far away from here. At a place called Emain Macha on Ireland." Then his voice took on a grave tone. "And I am going there to kill him!"

She saw this in her vision. There was nothing she would do to stop him. The stone did not lie and she would not change it. Not ever again, that is.

"Surely you will speak with him?" she pried.

"No. I am sent to kill him and return to Aoife," he flatly told her.

There was a long silence after that. The open land with its tall grasses spread out for quite a distance. Ahead there were mountains and a few patches of trees, but there were more mires and bogs and small rivers and ponds that blocked their path, forcing them to take alternate routes to get to where they were going. So much of it had changed from the last time Scathach had come this way. But then she had an escort of several Pict tribesmen as she traveled. She was suddenly surprised to see Aoife would trust her twelve-year-old son to walk through this alone, without fearing for his life. Didn't she know there were unknown beasts here? Perhaps she just didn't care.

They stopped and ate from the bit of supplies they carried, neither sharing their food with the other and after eating, pushed on without comment. Sometime before dark, Connla looked back to her.

"Do you have a son?" he asked.

"I have two," she replied.

"Are you going to see them?" he continued to question.

"No," she stated.

More silence followed.

Finally, it was Scathach who broke the quiet and spoke. She was curious. "Do you have any other relatives?"

He took a moment. "My mother has a sister," he told her.

That was good, she thought. At least Aoife told him that much. "Does she have a name?" she pushed.

"Scathach," he answered quickly, though she could see that it was like bitter fruit in his mouth.

Curiously, she had to know what Aoife had told him about her. "Have you seen her?" she questioned him further.

"No. Aoife says she is an old crone, withered with age and disease. According to Aoife, she is not expected to live much longer. In fact, Aoife thought her already dead for many years," he finished. "She hasn't seen her in a long, long time. And I've never met her. Though I don't see any need."

While his last statement was probably true, she was slightly disappointed to hear how Aoife had described her to him. At least he wouldn't get any impression that the woman he traveled with was of any relation. That made it easy to speak of things. But then she looked at him and studied him. She felt it was a good time to finally break her constant gaze at the ground before her. He was tall, taller than Cuchulain, she knew then. And he was handsome, she saw, but completely distraught. His entire life was constructed out of misery and pain. It wore well in his dark, forbidding eyes. They were scary eyes, she thought. She was forced to turn away. Evil lay there. She could feel it. Maybe there was a reason that he perished at Cuchulain's hand, she considered as she kept her eyes away from his. She would not fret after his death, she realized then. Her sister had made him the creature that he was and she would not attempt any interference with his destiny. No. He was doomed and she would not stop him from meeting his end. Yet wasn't that the main reason for leaving the island? Didn't she feel obligated to protect him, show him, teach him? No. Her days of teaching were over. She was no longer responsible for anyone but herself. She could do as she pleased...go where she pleased. She had to answer to no one but herself and her conscience.

That night, she barely slept. Dark dreams visited her, disturbing any rest she hoped to gain. She was torn between doing the right thing and doing anything at all. She tossed and turned all night. She could protect him, she knew. All she had to do was keep him from finding Cuchulain. She could take him with her, but for what reason? His heart was hard as rock, his blood cold as ice. He cared for no one. He was as wicked as his mother. No. She would not take him and keep him safe. But deep down, she wanted to. No. She would leave him! He meant nothing to her! He was evil!

She woke with a start. Connla was sitting by a small fire watching her. "You didn't sleep well," he commented.

"No," she agreed and sat up.

"Will you leave me today?" he asked.

She didn't know what to say. He caught her off guard. She wasn't ready for this decision yet. She needed more time. But there wasn't any more time. There was only the now, with one answer, but she didn't know which answer was the right one. The dreams came back rapidly in her waking mind. In the end, she finally answered him.

"Yes. I have to move south today," she said and sighed. Her heart ripped in her chest to know she was abandoning him.

She stood and brushed herself off, straightening her clothes as she did. Packing her things in silence, she gathered them together, threw them on her back and turned away from him.

He never moved from the fire.

A cold chill found her flesh and her spine tingled with fear. It was such a strange feeling. Fear was never a feeling she had ever felt and it was awkward. She turned back to him. He was watching her with cold, black eyes.

"It is yours," she told him.

"Will I see you again?" he asked then.

"Perhaps," she tried to smile.

"Where shall I leave it?" he stopped her from going a bit longer.

"Keep it with you always," she said. "It is a fine weapon."

He stood, walked to the tree and lifted the *Asi* sword from its scabbard where she left it for him. He tested it in the air, swinging it back and forth, feeling the weight of it in his hand. It was an excellent weapon, he knew. Not from around here, he also knew. He put it back and walked to the fire. "I will care for it with my life," he said to her.

Knowingly, she replied. "I know you will."

With that she turned and started walking.

After several steps, she heard him speak to her one more time. And her heart went to her throat and she swallowed it with every bit of pride she had left to give.

"I regret that we could not have been friends, Scathach."

She continued to walk, never turning around, never answering him, never stopping to change her mind. It was done. After today, she would forget him forever.

Scathach had gone her way, far to the south and then to the west. The Sayan Mountains seemed so close to her. The Altai were there too, she remembered. She would visit there again she hoped, but not this time. There was something that had to be done first. It was as if all things would be made right if she could just do this one final thing. And then she would rest, she told herself. She would settle and relax and live. And when the task was completed she returned—all the way to the northwestern coast of the Caledones—to a place where one island meets the other.

She stood there for the longest time looking off at the Cullin Mountains. Even from this distance they seemed impending. Her life on *Eilean a' Cheo*, the Isle of the Mist, where the Shadowy One lives, was over. And as the setting sun fell entirely from the sky she climbed into the small boat and moved out to sea, to another island she had hoped to see. She was greeted there with a warm welcome.

"It has been a long time," he said to her.

"Longer than it needed to be," she replied.

"Will you be staying?"

"As long as you will have me," she answered.

"I see you have brought gifts."

She opened her sack. "Yes," she told him.

He looked among the contents with satisfaction.

"You are pleased?" she asked him.

"The books I buried at your village. You have returned with them. I am deeply impressed," he said smiling. He never thought he would see them again. And then the last item fell from the sack. He lifted it with tears in his eyes. "Homer's Iliad," he said, holding it to his chest.

Piladius cried.

...END...

CPSIA information can be obtained at www.ICGtesting.com
Printed in the USA
BVOW07s0859110614

356045BV00003B/652/P

9 781424 176113